LEGACY OF LOVE

"Don't go, Grant..."

His voice was hoarse. "I'll stay as long as you need me." In the next moment his lips covered hers in a hard, demanding, fiery kiss. Gone was the gentle, playful caressing as his rugged masculine desire overtook them both. His strong arms engulfed her, pulling her completely to him, molding her to his hard, virile body. His lips sent pangs of passion shooting through her limbs. The moments hung like eternity and she was lost in his arms, in his animal magnetism, in his kiss....

CAPTIVE DESIRE

"Do you want me to treat you like a woman?"

Charly's undoing was her next challenge, and she knew it the minute she uttered the words. "I don't think you know how. You've been away from a woman for a long time!"

"Not as long as you think. I haven't claimed celibacy yet." In one swift movement he stood, encircled her in his arms, and kissed her with such skillful fervor that Charly clung weakly to his back. Her heart beat rapidly and she responded to his demanding lips in spite of herself. She was unable to resist, unwilling to stop him. A soft moan escaped her. In another moment she was lost to this ruffian she barely knew....

The Best Of

Tate McKenna

LEGACY OF LOVE
&
CAPTIVE DESIRE

LEISURE BOOKS NEW YORK CITY

A LEISURE BOOK®

September 1992

Published by

Dorchester Publishing Co., Inc.
276 Fifth Avenue
New York, NY 10001

If you purchased this book without a cover you should be aware that this book is stolen property. It was reported as "unsold and destroyed" to the publisher and neither the author nor the publisher has received any payment for this "stripped book."

LEGACY OF LOVE Copyright © MCMLXXXIII by Mary Tate Engels

CAPTIVE DESIRE Copyright © MCMLXXXII by Mary Tate Engels

All rights reserved. No part of this book may be reproduced or transmitted in any form or by any electronic or mechanical means, including photocopying, recording or by any information storage and retrieval system, without the written permission of the Publisher, except where permitted by law.

The name "Leisure Books" and the stylized "L" with design are trademarks of Dorchester Publishing Co., Inc.

Printed in the United States of America.

LEGACY OF LOVE

To Noel, Brent, & Shane, who inspire my life.

CHAPTER ONE

"Damn! Why would Daddy do a thing like this to me?" Morgan kicked stubbornly at the sturdy Colorado-rock fireplace, as if the blow would diminish her wrath. A merrily crackling fire dispelled the early April chill, but not the frigid tension in the room.

Her oldest brother, Brett, chuckled mercilessly. "To legitimatize you, little sis. He was just old-fashioned enough to want his darling daughter to be married before she lives with a man!"

Morgan struggled to restrain the urge to slap him. In years past she wouldn't have resisted, but at twenty-five she was a child no longer. Instead she opposed him angrily. "I didn't live with— Oh, what's the use? Damn you, Brett! I'll bet you had something to do with this! As the official lawyer in the family, you helped Daddy draw up the will. It's a male chauvinistic deed! How could you do this to me? Your own sister!"

A fleeting glance of pity crossed Brett's golden eyes as he professed with candor, "Morgan, I—believe it or not—I didn't have anything to do with it. This was all Dad's crazy idea. Honest to God, it was! There was nothing I could do about it. He was adamant. Why would I—"

Her tawny brown eyes spit fire at him as she interrupted. "I don't believe you! You just want to get all the family's property in the hands of the men! You and Adam!"

He threw his hands in exasperation. "Morgan, be sensible. I have all the property I can possibly say grace over. And I of all people wouldn't force anyone into marriage. God knows, I wouldn't do that. I don't care what you do—or who you do it with!"

"There you go again!" Morgan insisted.

"Look, honey. How do you think it looked to Dad when you traveled all over Europe with a mixed group of men and women? He knew what you were up to! He was no fool, just old-fashioned."

"But we were just friends. We didn't—"

"And then you went to Greece alone with André? Come on, Morgana dear. Be reasonable. How much innocence did you expect Dad to swallow?"

"But why did he want to make it a part of his will? What does having a husband have to do with keeping that stupid, run-down ranch property?" It was beyond her understanding.

"Because he felt that it would take a man to make a go of any ranch." Why did Brett sound like her father when he said that?

"Well, I'll show you . . . all of you! I'll make it work, by myself!" Morgan folded her arms defiantly, hugging her chilled body in the process. She wore a creamy turtleneck sweater that clung to the swell of her breasts and tucked into the trim waist of her tan tweed skirt. The deep brown velveteen blazer matched the sable of her exquisite eyes and contrasted sharply with her golden crown. The long, silky-blond tresses were tucked into a noble chignon, befitting the austerity of the day. There was an air of richness—of class—in her attire, but actually Morgan couldn't wait to get back into casual clothes and let her hair down.

"You'll make it work?" Brett's laugh was a sneer. "What do you know about ranching? You grew up in Denver's suburbs. The only ranch you know about is a dude ranch!"

A determined expression spread across Morgan's face, lighting her spicy brown eyes and radiating her creamy complexion. "Then that's what I'll do with it. I'll turn it into a dude ranch! And I'll make it profitable. Then what'll you do about it, Mr. Bigshot Lawyer? Do you think that'll settle the will . . . or will you devise another way to get that property for yourself?"

Brett glared at her with a satisfied smirk. "Don't forget about the stipulation to be married within a year."

"Well, at least I have twelve months to accomplish that! I'll worry about it later."

"Worry about what later?" Adam, the third Cassity sibling, entered the room. Sensing the friction, he didn't wait for an answer. "What's going on between you two?"

"Little sis is upset over Dad's will," Brett sneered.

Adam nodded. "That's understandable. Who wants to be forced into . . . anything? Especially Morgan! What in hell possessed the old man to do such a crazy thing?"

Morgan unfolded her arms and, motioning, muttered sarcastically, "His lawyer advised him."

"Now, Morgan, I told you—"

Adam's keen sense for keeping peace motivated his interruption. "How about a drink? It's been a grueling day. Reading a will isn't exactly my idea of fun!"

Morgan flashed, "I'll drink to that! Make mine a double!"

Brett looked sharply at her. "Since when did you start drinking doubles, little sis?"

"Today! Since my own brother and my own dear departed daddy gave me the shaft!" She was near tears as she grabbed the small, old-fashioned glass Adam slid toward her and spilled a little of the pungent liquid over her hand. Perhaps she could get drunk and obliterate the events of this day from her weary mind.

Adam and Brett exchanged comments. Suddenly they were business partners with common interests, the men in the family —the decision-makers!

Meanwhile Morgan climbed onto a stool and leaned on the counter, attempting to assuage her anger with the glass of Scotch. It wasn't working, but it kept her busy. She had never felt so miserable in her life. How could her father do this to her? And she'd thought she was the apple of his eye. Ha! He must have hated her! After all, not only was there the crazy stipulation about her marrying, but the way the estate property was divided was decidedly unfair. Brett and Adam got the profitable land, the apartment buildings in Denver and Santa Fe. The business offices in Denver were also split between the brothers. Didn't he think she could manage business affairs? Even the gorgeous home Brett and his ritzy wife lived in was given to them.

And what did she get? The run-down ranch where they all

played cowboys as kids! Her father had bought it as a getaway place for his rambunctious family, providing room to roam. *Here's a chance to get back to nature,* he used to say. Hell, nobody had gotten back to nature down there in five years! Everyone was too busy. Brett had opened his new law office and Daddy had helped with that. Adam had been working his way through law school for years, it seemed. And she had been . . . well, maybe somewhat of a disappointment to her father. She had dropped out of college her senior year, opting for travel in Europe with friends. Persuading Daddy to finance the trip with her education money had been a real coup! She remembered the confrontation with the distinguished, gray-haired man.

"But, Daddy, this will be my education! Imagine going to the Louvre in Paris, London, Spain, Italy . . . Germany! Oh, Daddy! What could be a better education that that?"

He leaned back and puffed on an ebony pipe. "Yes, Morgana, it would be an education, of sorts. But it won't take the place of a college degree."

"Daddy, this is the chance of a lifetime! I just can't miss it! I won't!"

He puffed slowly, wondering how many times he'd heard those very statements from his energetic woman-child. His daughter had never wanted to miss a thing: she relished life's adventures. At least she knew what she wanted—and didn't want! Sighing, he acquiesced. "All right, Morgana. I never could oppose you. I'll arrange it with the bank tomorrow."

"Oh, Daddy, I love you!" She had hugged him quickly before dashing off. . . .

The drink sloshed against her lips and she licked it away, reluctant to lose a drop. Apparently the only way Brett Cassity, Sr., could oppose his beautiful, headstrong daughter was in death. And he had done it sufficiently. *Damn him!*

"Morgan! You'd better slow down on that drink! We'll be carrying you to your room if you keep that up!" Brett was acting very self-assured now that he was the leading male in the family and had received the first-born inheritance from his father. The fact that he was six years older than Morgana and four years Adam's senior had always given him the edge. Now—today—that gap seemed even larger to Morgan.

"Oh, shut up! Don't tell me what to do!" Morgan snapped.

"Hello, Morgana, darling. How are you doing now?" Brett's wife, Alise, breezed into the room, looking especially lovely and extremely happy for someone who had recently experienced a death in the family. Of course Brett, Sr., wasn't *her* family, not her blood relative, anyway. And by virtue of being married to Brett, Jr., she had come out on top of the estate heap. *Damn her, too!*

The world, it seemed, was against her. Morgan kept her back turned to Alise to avoid conversation.

"Hello, Alise," Brett said tightly. Anyone could tell the relationship between them was strained. Is that what Daddy wanted for her? Marriage, ha! Maybe Brett hadn't influenced their father, after all. He had denied wanting to force anyone into— "Morgan isn't very happy, as you might understand."

"Well, it's been a difficult day." Alise's fluid voice slithered around the room. "I'll agree, Morgan. The will is unfair. You could contest it, you know. Shall we go, Brett? I'm tired."

"Sure, Alise." Brett returned his half-empty glass to the bar. "See you later, Adam. Morgan, cheer up. You'll feel better about this tomorrow. We'll work something out."

"Don't bother," muttered Morgan bitterly.

As the handsome couple left the room, Adam attempted to comfort his sister. "Morgan, I'm going skiing at Purgatory tomorrow. Why don't you go with me? I'm meeting an old friend. It'll be fun—a little relief from the strain of the last few weeks. This is probably the last snow of the season."

Morgan considered it for a moment, then demurred. "I don't feel like skiing, Adam. It sounds like too much fun," she muttered miserably, gazing into her rather blurry, empty glass. "Anyway, I have a job now. This is what Daddy's always wanted me to have. A job. And responsibility. Now I have both. And without a precious degree, too."

"What the hell are you talking about, Morgan?" Adam looked curiously at her, wondering if she was just drunk or completely out of her head.

"I'm going to turn that stupid ranch into a dude ranch and open for business the July fourth weekend. I'm going to settle down and be respectable. Maybe I can find myself a good ole cowboy to marry and have a dozen kids and spend my mornings cooking for the chuck wagon and my afternoons mending fences. Maybe that'll satisfy everyone."

"Morgan, you're talking crazy!"

"That's what Daddy wanted, isn't it?" Tears burned her eyes as the drink helped to reduce her anger to salty liquid.

Adam shook his head, and gentle brown eyes that matched hers revealed his sympathy. "No, I don't think that's what he had in mind. . . ."

"What, then?" Morgan implored.

Adam was at a loss for sufficient words to explain his father's rash rationale. "Well, I think maybe—"

"He wanted me to settle down!"

Adam sighed. There was no appeasing her. "Maybe so, Morgan. But actually I think your idea for a dude ranch is a good one. I read just the other day that the urban cowboy craze has influenced a current trend for dude ranching."

"Really?" She stared at him blankly.

"Oh, yes. Of course, July fourth is only three months away. That doesn't give us much time. . . ."

"Us?" she questioned, lifting her brown eyes to his.

"I'd like to help you get started. I don't take my bar exams until June, so I can't really be an official lawyer until after that. I had planned to work at Brett's office doing research. However I would enjoy working on the ranch, plus it would certainly provide the solitude I need to study for the bar. I want to help you, Morgan. Honest!"

Morgan's eyes narrowed as she answered in mocking tones. "Is that guilt creeping out? Feeling a little sorry for kid sister? Well, don't!"

He shrugged and grinned, determined not to let her set him on edge as she had Brett. After all she had a right to be upset. "A little guilt, maybe. Definitely not sympathy! You can do anything you set your little head to do, Morgan. Tell you what . . . I'll ski at Purgatory for a few days, then drive on over to the ranch at Vallecito. That'll give you time to pack and drive down. I'll meet you there!"

Morgan smiled up at Adam with tears glistening in her sad eyes. "Oh, Adam . . . thanks!" And as she hugged her brother's broad shoulders, the sharp memory of similar occasions with her father pierced her brave facade. . . .

The phone's abrupt ringing assaulted the soothing quiet, jangling loudly against the bare windowpanes and bouncing off the walls of the nearly empty rooms. Morgan's boots echoed as she walked hurriedly toward the newly installed instrument.

"Hello . . ." Her voice sounded strange after two days of relative silence in the old ranch house.

"Morgana?"

"Who else?" She recognized Brett's voice right away. What the hell did he want?

His voice was light. "Just checking on you. Have you heard from Adam?"

Instantly she was defensive. "Nope. He's due here today or tomorrow. And he's going to help me this summer, Brett. He offered and you agreed. Don't try to persuade him to return to Denver." It would be just like him to try to convince Adam that he was needed elsewhere, like in the law office.

There was a small pause and Morgan could hear Brett's sigh. "There's been a change of plans, honey."

Honey? Damn him! What does he want? "Brett! Don't do—"

"Listen to me, Morgan," Brett interrupted. "Adam's had a little accident. Nothing too serious, but it does alter your plans with him."

Morgan halted, heart pounding. "Little accident?" *What, now?*

Brett spoke quickly. "Adam broke his leg skiing. He's okay, just incapacitated with a full leg cast."

Morgan couldn't believe her ears. "Broke his leg? Skiing? Is he all right? Where is he?"

"He's in Durango's Mercy Hospital. I've talked to him and he's fine. Morgan, I want you to check him out of the hospital, since he was admitted overnight. I've arranged for an air ambulance to fly him back to Denver today. Will you go to the hospital and see that everything goes smoothly? I want him treated well. Can you do that?"

Morgan sighed. "Of course I can. But, Brett . . . what about the ranch? What—"

Brett's voice was abrupt. "Scratch it for now, honey. You can't do it alone."

Stunned, she answered, "I'll let you know when Adam's plane is due in Denver." As Morgan's hand replaced the receiver, her grip tightened until the knuckles were white with determination. Through thin lips she muttered, half aloud, "No, brother dear. I won't scratch it! I'll show you I can do it alone!"

Morgan's boot heels resounded in the hospital hall as she determinedly strode toward Adam's room. She pushed open the door and a slight gasp escaped her startled lips. She hadn't really considered her brother's appearance: that he might look different. Sitting in that stark-white hospital bed, he appeared so . . . oh, God! . . . *hurt* . . . with his leg stretched out and wrapped in that chalky cast. Even his usually tanned face was pale and drawn in pain.

"Adam! What in the devil did you do to yourself?" She crossed the room and kissed his forehead. It hurt her to see him in such a condition, and she completely forgot about their plans for the ranch.

Adam managed a tight chuckle. "What a way to end the skiing season. There just wasn't enough snow to cover all the rough spots. I should have known better! It was so quick, Morgan. One tip hit a rock and—wham! If it weren't for Grant here, I would probably still be out there on that slope. Nobody with any brains tackles the back side of Purgatory this time of year!"

Morgan winced as she listened to Adam's account. Finally she swung her gaze to the man who stood by the window and gave him a formulated smile. "Thanks for helping my crazy brother. I am so glad you were there!"

"Grant LeMaster," Adam offered, "meet my kid sister, Morgan Cassity."

The man's lips curled into a smile and his blue-gray eyes boldly assessed her. "I'm glad I was there, too, especially now that I get to meet his attractive sister. I guess Adam and I were both a little crazy yesterday. We knew from the ski reports that the snow was spotty. We just had to challenge the mountain one more time!" He laughed and shrugged his lean shoulders.

Morgan propped her fists on her slim hips. "And a fine price you're paying, Adam, for the big challenge!" Her jeans were designer labels, her burgundy sweater velour, and she drew up to her full height of five feet, three inches . . . maybe four with the cowboy boots. It was the only time she'd ever been able to tower over her tall brother, and she relished every minute. "What would you have done if Grant hadn't saved you? My God, Adam, that's dangerous!"

Adam grinned sheepishly. "Save the lecture, Morgan. I'm lucky and I know it. Grant performed a regular Boy Scout act by dragging me two miles, and I'm no lightweight! It was a tough day for both of us."

Morgan turned to the stranger with renewed appreciation. "Well, Grant, that's quite a remarkable story. A simple thanks hardly seems enough." She was, for the first time, fully aware of the man outlined by the light from the window. He was tall and hard-muscled with a rugged, western appearance. The worn jeans, the soft chambray shirt, even the scruffy boots seemed to be a part of him, his look. Morgan delighted in the raw masculinity of the man, from his long, straight legs to his narrow hips, the squared span of his shoulders, the unkempt shadow along his jawline, the sprinkling of gray hair at his temples. He reminded her of the men in Europe, only his attire was different. But those steel-gray eyes . . . they smoldered with forbidden excitement. . . .

Morgan suddenly realized that she was staring open-mouthed at this stranger! She clamped her lips shut, then unable to resist, asked, "Don't I know you from somewhere?"

The tanned skin around his devilish eyes wrinkled with his laughter. "Hey, that's my line! I doubt if we've met. I think I'd remember you, Morgan."

She forgot they were standing in a hospital room, that Adam was watching this exchange between them. "Have you ever been to Europe?" The question dwindled at the end, for she knew the answer. Perhaps he was the type of man she had searched for all over Europe. Perhaps . . .

"Hey, remember me?" Adam jolted them both to the stark reality of the hospital room. "I thought you were going to spring me from this prison, Morgan!"

"Oh, I am, Adam. The, uh, plane should take off for Denver

in about an hour. I've already checked you out of the hospital, and we're just waiting for an ambulance to take you to the airport. Are you ready to go? Where are your things?"

He pointed to the disarrayed heap of clothes stuffed into a large plastic bag supplied by the hospital, and Morgan busied herself organizing them.

"Morgan." Adam's hand reached for hers. "I'm sorry about the ranch. Really, I am."

She flashed him a warm smile and shrugged off his concern. "Don't worry about that at all, Adam. I'll just hire some wrangler here in town to help me out." Her eyes settled immediately on the rugged cowboy appearance of Grant LeMaster and spontaneously asked, "Grant, you look like a pretty good cowboy. Could you use a job?"

Grant's gray eyes flickered briefly from Adam's to Morgan's, where they rested approvingly. "Well . . . yes, you could say that," he drawled.

Adam raised up on his elbow. "Morgan, this man's no more a cowboy than I am! He's a writer—"

Grant rocked back on his cowboy-boot heels and shrugged his angular shoulders. "I just do a little free-lancing. Right now, I'm—uh—between assignments, as they say. And I'm always looking for unusual jobs."

Morgan's confidence grew as she realized that he was indeed interested in working for her. "Well, I don't know how fascinated you'll be with my ranch, Grant, because it's going to be a hard job. It'll take a real man to work it."

A slow smile parted his insolent mouth, and Morgan noticed a slight indentation in his shadowy chin. "I think I qualify, but what a challenge!"

"Well, what I mean is . . ." Morgan stumbled over her words. "It's very hard work and . . . I don't know if you . . . I mean, a writer isn't exactly very physical . . . I need someone who can really work, not stand around and take notes!"

Grant folded his sinewy arms and flashed a quick grin at Adam. "Let's see now. You want someone who's a real man, who's physical, and who doesn't stand around taking notes. Tell you what, I promise not to take notes! The other, I guess I'll just have to prove! You're a tough boss, Morgan."

Adam howled with laughter. "My God, Morgan! This man's —"

But he was interrupted by a firm hand on his shoulder and Grant's affected drawl. "I'd be mighty pleased to help you at the ranch, ma'am. And I'll try hard to be a real man." He paused and Adam again hooted with laughter while Morgan burned inside at their teasing. Then Grant added in a serious tone, "Only trouble is, I'm not alone. I have a six-year-old son. Would you be willing to take us both?"

"Sure. Why not? I can't pay you much, but it'll be a regular salary, for a change. And of course you can have room and board at the ranch." She didn't think that a child would create any problems.

"Regular salary?" sputtered Adam. "Morgan—"

Again he was interrupted by Grant's determined voice. "Now, Adam, don't worry about Morgan. I'll do my best to take good care of your sister."

Adam chuckled and shook his head. He commented sarcastically, "I'm not worried about her, Grant. I'm concerned about you!"

Grant's laugh came from low in his chest as he cast a confident glance at Morgan's petite figure, then back to Adam. "I can handle myself. You just take care of that broken leg and don't worry about Morgan and me. We'll manage just fine."

"Of course, we will," agreed Morgan as a nurse and two medics bustled into the room.

The nurse's ever-optimistic voice entoned, "Good afternoon, Mr. Cassity. Are you ready to go home?"

Morgan and Grant stood by helplessly watching as Adam was skillfully maneuvered onto a stretcher. Morgan clutched the small duffel bag containing Adam's clothes and followed the short caravan down the hall. Silently she wondered what Adam would have done without Grant yesterday on that cold mountain. She shivered at the chilling thought and was filled with a tremendous sense of gratitude—and a little intrigue—for Grant LeMaster. She watched his ambling gait as he walked in front of her and chatted briefly with the EMTs who had taken charge of Adam. He might be a writer, but he looked as though he spent more time being a cowboy. She could picture him astride a quarter horse, cutting dogies and riding the range. And he probably whiled away his nights doing the cowboy two-step. She wouldn't object to dancing close to him . . . those broad, lean shoulders— What was she thinking? She had just hired the man! She had to retain some sort of supervisory distance between them, didn't she?

Morgan drove behind Adam's ambulance and Grant's burgundy Suburban to La Plata Airfield, outside of Durango. She noticed a child's head bobbing around in the vehicle with Grant, but paid little heed. At the airport she pulled to a stop next to the red and white ambulance, just as a slight child darted from the Suburban to a small Cessna plane parked nearby. Must be the son Grant referred to, she thought absently.

Grant diligently accompanied Morgan and Adam to the air ambulance, where a nurse and the pilot awaited their injured passenger. Morgan's apprehension grew as the nurse explained the various emergency equipment aboard. There was something about seeing her brother in the midst of IVs and oxygen masks and stethoscopes that was frightening. After trying to reassure Morgan that this kind of trip was very routine in the accident-prone ski area, the nurse smiled at Adam. "Well, are you ready to go?"

Morgan leaned over her brother's pale, drawn face. "Adam, you'll be home before you know it. And Brett will meet your plane when you arrive. I'll call him as soon as you take off." She tried to convey a positiveness that she really didn't feel.

Adam smiled wryly, apparently trying to cheer her, too. "Yeah, and he'll probably have the whole damn place snapping to attention."

Morgan smiled and patted his shoulder. "Yes, it'll undoubtedly beat the reception you got here. You know how Brett likes to get things done."

As she kissed his taut cheek, Adam murmured, "You've got yourself a real man, Morgan. Handle with care."

He shook hands with Grant, and within moments they had shoved Adam's stretcher inside, the doors were closed, and the plane began to taxi down the runway. As she watched the plane take off and rise rapidly to clear the mountains, a sob rose within Morgan. Aloud, she voiced her fears, seeking the reassurance that Grant was only too glad to give. "Do you think he'll be all right? We don't even know them and he's so—"

Grant's voice was strong beside her. "Of course, Morgan. Adam's case is routine." His arm encircled her shoulders and he pressed her to him, repeating essentially what the nurse had just told them. "They do this all the time. You saw the equipment on board. It looked like a hospital. He'll be just fine."

Morosely she watched the plane disappear in the azure Colorado sky, and Adam's curious statement about Grant returned to her. Who was this man who stood so tall and reassuring beside her? Was it a mistake to hire him? After all, she knew absolutely nothing about him except that he was a friend of her brother's. What did Adam mean by "handle with care"?

She turned to face Grant, and his hand slid to rest lightly on her arm. For a long moment each looked into the other's eyes. He had touched her easily, naturally. And she had been receptive to his offering. Now she gazed closely into gray eyes that hinted of mystery. Tiny laugh lines fanned out from the corners onto tanned cheeks. His nose was straight and flanked by a crease on either cheek that led past his mouth. His squared jawline was covered with short, dark stubble where he had apparently not bothered to shave. Her eyes traveled back to his mouth where the lower lip protruded provokingly. Instinctively she swallowed, trying to eliminate the choking knot in her throat.

He broke the spell by squeezing her arm. "Morgan, come and meet my son." Then he moved a few steps away from her and called, "David! Come over here!"

In a moment the young boy stood before them, a slim, lithe child. His hair was jet black and he gazed soberly up at Morgan with the most beautiful ebony eyes she'd ever seen. Instantly she was reminded of the large-eyed Indian children painted by De Grazia, one of her favorite western artists.

Grant squatted down so that he would be eye level with the child. "David, this is Morgan Cassity. Morgan, meet my son, David."

Morgan extended her hand and he took it timidly. "It's nice to meet you, David." She smiled. This child was obviously of American Indian heritage. The traits must come from his mother, because Grant certainly didn't look . . .

Grant related the plan. "She is Adam's sister, David. And we are going to work on her ranch for a while. Would you like that?"

A distinct light crossed David's eyes as he acknowledged to Grant that the idea pleased him. Taking his son's hand, Grant stood. "Are you ready to go, Morgan? Why don't you lead the way?"

"Do you need to pack or get your things?"

He shrugged. "We live rather simply. Show us your ranch— we'll pick up our things later." He adjusted a handsome, dove-colored Stetson and led David toward the Suburban, talking and pointing at the planes that were parked nearby.

As Morgan watched them, she felt that there was something incongruous about that gorgeous hat. It was too . . . expensive. And so was the Suburban. But she shrugged and headed for her Camaro, grateful that at least she had found someone to help her now that Adam was unable.

Grant turned to her before reaching his vehicle. "Don't forget to call your brother in Denver about Adam. Just use the airport phone."

She nodded meekly. How could she have forgotten about Adam so soon? But she had.

Morgan's white Camaro headed over hills, into valleys, followed by Grant's large, burgundy, four-wheel-drive vehicle. They drove the twenty miles away from the small town of Durango, into the beautiful narrow valley where the ranch was located. The entire area backed up to the San Juan Wilderness and was a favorite of sportsmen and naturalists alike. As Morgan drove into the familiar rutted driveway, the place seemed suddenly very remote. And she was here alone with a stranger.

She crawled out of her compact car and watched the lean cowboy behind her alight easily from his sturdy vehicle while the boy ran over to a broken-down fence and proceeded to climb around. Grant ambled toward her, glancing curiously around him at the run-down ranch. Being all alone, the only sound they heard was wind rustling through giant ponderosa pines.

Apprehensively Morgan wondered what in hell she was doing. She had actually put herself in a very dubious position—out here so far from civilization with a perfect stranger. But surely Adam would have warned her if he thought she would be in danger. *No*, she tried to assure herself, *he's perfectly safe. Adam said it would be fine. "You've got yourself quite a man"* rang in her mind.

"You're going to turn this place into a dude ranch, Morgan? You've got a big job before you," Grant said, shaking his head dismally.

Morgan nodded solemnly. "*We*, Grant. We have a job before us. That's what you're hired for, remember? We have a dude ranch to put together before July fourth."

His dark brows arched. "July fourth? You're pushing it some, aren't you? I don't think we can get it ready by then."

She shrugged. "I've already advertised. And I have one family, friends from Denver, committed as customers. So we have to. Adam thought we could do it, if we work very hard. If you're not willing, now is the time to back out."

He pushed the cowboy hat back on his head with his thumb. "Well, if Adam could do it, that's good enough for me." He gazed at her steadily with gray, penetrating eyes. "I'm not a quitter. Especially before I've begun. We'll stay, Morgan. And we'll get the job done before July fourth, if that's what you want."

She smiled spontaneously, warmly responding to his avowal. "Great! That's what I wanted to hear. I think we can do it, too, Grant." She took a few steps up toward the high porch of the ranch house.

"I'm sure David is hungry by now. Where can we eat?" He took a step after her, but still had to look up to where she stood.

"You can fix yourselves sandwiches in the ranch-house kitchen. Sorry there isn't much food around here yet."

He propped a booted foot casually on the step above him and leaned an elbow on his knee. A little caustically he said, "One important thing you'll need here is lots of food. And you'd better get used to cooking a decent meal because when you have a hardworking crew of wranglers and a houseful of guests, a sandwich won't do."

Morgan's sable eyes hardened. "I'll hire a cook when that time comes, Grant. But will a sandwich do for tonight?"

"Sure, David and I are hardy. We can make it on anything." He ascended the stairs and suddenly was towering beside her.

"Incidentally," she directed tersely, "you'll sleep in the bunkhouse. I'll get you some blankets. And breakfast will be at eight."

His directive was equally as terse. "You'd better make it at six. We have work to do. Anyway, you'll have to get used to the early hours."

"My, my! What would I do without my *hired hand* who informs me about all the things I'll have to do on my own ranch!" She turned away sharply and disappeared into the house, her straight, golden hair trailing midway down her back, like fine silk just waiting to be spun.

CHAPTER TWO

Fragrant whiffs of cooking bacon breezed over Morgan's sleeping form, filling the darkened room with delicious morning smells. She stirred, turned over, and buried her head deeper while her golden hair fanned on the pillow. Then something— maybe it was the aroma of coffee mingling with the bacon— brought her to full consciousness. She lay very still, determining where she was and just who would be creating such a delicious disturbance.

Sitting straight up in bed, she knew! Grant LeMaster! He was in the house! What was he doing in *her* house? She was up in a flash, grabbing her silken robe, dashing down the hall. The old house was a rambling ranch-style with three large bedrooms located in a separate wing that was isolated from the activity area. Morgan had set herself up in the enormous end bedroom that her parents had shared, so it was quite a jaunt down a long L-shaped hallway to the source of the curious activity that had awakened her.

"What are you doing in here?" Morgan demanded on approaching the brightly lit kitchen.

Grant LeMaster, hired hand turned cook, looked up from his skillet and smiled warmly. "Morning! Coffee's ready. And breakfast will be in a few minutes."

Morgan propped her fists on her hips, forgetting to hold the robe together, so that her shapely legs were quite visible beneath the very short nightie. "Just what in hell are you doing?" She gulped and could have bitten her own tongue as large dark eyes peered at her from behind Grant. *The kid!* She had forgotten him! And there he was—awake as an owl!

Grant smiled indolently. "Well, David is working on cinnamon toast and I'm doing the bacon. How do you like your eggs?"

"Eggs?" Morgan blanched at the thought. She pushed the robe around her and quickly knotted the loose belt. Closing in on him, she muttered through clinched teeth. "What are you doing in my house? At this hour of the morning? And fixing all this . . . food!"

He gazed down arrogantly at her. "I told you six o'clock. We're late already. There's a full day's work to do, Morgan. I suggest you start with a cup of coffee." He nodded toward the busily perking pot.

Exasperated by the niggling thought that he was probably right, she moved numbly toward the pot, filled a mug, and slumped at the table. "Now that I'm awake, I may as well stay up. My God, what an hour! It's profane to rise before the sun. And to be so cheery about it."

"Oh, the sun's up. Has been awhile. You'll have to set your alarm if you can't get up naturally at this time."

"Naturally? This is the most unnatural thing I've ever done! Who ever gets up *naturally* at this hour?" She glowered sleepily into the face of the small boy who had approached her silently.

"I do," David said quietly. "Would you like some toast?" He held a platter of bubbly brown toast.

She looked closely into those dark, somber eyes and was struck by the depth of emotion they revealed. There was no reflection of herself; only his own sensitivity was apparent as he stared steadily at her.

"I . . . why, yes, David. It looks delicious." She reached humbly for one of the pieces of toast with their marvelously rich topping. "Where did you learn to make such great cinnamon toast?" She nibbled a bite, just for David's sake, and found it delicious.

Solemnly the child nodded to the tall man who beamed at him with pride. "From Grant." David put the platter of toast in the center of the table and sat quietly munching a taste of his own fare.

"Grant?" She arched her eyebrows at the man. "Well, isn't *Grant* clever!"

The man smiled satirically as he set heaping plates of bacon and eggs before her and David. "I try."

In a low voice she muttered, "Whatever became of *Dad,* or *Papa?"*

He lowered himself into the chair next to her. "David and I have a very friendly relationship. We're pals, aren't we, partner?" He tousled David's straight black hair affectionately.

"If you're his pal, who's his father?" She couldn't seem to avoid her tartness this morning.

Grant turned his steel-cold gaze on her. "Look, I'll handle the management of my son. You take care of your business at the ranch. So far you haven't done so hot at your job, so don't tell me how to do mine!"

"How the he—" She stopped abruptly, remembering the child across the table from her. Evenly she tried again. "How can I, when you enter *my* home and start your business in *my* kitchen before I'm even out of bed?"

"Well, someone had to do it! I expected food on the table at six. We have a full day ahead, so eat up." He motioned to the pile of scrambled eggs on her plate.

"You expected—" She glared at Grant, then caught sight of large eyes set in a small dark face watching for her reaction. She forced her lips into a tight smile, picked up the fork, and began pushing the egg around for just the right tiny bite.

Silence hung heavily in the air while Grant and David finished off the entire plate of cinnamon toast, and Morgan struggled with each minuscule bite she took. Breakfast at six! How awful! And all this food! She remembered the marvelous croissants and coffee in the little French cafés. There, they slept as late as they wanted. And the doughnuts . . . and the little German bakery shops where they rode their bikes to savor the marvelous delicacies before choosing the perfect thick sweet rolls and an extra bag of shortbreads. Oh, that was nice. . . .

A voice jolted her back to the six o'clock breakfast and Grant LeMaster. ". . . and while I'm making a quick assessment of the buildings, you begin making a list of supplies. Start with meat and potatoes. I'll be back shortly and we'll tour the property. We need to know the condition of the trails and just how far the ranch goes. Later we'll go into town for supplies. We can't do a thing without equipment and supplies."

Morgan stared numbly at Grant as he left his plate in the sink. How dare he issue orders to her like that? Just whose ranch is this anyway?

"And you might clean up this kitchen while you're thinking about supplies." As David headed out the door, Grant stopped beside her. In a low breath he said, "And get dressed. I don't know how many mornings I can endure staring at those barefaced nipples over coffee."

Morgan came to life as she hopped to her feet. "Bare—! Well, we'll take care of that problem right now! You get out of my house! How dare you say that to me! I think one of the first things on the supply list will be a hot plate so you and David can cook your own breakfast out there and leave me alone!" She motioned toward the bunkhouse with a slim hand, which Grant immediately enclosed between his palms.

The sensuous warmth from his hands pulsed through her as his velvet voice permeated the air. "Now, now, hold your temper. We have a certain image to uphold for little David," he admonished sarcastically.

Her voice was shrill. "I don't give a damn about image! And I don't intend to face you over breakfast every day at six! You can fix your own meals and stay out of my house!" She pulled her hand from his and tucked it securely under her other arm. Damn him, anyway! He had her perspiring at this hour!

His lips moved close to her face, showing his white, even teeth as he spoke. "We're wasting time, you know. It's nearly seven. I have work to do and you have . . . enough to keep you busy. I'll be back in an hour. Be ready." He turned his broad back on her and strode out.

There was something so smug and authoritarian and . . . commanding about him that infuriated Morgan. Worse yet, he was undoubtedly right! She stared at the closed door for a few moments, stifling the urge to sling her coffee cup after him. Instead she refilled it and stomped angrily to her room. Getting dressed was her first priority. After what he'd said to her, she didn't dare appear until she was completely decked out.

She tugged on her designer jeans and pulled a chocolate brown sweater over her head against the chill of the April morning. Damn Grant LeMaster! What had Adam said about him? Quite a man? What could Adam possibly have seen of value in the man? Maybe he didn't know Grant very well. Maybe Grant just picked him up on the ski slope! Oh, dear God! Could it be that he was a total stranger to them all? She made a mental note to contact Adam immediately . . . at least, as soon as normal people woke up! Whatever had drawn her to this man's sex appeal in the first place? He was attractive, in a rough-hewn sort of way. But she was wrong to compare him with the European men. He was nothing like them. There wasn't a polite bone in his body. He was an arrogant bas—

The ringing of the phone blasted into her angry thoughts. Almost spastically she reached for it, wondering who could be calling her so early.

"Morgan, did I get you up?"

"Brett! What do you want at this hour?" Suddenly a sinking fear hit her. *What's wrong now?* So much had happened lately, she was getting paranoid.

"Aw, your warmth is showing, Morgan. Just thought I'd check on you before I go to work. And I wanted you to know that Adam arrived safely."

"Mostly to check on me, I suppose," Morgan snapped.

"You might say I'm concerned about you. Matter of fact, I don't think it's a good idea for you to stay at that ranch by yourself. I want you to come on back to Denver. In only six weeks or so Adam will be able to help you. By then maybe all of us can come down for a few weekends and help you get the place in order. You'll just have to wait a few weeks to get started."

"Come back to Denver?" Slowly she seethed inside. "Brett, I don't have to stop my life just because Adam broke his leg. I have a job to do here, remember?"

"Morgan, it's too dangerous for you to be there alone."

"I'm not alone. I've hired a . . . a cowboy, a wrangler," she spouted proudly. She wouldn't tell Brett what a jackass he was!

Brett's chuckle infuriated her. "Yeah, well, Adam and I have discussed that. And we've agreed that you can't manage it alone. And that dude's no cowboy. He's a writer and knows nothing about ranching . . . dude or otherwise."

Suddenly she was defending him. "He certainly does! Why, we're assessing the property today and going in for supplies later. I'm busy, Brett. And I'm not closing up here to return to Denver until you and Adam determine when I can go to work."

"Morgan, you're impossible. And goddamn stubborn!"

"It's a family trait, brother dear," she grated into the phone. "Gotta go. I have a ranch to run. Thanks for your concern." With a snap she hung up the phone. How dare he tell her what to do! She'd be damned if her brothers would manage her life! She'd run this ranch or die trying! She was still shaking with anger when a scraping noise, like a heel on the bare floor, attracted her attention. Whirling, she encountered the chiseled face of Grant LeMaster standing in the doorway to her bedroom!

"What are you doing here?" she demanded.

He folded his arms and looked at her. "Seems I've already heard that question this morning. I see you haven't cleaned up the kitchen. Do you have your supply list made?"

"And I'm getting tired of asking the same questions over and over! What are you doing in my bedroom?" she sputtered again.

His smile was mocking and those gray eyes raked over her. "I thought you could use some help."

"Well, I think I can manage to dress myself! Now you get out of here!" Why wouldn't they leave her alone? All of them! And why had she defended this arrogant, brazen man to her brother? Morgan knew nothing about him, except that he put her on edge . . . and that his eyes were daringly gray. Defiantly she exposed what she did know about him. "I understand that you're not a cowboy, after all. Why did you pretend you were?"

"I didn't. You jumped to that conclusion. However I'm not a complete stranger to horses. Even tried my hand at rodeoing. I came along for the creative experience."

"Creative experience? What the hell do you mean by that?" She felt more manipulated by the minute.

"Just a fancy way of getting experience that I might be able to incorporate into my writing sometime."

"You're going to write about this? My ranch? *Me?* Oh, no you don't! You may as well hit the road now. I need someone who can work, not write!"

"I told you I could handle the job. And I intend to. Anyway, I told Adam I'd look after you. I can't go back on my word, now, can I? Not with him laid up with a broken leg. Now, if you'll get your boots on, we can be on our way. I'll be doing your job in the kitchen while I'm waiting for you, Morgan." He turned on his heel and left her fuming.

"My job is *not* in the kitchen!" she yelled at his receding back. Grabbing the fancy cowboy boots, she tugged them on and stuffed her jeans down into them. Furiously she brushed her silken hair to a shine then braided it quickly, letting it drape over one shoulder. A little lip gloss was the only makeup she bothered with today. After all, whom would she see? Only Grant LeMaster.

First Grant insisted that she accompany him through the outbuildings of the ranch. Dismissing the earlier sharp words, they somehow managed to discuss the pros and cons of which buildings would be needed for immediate use, which needed only painting, which needed remodeling.

Little David hopped, ran, and hid in the empty rooms, staying close but not underfoot. He was a quiet, undemanding child and Morgan found that she didn't mind having him around at all. It was his father that disturbed her.

Then they toured the far reaches of the ranch in Grant's Suburban. The four-wheel-drive vehicle was well suited to the rough roads that plunged through the rugged terrain, and Morgan was grateful for it. She was sure her Camaro couldn't have made it. As they drove along, she pointed out landmarks of the property and Grant dictated items for her to jot down on the supply list. Polite but terse conversation was kept to a minimum. After all this was business.

Following a brief lunch, which they all chipped in to prepare, the three of them set off for town. They spent some time in the hardware store, choosing the tools Grant thought he would need. Then he asked Morgan to do the groceries alone.

"I'll be back in an hour to pick you up, Morgan. David and

I will just pack up a few items from our apartment. See you soon."

"Okay. Can you think of anything else you'd like to have? What about you, David?" She smiled at the boy, whose ebony eyes gazed steadily at her.

He shrugged without a sound.

"What about doughnuts? And Cheerios? Every kid likes those."

His dark eyes traveled questioningly to Grant, who nodded with a wink. "Yes. I'd like that," he told her unemotionally.

She had never seen a more placid child. He didn't even get excited about doughnuts.

"And plenty of fresh fruit and vegetables. Growing boy, you know. And we've gotta take care of those good teeth," Grant added.

She glanced at him. "Spoken like an earnest father."

"Thank you, ma'am. Nicest thing you've said to me all day," he quipped. "Maybe there's hope for us yet, Morgan."

"I doubt it," she said as she opened the door. "If you just do the job I need, I'll be happy."

Grant nodded briskly. "That should be easy enough, because I'm going to do the job. Together, we'll make it." His steely gray eyes reassured her, and she crawled out of the large vehicle believing him.

Morgan glanced at the presumptuous father and unassuming son as they drove away, knowing that when they brought their belongings to the ranch, it clinched their staying more firmly. Is that what she wanted? Could she work with Grant LeMaster? He'd promised to do the job she needed. But what she really needed was a husband. Oh, God—what made her think of that just now? She clutched the grocery list and headed into the supermarket.

By nightfall Morgan slipped gratefully into bed. Supplies and tools had been bought and stored in appropriate places, ready for the busy ranch life ahead. Dinner had been such an obstacle for Morgan that Grant and little David had prepared the pork chops and mashed potatoes, while Morgan was relegated to the salad. Few words were spoken as the three sat at the table together to eat . . . again. Grant had not gotten the threatened hot plate along with the other necessary supplies today. So Morgan knew they would face each other again over the table in the morning. What an event to anticipate . . . with dread!

Finally Grant and David had moved into the bunkhouse, symbolizing to Morgan their intent to stay. She would have to face Grant LeMaster every morning, whether she wanted to or not. However there was some security in having him here. He would help her realize her goal. He had assured her of that.

Morgan gazed through the window as David struggled with a small suitcase and a large box of toys. Actually it wasn't very much for a child. But Grant had brought even less—two suitcases, one of which was square and could be a portable typewriter case. If so, he apparently had only one suitcase of clothes. He needed a job more than she realized. The move was quickly accomplished, the bunkhouse door closed, and the father and son were in to stay.

If Morgan thought she was tired that first night, it was nothing compared with how she felt by the end of the week. Each day began at six, despite her protestations, and ended, gratefully, at dusk. Then there was the evening meal to contend with. Most of the time Grant assisted, directing all of Morgan's efforts. And that was fine with her. She had no desire to take over the kitchen duties. Even little David seemed more comfortable in the kitchen than Morgan and more willing to do chores that needed to be done.

Morgan often watched the little boy in amazement. She had never seen such an agreeable child. Grant must be doing something right as a father, she thought, shaking her head, even if he did allow his son to call him by his first name.

By Saturday, Morgan was stiff and sore from the physical labor she had done all week. The muscles she used were totally different from the ones needed for a tennis match or day of leisurely swimming. At dusk she trudged toward the front stairs and sat wearily on the top step. Grant joined her, removing his straw working hat and wiping perspiration from his brow with his shirt sleeve. No words were necessary, for both were too exhausted to converse. They just watched David's energetic playing in the evening shadows.

Finally Morgan commented, "I don't know where he gets the energy to continue. He never seems to run down."

Grant smiled at the young boy, who played a game of hopping and tossing a small stone. "One thing's for sure. He sleeps well at night. I must admit, Morgan, he has really enjoyed being on the ranch this week. It seems to be a good place for him, and I'm glad you agreed to let him come. Not everyone would do that."

"He's a delightful child, Grant. In fact, he's about the quietest kid I've ever met. And he's very beautiful . . . or should I say, handsome," Morgan said sincerely.

"Yes, he is," agreed Grant, honestly.

"I suppose he looks like his mother . . ." Morgan began hesitantly. She couldn't help wondering about the child's mother . . . Grant's wife.

But Grant just nodded and grunted, "Uh-huh." He'd never offered any information about their lives, or why David was living with him instead of his wife . . . or former wife. The situation must be severe. What judge in his right mind would award a child to a father who had such an unstable life-style? Perhaps David's mother was dead?

Abruptly Grant changed the subject. "Do you have any plans for supper?"

She grinned and shrugged. "You know me. We'll whip something together, as usual."

"Why don't we go into town for a pizza tonight?" he suggested. "It's been a rough week and that would be a good treat for all of us!"

Morgan shook her head tiredly. "All the way into town for a pizza? It's so far and I'm so tired, Grant," she groaned.

"Well, I would suggest take-out service, but I don't think they'd deliver," he said wryly. "Come on, Morgan."

She looked into his smiling, tired eyes. "Do you really mean it? You'd drive all the way into town for a pizza?"

"Only if you'll go, too. Tell you what. You take a nice, warm bath and relax a little. David and I will shower and meet you in an hour. Then we can make our little jaunt into town together. It'll be fun."

"You're serious, aren't you?" She stifled a yawn. "I'm afraid if I get in the tub, I won't be able to get out again."

"Then I'll come and get you." He smiled and touched her nose. "If you don't want my help, meet us here in an hour." Turning, he started toward the bunkhouse. "Come on, David! Race you to the shower! We're going to town for pizza!" Grant suddenly exhibited a spurt of energy and ran laughing with his son across the yard.

Morgan sat in the dark for a few minutes, listening to the happy sounds of father and son before hurrying inside. If she could believe him—and she certainly did—she had better get her own bath and dress herself. Tonight she was going out, even if it was only with Grant LeMaster and his son.

Within the hour the three of them took off for town in high spirits. Grant drove the Camaro this time and David delighted in riding in the small car. To him everything was an adventure— it was a pleasure to watch him. The child's innocent joy was contagious, and soon Grant and Morgan abandoned their constant digging remarks. Pleasure was imminent, in spite of the stubborn characters involved. Was it possible that they could converse civilly? Enjoy an evening in harmony? Be polite to one another? Even go so far as to joke and laugh . . . together? It was happening . . . and they were led by a child.

Grant scanned the menu, then solicited opinions. "How hungry are you tonight? Should we share a large pizza?"

"Oh, yes! I'm starved!" agreed Morgan enthusiastically. "I'll have black olives, pepperoni, and anchovies, please." She glanced idly around the semidark pizza parlor. The decor reminded her of an old western saloon with low-hanging lamps over round tables and a makeshift bar along one wall. The only modern concession was the line of electronic games in the back.

"I want just sausage," David's small voice chimed in. "No peppers or 'chovies and *no* onions on mine!"

"Olives, not onions," Morgan corrected. "You'll like olives."

"No, I won't! I don't like olives or onions! Blah!"

Grant spread his hands. "Okay, okay! Let's start again. Could you two compromise, please? Morgan, I must admit, even I don't like anchovies."

She glared at him. "Can't we split it up—half and half?"

He leaned toward her with a twinkle in his eyes. "How would you suggest doing that? Half for you and the other half for David and me? Can you eat that much?" He glanced up at the patiently waiting attendant. "I'm sorry. Why don't you take the next order while we discuss this?"

"Can't you make a decision, Grant?"

"Oh, I can. But trying to please you two is impossible! What about drinks?"

"Coke!" David cried.

"Root beer!" Morgan voted, laughing.

"Morgan, how about a Coors?" Grant said in mock exasperation.

"That'll be fine." Morgan snapped her fingers. "Tell you what, Grant. Hurry up and order whatever you feel David will eat. I'll concede. It doesn't matter to me. What David and I really want to do is play Pac-Man!"

"What's Pac-Man?" David looked up at her curiously.

"What's Pac-Man! Where have you been keeping this child, Grant? Come on, David. I'll show you! You make the big decision and order for us, Grant. We have confidence in you." She and David sorted through her purse for quarters. As they started toward the electronic games, she heard Grant ordering.

"We'll have three separate pizzas. One with anchovies, pepperoni, and black olives, one with just sausage, and the other . . ."

Soon he joined Morgan and David, watching in amazement at David's dexterity in maneuvering the little electronic gobbler. They took turns, but the small boy proved his skills to be sharper than either of the adult's. Totally absorbed in watching Grant's game, Morgan rested her hands casually on his angular shoulders, rooting for the round gobbling blob. It was only when the game was over that she realized she was brushing against him so easily.

Grant rose and draped a long arm around both her and David. "Our pizza's getting cold! Let's leave Pac-Man for another time."

Morgan smiled up at Grant, feeling slightly warmed by his closeness. She tried to pretend that his sudden familiarity didn't matter to her. But she knew better. His touch set her on fire.

Morgan insisted on buying an ice cream cone for David before leaving town.

"Yes, yes!" agreed David, showing definite enthusiasm.

Grant nodded to the west. "Swenson's is just down the street. I have an errand to run, so I'll meet you there in a few minutes."

"Okay," Morgan agreed, taking David's hand.

"What kind of ice cream do you want, Grant?" the boy asked his father.

Grant shook his head. "Oh, I don't want any ice cream, son. You go with Morgan and enjoy it." He didn't notice the expression of disappointment on David's face.

But Morgan did. "I can't decide between Peanut Butter Fudge and Cherry Cheesecake, David! How about you?"

He looked up at her with renewed interest. "I like Bubble Gum," he admitted, smiling.

Morgan returned the smile, and they started down the street hand-in-hand. They were finishing off their sugar cones when Grant drove up and honked.

As they climbed into the small car, David smiled cheerfully at Grant. "You missed the most fun, Grant! Morgan let me taste her ice cream and I let her taste mine! Next time we're going to try different kinds!"

Grant smiled at David, "Great, son." Then to Morgan he raised dark eyebrows. "Next time?"

"Sure." She nodded, a twinkle in her deep brown eyes. "We have twenty-nine other flavors to try!"

With a knowing gaze he uttered triumphantly, "For someone who didn't want to come in the first place, you certainly ended up having a good time."

"Yes." She smiled, ignoring his gloating attitude. "David and I had a great time."

As they drove home in the dark, they sang along with the radio until they realized that there were only two off-key voices. David had drifted off to sleep, curled up in the backseat. As they pulled into the driveway, Morgan placed her hand gently on Grant's arm. "This was a good idea, Grant. Thanks for making me go."

"I'm glad you went, Morgan, but I have the distinct feeling that no one could make you do anything you didn't want to." He paused and reached for a paper bag under his seat.

Morgan's breath caught in her throat at his statement, for she knew how wrong it was. Her father would make her do something she didn't want to do—marry!

"Here's an even better idea," Grant directed, handing her the brown bag. "Here. You get the glasses filled and I'll join you as soon as I tuck David in bed."

She looked at the telltale shape of the item he gave her and giggled. "You're full of great ideas tonight, cowboy!"

He was gone before Morgan had time to change her mind or to decide if this was the proper behavior for a boss-employee relationship. A glass of wine certainly sounded great right now. It had been a long, hard week, and they deserved a little relaxation.

By the time Grant arrived, Morgan was trying to light a fire in the fireplace. The wineglasses were filled and the remaining wine was in the refrigerator being chilled.

"Here, let me." Grant took over the fire-making chore, as he had taken over so many jobs around the place. Soon a friendly fire was licking around the logs. He settled heavily at the other end of the sofa from Morgan. Before saying a word, he drank several sips of wine and leaned his head against the back of his seat. His eyes were closed for several minutes and Morgan noticed that tired lines of fatigue were visible on his still countenance.

She tried to turn away from Grant's powerful, if tired, profile and concentrated instead on the growing fire. She sipped her wine but, despite its relaxing effect, she still felt his energy in the room. Finally she asked quietly, "Did David go back to sleep?"

Grant answered without even opening his eyes. "He didn't wake up. I undressed him and hauled him to bed, and he still didn't move. He's exhausted, but I think he really loves the ranch life, Morgan."

"Well, can you blame him? I suppose he's been cooped up in an apartment with you. This gives him room to roam."

"Yes. And he's missed that."

"Missed it? Did you have a ranch before . . ." She halted. *Before what?*

Grant opened his eyes and reached for his wineglass. "David's been with his grandmother. He hasn't lived with me very long."

Morgan couldn't retain her curiosity. "Where is his mother?"

He took another huge gulp of wine. "She's dead."

Morgan swallowed hard. So the mother was dead and the grandmother had cared for this child. Finally Grant had decided to take care of his own child.

"How long ago?" she asked gently.

"She died in childbirth."

In childbirth? Did that happen nowadays? Morgan thought in horror. How awful! To lose your wife and be left with an infant, all at once. "Grant, I'm so sorry. It must have been hard. But you have done a remarkable job. He is a terrific kid. I mean that sincerely."

He looked at her, puzzlement in his soft gray eyes. He studied her for a moment before answering. "His grandmother did that. But I agree, he is a pretty neat kid. And you should see him ski. He skied Bull Run at Purgatory with Adam and me the day Adam fell. That's a black slope, the most difficult. He even helped me move Adam. Yes, he's a special kid."

"I can tell you're proud of him," Morgan smiled.

Grant chuckled. "I guess I'm bragging too much, aren't I? But I'm really like a new father."

"How long have you had David?"

"Two months. Adam has been helping me with some legalities. You know, everything is complicated these days. That's why we met at Tamarron. The skiing was just a diversion."

"How did you meet Adam? I've never heard him mention you, Grant."

Grant laced his fingers behind his head and leaned back on them. "Adam and I met in college in an investigative journalism class—we had an assignment together. I don't know why he took that damn course. Maybe he wanted to know how investigative reporters think so he could defend against them someday."

"Grant!"

He sighed heavily. "Face the facts, baby. The legal system is just a game, too, you know. Anyway, after that we became drinking buddies. But he went on to law school and I went on to . . . whatever I've been doing. The only time we can get together is an occasional skiing trip."

She raised her eyebrows. "I'm surprised you went to college with Adam. You look—"

"Older?"

She laughed good-naturedly. "Frankly, yes."

He moved his hands, leaving one arm relaxed across the back of the sofa. "I am. Thirty and counting. I spent my young and sensitive years in Nam. That's why I have these gray hairs." He laughed and ran long fingers through the gray strands at his temples.

In an action beyond her control Morgan reached out with one hand and ran her fingers through his hair, too. "Was it bad?" she asked softly.

His chuckle was a sarcastic grunt. "Yeah. It was . . . horrible. Sometimes I—" His hand closed over hers and held it against his cheek, then slid it to his lips, where he kissed her palm. His eyes were closed, and he seemed to revel in the softness of her hand on his face. It was like electricity searing through her arm and body until she finally pulled away from his fiery touch.

He took a quick breath and adroitly changed the subject. "What about you, Morgan? What were you doing before you became a rancher?"

After his revelation of years spent in Vietnam, Morgan was almost ashamed to tell him she had frolicked away the last few years. "I . . . I went to college at the University of Colorado."

"Your major?" Obviously he was looking for something they had in common.

She paused, fearing they had absolutely nothing. "Liberal arts. But I didn't graduate. I . . . quit to go to Europe with friends." Why did she feel guilty about that? At the time, she thought it was a great idea.

"Europe? Wonderful! Where did you go? I've always wanted to see Europe. Tell me about it."

His enthusiasm dispelled any feelings of chagrin she had about the overseas trip. They talked late into the night as he eagerly questioned her about her trip to Europe and she regaled him with tales of her adventures and impressions. The bottle of wine was empty and the fire had burned to glowing embers before they realized it.

"My God, Morgan, it's late. I've got to go."

They both stood at the same time, eyes meeting in an unspoken surge of emotional attraction. The fragile bond between them had definitely been strengthened tonight by the fun and laughter, the wine and conversation.

Morgan smiled. There was a catch in her voice as she tried to convey her feelings. "Thanks for insisting that we go out tonight, Grant. It was . . . wonderful. And so was the wine."

"I enjoyed it, too, Morgan." His voice was low and apologetic. "I'm sorry that I've been a little rough on you this week. But there's just so much to be done around this place, and if you want to get it done by July . . ."

She shrugged, her deep brown eyes captivating him thoroughly. "I understand. I need someone like you, Grant. You've already been a great help. . . ." Her words dwindled at the end, as his hand cupped her face and turned it up to meet his feathery light kiss. "Don't go, Grant . . ." she breathed against the sensuous curve of his lips. Tonight he was more than the man she had hired—he was that mysterious stranger she had first met . . . and more. Much more. She trembled inside at the touch of his mouth against hers, but did not shy away from it.

He kissed her again, lightly. "I don't want to . . ." They stood close, still not touching except for his hand capturing her face, their eyes locked in tormented disquiet. She could hear his steady breathing and wondered if her own stifling gasp was obvious.

She choked out the words. "Stay for the summer . . ." Morgan closed her eyes for another kindling of lips and passion and braced herself for it by placing her hands on his waist. Her fingers gripped the worn leather belt that hugged his lean hips. She could feel the warmth radiating from his body and the quivering of rock-hard muscles as her hands grazed his broad back. Drawn to his unleashed power, she swayed into him and nestled her head into his chest, breathing in the delicious smell of his warmth.

His voice was hoarse. "I'll stay as long as you need me." With gratitude in her eyes she looked up at him and he bent down to her as if to drink in her liquid gaze. His lips covered hers in a demanding, fiery kiss. He gently caressed her back, moving his hands in enticing strokes, finally settling on the soft curves of her breasts. Soft gasps escaped from deep in her throat as he feathered light satiny kisses along her smooth neck. His strong arms engulfed Morgan, pulling her completely to him, molding her to his trembling body. His tongue again teased her lips apart to taste her sweet mouth, sending a torrent of hot passion coursing through her body. The moments hung like eternity as she was lost in the ecstasy of Grant's arms, his kiss, his overwhelming magnetism. Morgan did not pause to wonder why she was drawn to the strength of this man she barely knew. But she melted inside with the unmistakable pleasure of his touch. And she never wanted it to end.

Morgan's arms reached up to the strength of his shoulders, clinging, pulling him down to her. There was no escaping his demanding mouth, his encompassing arms, his unyielding passion, his steel-gray eyes. Slowly she realized she hadn't pulled him down to her at all. He had effortlessly lifted her off her feet to meet his searing kiss! He held her firmly with one arm around her back and the other grasping the soft curve of her buttocks. She moaned as her breasts were crushed against the firm muscles of his chest and her nipples hardened at the pleasurable friction. Lost in the ever-mounting sensations, she gently traced her tongue along the outline of his ear with quick, flicking strokes. Grant groaned, sinking both his hands into the soft flesh of her buttocks, pulling her closer to his ever-increasing desire. He opened his mouth against her moist lips, easing his tongue across the ridge of her teeth, possessing her tongue with his own.

Morgan unclasped her arms from behind his neck with a shudder, and pushed on his shoulders with a determined sigh. This had to stop; they both had responded too eagerly to what began as a casual kiss! Her feet dangled helplessly as she awaited Grant's response to her withdrawal.

He lifted his passion-darkened face from hers and whispered hoarsely, "Morgan, I . . . have to . . . go. Or I'll never stop." Releasing his hold on her, he allowed her to slide down the long length of his chest and thighs.

As her feet touched the floor, she clutched at his arms momentarily, steadying herself. "Grant, I . . . this can't go on . . ." She dropped her arms to her sides, feeling weak and shaken.

He shook his head and ran his long fingers through his dark, unruly hair. "You're right, Morgan. We have to work together."

Her eyes were pleading. "It . . . it won't happen again, Grant.

It can't. But . . . please say you'll stay the summer. I . . . need you." *Oh, God, I want you!*

He nodded mutely, not daring to speak or touch her again. If only she knew how badly he needed—desired—her, she would send him packing tonight!

As if she could read his mind through those smoldering gray eyes, Morgan whispered, "You'd better go now, Grant." She smiled faintly, suddenly feeling shy before the tall man who had kissed her so thoroughly, literally sweeping her off her feet.

Without a word he turned around and was gone. Weakly Morgan sank onto the sofa, staring into the glowing embers in the otherwise dark fireplace. *Oh, dear God, what's happening to me? Am I so gullible, so vulnerable that I can't resist this man? Or am I falling in love . . . again?*

CHAPTER THREE

The sun, streaming brilliantly over Morgan's bed, finally aroused her. Or was it the wonderful aroma of perked coffee? She stretched lazily, arching her stiff back and flexing sore, shapely leg muscles. Yes, there was definitely coffee brewing somewhere in the house, and she knew she had to have some. With a great deal of effort Morgan rolled out of bed and clutched the blue silken robe around her. She shuddered involuntarily as she splashed ice-cold water on her face, trying to wash away the wrenching effects of the late-night wine she and Grant had shared. What she really needed was to brush her teeth and drink about a gallon of coffee. *Oh, damn! Why did I do that last night?* But, deep inside, she knew. She knew, but wouldn't admit it, didn't dare think it.

She stumbled out to the massive den, where Grant was intently concentrating on writing. Dear God, he was handsome as he sat with his bare feet propped up, long legs stretched out, dark head bent over his work. His long arm reached absently for his cup of coffee, bringing it to his lips for a long gulp. *Those lips!* Morgan tingled as she recalled the provoking disorder his sensuous lips had created within her. *Oh, no!* What in the world was she thinking? She was the boss around here and wouldn't allow *that* to happen again! They had both agreed to it! She shook off the mixed feelings, cleared her throat, and quickly headed to the kitchen and much-needed coffee.

Finally, completely recovered, she joined Grant, steaming cup in her hand. Before she had a chance to speak, he smiled and remarked cheerfully, "Good morning, beautiful. How are you this morning?"

She eyed him narrowly. "How can you be so chipper? And why are you up so early?"

He chuckled. "Aw, did the wine bother you? Feeling a little thick-headed?"

She didn't like his choice of words and turned her back on him, staring blankly out the window. "No. I just can't stand people who are so damned cheery in the morning."

"Well, somebody's got to present a pleasant face to David. And what good is a grump?"

Her comment was short. "You're the father."

"And I thank God for that kid every day! I'll do whatever is necessary to keep him, too! I don't give a damn if I have to get up at the crack of dawn every day! If you don't like it, we'll leave now!" The words exploded from the previously placid form of Grant LeMaster, echoing the fervor of his convictions through the nearly empty ranch house.

Morgan blanched beneath his barrage of angry words. "Grant, I . . ." she attempted weakly, turning to him. "I didn't mean to offend you. I know how much you care for David. And I certainly wasn't hinting that you . . . you two . . . leave. I'm sorry. I shouldn't have said that."

He sighed and ran his hand over his face. "So am I, Morgan. I . . . I guess we're both a little testy after last night. And I'm much too sensitive about David. I'm still learning how to be a father to him."

She stepped toward him. "You . . . you're a wonderful father, Grant."

He laid his notepad aside and rose to refill his coffee. There was a heavy silence for long moments as they stood facing each other, coffee cups gripped tightly in anxious hands. Tightly he said, "Look, Morgan, this is a miserable way to begin the day. Let's try to forget what just happened." He turned on his heel and disappeared into the kitchen. "More coffee?" he called.

"Yes, please."

He ambled back and poured the steamy black liquid into her

waiting cup. She felt very bleak, knowing she had created the disturbance between them. An idea took form, and she heartened, thinking that perhaps she could salvage some semblance of their relationship.

Morgan sat on the couch opposite him, wrapping her hands around the warm cup which she set on her knees. "Grant, this has been a rough week. Since today is Sunday, let's take the day off and do something fun."

He raised dark brows. "What do you suggest?"

"Let's have a picnic! I know a great spot. David will love it and there's even a stream where we can fish! How about it, Grant?"

He smiled rigidly. "Okay, Morgan. It does sound like fun. And I know David would love it. Maybe we would enjoy it, too."

"Oh, we would . . . will! It's a beautiful place, Grant. I haven't been there in years, but we used to go there as kids. And I remember how much we loved it." She smiled happily, her eyes glowing with anticipation of a day spent with Grant.

They didn't bother with breakfast but packed a huge lunch for the picnic. David was content with a bowl of cereal, and babbled excitedly about the prospects of fishing. He helped Grant string the fishing rods for his first attempt at trout fishing. Expectations were high as they set out in the Suburban for the promised paradise in a hidden valley somewhere on the ranch.

It was one of those absolutely beautiful Colorado days in April with a perfect cerulean sky and brilliant sun to warm the early-morning chill. The tinge of frost that covered everything had melted, leaving a glistening accent on the world.

"What a gorgeous day! I'm glad we decided to do this! Aren't you, David?" Morgan smiled happily at David's bright face.

His large dark eyes were lustrous with excitement he could barely contain as he exclaimed, "I'm going to catch the biggest fish today! I can't wait! Can I cook him, Grant? Can I? How much longer till we get there?"

Grant's voice was teasing. "Now, wait just a doggone minute! You'll be competing with a champion trout fisherman today, David! You don't know what a great fisherman your dad is! But if you happen to catch any fish, of course you can cook them."

Morgan protested stoutly, "What makes you guys think

you're the only ones who can fish? I'll give you some stiff competition! Guaranteed!"

"Morgan?" David's voice was still timid around her. "Can you fish?"

"Sure." She grinned. "I'll show you. Turn here, Grant." She pointed to a narrow, almost obliterated road with two faint tire tracks. "It's been a long time since this road was traveled. Wonder if it's still passable."

"Sure, we can make it," Grant surmised as they bumped along on the old roadway.

"You know, David," Morgan recounted, "when I was a little girl, just about your size, my family used to come here for picnics. We'd spend all day fishing and playing games and hiking. It was such fun. . . ."

His small voice broke into her reminiscences. "Your father and mother brought you here?"

"Yes." She nodded, recalling those warm, carefree days.

"Just like today?" he asked innocently.

A knot lodged tightly in her throat as she nodded mutely, finally murmuring, "Yes, David. Just like today."

Suddenly the Suburban lunged sharply forward and ground to a halt. Quickly Grant started the motor and backed the vehicle out of the rut, then cut the engine again. **"Well, folks,"** he announced, "this is as far as we go."

Morgan looked around. They were completely surrounded by shrubs. "That's okay. We're close to the stream. Seems to me this is as far as we ever drove. It's not very far, and we can just load up and walk. Can't we, David?"

"Sure. I'll carry the fishing rods! Let's go!" The beauty of excitement filled his small face, and the emotion of the previous moment was lost beyond his understanding.

"Here, son, you carry the rods. I'll get the food and cooler. Morgan, can you get the tackle box?" Grant distributed the various paraphernalia.

"Yay! I hear the water!" David grabbed the proffered fishing rods and took off with a hoot.

Morgan and Grant reached into the back of the Suburban at the same time for the remaining items. He grasped the portable cooler with one strong hand and glanced at Morgan.

"Need any help? Do we have it all?" He glanced down to see her clutching the tackle box in one hand, her other arm wrapped around a large, colorful quilt.

Their eyes met over the quilt and turbulent thoughts raced in both their minds. Grant broke the uneasy silence. "This was a good idea, Morgan. David loves it already."

She nodded, unable to smile as she looked into the depths of Grant's bold, blue-gray eyes. "I knew he would." She dropped her eyes, unwilling to meet his gaze any longer. Maybe this was a mistake for her.

"Is this hard for you, Morgan? Coming to this place so soon after your father's death?" His voice was serious and understanding.

A shrill voice echoed from beyond the tree line. "Grant! Come on!"

Morgan looked up quickly. "I'm fine, Grant. Let's go. David's going to catch the first fish before we even get there!"

And David did manage to catch the first fish! Then, amid great shouts of joy, he almost lost it. If it hadn't been for Grant's great fish-saving act, the fish would have been free again. But, true to a father's dedication, Grant lunged after the squirming fish, salvaging it for his young son. The fact that he had leaped into the ice-cold rushing stream was not important. The heroic act had prevented a catastrophe for David, and what did it matter that Grant's jeans were now thoroughly wet?

Both David and Morgan screeched with laughter and delight as they pulled their hero from the icy depths. He handed the slick fish to David with the admonition, "Last chance, son. Hold on to him this time." The meaning was clear to all. He would not dive into the chilling waters again.

"Oh, I will! Thanks, Grant! You saved my fish! Can I cook him? Can I?"

"Sure, son," Grant muttered through clenched teeth. He stood dripping water from drenched jeans that clung to his masculine shape.

Assured that the precious fish was safely in the creel, Morgan turned her attention to Grant. "Oh, my God, you're wet, Grant."

His eyes snapped at her. "Keen observance, Morgan!"

"If it'll make you feel any better, you were magnificent! You're now a hero! I'm sure David will never forget it. And neither will I." She couldn't control the peals of laughter that flooded her as she recalled his antics. "You should have seen it, Grant. Such great form! Why, the Denver Ballet Company would have been proud!"

He pushed past her, muttering for her ears only, "Doing a goddamn water ballet and freezing my ass off, and all you two can do is laugh!"

She couldn't resist quipping, "What do you expect us to do? Remove your pants and hang them on the line to dry?"

He turned around slowly to face her, an expression of bold vengeance on his face, and for a frantic minute she feared that is exactly what he would do. "Don't tempt me, my dear!" Then he wheeled around and stalked toward the Suburban.

"Where are you going, Grant?" Surely he wouldn't go back to the ranch so early and ruin their day.

"Oh, I wouldn't spoil your fun!" he called sarcastically. "Thank God I keep cutoffs in the jeep. Otherwise I could freeze my ass off, and you wouldn't care!"

"Oh, yes, we would!" Morgan answered, but he didn't acknowledge hearing her. So, she turned back to help David bait the hook for the next big battle. "Now, we're going to hold on to the next fish, aren't we, David?"

He nodded enthusiastically. "The next one . . . oh, boy!"

Grant returned shortly attired in a pair of very worn cutoff jeans. Morgan tried not to notice where the fringe graced the hard muscles of his legs as he climbed the rocks to just the right spot. He braced himself, and the corded muscles of his legs strained boldly as he cast his fishing line expertly into the dark holes. Undoubtedly he had fished for trout many times before, for he exhibited skillful knowledge as he quietly flicked his wrist and maneuvered the shiny artificial fly on the end of his line.

Meanwhile Morgan and David laughed and talked and scooted around on the lower rocks, clearly visible to any fish who might care to take notice of their loud, fun-filled activities. Yet they continued to pile up the fish and caught five between them in a period of two hours.

Morgan helped David untangle his line, and David returned

the favor by assisting when she caught her first fish. Morgan was so thrilled, she was shaking as she tried to unhook the squirming thing.

David bent over the prize with her, warning, "Don't drop it, Morgan. I don't think Grant will dive in the water again."

"I can guarantee it!" Grant's voice boomed behind them. "What's for lunch? I'm starved!"

Morgan dropped her fish pompously into the creel with David's catch and winked at the little boy. "Who cares about lunch? We have fish for supper! And David gets to cook them all!"

"Yay!" David clapped his hands in delight. "Morgan, I thought you came out here when you were a little girl," he chirped teasingly. He stood on a rock and towered above her blond braided hair.

She looked up curiously at him. "I did, David. I was just about your size."

He propped his hands on his hips and beamed down at her. "Well, I'm bigger than you! You're still a little girl! And lots more fun than Grant!"

"Little girl?" she sputtered, trying to tickle him before he jumped off the rock and dashed away, laughing at his own joke.

Grant howled with laughter and swatted her on the rear. "Come on, *little girl!* Let's eat! This man's starved!"

Chuckling, Morgan grabbed the quilt and followed her hungry fishermen, who were already trudging across the field.

"Over here!" yelled David, always ahead of them by at least twenty paces. "Let's eat here under this tree!"

As they approached the tree-shaded, grassy area, Grant agreed. "It looks just about perfect, David. Now, where's the food?"

Morgan spread the colorful quilt on the ground, and the three of them gathered around the food basket like rapacious predators scraping for sustenance.

"Stand back, you graceless vultures!" Morgan rebuffed. "I shall distribute this gourmet's delight in due turn. A sandwich for you and a pickle for you." She bowed first to David, then to Grant, both of whom obliged with large grins as the diminutive chef took charge.

"I thought you weren't inclined toward kitchen duties," Grant teased between bites of ham sandwich.

"Oh, I don't mind the gratification. It's the preparation I despise! And out here, this is fun! David, eat your sandwich before you start on the cookies."

Grant opened a diet soft drink and passed it to her. "It is fun, Morgan. This idea of yours was a good one."

"Well." She smiled. "I had to come up with something that would compare with the pizza night."

"This is funner," David said enthusiastically. "I like to fish!"

"I do, too. And I thought you would," Morgan agreed as she leaned back against the large tree trunk and sipped her drink. "Wow! I didn't realize how hungry I was! Is there another sandwich?"

"I knew you'd be starving by now. But I tried to restrain myself as long as I possibly could. Didn't want to ruin your fishing. That's my supper you're catching." Grant chuckled.

"And I get to cook them 'cause I caught the most!" chirped David, happily. "Can I go for a walk, Grant? Over there?" He pointed across the field.

Grant nodded. "If you stay within shouting distance. That means right around in the clearing so I can see you."

"Yes, sir," agreed David, grabbing a handful of cookies before he darted away.

Morgan shook her head in awe. "There he goes again. Where does he get the energy?"

"Well, he didn't stay up until after midnight last night drinking wine and talking!" Grant observed with a knowing smile. Emitting a thoracic groan, he eased himself to a reclining position and folded his hands under his head.

Morgan pulled her knees toward her chin and tried not to pay heed to the corded muscles bulging along his arms and chest. Those powerful arms had held her so soundly last night, easily eliciting her very feminine response to his masculine will. However she couldn't deny her own yearning for his touch. But that was last night when she was lulled by the wine and his virile appeal. After all she wasn't a zombie! Today, in clear light, she viewed things differently and she determined to let him know.

She looked away from him and studied the outline of trees against the azure sky. "Grant, about last night—"

His quick reply interrupted her words and train of thought. "Look, Morgan, I feel entirely responsible for that. I brought the wine, and initiated everything else. I can understand your position. If you don't want it to happen again, I can assure you it won't. I just find you attractive, and responded accordingly. If you don't like it, then . . ." He shrugged angular shoulders and shut his eyes. There was an air of indifference that infuriated Morgan. He had taken the words right out of her mouth, twisted their impact, and discounted their justification.

"It's not that I didn't like it . . . well, what I mean is—" She stopped abruptly. *Here I go again! Tongue-tied and stumbling over my words like a fool! Damn him, anyway!* "Grant, I just don't want that sort of thing to become a habit. I mean, that could be . . ."

"Dangerous?" He laughed. "Don't worry, Morgan. I'll back off. I can take a hint! Do you have someone else? Is there another man in your life? Just give me the word, and David and I can make ourselves very scarce."

"Oh, no." Her answer came too fast and she took a deep breath and tried to slow her words. "Not at the moment. Actually, I . . . while I was in Europe, most of my friends married."

He rolled over on his side, bending his arm to prop his head. "I mean it sincerely, Morgan. If you want a weekend in privacy, just say the word. We'll be gone in a second."

His seriousness about the rather pointed subject brought a warm blush to her cheeks, and she laughed lightly in an effort to ease her nervousness. "If the occasion arises, I'll be sure to let you know, Grant."

Grant smiled and nodded slightly in agreement with Morgan's blithe promise, those steely-gray eyes of his lingering over her knowingly. Then his gaze turned to encompass the majestic mountains that lined the horizon. "What a beautiful place to grow up. I would love for David to have this kind of freedom and fun. Look at him. He's really enjoying this, Morgan."

She grinned at the vision of the young, dark-haired boy chasing butterflies. "Hmmm . . . it is great for kids. I can remember romping through this field doing exactly what he's doing."

Grant took a deep breath. "Clean, fresh air . . . no smog. Peaceful and quiet . . . no cars honking or jets breaking the sound of silence. Did you come here often with your family?"

"When I was young, we came down here from Denver every holiday from school. Spent every summer here." She picked a long grass and chewed the sweet, juicy end. "When I was about ten—Do you want to hear this?" She stopped abruptly, unsure of his interest.

"Please go on, Morgan," he encouraged.

After a pause she continued. "Our mother died when I was about ten, leaving me as the only female in a very male-dominated family. My two brothers and father loved the winter sports available nearby and the country life the ranch provided. I was a part of those activities, too."

"Did you enjoy them?"

"Yes, but . . ." she answered slowly, "I suppose it wasn't enough for me. As I grew older, the peace and quiet was too dull for me. I wanted to travel."

"So, you took off for Europe," Grant added.

She shrugged. "Well, actually, in the last five or six years, none of us have used the ranch very much. My brothers were extremely busy with college and law school. I attended college for a few years, then had a chance to go to Europe with friends. I decided to quit school short of my degree, much to my father's chagrin."

"He wasn't in agreement with your decision to go to Europe?" Grant inclined his head toward her, detecting a growing terseness in Morgan's words.

"Of course, Daddy tried to convince me to finish college. Eventually, though, he agreed for me to use the rest of my education money for the trip. I guess my tour of Europe lasted longer than he expected. I was there three years. However I didn't realize just how much he was opposed to my . . . life-style . . . until he died."

After a moment Grant asked, "Did you come from Europe for your father's funeral, or were you here in the States?"

Somehow Morgan appreciated his sincerity. She hadn't talked much about her father's death and Grant seemed a willing listener. With a sigh she said, "I was in Amsterdam when I got the call. I hadn't seen him in three years. But he wasn't ill. The doctor said he probably had no symptoms before the sudden heart attack. He just died. It was quick." Her voice was flat. The pain of his death was still there, but had been dulled by her anger at his will.

Grant's voice was low and sober. "I'm sorry, Morgan. I know you and your father were close. Adam said you were your daddy's darling."

She nodded. "I thought we were close, too. But the will that Daddy left for us changed my mind about some things. Did Adam also tell you about that?" Morgan couldn't soften the hard tone that edged her voice.

He shook his head. "We didn't talk about the will."

She traced the colored shapes on the quilt aimlessly. "From the way the inheritance was distributed, you'd think he hated me."

"That bad?"

"For me, yes. Adam and Brett received the office buildings in Denver that are already money-producing real estate. I got this run-down ranch. All they have to do is maintain what's already functioning. I have to start from scratch."

"But just look at the challenge you have, Morgan! This place is beautiful . . . and promising."

Morgan's brown eyes glistened with hurt anger. Obviously Grant was just trying to bolster her. "To hell with challenge! Who wants to work so hard that you get calluses on your hands and blisters on your feet? Not me!"

Grant reached for her hand and pressed the palm to his lips, his tongue gently circling her sensitive flesh, sending tingles up her arm. His breath was soft and warm as he spoke into her hand. "That's what you hired me for, remember? I'm supposed to be the one to get calluses and blisters. And I still think you got a bargain." He kissed her palm, then turned it over to brush the rough knuckles with the softness of his lips.

Morgan tried to control her breathing as she answered, "You don't understand how Daddy has interfered in my life with his demands. He has just ruined it for me!" She tried to pull her hand away from Grant's tender, evocative caresses which were draining all rational conversation from her mind. "Please, don't do that, Grant." Even though his lips and tongue had only grazed her hand, it was enough to stimulate alarming impulses inside her. His power was too magnetic for her to break away, and Morgan felt helplessly drawn to him.

Sitting up, he moved urgently closer, his arms enveloping her in a crushing embrace. "Morgan, Morgan, come to me . . ." His insistent words faded into a soft gasp just before his lips closed over hers. His tongue lightly teased her lower lip, then tickled the delicate outline of her upper lip, finally persuading her mouth to open for further intrusion.

At his touch Morgan immediately forgot her resolution of just moments before. Willingly she gave in to the soft pressure of his mouth, the tender probing of his tongue. The exquisite sensations that washed over her were too overpowering, too wonderful, to stop. Not just yet, anyway. She moved still closer to Grant; her fingertips playfully twirled the hairs at his nape. Grant, feeling her body melting into his, her soft feminine curves pressing against his tautening muscles, nuzzled his mouth along the sensitive line of her shoulder. Her hands began a slow dance of pleasure up and down his spine. This was like nothing else she had experienced. No one, not even André, had made her feel like this.

Grant slowly moved his mouth to repossess the softness of her lips, his probing tongue promising, urging, tempting. His warm hands slipped under her sweater, and reached around her ribs, his long fingers splayed against her sensitized flesh. As she clung to his shoulders, his hands shifted upward, gliding gently but skillfully over her soft breasts. His searching hands cupped each generous mound, and her sensitive tips swelled, drawing forth a surprised gasp from Morgan. Neither of them were aware of the small figure who galloped happily toward the shade tree.

"Hey, Grant! Look what I found!"

The small child's shrill voice stopped their passion cold and both Grant and Morgan jumped. Grant groaned softly and quickly pulled away from Morgan's warm body, folding his hands casually under his head. Morgan jerked back against the tree, tugging her sweater evenly around her hips.

"What, David?" Grant managed to mumble.

"See the grasshopper I caught?" David's shining face glowed blissfully while his grimy hand clutched a kicking green insect.

"That's great, son," Grant responded, showing amazing interest in the creature.

"Can we use it for fish bait? Are you ready to go fishing again?" Large, dark eyes looked down, questioning.

"Oh, uh, not yet, David. Why don't you see if you can catch a few more grasshoppers? Here, you can put them in this empty sandwich bag."

David eagerly complied with his father's request and brought a smile to Grant's face as he ran off again. There was an uneasy silence and a sudden gust rustled the leaves of the shade tree.

Grant's steel-gray eyes met hers. "Morgan, I—"

Morgan shifted her position and gazed at him honestly. "You don't have to explain, Grant. It . . . it was as much my fault as yours. But it just can't keep happening. I have a ranch to run and . . . you have your work. At this rate the place will never make it."

"Perhaps your father left you the ranch because he had confidence that you could build it into something beautiful as well as useful."

"With the stipulations surrounding the damn thing, I have to make it work . . . or lose it. Oh, yeah, he forced me to do what he wanted." Resentment steeled her voice.

"What do you mean by that? What stipulations?" Grant puzzled.

"Well, part of the provisions are that I have to make the ranch profitable within a year, or share the ownership with my brothers. If I just let it sit, believe me, I'll lose it. They'll take over."

"Profitable in a year? That's damn near impossible for any business, especially a tourist-oriented one. My God, Morgan—how could he do that to you?" Grant's voice rose as he sat up, looking at her in amazement. "So that's why you're so determined to pull this thing together in a hurry."

Morgan's eyes flashed deep bronze in her angry response. "You're damned right I am! I'm determined that this is one thing they won't run in my life! They've tried, already. Adam was willing to help, which was fine. But when he broke his leg, Brett called to tell me to return home until they could help me. See, they still want to keep me under their thumb! Just like my father did! That's what Daddy intended when he left the will so confined in legalities."

"Do you think he was pushing you to independence?"

She looked at Grant curiously. How much did he actually know about her? She admitted, "He wanted me to settle down to one thing. And to stay in this country." Did she dare say "settle down to one person"? "With this will, he has forced me to change my life and do what he wanted me to do. And I resent that. My brothers weren't forced to change anything. Their lives are the same . . . or better. They now have additional income and property."

"Don't forget," Grant advised, "they also have additional responsibilities. Keeping businesses going isn't easy, Morgan."

She sighed. "Oh, I know that. But apparently Daddy didn't think I could handle a business, so he gave me this stupid ranch. And even that is dampened by restrictions. Thank God there's also a trust fund set up for me and I can borrow from it without cosignatures from my dear brothers!"

Suddenly Grant's features were alive with enthusiasm. "Morgan, in all modesty, we have made an excellent start on the ranch. And I love the challenge of what can be done with it. I'd like to help you make a profitable business of it. Now, I don't know if it'll be earning its own way this summer. That seems a little too soon. But we can give it a try! How about it? I told you I'd stay the summer. And I will. I believe we can make it if we work together!"

Morgan looked at him doubtfully. Why was he so eager to help her? Was it the challenge—or her? "Of course, Grant, I would love to show Adam and Brett that I can be successful without their influence. But I don't know . . ."

Confidence was evident as Grant encouraged her. "Together we can do it, Morgan! I'm sure of it!"

She smiled at his little-boy zeal. "Grant, you don't know anything about ranching and neither do I."

He shrugged. "We'll learn together. Now let's go find my son before he catches all the grasshoppers here!" He caught her hand and they ran across the green, grassy field . . . together.

* * *

Although the hour was late, Morgan paced the living room. Her thoughts were jumbled, confused, wrangling inside her until she could scream. She reflected on the day spent with Grant and David. It had been glorious, a time to remember with joy. And then there was the arrangement she and Grant had discussed. Actually she could find no fault with someone wanting to help her. It gave her some assurance and peace of mind regarding the ranch. But another thought had been tearing at her mind since their agreement. If he was going to stay the summer, then why not—? No! How could she? She hardly knew him! And yet she would have to do something . . . sometime. That was another proviso of the will. One that she hadn't told Grant. She could offer him the stability that he needed for David as well as the fifty-thousand-dollar wedding gift. It would be worth the money to her, for she had no great need of it. But Grant did. Would he do it?

Beleaguered by her own wildly racing thoughts, she roamed through the large ranch house. If she could convince him that he would benefit, too, then maybe he would help her. She glanced out the back window nervously. A small yellow glow outlined the bunkhouse door. He was still awake! Well, why not try?

With sweating palms Morgan gripped the doorknob and bolted across the backyard to the bunkhouse. She would simply try before she lost the nerve. Gnawing questions continued to bedevil her even as she approached the smaller building. What if . . . he refused? What if . . . he left her now? What if he wouldn't even stay the duration of the summer to work? What if . . . this ruined everything?

What if . . . oh, God . . . he said *yes?*

Morgan paused for a moment to gather her strength and listened to the clicking of his typewriter in the quiet night. He was working . . . poor guy. After all the toil of this exhausting week he still tried to write! Didn't that prove his need for the deal she was about to propose?

She knocked lightly on the door and waited, dread engulfing her like a chilling fog. The typing stopped and Morgan held her breath. She could hear him walking across the floor, but wasn't quite prepared for his rugged, masculine figure outlined in the open doorway. His shirt hung loosely, unbuttoned and barely hiding the crisply curling mat that spread across his chest.

"Morgan? What's wrong?"

"Grant, I—" When she finally found her voice, it came out embarrassingly shaky.

"Morgan, are you all right?" Grant's hand reached out to her, and, incredibly, she moved away from him. He placed his outstretched hand on the door facing, obviously perplexed by her strange behavior.

She had to say something to him! She was here before him! Oh, God, what would this do to her life? With a rush of breath and courage she expelled, "Grant, will you marry me?"

CHAPTER FOUR

The shocked expression on Grant's face disclosed all Morgan needed to know at the moment. Grant was appalled, angered, probably even repulsed by her question. He would depart as soon as he could gather his son and their meager belongings. Morgan was sure of it. She had destroyed what little working relationship they had. It would never be the same even if he stayed. But he wouldn't do that. Couldn't. Now he would leave her alone on the ranch—in fear of having his already difficult life completely ruined by this crazy female who asked for his hand in marriage after knowing him only one week.

Unsteadily Morgan turned away from him, bitter tears stinging her eyes. She hated this degradation—all because of her father and his unreasonable demands. Damn him!

As she started away, she heard Grant's laughter. He was actually laughing at her . . . amused at her ignoble invitation to marriage. Damn him, too! Oh, how she hated him! His low laughter rang in her head until she wanted to scream. And run. So that is exactly what she did—or tried to do.

Forceful, masculine hands restrained her efforts, gripping her, wrapping her into his steel-hard arms . . . warm, secure arms that had held her before. Only now they seemed to be binding her, coercing her into the shame of confronting him. His hand cupped her chin, lifting the angry-sad face so that he could see the tears that trailed her cheeks.

His voice was harsh. "Morgan, what did you say?"

She clinched her teeth, determined not to cry anymore—and not to humiliate herself before this man again. Once was enough —more than enough for Morgan Cassity.

"Get your hands off me!"

His breath was frosty in the cold night air as he rasped, "Don't run away from me, then! Talk to me, Morgan! It's not often that I'm asked to marry. And I want to know why. It's not for love!"

She almost spat her words. "No! It's not for love! It's for . . . for business!"

"What?"

Morgan's sable eyes flashed at him wildly. Oh, why had she ever done such a thing? "I . . . it's . . . oh, why don't you just go on and leave me alone? It's what you want to do! Just pack up and get out of here! Then you can laugh all you want to! Oh, yes, Grant LeMaster, you can laugh about the hysterical female who asked you to marry her one miserable night! And let go of me! You're hurting my arms!"

He eased up slightly on her arms, but didn't let go completely. "Then let's go into the house and talk about this. I'm intrigued by your question. And curious about your reason."

"And don't forget amused by the idea!" she hissed.

"No more laughter, I promise."

"I have nothing to say to you." She regretted even mentioning it, hoping he would let the subject drop . . . knowing he would not.

"I'm interested in the proposal," he persisted.

Morgan's eyes narrowed, as she doubted his sincerity. "It would make great writing material, wouldn't it?"

With a resigned shrug Grant's arms slumped to his sides. "I wouldn't do that to you, Morgan. Surely you know that."

Now that she was free from his fierce grasp, Morgan turned away from him. How could she trust him? She didn't even know him. And she had been fool enough to ask this strange man to be her husband!

Grant's ragged voice broke the stillness of the night. "Morgan, what if I said yes? Yes, I'll marry you."

She stopped midstep and took in a shaky breath. Had she really heard right?

"Morgan, the answer is yes." The steel edge of his voice cut into her, and she knew she had to answer him. But what could she say? How could she explain? Did she really want this?

Morgan's voice was unsteady as she asked, "Are . . . are you sure?"

"Frankly, no! How the hell can I be sure when I hardly know you? But I do know one thing. You're in trouble or you would never have posed such a wild proposition. Maybe I can help you a little, Morgan. Are you pregnant?"

"No!" She wheeled around to face Grant and encountered his darkly concerned face and long arms folded across his chest. He was just like all the others. Maybe Adam had done too much talking to his friend. Maybe he told Grant she had spent the last few years in Europe . . . with different men! Oh, how could he? "No, I'm not pregnant! And I'm not in trouble!"

"Then why do you want me to marry you?"

"I don't! I mean . . . er . . . I can't help it!"

"Can't help it? You have a compulsion for marriage?" Amusement played at his lips, infuriating her further.

"No, I certainly do not! And I would never have asked you if I hadn't been out of my mind . . . temporarily, that is! Now I'm sane again, so just forget it!"

"Ah, you're too late to rescind the proposal. You've asked, and I've accepted! Now let's go inside before we freeze, and discuss the upcoming nuptials!" He steered her firmly but gently toward the back door of the ranch house, and before she knew it, they were sipping hot chocolate and she was pouring out the entire miserable story of the stipulations in her father's will.

"So it would be a union for business purposes only. There would be none of the . . . uh . . . usual privileges of a marriage," Morgan explained tactfully.

Grant looked at her sharply. "Do you mean sexual privileges?"

Her eyes met his defiantly. "Exactly."

He shrugged. "My concern was regarding the sharing of property and . . . custody."

His attitude afforded considerable relief. At least he wouldn't bother her about sex. "David?" She hadn't even thought of the boy. "Oh, I would never interfere with your relationship with your son, Grant."

"I'd want it in writing."

She shrugged. "Fifty thousand is mine—ours—upon marriage. I will give it all to you if you'll stay long enough to get the ranch working smoothly, say, the end of the summer. At that time you can have the money. No strings attached. But I want to retain the ranch in my name. And I'd want it in writing."

He pursed his lips thoughtfully. "Sounds reasonable. You keep the ranch, I keep the kid. By the end of the summer we should be even. Is it a deal?"

Morgan nodded in full agreement. "It's a deal!" She smiled wanly and extended her hand. Their hands clasped to seal the strangest arrangement either had ever dreamed of . . . in all their traveling or writing. The run-down little Colorado ranch would be the location of the most unique and unusual summer either had ever experienced.

The next day they went into town for the necessary blood tests that would precede the bizarre arrangement-marriage. They talked to a lawyer who would draw up the marriage agreement they both would sign, detailing the items they desired. There were some basic issues here, and love was definitely not one of them.

Morgan and Grant rode back to the ranch in strained silence, each seemingly lost in sober contemplation. Finally Grant suggested, "Morgan, I think it's about time we considered hiring some additional help. We'll certainly need it when time grows closer to opening the ranch, and it would be nice if we had someone by then that we knew and could trust. I could use some help now with the corrals and barns, and I'm sure you could use help in the house."

Morgan looked at Grant sharply. "Let's get something straight right now. The house is *not* my domain! I will not be in charge of the kitchen! Nor of the house!"

"Nor the bedroom?" He chuckled.

"Right!" she reaffirmed adamantly.

"Well, then, it's time we hired someone to be in charge of the kitchen! And the house as well!" A muscle twitched menacingly in his tight jaw, and Morgan grinned at the reactions apparent in his very masculine profile.

She just couldn't resist taunting him. "And what about the bedroom? Do you have someone in mind?" A mocking sweetness dripped from her voice as she folded her arms and glared at him, waiting for an answer. She would be damned if she would allow his liaisons on her ranch, and they may as well get that straightened out right now.

"I'll keep my bedroom activities as discreet as you do," he answered brusquely. "As for the rest of the house and grounds, yes, I do have someone in mind. I know an older couple who live in Durango and are having a tough time making a living these days. He's an old ranch hand and cowboy with a multitude of skills, but people are reluctant to hire him anymore because of his age. I think a ranch the size of yours would be just about perfect for him. And I'm sure his wife would be willing to take over the kitchen duties, including early-morning breakfast."

Morgan listened intently, ignoring the jabs at his discreet bedroom activities and her awful early-morning breakfast attempts. The fact was they *had* reached a point when they both needed more help around the ranch. And they definitely would be hiring someone in a month or so. Why not now? Plus, it would be nice to have someone else, besides David, on the premises to ensure they weren't completely alone after the marriage. Grant would be forced to go elsewhere for his "discreet bedroom activities." He wouldn't dare flaunt his promiscuity in front of them.

Morgan nodded in agreement. "I certainly agree that we need help. And this couple you know sounds suitable. I'd like to meet them before a final decision is made, though."

"Certainly. I'll arrange it for our next trip into town," Grant allowed.

"Good. Then maybe he could help you get the wild horses down at Ignacio," Morgan replied.

"Wild horses?" The vehicle lurched a little.

Morgan smiled sheepishly. "Actually, it was Adam's idea to buy unbroken horses and break them ourselves for saddle or pack. They're cheaper. So I bought a couple of horses from a rancher near Ignacio. Grant, they're not wild . . . just a little green. They don't take to riders well yet."

"My God, Morgan! Do you know how goddamn much trouble unbroken horses can be?"

She shrugged and answered honestly, "Never thought much about it."

His tone showed his agitation. "Well, hell, woman! Who's going to break them?" The minute he said it, *he knew!*

She paused before saying, "Who's in charge of the corrals?"

"I'll be damned! It's been years since I've saddle-broken a horse! Do you want me to kill myself?" He was still quite impassioned.

Morgan raised her eyebrows and quipped, "Not before the wedding. I figured if I took care of renovation and purchasing, you could handle training . . . and early breakfasts for the Rocking M Ranch!"

"Rocking M Ranch? Seems to me you should name it Lazy M Ranch—that would be closer to the truth!" Grant scoffed.

"Now, now, darling. Don't be bitter! Can you believe we're having our first lover's quarrel? And we aren't even married yet!" Morgan figured she had pushed Grant about as far as she could in this first bout. After all, she knew she needed him. His business sense would prove valuable, as would his strong back. But he had a stake in this project, too. It was to his benefit to make the endeavor profitable by summer's end. Then he could leave with the fifty thousand, free and clear. Not a bad salary for a summer's work. And Morgan could go about her life, free of the entanglement of a husband. It couldn't come too soon for her. But first Morgan had a wedding to attend. Her own!

Morgan stared at the distant, white-tipped mountain peaks. They were so steady and peaceful and constant . . . always there, always dependable. Their steadfast significance gave her the strength she needed to endure this, her wedding day.

Grant would return soon. He had surprised her by saying that he and David should be dressed appropriately for the wedding. The two of them headed for town early, with a promise to return soon for her. She didn't know why he wanted to bother with a suit for this facade of a wedding, but it forced her to thinking of wearing something besides her jeans and velour sweater. Maybe he thought of himself as a "landed gentry" now and felt he should dress as befitting someone of his status. Ha! She supposed she would raise his status considerably with this marriage. Just for the hell of it, she should wear her scrubbiest clothes. She smiled involuntarily at the thought. It would serve him right!

The noise of a vehicle in the driveway attracted her attention, and Morgan turned away from the glorious mountains. Sure enough, there were Grant and David climbing out of the burgundy Suburban. They were both dressed to the teeth. Even little David sported a pair of new leather cowboy boots, beige slacks, and a dark brown sport jacket with western cut to the coat. It fit his little shoulders perfectly, and he looked so handsome. When he turned around, she could see that his small, dark face was aglow with a broad smile.

Oh, God, what was all this going to do to David? She hadn't even considered him until this moment. What was he thinking? Did he want her as his new mother? *Mother!* She had not even talked to him about it and wondered what Grant had told him. It had all happened so fast, they had not really discussed the boy. All she knew was that she wasn't to interfere with the custody of David when the divorce came about. But that didn't mean she couldn't be friends with him. Maybe not a mother—she shuddered at the thought. But they could be friends.

The joyous expression on David's face was too much for Morgan. She just couldn't ruin his day by dressing in her oldest clothes. She dropped her robe and opened the closet door, searching for something appropriate . . . something *comme il faut.* Her eyes fell on an exquisite designer dress that she had purchased in Paris last year. She had only worn it a few times— Once to a friend's wedding and again in Greece with André. *André.* She had bought it with André in mind . . . knowing he would love it. Her bronze eyes flickered at the memories, acknowledging bitterly that it now seemed justifiable to wear the ivory-colored garment to her wedding. Morgan quickly slipped her arms into the long sleeves which were cuffed tightly with tiny, pearl buttons at the wrists. The bodice clung softly to her curves, caressing the swell of her bosom. It was impossible to avoid the creamy stretch of cleavage visible in the deeply plunging V neckline. A small, tie-belt hugged the slim waistline she had hidden all week under jeans and a bulky shirt. Morgan surveyed her reflection in the full-length mirror, wondering briefly if the dress was too seductive for her wedding. She turned, and the skirt swirled gently around her knees, brandishing beautiful, cutwork embroidery. Splendid! It's not too alluring, she decided. Just impressive. Maybe Grant would find his new bride attractive in this. She smiled wryly to herself. *Why do I care what Grant thinks of me? This is just a business deal for both of us.*

She ran a brush through her flaxen hair, letting it hang loosely over her shoulders. Maybe David wouldn't be too ashamed to have her for a new mother, even if she was only temporary. She sighed heavily. *Well, let's get on with it!* Morgan opened the front door, where David and Grant stood waiting. There was a clumsy silence as the trio stood under one another's visual scrutiny.

David was the first to speak. "Wow, Morgan! You look beautiful! Why don't you wear that dress here at the ranch?" His innocent honesty embarrassed her.

Morgan blushed prettily, avoiding the gleam of approval and unhidden desire in Grant's eyes. Purposely she spoke to David. "Thank you, David. You look so handsome today, I felt I should wear something nice to accompany you."

"Well, it's sure nice, isn't it, Grant?" David's dark eyes glistened brilliantly at his father as he reached for Grant's hand.

"Oh, it's . . . very . . . nice," agreed Grant, with a wicked grin for Morgan and a wink for little David.

Morgan was amazed at David's reactions to her appearance. Was the kid wise beyond his years? Or was he wise because of living with a bachelor father? Well, what should she expect? The man who was to be her husband stood there agog, his slate-gray eyes fairly bugging out of his head. Maybe the dress had done more than it was meant to. She certainly didn't want him to think . . . But that had been spelled out with clarity. Morgan lifted her chin proudly to meet his steady gaze.

Grant's knowing eyes roamed down the V neck of her dress, then back to her flushed cheeks. "Yes, Morgan. I'm very fortunate to be standing by your side today. You are gorgeous, even if you are a little girl." He reached to take her hand, but she brushed by him coolly.

"Spare me the hearts and flowers, Grant. It will do you no

good. Besides, we both know what this is all about," she muttered close to him.

Undaunted, he managed to open the Suburban door before she could reach it. "Speaking of flowers, I thought you should have a bouquet for your wedding." He produced a small assemblage of tiny forget-me-nots surrounding a white orchid and thrust it into her hands.

Instinctively her fingers lightly caressed the smooth petals of the orchid. It was a beautiful gesture and Morgan was touched. "Thank you, Grant," she murmured, keeping her head lowered as she climbed into the front seat. It wouldn't do for him to see the sudden swelling of tears that filled her eyes. Did he really care? He seemed to be trying to make this a special day. Sighing, she wondered if anyone really cared that she was being forced into a marriage today. Her family didn't even know. It had been decided that they would be notified later.

The trip into town was extremely quiet and strained. Morgan tried to ignore the fact that Grant looked very dashing in his beige, camel-hair blazer with stitched detailing and double-point back yoke. His champagne-colored silk shirt was complemented by a western bolo tie with silver concho slide inset with a huge turquoise stone. The thing must have cost him a fortune, unless it was a gift from his former wife's family.

Under normal conditions Morgan wouldn't even attempt to hide her admiration for the handsome man beside her. But these weren't normal conditions. She felt doomed to endure a marriage she never wanted . . . with a man she hardly knew. And she was definitely the reluctant bride.

The strange marriage contract was signed first, the stipulations in agreement with both parties. He wouldn't interfere with her property. She wouldn't contest his child custody. They stood somewhat nervously before the justice of the peace, who was, surprisingly enough, a woman. She read the age-old vows methodically from a dog-eared little book, smiling presumptuously at the tall, steely man and serious young woman before her. Their stony expressions didn't change throughout the short ceremony.

When she reached the part about the ring, Morgan gazed uncertainly at Grant. It hadn't even occurred to her that a ring would be necessary. However Grant smoothly reached into his pocket and produced a small round thing which he proceeded to slip onto her finger, repeating something about "with this ring I thee wed."

Morgan looked down and gasped silently. Wrapped around her finger was an absolutely beautiful crafting in silver with inlays of deep, dark turquoise. Her startled bronze eyes raised to meet Grant's just as the justice of the peace entoned, "All right, you may kiss your bride." *It was done!*

Morgan watched as his taut face approached hers, bearing down, closer and closer until she felt his warm lips on hers, tenderly claiming his wife before witnesses. The long moments were finally interrupted by loud applause and cheering from their smallest spectator. "Yay! It's over! Now can we get some ice cream like you promised, Morgan?"

Grant released her then, and Morgan turned from her husband to look at David with a grateful smile. "Sure, David. I think I'll celebrate with Doom's Day Licorice!"

As they left the building, Morgan slowed, purposely allowing David to run on ahead. She touched Grant's arm with her left hand, where the ring gleamed boldly, almost ostentatiously.

"Grant . . ." she began hesitantly. "You really shouldn't have gone to all this expense. The ring is . . . just magnificent." Her sable eyes were large and round and serious.

His unwavering gaze settled on her. *Those eyes . . . those beautiful, blue-gray eyes.* "I couldn't find a diamond I liked on such short notice."

She shrugged. "Diamonds are forever, like the ad says. And we both know this marriage is just temporary. Is it turquoise? I don't think I've ever seen turquoise so green." She held the ring out admiringly.

He nodded tersely. "That ring has a legacy, Morgan. The reason the stone is so rich and green instead of the usual turquoise blue is that it came from a special mine in Utah. Thunder Mountain turquoise is very valuable today because that mine has been closed for about twenty years. So it's rare."

Morgan pursed her lips as she examined the ring anew. "How interesting. And the legacy?"

Grant took her hand and cradled it tenderly in his own, looking deeply into her eyes. "It is said that the one who wears this ring will be forever loved." He lifted her fingers to his lips and kissed them repeatedly.

As his lips played sensuously with her fingertips, she asked nervously, "Do you believe that myth?"

He shrugged with a slight smile. "We could make it happen."

She shook her head vigorously, knowing what he was insinuating. Then a terrible thought struck her, and with a shaky voice Morgan asked, "It didn't belong to David's mother, did it?"

His fingers tightened on hers. "Hell no! I bought it for a very beautiful woman, my wife. The ring is yours, Morgan. Make of it what you will!" Grant dropped her hand and turned away, leaving her feeling like a first-class heel.

She grasped for his arm. "I . . . Grant, I'm sorry. I didn't mean to diminish its intent. I'll wear the ring . . . proudly." She managed a faint smile.

A childish voice interrupted calling loudly, "Grant, Morgan, are you ever coming?"

"Sure, son, we'll be right there," Grant replied.

"Grant"—Morgan gripped his arm as she watched the small boy wistfully—"I hope David doesn't get hurt by all this."

Grant's voice was matter-of-fact. "We'll all be affected by this marriage of ours, Morgan. There's no way we can avoid it. The acts of adults always affect the children, in one way or another. But I'll do everything I can to protect David as much as possible. I only hope you'll do the same." Grant started walking and Morgan followed.

Yes, they all would be affected by this marriage . . . and maybe even hurt. Nothing that manipulated people's lives ever left them completely unscathed. She knew it, and now felt guilty because she had dragged little David into her business marriage. Very guilty.

However if Grant cared so much for his son, why had he been willing to enter into the deal? The answer was clear. There was a large amount of money in this agreement for him. Grant had money to gain and nothing to lose . . . only time.

The fingers on her right hand involuntarily caressed the silver wedding ring. Morgan sighed and followed her new husband. Summer wouldn't end soon enough for her.

* * *

After the ice cream it was business as usual as they stopped by to meet and hire the older couple Grant had recommended. Boyd Simpson was a wiry, lean man in his late fifties. He had a ready smile and walked with a limp. Grant arranged to meet him the next morning to travel to Ignacio for the unbroken horses.

Willa Simpson, Boyd's wife, was a simple, happy woman who tousled David's hair affectionately and agreed to manage the ranch house, and especially the kitchen. Morgan could tell they would have a great alliance. She liked the Simpsons at first meeting and admitted ruefully that Grant was right about them. They would be good additions to the Rocking M.

Morgan and Grant spent the afternoon of their wedding putting the finishing touches on the repaired corral and barn in preparation for the first influx of animals the following day. By nightfall David was eager for his bath and bed. As usual Grant took care of the child, tucking him in bed in the bunkhouse. Morgan thought she had seen the last of her husband as she slumped exhaustedly in front of the unlit fireplace. She sat alone, begrudgingly recalling that this was her wedding day . . . and night. She was feeling very sad and melancholy when she heard a sharp knock at the back door, followed by the definite sounds of someone entering.

"Morgan?" Grant's voice questioned.

It was only her husband. *Husband!* How strange the word sounded.

Without even glancing up she acknowledged him. "Yes? What do you want?"

"Just thought we'd celebrate. After all, it is our wedding night."

She looked up sharply then and caught sight of the bottle of champagne he brandished. "Celebrate what? My compliance?"

His answer was just as sharp as hers. "*Your* compliance? What about mine?" He set the bottle on the kitchen counter and began to work diligently on the cork.

Morgan's tart voice followed him there. "You? You haven't been compromised! You have nothing to lose! And only money to gain! Not a bad deal, Grant LeMaster!"

The cork popped loudly, punctuating her remarks.

Quietly he crossed the room and bowed graciously as he handed her a glass of the bubbly liquid. "For you, Mrs. LeMaster." His tone was smoothly vicious. "And you have nothing to lose but the ranch! Shall I leave now? You can pick up the wild horses with Boyd tomorrow. And you can break them yourself. And you can—"

"All right, Grant! I do need you. And I realize you're here at my request. Actually I'm very grateful that you'd be willing to marry me . . . someone in my condition!" Her eyes softened.

His eyes traveled over her, and his tone was debasing. "Are you trying to tell me that you are pregnant, after all?"

She laughed mockingly at his angry tone, enjoying the tingling on the tip of her nose as she took a drink of the champagne. "I told you I'm not pregnant. I just meant the conditions of my father's will. There aren't many who would be willing to take a wife under those conditions. Of course, I've tried to make it profitable to you. You're a little edgy tonight, husband dear."

"Just matching your mood, my sweet little wife."

Morgan stared defiantly into his belligerent eyes, then turned away to the empty, black fireplace. In a moment she spoke. Gone was the bite in her tone and, in its place, a touch of melancholy. "Look, Grant, I'm afraid I'm a little bitter tonight. This is not the way I had imagined my marriage would be, and I'll admit, I'm not in a very good mood. I had hoped for love somewhere along the way. I . . . I don't want you to leave the ranch, Grant. You know I need you this summer. I guess I'm just a little uptight tonight."

"Believe it or not, I can understand what you're saying, Morgan." He motioned to refill her glass. "Drink up, darling. It'll help you relax. You sound as though you need it."

Morgan's sorrel eyes narrowed distrustingly. "So I'll be more agreeable to grant you sexual favors on your wedding night?"

His taunting grin infuriated her. "I don't expect any favors. You made that perfectly clear at the beginning, Morgan."

She sat up straight, her blond hair swinging furiously across one shoulder. "And I meant it, too! Oh, you've been very nice all day. But all the champagne and nice flowers and beautiful rings in the world won't make me change my mind!"

Grant leaned his head back and gulped long and loud, emptying the glass before turning his devil-like eyes on her. "Oh, I don't expect the virtues of life to change your hostile mind, Morgan! It'll be pure, unadulterated *lust* that does the trick! Enjoy your celebration alone, Mrs. LeMaster." He turned on his heel and strode out, leaving Morgan to spend her wedding night in silent isolation.

CHAPTER FIVE

"They're back, Morgan! The truck is here! Come on! Let's see the horses they brought! Oh, boy!" David's small, bright face flashed through the darkening shadows of evening as he darted off to greet Grant and the new ranch foreman, Boyd Simpson.

Her muscles aching, Morgan laid aside the pitchfork and surveyed the area where she had spread fresh, sweet-smelling straw for the new animals. She smiled to herself, proud of a job well done. Yes, they had done a lot in the last week toward turning the run-down ranch into a workable one. Most of the work had centered on getting the barn and corral ready for these horses. She and David had helped Grant with the repairs, hammering on stalls, doors, and feeders. Living, or rather, working together had been somewhat strained for a day or two after the wedding. But there was so much work to be done, they had adopted a brother-sister relationship. It was an easy posture to assume, since theirs was certainly not a typical husband-wife alliance.

Today, while Grant hauled the new horses from Ignacio, she had been in charge of cleaning the stalls, spreading clean hay on the floor, and stocking the oats in the feed bin. She had completed the tasks and was satisfied that everything was ready for the new animals. Grant would be pleased. *Why does it matter what he thinks?* she wondered stubbornly. *It shouldn't. But it does.*

Morgan looked down at her red, raw hands. The palms burned

unpleasantly. She turned them over and examined the broken blisters. With a pang of regret she remembered the time Grant had kissed those palms so tenderly and promised he would be the one getting blisters and calluses. That was before their marriage, though. Things were different now. He didn't care about her blisters.

Confident that the old barn was fully prepared for their first animals, Morgan started toward the happy sounds of David and the two men. She knew that danger as well as immediate responsibilities came with the acquisition of the unbroken horses. Grant had reminded her about the real necessity for insurance for the ranch. It was a detail that she had never been concerned with. But now, with animals on the property and employees as well, their liability was great. What would she have done without Grant here to make sure about these things?

However these new responsibilities were indications that the dude ranch was becoming a reality, not just an idea. And she had to admit, if only to herself, that Grant had been a major contributor to that reality. Bitter as their exchanges had been, Morgan had confidence that Grant would stay and work through the summer. After all, he had committed himself. And so had she. The silver and turquoise wedding ring gracing her third finger was proof of that.

Morgan rounded the corner of the barn, and a small fist of desire knotted in her stomach as she caught sight of Grant. Even in the growing shadows of evening, she could see those mesmeric gray eyes and the squareness of his jawline as he worked to open the back of the huge truck they had rented for hauling the horses. He was lean and ruggedly appealing, looking every inch a cowboy tonight. It was hard to believe his claim to be a writer. Morgan bit her lip in frustration at her own sudden desires. Oh, lord, he was handsome! If only she weren't so indebted to him . . . if only she hadn't been forced into marrying him . . . perhaps he would appeal to her. Well, hell! Who was she trying to fool, anyway! He *did* appeal to her! She was inexorably drawn to this arrogant, virile man she had married, even though she fought against this primitive urge. She just couldn't help it! If only they could get along!

Grant turned toward her and their eyes met for a moment in

the dusky light. It was no more than a brief hesitation, but the impact left Morgan unnerved and puzzled, wondering what he was thinking about this strange, stubborn bride he had taken. If she knew, she would possibly be astounded. Possibly . . .

Without betraying his thoughts Grant uttered a low, muffled greeting, but continued with his chore, giving her no more attention than a fence post.

However the older man caught the glance and mistook it for something else. He grabbed the chains on the truck and muttered roughly, "Go on, son. Tell her hello like you mean it. I'll get this." By his statement Boyd had made the situation obvious, leaving Grant no alternative but to comply.

So he stepped awkwardly to Morgan, his disdainful eyes cutting into her. Oh, how he must hate her! As he moved close for the kiss she knew was coming, she closed her eyes and flinched inwardly at his touch. A rough hand reached for her shoulder and warm lips grazed her face, ever so close to her lips, yet not quite on them. He had purposely avoided their contact, but she was the only one who knew. He obligingly endured the kiss, just as she did. Having others around was going to be more difficult than she had figured. Could she endure this marriage farce? And it was just beginning!

"Come and see the horses you bought. They're fine-looking animals," he estimated. Grant's attention to her was minimal, as he was far more interested in getting the snorting, restless animals out of the van.

Moving the agitated horses proved to be a hectic job, with both men straining for control, Morgan opening gates, and David wide-eyed with excitement. He seemed to be everywhere at once —in front, behind, in each doorway—always in the wrong place at the wrong time. The horses were excited and nervous, and all three adults pulled David out of the way of sharp hooves at least once. Grant's calm instructions to the child went unheeded until finally in exasperation the father exploded, "All right, David! No more moving around! Stay right where you are and don't move. You're in the way and going to get hurt!"

It must have been the first time Grant had raised his voice to David, for the boy looked as though he had been struck. Recoiling with real trepidation coupled with embarrassment, David ran out of the barn.

"David! David!" called Grant, as he latched the final stall.

Morgan followed the upset child far enough to see him enter his room in the bunkhouse. But Grant's harsh voice halted her continued progress.

"I'll handle him, Morgan."

She wheeled around and snapped, "Now look what you've done! You were too harsh with him!"

His eyes narrowed. "He purposely disobeyed me!"

"Well, did you have to yell at him like that? He was excited. He's just a little kid, Grant!"

"I expect him to obey me, especially when it regards his safety! I didn't want him trampled by wild horses!" Grant propped his fists on his hips and glared at her.

Morgan matched his aggressive stance. "Neither did I! But that's no way to talk to him."

"I'll deal with my son as I see fit. And I don't expect you to interfere! *Comprende?*" Grant's tone was hard.

"Oh, I understand perfectly well. You are such a pig-headed mule, nobody can tell you a thing! Even when you're wrong!"

"If you'll shut up and move out of my way, I can go and talk with David!"

"What are you going to do—apologize?" Morgan mocked. "That certainly doesn't sound like the stubborn jackass I know!"

"That's part of the problem, Morgan. You don't know me at all!" he asserted through clenched teeth. Brushing past her, he headed resolutely for the bunkhouse.

"But I married you anyway," Morgan murmured miserably, half to herself. An overpoweringly ominous feeling that she had made a very big mistake settled over her like a huge net. And she was trapped in the middle of that net with no way to escape.

Morgan slammed the door to her room. She was so agitated after her confrontation with Grant that her eyes smarted with angry tears and her stomach churned nervously. Never had she felt so frustrated and helpless in her entire, pampered life. Morgan paced the floor, feeling like a trapped animal. She glanced up at her reflection in the mirror. *And a wild animal, that,* she mused wearily. Her hair had been braided earlier, but now shabby golden strands hung loosely around her ears and face. *Like a lion,* she thought with sordid amusement. *What I really need is a relaxing bath. Ah, yes. That sounds great!*

Morgan adjusted a couple of her favorite Johnny Mathis records on her old stereo, lit a tiny votive candle, and filled her tub with very warm, scented water. She stripped off her dusty clothes and brushed through her tangled hair, twisting it neatly on top of her head. Sinking slowly into the marvelous, soothing water, she let it lap hungrily around her shoulders and neck.

The sensitive sounds of Mathis, the flickering candlelight, the balmy lilac fragrance, and the refreshing water massaging her gently all served to heal the tumultuous passions that filled her being with turmoil. Here, in her quiet, private domicile, Morgan could forget Grant LeMaster and the ranch and her complicated life.

Was that a door slamming? Morgan listened intently but could only hear the melodious sounds of Mathis singing "Chances Are." She mouthed the familiar words to the cherished old tune, wondering what her chances were of lasting through the summer on the same premises with Grant.

Did she hear voices? Morgan inclined her head toward the door but was serenaded by Mathis's lovely "Small World." She smiled foolishly to herself. *Dummy! You're hearing things! Funny* . . . She hummed along.

She sang softly to herself as she lathered her legs. "Fun-ny, just because de-dum de-dum . . . hummm . . . hummmmmmm . . ." Morgan smiled as she hummed the tune, making up self-mocking words here and there. Somehow the singing plus the teasing released her tension. She pushed tepid water around her neck, then stopped . . . sure she heard voices.

She listened, and it was quiet again. There was only one way to find out for certain and that was to climb out of the warm, wonderful tub and investigate! It was probably just her mind playing tricks on her, but just in case . . . Damn! This was yet another annoyance in her evening. Even the solitude of her bath was interrupted! She wrapped herself in a thick towel and, swathed in steam, stepped from the bathroom to her bedroom.

Just as Morgan dropped the concealing towel and reached for

her robe, the door to her room opened! For a split second she was filled with horror, and her mouth opened to utter the scream that filled her mind, but refused to form a sound. Then her brain registered that the man standing in the open doorway, gaping at her nudity, was none other than her husband!

She finally managed, "Grant!"

With suitcases in each hand he stood frozen, ogling in typical male fashion at the curving female shape before him. His gaze steadied, and those penetrating gray eyes darkened with passion as he closed the door with his foot. My God! he thought. She was beautiful! Could he . . . could he actually carry this fakery through for the entire summer? Without touching her? He wanted to sweep her into that bed this very minute . . . He'd never come so close to wanting to force—Oh, god, no! What was he thinking? This was his *wife!* Grant's voice was hoarse as he mumbled, "Sorry, Morgan . . . I shouldn't have barged in like this. . . ." His eyes never left her quivering form.

Hastily Morgan clutched her abandoned shirt to her nude figure. It covered her breasts adequately enough, but not her legs. "What are you doing in here?" she demanded, her voice still shaky from the surprise appearance of a man at her door. But this particular man was now her husband. What did he want of her?

Grant's cool gray eyes claimed her long, bare legs and creamy, uncovered shoulders. A few strands of her long, flaxen hair had worked free from the twist and temptingly reached one shoulder. Her bronze eyes were still wide with fright, only now tinged with the anger—or was it fear—that trembled through her body.

In a slow, well-modulated voice he declared, "Mrs. LeMaster, your husband doesn't sleep in the bunkhouse any longer." He tore his eyes away from her and set one of the suitcases against the wall, then moved toward the closet with the other. It was obvious he had no intention of leaving . . . at least not right away.

Morgan took advantage of the time his back was turned to slip quickly into the shirt and grab her jeans, jerking them furiously over her bare hips. This was no time to bother with underwear. Under the circumstances it was far better to be attired in her discarded work clothes than the flimsy robe. Covering her body also gave her renewed strength to combat this brazen intruder.

There was something about being stripped of one's clothes that also tore down defenses. Now Morgan's offensive was powerful. And loud.

"Where the hell do you think you're going? You're *not* sleeping in my room! Get out of here, Grant! Do you hear me? You are not spending the night in *my* room!"

His back was infuriatingly turned to her as he arranged his suit and a couple of clean shirts and jeans in one small corner of the closet. Sarcastically he drawled, "Oh, yes, at that decibel level, Morgan, even the coyotes in the distant San Juans can hear you! Hold it down a little. You'll disturb David."

"David! Where is he?" Involuntarily she glanced toward the door, half expecting the little fellow to saunter in.

Grant's insolent lips curled into a smile. "He's happily settled in the bedroom down the hall. Nice accommodations for a boy. Must have been your brothers' room. David's delighted with the bunk beds and those atrocious cattle horns mounted on the wall—"

Morgan interrupted his insidious rambling. "Grant, don't tell me you've already moved David into this house!" Moving David into the house was a devious act aimed at making Grant's own expulsion more difficult. He was maneuvering her, damn him. And using the child to accomplish his own sordid intent.

Mock surprise aggravated her. "What's wrong, Morgan? You don't mind David using your brothers' old room, do you?"

Caught off guard, she answered, "Well . . . no, but . . ."

"Good," he responded, "because he's all tucked in bed. I'd hate to disturb him now. And you'll be pleased to know that David and I settled our differences before I put him to bed. I apologized for raising my voice and explained where he went wrong. I feel much better, and I'm sure he does, too. Don't you, Morgan?" Amusement played around his rakish eyes.

"Oh, yes, Grant. I'm very relieved. It takes a big man to apologize and especially to inform a six-year-old where he went wrong!" Her sarcastic tone matched his.

A pause in their caustic conversation allowed the soothing tones of Johnny Mathis to filter between them. "What I Did for Love" brought a devilish smile to Grant's countenance. "See, Morgan, even Johnny Mathis understands that some things are done in the name of love. David understands that I scolded him out of my love for him. Surely you can accept that."

Morgan's eyes narrowed. "I doubt that you do anything out of love, Grant. David may believe you, but I don't! And I'm sure he won't mind if you bunk in with him, because you are not sleeping in my room. Now, get out!"

"Not just in your room, my sweet little bride, but in your bed." His voice and quiet and calm, considering his brazen assertion.

"You are not!" Morgan angrily confronted him, hands on her hips, furious with this tall imposing man who came into her room and claimed her bed! No matter that he was her husband! She drew herself up, bitter that she wasn't a little bit taller. Well, she'd show him what a hellcat she could be if he even tried to stay with her!

He faced her boldly. "I am your husband, Morgan. And you are my wife. Mine!"

There was something about his arrogant stance, the square line of his jaw, the unmistakable glow of passion in his eyes that made her want to slap him. As if by a reflex, and without thinking about her actions or their consequences, Morgan raised her arm to hit Grant. But his reflex was even quicker. His large hand flashed up to grasp hers cruelly before it could deliver its stinging blow. Her other hand knotted into a fist and pummeled Grant's shoulder before he grasped it too, capturing both of her hands to prevent the hurt she so desperately wanted to render.

As Morgan wriggled to free herself from the man she hated and so savagely wanted to wound, he held her ever firmly, pinning her arms to her sides and her body to his. The salty smell of his body accosted her senses as he hissed in her face, "Don't ever try to hit me again!"

"You . . . you crude barbarian! You smell like a bear! Let go of me, damn it!" She was surprised—and repulsed—by his controlled assault.

Grant shifted her even closer. "Why? So you can beat me up? Uh-uh. I like this better." And he covered her mouth with his in a vicious, scornful kiss that lacked everything except force.

Morgan had never been kissed—or treated—so roughly before, and she reacted with all the ferocity she could muster against this man who held her brazenly against his taut thighs and insistent masculinity. Her tender lips throbbed from his attack, and still he refused to stop. With her hands held so tightly Morgan's only weapons were her feet, so she began to kick at him. She was oblivious to the fact that her bare feet could render no harm, since he wore his scuffed, leather boots. However her renewed attempts at escape were enough to arouse his anger, and with her arms still pinned, he easily lifted her kicking, squirming body to the bed, where he unceremoniously dumped her.

Morgan was entirely helpless as he covered her protesting, wriggling body with his weight, grasping her legs on either side with his own as he moved over her, making no effort to hide his arousal. His mouth was alarmingly close to hers as he rasped, "Don't think you can overpower me, Morgan! You don't have a chance!"

Morgan was furious! She was being ravaged by her own husband, and who would ever believe her! Through clenched teeth she muttered, "Go ahead, damn you! Rape your wife, and . . . I'll sue you!" As the harsh words left her mouth, angry tears filled her flashing bronze eyes.

Grant's laugh was low and vicious, as he immediately released her hands, leaving them weak and limp. He shifted his body, still trapping her legs with his own, laughing wickedly. "Oh, no, Morgan. I won't force myself on you. You'll have to want me, first," he threatened as he slipped the fingers of one hand just beneath the unsnapped waistband and zipper of her jeans. He traced slow circular patterns, enflaming the sensitive skin of her belly, moving to continue the delicious sensation down the smooth curve of her hip, lingering on her satiny flesh. Morgan steeled herself to what he might do next, fearing her body would betray her resistance. She could feel his fingers gently stroking, gradually decending to her most secret center of desire. Unwillingly she arched toward his searching fingertips, even as she struggled to find words to make him stop.

Morgan's voice trembled with emotion. "So you've proven that you're stronger than me, Grant. What more do you want?"

Passionately he rasped, "You. I want you, Morgan!"

"No! I told you! Grant, you promised! Please . . ."

In the silence that followed Morgan's plea, the Mathis record lulled its sweet tune. "If we only have love . . ."

Grant's voice echoed his remorse. "But we don't, do we, Morgan? There is no love in this marriage. It means nothing that you are my wife. Because there is nothing between us. Nothing . . ." With a low moan he rolled away from her. Sitting on the edge of the bed, Grant cradled his head in his hands. "Oh, God, Morgan. What are we coming to? Can't we have a decent conversation without talking about raping and suing each other? I . . . I don't know what happened to me. I only wanted to talk."

"Talk?" Morgan almost spat at him, scrambling to a sitting position in the middle of the bed. "That's what this is all about? You intrude into my privacy, move your things into my bedroom, and . . . assault me, so we can talk?"

He turned to face her, a crooked smile tugging at his lips as the humor of the situation registered in his passion-crazed mind. "Yeah, something like that." He grinned. "I know it's a little abrupt, but we cowboys lack certain social graces."

The honest expression on his face, the little-boy grin that softened his eyes, the open apology written all over him, brought a reluctant smile to Morgan's face. They both had lost control for a few minutes . . . and they both knew it. "I'll have to admit, you are lacking in social graces, but not in brute strength. I have no doubt that you can break those wild horses out there tomorrow."

Wryly he admitted, "Brute force. But I'm not trying to break wild horses tonight, am I? Just trying to talk to . . . my wife."

Morgan shivered at his words, running her hands over her arms, hugging them unconsciously. "So talk."

Taking a deep, ragged breath, Grant began pacing the floor while he talked. He was still obviously quite shaken by the events of the evening. Or was he simply tormented with unsatisfied desires? "David and I have moved into the ranch house. I won't stay in the bunkhouse any longer."

"When did you decide that?" Morgan was relieved to get some small distance between them.

Instead of answering her question per se, he explained, "After discussing the Rocking M's housing situation with the Simpsons, I know that they like the idea of living in the large bunkhouse.

It has the privacy they need, as well as a bath and room for a small kitchen. We can renovate it easily enough for them. Then the smaller bunkhouse can be used for the temporary wranglers that we hire just for the season. The Simpsons do deserve the larger one. Agreed?"

Morgan answered with a sardonic smile. "My, my, aren't you generous! Giving up your nice bedroom to the Simpsons! Why, Grant, how gallant of you!"

"Honestly, Morgan, did you expect to give them the room down the hall and let your husband continue to sleep in the bunkhouse?"

Morgan shrugged with a grin. "Sounds fine to me. That's the way it's been working out so far. Now that you've given up your bunkhouse, where do you expect to live? Here?" She folded her arms across her breast.

Grant matched her action, but looked ever so masculine with his wide stance and gray eyes glaring into her. "David is settled down the hall, and I intend to live with my wife."

Morgan's brown eyes narrowed at him. "Grant, we agreed . . ."

"I know what we agreed. And regardless of what happened tonight I promise there'll be no more . . . brute force. I'll set up my office in the little room next door and sleep in there. No one will know it but you and me. Does that satisfy you?"

She agreed, somewhat skeptically. "Looks like you have it all figured out."

"What I didn't figure on was what happened tonight." His voice was suddenly low and gentle. "Morgan, look at me. I'm . . . I'm sorry about what happened. I didn't intend to lose control like that."

Morgan blinked and looked down. "I guess I lost a little control, too, Grant. I pushed you . . ."

"Let's let it drop. I . . . I'll just get clean clothes and use the shower down the hall. I have a big day tomorrow. Boyd and Willa are moving in, and I intend to ride at least one of those wild horses." Grant moved quietly to the closet and took the clothes he needed, then left her alone without glancing back.

Morgan sat curled up on the bed for long, lonely moments. For some strange reason she felt very sad and mixed up after

Grant left her. She could hear him moving about the room next to hers and wondered what he was doing. Then she rebuffed herself for even caring. Deep down she feared her own feelings toward this steely man who had just left her bedroom. He had excited her with his touch, even though their meeting had been stimulated by anger. It wasn't his anger that excited her. It was his eyes and the smoldering emotions hidden there. She longed to feel his arms around her again and his lips on hers. But gently this time. She didn't want to feel his angry, punishing lips ever again. Yet, according to his promise, she wouldn't feel his lips again . . . unless she desired it. At that thought she tenderly touched her bruised lips, knowing she desired Grant very much.

As Johnny Mathis crooned soft lyrics of forever-after love, Morgan wondered if it could possibly be love she felt, or just desire.

CHAPTER SIX

By ten the next day Willa and Boyd Simpson were moving into Grant and his son's ex-bedroom. As soon as their things were unloaded from the small pickup truck, Grant and Boyd went off together to see about the horses and start their day's work. Morgan stayed with Willa, trying to make the rugged old bunkhouse look like a home for a woman.

"I found these curtains in the back closet, Willa. They should fit the windows." Morgan unfolded the chintz material for Willa's inspection. "How do they look?"

"Yes, I think they'll do fine." Willa beamed at the feminine addition to the rather barren room. "When we get curtain rods . . ."

"I have everything we need right here." Morgan motioned to some equipment she had left near the door. "I'll put them up while you finish unpacking."

"Thank you, Mrs. LeMaster. But I can do that if you have more important things to do."

Morgan pulled a chair over to the window and stood on it to align the rod correctly. "Right now the most important thing I have to do is to make sure you and Boyd are settled and comfortable. And please, Willa, call me Morgan. I want you to be my friend as well as Grant's. As closely as we'll all be working and living, first names will be much easier."

Willa smiled amiably. She had a beautiful smile and a lively twinkle in her blue eyes that spoke of a gayness that still pervaded her spirit. And Morgan liked that. *Yes,* she thought. *We'll get along fine.*

Willa halted and assessed Morgan honestly. "You know, Morgan, you and Grant seem to be an ideal couple. I think he made a real good choice for a wife."

Morgan couldn't hide her mirth at what Willa had intended as a compliment. Wouldn't she be surprised at the "ideal couple" if she knew Morgan had done the choosing? "Thanks, Willa, but you know I wasn't actually his first choice. Grant was married first to an Indian woman. She was David's mother." Morgan felt it best to get the facts about David's parentage out in the open at the beginning. Of course Willa probably knew Grant's first wife, or knew about her.

Willa cast a puzzled glance at Morgan, who busily hammered the curtain rod in place. "No," she said thoughtfully, "I didn't know her. But it seems he said something about you being newlyweds the day you stopped by to hire us."

"Yes," Morgan agreed, silently amused at the term *newlyweds.* It hardly described their status. "In fact, the wedding was just last week." She stood back to see if the curtains hung evenly.

"Then you're still on your honeymoon!" Willa exclaimed, delighted with the romantic notion. "Now if there's ever a time that you and Grant want some privacy—you know—just give me the word. Boyd and I'll see that little David is completely entertained."

Morgan's fair complexion colored immediately at Willa's bold suggestion. "Oh . . . uh, thanks," she mumbled. *Honeymoon, indeed!*

"I didn't mean to embarrass you, honey." Willa chuckled knowingly. "But I was a newlywed once myself, and I remember. It must be difficult to marry and become an instant mother. And I know it's inconvenient to have us around the ranch all the time."

Morgan answered stiffly, "Actually, Willa, our main concern is to get this ranch running smoothly this summer. And you and Boyd were hired with that purpose in mind."

"Oh, I didn't mean to interfere . . ."

Morgan smiled tightly. "You didn't, Willa. But we all have

lots of work to do before July fourth. Now would you like to see the house and the rest of the ranch?"

The older woman nodded. "I especially want to see the kitchen. Grant made such a point of making sure I could cook, I'd like to see the place where I'm to do it." Willa was slender and rather lithesome. She and her husband were in their late fifties and both emitted a calm strength, a cohesiveness that had enabled them to remain serene and happy through life.

Morgan led the way to the kitchen and thought with an inward smile how this steadfast couple resembled each other—just a little—as many couples seem to do who live together for a long time. She wondered if she and Grant would . . . but no. There wouldn't be time for that. They wouldn't be together very long . . . only one summer.

Morgan stepped to the back door and indicated for Willa to precede her. "Here it is, Willa. The most important room in the house! At least the men around here think so!" Both women giggled in agreement about the importance of a full plate of appetizing food to a contented ranch hand. Morgan eagerly confessed that she was only too glad to relinquish that responsibility to Willa. The uncomfortable tension of moments before was behind them.

Hereafter Willa would be careful to skirt the sensitive issues of Morgan's marriage and motherhood. Otherwise they would get along fine.

They examined the kitchen and toured the house, then the women walked toward the barns. They ended up at the corral fence where they watched Boyd and Grant tending to one of the horses. Both men were intense, working to adjust the saddle, stirrups, and reins. Suddenly Grant lifted his boot to the stirrup and heaved himself smartly into the saddle. Boyd moved back quickly, stumbling against the fence in his haste. And the big horse on which Grant perched went crazy! He jumped and hopped stiff-legged, twisted, turned, galloped a stretch, then stopped on a dime and whipped around in a circle. It was that last circle that got Grant.

Morgan watched, horrified, as Grant flew through the air, almost in slow motion, and landed with a thud on the hard earth. A masculine voice hurled angry expletives through the air, then all was quiet as everyone strained to know the fate of the Rocking M's newest bronc rider. Dust filled her nostrils before Morgan realized that she had scaled the fence and entered the corral at a dead run. As she reached Grant, his gray eyes gazed up foggily into hers. He stared for a moment, as if wondering who she was . . . or, more likely, what she was doing there.

"Are . . . are you all right, Grant?" she questioned breathlessly.

He nodded abruptly and started to get up. Involuntarily she reached for him, not actually helping, just gripping his arm reassuringly. His muscles tightened under her clasp.

Boyd's shout interrupted the moment. "Come on, Grant. You've got to mount him again! You can't let him go free after this. You've got to break him, son!"

Grant broke away from her, as if mesmerized by Boyd's voice. Morgan could hear him muttering, "I'll take him even if I break every goddamn bone in my body . . . I can do it!" Boyd shouted at her to get out of the way and Morgan quickly obeyed, clambering to the top of the fence rail near where Willa stood. Boyd was right, of course. Grant had to show the animal who was boss, who was superior. He had to ride the horse, too, for his own self-esteem. Morgan knew it had to be done. And yet she also knew the pain her husband was enduring. She had seen the dullness of his eyes and knew he was hurting. Flinching with each jolt of Grant's body, gasping every time his frame swayed in the saddle, Morgan mentally suffered the ride along with Grant. Finally, when both the man and horse were swathed in great sweaty lather, the animal stopped jumping. He stood stockstill for a few seconds, heaving, during which time Grant gathered his strength for another onslaught.

But Boyd shouted triumphantly, "Whoopee! He's done, Grant! Finished! You did it! Now walk him around. Just keep him moving for a while."

Grant did as Boyd instructed, and Morgan breathed a sigh of relief . . . proud as hell of Grant. Yet a niggling thought inside her refused to withdraw. Their alliance had placed Grant in the hazardous position of breaking those horses . . . or else. And he was too stubborn to quit. Morgan knew that breaking horses was always risky, even for experts. Grant could have been crippled . . . or killed . . . because of her!

She knocked faintly on his door, not wishing to disturb him if he was already asleep. A groaning mumble answered her knock and Morgan opened the door slowly, saying, "It's me, Grant. I . . . have something for you. For your back." She eased into the darkened room where he lay, half stretched out on the narrow bed. At one time this had been her room, and she had slept on this very bed on which Grant tried to make his lengthy body fit. He sprawled with one knee bent and one arm flung over his eyes, and he looked . . . oh, so very masculine lying there.

He didn't move, but verbally acknowledged her presence with barely a civil, "What do you want?"

Morgan swallowed hard as her eyes accustomed themselves to the darkness. She could see his angular form more clearly now. He wore no shirt to hide dark, curly hair that spread across his chest, trailed his flat belly, and ended in an enticing line beneath his shorts. The sight of his virility thrilled her, awakening bold desires that had never been stirred. *Not even with André.*

"Grant? Maybe this will help." Morgan was suddenly timid before him. She wanted to touch him, and yet . . .

Grant moved his arm upward a little, so that he could see her. It was hard to believe this shy form standing nearby was the same little hellcat he wrestled to the bed only the night before. She was like an apparition, with her golden hair flowing over the shoulders of a pale dressing gown. Her dark eyes were so serious . . . oh, God! She was so beautiful! "Morgan?" It was a question, as if he could hardly believe it was her. "What—"

"Well, who else? Come on. Sit up. Drink this. It'll help you relax." She handed him a small glass.

He reached for it, rough fingers touching hers in the process. "What is it?" He raised his body with a groan and gave her a curious glance.

Sighing, Morgan joined him on the bed, sitting cautiously on the edge. "This is what's left of the champagne. I . . . thought you might like some tonight. It's all we have in the house right now. I suppose a stiff shot of whiskey would suit you better, but—"

He interrupted abruptly. "This is fine. Thanks."

"How do you feel?" She watched him gulp the drink.

He looked at her solemnly, his ashen eyes tired and dull. "Like hell."

She nodded, as if knowing that would be his answer. "Finish your drink, then turn over. I'll rub your back with this deep-heating stuff. Willa loaned it to us. She says it's the best for aching muscles."

Grant eyed her closely. "Am I dreaming, Morgan? You graciously bring me a drink . . . and now you're offering to rub my aching back?"

She nodded with a sheepish smile. "I guess I've got a bad case of the guilts, Grant. I'm . . . I'm sorry I put you in this situation of having to break those two wild horses. I just realized today how very dangerous it is. And I know you didn't bargain for that when you—"

With a loud groan he stretched out on his belly. "I didn't bargain for a lot of things, Morgan. But then neither did you. I just chalk this one up to experience. One down and one more to go! While I've got you here, and you're in a sympathetic mood, let's try Willa's remedy. What are you waiting for?"

Morgan looked at the broad, sinewy back before her and began to touch him gingerly. His muscles were tense and hard, coiling tighter as she ran her slim hands over him. Lightly at first, she covered his muscular back with the menthol-fragrant ointment, then moved to retrace the taut expanse of masculinity with more ardor. When he obviously flinched at her touch, she asked apprehensively, "Did I hurt you?"

A rough laugh escaped his lips. "You didn't, Morgan. But that damn horse certainly did his share. Ahhh, my arms feel like they've been pulled from their sockets. But don't stop. Right there, Morgan . . . ooooh, that's nice, honey . . ." His voice was almost a guttural groan.

Morgan proceeded to do as he instructed, kneading his shoulders, massaging his well-knit forearms, manipulating the cords that led from his backbone around his ribs. She enjoyed the task, reacting easily to the warmth created between her manipulating hands and his tight-muscled body. The ointment seemed to create a magnetic field, attracting her to his radiating appeal.

"There, how's that? Feel better?" Morgan murmured.

"Ummm, yes." He sighed, shifting to a more comfortable position. "Don't stop, Morgan. This almost makes me glad I married you."

"Almost?"

"Um-hum," he mumbled.

She continued to massage him deliberately, smiling to herself at his teasing jab at their marriage. Last night she would have taken offense. But tonight, after seeing the risks he took today— for her and the ranch—she knew that she was asking a tremendous amount of him. Perhaps too much. "Grant . . ."

"Hummm?"

"I'm sorry about the deal with the wild horses. I . . . I think it's too much to expect you to break another one. You're right. This wasn't in the bargain . . . and I shouldn't ask it of you."

"You getting soft, Morgan? We haven't even tried Blue Velvet yet. He's tomorrow."

Morgan's voice was urgent. "No, Grant. Please . . . don't ride again tomorrow. Rest for a few days."

"Tomorrow's the day, honey. I'll ride him or . . ." His words dwindled toward the end and were unintelligible.

Morgan leaned forward trying to catch his words and failed to notice the relaxed nature of the taut muscles which she had massaged into submission.

"Grant, I can't let you ride again tomorrow. I just didn't think about how dangerous breaking horses can be . . . especially for a relative novice. Not that you're . . . well, you were pretty good today, Grant. But I can't let you take that risk again. In fact, I want to sell Blue Velvet. And from now on we'll buy horses that are already broken. That's what we'll do. We need some pack horses or mules, anyway. Maybe we can strike a trade. I . . . just don't want to risk . . . my husband . . . with those wild horses again. Why, if anything ever happened to you, Grant, and you were injured, I'd never forgive myself." She paused, amazed by her own admissions. "Grant?" She halted and leaned closer, listening to his steady breathing. Grant was asleep and hadn't heard a thing she'd said.

Morgan sighed and stood up, surveying the prone man who slept so soundly before her. One of his legs sprawled across the bed, the other hung half off the side. He looked so damned uncomfortable, she wondered if she should wake him and . . . what? Offer him her bed? She acknowledged that he would be able to rest better. But would she? Could she possibly think of sleeping next to him? My God, she could hardly stand to look at him now! Quickly she turned away from his appealing virility and retreated from the room, frustrated, puzzled, bedeviled by the man she called her husband.

The next morning, true to her promise, Willa cheerfully prepared breakfast for everyone. In fact, by the time Morgan stumbled in, the men had finished and already left for work.

"They're repairing that blue devil's stall this morning," offered Willa.

Morgan stirred her coffee absently. "Repairing a stall? What's wrong with it?"

Willa poured herself a cup of coffee and joined Morgan at the table. She chatted happily, omitting the answers Morgan sought. "My, my, how that bunch can eat! Do you know that little David ate five pancakes! And Grant—"

"You fixed pancakes for breakfast this morning? Well, no wonder they're all so happy with your cooking, Willa! I've never served pancakes in the morning. They must think they're in heaven!" Morgan laughed. "That's just something I can't face so early in the morning. Boy, am I glad you're here."

Willa reached over and patted the younger woman's hand. "Not nearly as glad as I am to be here, Morgan. Boyd and I are real honored that you and Grant decided to hire us. There aren't many people willing to do that nowadays."

Morgan smiled easily across the table. "Well, the feelings are mutual, Willa. We need your help to make this ranch work. Now what's wrong with the stall? I know it was fine yesterday."

Willa shook her head in dismay. "That blue devil of a horse kicked the walls down during the night. He made a huge hole in it and, if he'd had more time, would have knocked the whole stall down! That one's a bad animal."

Morgan shrugged. "Well, maybe it'll keep them busy today and they won't try to break him. I'm going to sell him as soon as I can. Blue Velvet . . . he has such a beautiful name. Why can't he live up to it?"

Willa chuckled. "Oh, he lives up to his name, all right. You know what the rodeo bronc riders say about a horse with *velvet* in its name. . . ."

Morgan looked up curiously. "No, what?"

Willa sipped her coffee before answering. "It's the meanest horses that get the name *Velvet.*"

Morgan frowned. "Couldn't be meaner than that one yesterday!"

"Oh, sure." Willa shrugged. "That one Grant rode yesterday was a pussycat compared to some. I remember one time on a ranch out in Montana. I was very young, mind you. But there was an Appaloosa stallion named Calico Velvet that nobody could ride. Boyd was breaking horses every day and had tried that spotted devil three days in a row . . . and three times had been bucked off! On the fourth day I got it in my head that I could ride that horse. So I saddled him and, oh, he stood so still. I thought he was gentled by all the riding of the past few days, but he sure fooled me! As soon as I touched that saddle, he jumped higher and longer and rounder than he ever had . . . at least, it felt like he did! But I stayed on him and by the end of the ride, that horse walked me around the corral and all the hands—the men—gathered on the fence rails and applauded! Gosh, those days were long ago!" A happy glimmer lit Willa's blue eyes as she recalled that glorious day in her past.

Morgan smiled warmly. "Willa, that's a beautiful story. I'll bet Boyd was proud of you!"

"Proud?" Willa scoffed. "He was madder'n a wet hen! Didn't speak to me for two days! Said I could have killed myself!" She shook her head as she rose and finished cleaning up the dishes.

Morgan's finger ran slowly around the rim of her cup. The reason for Boyd's anger at Willa echoed in her mind and she shuddered at the thought. Grant could have gotten himself killed yesterday on that horse. And it would have been all her fault. *All her fault.*

Willa's laugh interrupted Morgan's morbid thoughts. "You know something, Morgan? Boyd wouldn't admit he was proud of me, but he was. I could see it in his face. But I guess the most important thing was that *I* was proud of me! I'll never forget that day!"

"Well, I'm proud of you, too, Willa!" Morgan stated emphatically. Suddenly her attention was turned to the far corral. The blue-gray stallion was prancing and pawing, under the guidance of Boyd, followed closely by Grant. She stood up with a start, her voice shrill and nearly wild. "My God, Willa! They're going to ride him! They're going to ride Blue Velvet! Grant—"

Willa's gaze followed Morgan's, but her tone was quite nonchalant. "I'm not surprised. There's one thing cowboys don't tolerate, and that's to be bested by an animal. The sooner they break him, the better."

"Oh, no! He can't! He just can't!" Like a flash Morgan bolted out the door, running at top speed the distance to the far corral. In the time it took her to reach it, Grant was already astride the huge horse. Gasping for breath, Morgan gripped the fence rail and watched the dreadful sight of Grant clinging desperately to the wildly bucking animal. He hung on for long, agonizing moments of hell until—inevitably—he flew through the air once again. The landing was accompanied by loud curses, however, and he was on his feet, brushing the dust from his seat by the time Morgan could race to his side.

"Grant! Are you all right?"

He turned his steel-hard eyes on her sharply. "Morgan, get out of this corral! Leave me alone! I'm fine!"

Hurt and astonishment filled her heart at his words, and she sought a quick reason for standing beside him in the dusty corral. "I . . . I want to ride him next, Grant! It's my turn to try Blue Velvet!" Morgan couldn't believe her own voice. She had never ridden more than a very slow gelding in her life. And here she wanted to mount a wild stallion!

Grant waved her away. "Are you crazy? No, Morgan, I'll take him. He's much too dangerous for you."

The belittling remark in itself was enough to spark Morgan's vengeful spirit. But it also served as a reminder of the reason this horse had the name of Blue Velvet. "The meanest horses get the name of Velvet." Morgan was crazy with the thought of Grant riding this insanely wild horse . . . and getting hurt. A terrible knot clamped viciously in the pit of her stomach, choking her with fear and blocking out all reasonable thought. As Grant bent to retrieve his hat, Morgan moved past him. Reaching the spot where Boyd held the impatient horse, she ordered firmly, "Hold him still for me, Boyd."

Before Boyd or Grant realized what she was doing, Morgan had mounted the angry, feisty animal. As soon as her weight hit the saddle, Blue Velvet bolted free from Boyd's startled grasp and began his stiff-legged stint across the entire corral. He turned and twisted and jumped while Morgan held on gamely, her flaxen hair flying wildly and her small body jostling like a puppet.

Grant watched, astounded, consternation paralyzing him where he stood in the center of the corral. He didn't have long to wait for the gruesome sight of Morgan—his wife—hurtling over the bowed head of the devil horse and landing in a still, unceremonious heap in the dust. He wasn't even aware of his own hoarse voice repeatedly yelling her name as he raced across the dry earth to kneel over Morgan's unmoving form.

CHAPTER SEVEN

The balding doctor looked over gold, wire-rimmed bifocals at Grant. "Mr. LeMaster, the X rays show your wife has two broken ribs. She'll be in a lot of pain for the next few days. Her concussion is mild, but she'll need complete bed rest for at least a week, maybe two. Now we could hospitalize her, but if you think she can get the rest she needs at home—"

"Oh, yes, Doctor. I'll make sure of it. Complete bed rest." His eyes caressed Morgan, who lay very still on the examining table with her eyes closed. "We have an excellent housekeeper who'll help me take care of her. And I'll see that she stays in bed."

At that statement Morgan's eyes flickered open to give Grant a hard stare. But she said nothing.

The old doctor raised his eyebrows knowingly and laid an experienced hand on Grant's arm. In a lowered voice he advised, "And you must be very careful with your wife, Mr. LeMaster. She—uh—those ribs will be terribly sore for several weeks. You'll have to help her keep them wrapped with the Ace bandage and you may need to tighten or loosen it, as her pain dictates. She'll let you know, I'm sure."

Grant nodded seriously and winked at Morgan, who was in too much pain to see the humor in his response. "I'm sure she will. And I'll keep my distance, Doctor, believe me."

Grant assisted Morgan to her feet and wrapped a strong, secure arm around her as they walked slowly out to his roomy

Suburban. "Do you want to lay down in the back, Morgan? I can move the seat easily."

She shook her head. "Just help me into the front seat. I'd rather sit. Getting up and down is worse than staying up after I'm already here."

"Sure, Morgan." He settled her in the seat and drove very carefully back to the ranch. There she was greeted by a very anxious trio. Little David was curious and concerned, as was Boyd Simpson. But obviously the most upset was Willa. She hovered like a little hen, settling Morgan comfortably in the newly made bed.

"How about hot tea, Morgan? Does that sound good?"

Morgan nodded with a tight smile, just to please the older woman. She closed her eyes, and Grant followed Willa out of the bedroom. Outside, in the hallway, Morgan could hear their terse exchange.

Grant's voice rumbled. "Willa, she's very lucky. Just a couple of broken ribs and a very mild concussion. Doctor says she needs complete bed rest. Can you help me make sure that she gets it?"

"Oh, yes, I'll see to it, Grant. I'll take good care of her. It's the least I can do."

"I knew you would, Willa. That's why I didn't put her in the hospital. I figured we could keep a better eye on her here. I don't know what got into her. Why in hell would she tackle that wild horse?"

Willa's timbre-filled voice answered. "I'm afraid I put the notion in her head, Grant. It's all my fault."

"Your fault, Willa? How's that?"

"Oh, I told her about the time I rode a bronc in Montana. I'm sure she thought she could do it, too. I'm awfully sorry. I sure didn't mean to suggest something so dangerous to her."

Grant's voice was soothing as they walked away. "Now, Willa, I don't think you influenced her. That girl has a mind of her own. . . . I'm sure it was her own crazy idea. You are definitely not to blame. . . ."

Their voices floated away until Morgan was awakened by a male voice that rumbled near her. "Morgan, would you like to sip this hot tea Willa has made?"

She forced herself to wake up, moving painfully so that she

could sip the hot drink. "Yes, that feels good inside." She smiled up at her worried husband.

The concerned look on his face set his jaw firmly and increased the intensity of his deep-set gray eyes. His rough hand brushed her face—an involuntary move of affection and care.

"Hey," she coaxed. "Don't look so down. I'm okay. Just need a little rest."

He nodded. "Yes, I know. And here's your medicine. Doctor says it'll help you relax."

She gulped the capsule obediently, since she was in no position to resist Grant's wishes this time. "It'll put me to sleep, you mean. I . . . I want you to know something, Grant. Tell Willa—"

His hand pushed on her shoulder, settling her flat against the bed. "Not now, Morgan. You need to rest. We can talk later."

"Now!" Morgan's voice rose in defiance. "I want to talk now! Tell her it wasn't her fault at all. It was all my idea. I . . . I just didn't want you . . . you to get . . . hurt."

"Me?" he asked incredibly. "But, Morgan—why?"

She smiled weakly. "This could be you lying here, Grant. Or worse. And I'd never forgive myself. . . ."

"Oh, God, Morgan. You didn't . . . for me?"

Her eyes closed involuntarily and squeezed two tears out of the corners onto pale cheeks. She barely felt his lips kiss them away and couldn't decipher his mumbled, "Now, I've got to live with the guilt, little one."

The remainder of that day was a fog in Morgan's memory. She floated in and out of wakefulness, only aware of one face visible every time she awoke. The serious, concerned image of her husband filled her mind—she thought she was dreaming of him but he was real and didn't leave her side all day.

By nightfall Morgan rallied enough to sip rich, fragrant broth lovingly prepared by Willa. Grant eagerly helped her eat. Afterward he assisted as she hobbled to the bathroom.

Finally in a weak voice she called for him. "Grant?"

Outside the closed door he answered, "Yes? Do you need . . . help?" There was a helplessness to his tone.

"Would you hand me my robe? It's hanging just inside the closet."

"Sure." In a moment a masculine hand eased the bathroom

door open just enough to squeeze the blue satiny robe inside. "Do you want your nightgown?"

After a pause she answered, "No, I don't think I could get it over my head. This will be fine because I can just slip it on, if only . . ."

"What? Should I get Willa?"

Morgan refrained from the laughter that welled up inside her, knowing that it would hurt those ribs. But there was definite amusement in her answer. "Now, how would that look, Mr. LeMaster? 'Hey, Willa, would you come help my wife undress? I've never seen her like that!' "

His answer was quick and pointed. "But I have."

Morgan sighed in exasperation, not able to accomplish her painful task of stripping off the tight jeans she still wore. In frustration she gasped, "Then come in here and help me. You're my husband!"

Without hesitation the door opened and Grant stood there in all his glory, trying not to gape at her, feeling suddenly restrained.

Morgan ignored the expression on his taut face as she explained in a persistent voice, "All I need is for you to pull these jeans off my hips. I just can't bend over to get them down." She had shed her blouse and donned the robe, which clung seductively to her firm-nippled breasts.

Grant reached for her waist where the jeans were already unsnapped and unzipped, but continued to rest snuggly against her hips. Gently he tried to budge the skintight garment, averting his eyes from those prominent breasts, which lay just at eye level. "They're tight!"

"I know that! That's why I couldn't get them off! Pull harder, Grant! Come on! I can't believe you're suddenly bashful!"

His eyes darted to her face, as he rumbled, "Bashful is not my problem, Morgan, and you damn well know it!" Inserting his long fingers around the snug waistband, he firmly pushed the jeans over her hips, allowing his hands to trail her hips and legs as he removed the offending garment. Dropping the stiff denim pants on the floor, Grant stood before her, drinking in her half-clad body with hungry eyes. Her bikini panties had rolled into a narrow item that hid nothing as his eyes rested momentarily on her V patch before traveling upward to her breasts, then on to her large, brown eyes. As he looked deeply into them, Morgan watched a small muscle flex in his cheek, while his hands sought her.

Gently caressing her breasts, his thumbs circled the ripe nipples. Then his hands groped for the robe which hung openly inviting, barely revealing her tightly wrapped rib cage, reminding him of her injury. "My God, Morgan!" he admonished raggedly. "Cover yourself! How much do you think I can stand?"

Her wide eyes were not entirely innocent. "I . . . I didn't think about it, Grant. You know what the doctor said."

Tiny beads of perspiration lined his upper lip. "To hell with what the doctor says. I'm waiting on word from you."

Her eyes fogged with pain and she shook her head. "Please, Grant . . . help me back to bed."

With strained control he helped her across the room. When she was settled comfortably, he mumbled good night and hurriedly left the room. Morgan drifted to sleep to the unmistakable sound of the shower down the hall. Her dreams were vivid and numerous, alternating from running in the rain she thought she heard, to her wild ride on the devil horse. Round and round she went, up and down, jerking from side to side until she was again flying through the air! *No! Oh, no!* It was Grant flying across the sky! Grant was falling! Her own distraught screams woke her, and Morgan clutched frantically at the alarmed man near her, amid frenzied cries of "Grant! Grant, hold me!"

"It's okay, Morgan. I'm here," he soothed, caressing her perspiration-drenched forehead and rumpled hair.

"Grant? Are you really here? Are you all right?" She held him tightly, listening to his strong heartbeat and absorbing the secure warmth from his body.

"I'm fine, little one. You must have been dreaming." His hands were strong and reassuring on her.

"Oh, God, the dreams were awful! Hold me, Grant. Don't leave me, please. Just hold me tonight," she pleaded.

His powerful arms locked comfortably around her trembling body and he murmured, "I won't leave you, little one. I'm here whenever you need me." And he stayed with her the remainder of the night, reassuring her occasionally, caressing her when she cried out, loving her with gentle promises. She wanted him . . . needed him . . . had cried out for him. She clung to him now in her pain, but would she want his touch in the clear light of day when her pain subsided? Grant LeMaster spent the night in the glory of his wife's arms, but there was little sleep for him during the long, dark hours.

David's happy, young voice bolstered her even before his small, dark face appeared in the doorway of Morgan's bedroom. "I have something for you, Morgan. I made a picture for you!"

"Well, great! Let me see it!" Morgan had been plagued with headaches all week and this was the first day Grant and Willa had allowed David to visit.

"Too loud," they had said.

But Morgan had missed the youngest member of her little family and was delighted to see him now. She smiled teasingly and begged, "Give me a hug, David. I've really missed you this week. What have you been up to?"

He wrapped his small arms around her neck and hugged her tightly. He clung for only a brief second, but long enough for Morgan to realize that he sought her love. It was the first time she knew—*really knew*—that she was more to David than just an acquaintance of Grant's. Unexpected tears of joy sprang to her eyes as the small boy slipped away and exclaimed eagerly, "I've missed you, too, Morgan. We haven't done nothing fun all week. I haven't had any ice cream in a whole week! It's just no fun around here without you!"

Morgan frowned seriously, and gave Grant a disparaging glance. "No ice cream at all? How awful, David! We'll have to do something about that! I'm ready for some pistachio! How about you?"

David thought solemnly for a moment. "Rocky Road is still my favorite."

"That kid knows what he likes and he sticks with it!" laughed Grant from where he leaned against the doorjamb. He folded his arms across his chest and an expression of pure pleasure lit his face for the first time that week. David was definitely good for Morgan and he probably should have let him visit her sooner.

"I want to see the picture, David," Morgan encouraged.

Timidly the child held the paper up for her perusal. "See? You're not the only one who fell off Blue Velvet."

Morgan gazed curiously at the stick figures displayed on the paper. "I know this is Blue Velvet in the center, but who's this?" she asked, pointing.

"That's Grant!" he announced proudly. "See his big hat over here on the ground?"

Stiffly she nodded. "Grant rode Blue Velvet?"

"Yep." David smiled majestically at Grant, who suddenly seemed to cringe in the doorway. "And he broke him, too. Took all day, but he finally rode him!"

"Grant?" Morgan's voice rose in alarm as she looked to her husband for confirmation.

Grant shrugged with a meek smile. "Out of the mouths of babes."

Morgan looked back at David's innocent face. "I love the picture, David. I'll put it up on the wall, so I can see it every day. And you are a very fine artist!" She smiled warmly and pulled him closer for a quick kiss on his tanned cheek.

Grant stepped forward to end the visit. His little son had already revealed more than he wanted Morgan to know. "You'd better run along now, David. I think Morgan needs her . . . uh, her rest. This is about all the excitement she needs in one day."

"Okay. See you later, Morgan. Don't forget about the ice cream!" David smiled happily before skipping out of the room.

Morgan faced Grant angrily, her voice shaking with anticipation. "Grant, was he telling the truth? Did you ride that . . . *that horse* this week?"

He stood near the bed, hands on his hips. "My son doesn't lie."

She looked away from his steady gaze. "Grant, how could you? I told you I want to sell Blue Velvet. I don't want to take a chance of anyone else getting hurt on him. What if you'd been . . . what if . . ."

He sat on the edge of the bed and took her hand. "But I'm fine. Just a little sore, that's all. Don't you understand, Morgan? I had to conquer him, especially after he threw you. I just had to."

Her brown eyes filled with tears. "I don't want that horse

around here. And I don't want you to ride him anymore, Grant. You did all this while I was sleeping my life away. I would never have known. . . ."

He kissed her palm tenderly. "I appreciate your concern, Morgan. I've missed you this week, little one. There was no one to rub my aching back at night—"

Pink colored her cheeks and she smiled involuntarily through her tears. "Oh, Grant—" Morgan's arms encircled his neck, pulling him down to her waiting lips. Tenderly, passionately, his mouth caressed hers, trailing along her cheeks and licking away the tears. He then moved down her sensitive neck to the wildly pulsating hollow of her throat, murmuring, "Oh, God, you're warm and inviting in that bed, Morgan."

"And I can smell you've been working hard all day." Morgan giggled, wrinkling her nose at him.

Just as Grant's mouth covered hers again, hungrily seeking her delectable sweetness, Willa cleared her throat from the doorway and announced, "Supper will be ready in half an hour. Don't you dare hurt her ribs after all she's been through this week, Grant LeMaster!"

Grant stood clumsily, like a little boy caught with his hand in the cookie jar. He turned steely eyes to the older woman. "I can kiss my wife without injuring her, Willa!" He then turned and stalked out, leaving the two women alone.

Willa ignored his remark and continued talking with Morgan as if Grant had never been there. "Do you feel like having something solid to eat tonight, Morgan honey? I made some chicken soup for you."

"That sounds great, Willa. And I'm starved!" Morgan smiled enthusiastically. "Gosh, I'm glad you were here this week. What would we have done without you?"

Wistfully Willa said, "Without me you probably wouldn't even have tried to ride that devil horse."

"Now that's not true, Willa. I . . . it was my own idea. I'll agree, it was a foolish one but I have to take full credit for it. I . . . I just didn't want Grant to get hurt. He's not a real cowboy, you know. He's just doing all this for . . . to save the ranch." She couldn't bring herself to say he was working for her. Or was he? Hope sprang in her heart at the thought.

Willa raised her eyebrows. "Grant LeMaster can take care of himself, and he's more of a roughneck than you think. I know one thing, though. He'd do anything for you, Morgan. Well, I gotta get to my supper. I'll bring your soup in a few minutes."

After supper Morgan lay awake, pondering Willa's earlier statements and listening to the evening sounds of the family. The men went back outside for some late chores, and she could hear Willa clanking about the kitchen. Then Grant helped David with his bath and getting ready for bed. A good-night kiss from the little boy was the only contact she had all evening with the family. They were already functioning very well without her. Nothing was more miserable than to lay helplessly and listen to others' activities, knowing they really didn't need you.

Grant poked his head into her room with a large towel draped over his bare shoulders. "Do you need anything before I take my shower, Morgan?"

Her eyes lit up and she responded eagerly, "That sounds like a great idea, Grant. I'd like to take a bath!"

He looked at her sharply. "I think you should wait, Morgan. This is the first afternoon you've felt decent."

"All right, a shower then. It's been days since I've touched water! And I want a shower tonight. I think it'll make me feel much better. Come on, Grant. Help me up."

Reluctantly Grant approached her. "Morgan, I don't think you should be in the shower alone."

She laughed and threw back the covers. "What do you suggest? Want to go in there with me?"

"Don't tempt me, little one!"

She reached up, and he pulled her stiffly to her feet. It was an awkward movement, but it was the only way she could raise up without pain. She squeezed his hands. "I'll be fine, Grant. Just stay close by."

He stood helplessly as she gingerly made her way into the bathroom. Once again this little spitfire of a willful bride was getting her way. "Morgan, you aren't feeling dizzy, are you? Will you call me if you feel the least bit sick? If you lost your balance in the shower, you could be seriously hurt."

She smiled seductively at him. "Would you come in and get me if I called?"

His expressive eyes answered even before he assured her, "You bet!"

"I need this shower, Grant. I'll feel much better afterward. You'll see!" she promised and closed the bathroom door behind her.

Heaving a sigh, Grant sat on the edge of the bed, waiting impatiently until she finished. Oh, how he wanted to burst into that little room and take her. After all, she was his wife, and she had tempted him on more than one occasion—but he had promised. Damn! Why had he promised?

A few minutes later Morgan emerged slowly from the steamy bathroom, a glorious smile on her flushed face. She had tied the blue satiny robe loosely around her waist, and it clung to her still-damp breasts, outlining the prominent nipples. Her long hair was wet and dripped dark spots around the shoulders of the robe . . . and lower. Oh, God—how he wanted to jerk that robe away!

"I feel wonderful and . . . clean." She beamed. "Thanks for waiting, Grant. Now you go ahead and take your shower. I'm going to sit right here and dry my hair."

He hovered nervously, helping her to ease into the chair, plugging in the hair dryer. "How do you feel? Are you sure you'll be okay while I'm gone?"

She nodded, not aware of just how sensuous she looked with her face freshly scrubbed and that thin robe clinging seductively around her shapely body.

Grant turned away quickly, stepped into the shower, and adjusted the temperature to cool. By the time he emerged, shirtless and wearing casual shorts, Morgan was struggling to dry the long ends of her blond hair.

"I can't seem to reach all of it without hurting my ribs," she complained, offering him just the invitation he needed.

"Here, let me," he accepted willingly. He dried, burrowed, caressed the lengthy flaxen hair he had longed to knot in his hands. It was so soft and pliable, he was sure that Morgan's body would be the same if only . . . oh, God, if only . . .

Grant directed warm air on the hard-to-reach places, lifting the thick strands, parting the back, drawing sensuous circles with deliberate ease. When her hair was finally dry to the touch, he flicked the instrument off and proceeded with first the brush, then the comb. Morgan closed her eyes, relishing his languid manipulations. Finally his fingers continued with masterful exploits, massaging her temples and her nape.

His index fingers traced her jawline from her earlobes to her chin, lifting her face to him ever so gently. Since she was still sitting, he bent to meet her upraised, slightly parted lips with his luxurious kiss. She reveled in the taste of his mouth and marveled at the naturalness of it all.

Grant's hand trailed, quite naturally, down her arched neck, blazing paths of uncurbed passion through her veins. He tarried lazily over one firm, full breast. Morgan shuddered with desire as his thumb and forefinger rolled the already taut nipple playfully.

Weakly she fought her own dynamic response to Grant's fiery touch. "Grant, don't . . ."

He provokingly rubbed the tiny protrusion he held. "Don't deny what's happening between us, little one. You want me as badly as I want you," he murmured against her cheek. "Come to me. . . ."

As if drawn by an invisible force, Morgan reached up for him as he lifted her easily to her feet. Her hands pressed against his unyielding chest as she sought his lusty, powerful kiss. No more soft, gentle clinches, as with a low moan he crushed her to him vigorously, eliciting a sharp cry of agony from Morgan. Immediately the magic of the sensuous moment was broken, and Grant stepped back, muttering, "Damn! Did I hurt you, Morgan?"

She clutched her ribs and nodded, bending her head to hide the quick tears that sprang to her eyes.

"Morgan?"

She shook her head and the golden hair hid her face. "I'm . . . I'm sorry, Grant. I just can't—"

His voice was low and tense. "Morgan, I'll be careful. I swear it. God, I don't want to hurt you. But I want you."

"Grant, don't make unreasonable demands of me. I told you —"

Tightly he rasped, "Is it unreasonable for a man to want his wife?"

"Will you wrap this Ace bandage around me?" she demanded, holding up the beige item.

Grant looked at the bandage in her hand as if it were a foreign object that he had never before seen. *How could she make such a request? Didn't she realize what she was doing to him?* "Don't ask me to do that, Morgan," he said brusquely.

"Why not? I . . . need you, Grant. I can't do it myself. And the bandage helps ease the pain." She held the Ace bandage out to him.

He looked at it wildly, then back to her puzzled, chestnut eyes. "Nothing will ease the pain between us, Morgan, until you stop being so goddamn stubborn. Don't ask me to help you undress or to touch you again . . . until you're ready for me to stay!" Grant stalked out of the bedroom, leaving Morgan to hold the bandage alone and wonder why she had let him go.

He was right! She wanted him badly. And he had admitted that he wanted her. Why did she hold back? Why didn't she admit it? Was she scared of him? Of what would happen between them? Was she fearful of the pain? No—she quickly shoved that thought to the back of her mind. He had promised to be careful . . . that he didn't want to hurt her. Was she just too stubborn to give in to her husband? *To give in?* Why, she wanted him as much as he clamored after her.

Oh, Grant, I love you. Please come back to me to stay the night! She was astounded by her own thoughts—her own reluctant admission! *She loved Grant!* Was that it? Could it possibly be that she had fallen in love with this man she had chosen to be her husband? Her summer spouse? How did this happen? When? Her mind raced over their short, turbulent acquaintance . . . that fateful day in the hospital, his compliance on their wedding day, his arrogance the night he entered her room and announced he wouldn't live in the bunkhouse any longer. An irresistible smile formed as she recalled past scorching words, heated caresses, the feverish passion that engulfed them only moments ago. With a ragged sigh Morgan conceded that she loved Grant, and she wanted him to love her, too. Maybe that was why she hesitated. She wanted his love, not just his passion.

She could hear Grant's footsteps pacing the bare floor in the room next to hers, brief clanking of the typewriter, the crackling of paper being ripped apart. His voice rumbled through the stillness of the night with muttered oaths. The old floor creaked with more pacing. He was as miserable as she. Finally when she could bear the sounds and her own torture no longer, Morgan walked steadily to his room. She knocked softly on the door. Maybe they could talk. . . .

Grant swung open the door, standing in the shadows dressed only in his briefs, looking so wild . . . so angry . . . so very masculine. She wanted him close to her—but she knew there would be no turning back this time. He had made that perfectly clear. And she knew it was too late for talking. They were beyond that now. With a shaky voice she appealed to her husband. "Grant, please come and hold me. I can't sleep."

He looked at her, unflinching and bold. "No, Morgan, I won't come and hold you anymore. I . . . just can't. But I will come and love you."

She nodded knowingly and looked down, not believing what she was doing. She only knew that she wanted him, too. At that moment—since the first time she had met him—for many long, miserable nights she had wanted him. "Okay."

"What did you say, Morgan?" he asked gruffly.

"Yes." She looked up at him, her bronze eyes meeting his passionate gaze. "I said yes!"

His voice was low and urgent. "Then say it, Morgan. Say you want me to love you."

His labored breathing was audible in the pause before she finally yielded, her voice a tremulous whisper. "Come and love me, Grant. I want you to love me."

Without a word he cradled her somber face in his hands and kissed her waiting lips, her pink-flushed cheeks, her closed eyelids. "Come on, little one. I'll bandage your ribs first. I . . . don't want to hurt you."

He led her into her bedroom, untied the shimmery robe and let it fall into a limp circle around her feet. With a sharp intake of tortuous air Grant's dove-gray eyes meandered down the gleaming whiteness of her breasts, her softly curved hips, her inviting thighs. Morgan stood brazenly exposed to Grant's blazing gaze, then passed the flesh-colored bandage to his hot, slightly trembling hands.

"Do you know how to do this?"

His voice was somewhat unsteady. "What? Oh . . . yes, I think I remember how the doctor wrapped it." He bent toward her and began to wind the bandage clumsily around her ribs while Morgan held her breasts up and out of his way. She hid the rosy tips from his close scrutiny and, shutting her eyes, pretended that he wasn't devouring her body with his eyes. And she tingled with anticipation.

"Is this too tight?" His fingers brushed her skin.

She shook her head and felt her hair ruffled around her shoulders, generating a shivering wave of desire down to the tips of her toes. He felt the tide, too. She was sure of it.

Slowly he spoke. "Morgan, you're beautiful. I've wanted to hold you, to touch you long before our wedding." His fingers swiftly clasped the bandage's end and pushed her hands away from the creamy mounds they hid. He then cupped them gently, moving his hands over them with sure gentle pressure. "Do you know how I've ached for you, little one? Do you know how hard this has been to work and live with you . . . and never touch you?" His skilled fingers rubbed lightly on the soft tips while he talked. "I hoped—prayed—that you would come to me. I knew you wanted me, too. Oh, God, the waiting has been torture!" By the time he stopped to take a breath, her nipples were prominent affirmations of Morgan's own aching responses to Grant's touch.

Her voice was a tight whisper. "How did you know? I didn't say anything to give you that impression."

His lips were close to hers, and his hands continued to caress her breasts maddeningly as he spoke. "You didn't have to say a thing. I could feel it. I saw beneath that angry exterior. I figured it was worth busting a couple of broncs to have you."

She shook her head. "I'm not worth risking your life over, Grant. I've felt guilty for setting you up to ride those broncs. I was so worried about . . . my husband."

His hands moved slowly downward to trace the shadowy outlines of her form, her waist, her hips, her thighs. "Suddenly, that word sounds right. Tonight I will be your husband, Morgan." He lifted her and carried her to the bed, lowering her tenderly on her back and kneeling beside her. He moved to touch the silky curve of her inner thighs, then to stroke her intimately.

His tongue began a sensuous journey along her thigh, trailing a path of kisses across her abdomen, then moving up to settle gently on a pink-tipped breast. Morgan quivered with unclaimed desire as his hands continued to explore her sensitive body.

"And I will be your wife—" She gasped softly as his lips brushed hers then sought again those delicious peaks, his tongue flicking in a sensual rhythm that threatened to drown her. She reached out to steady herself. "Grant . . . oh, Grant—"

"Do you want me?"

"You know . . . I do . . ."

"Then touch me. Let me know—" he rasped.

Tentatively, almost modestly, Morgan reached out for him. Her slender fingers raked curiously over Grant's chest and the small, erect male nipples. Her nails combed outrageously through the crisp mat of hair and followed its trail down his flat belly to the elastic waistband of his briefs. It was an easy effort to push them over his slim hips, but her hands halted abruptly when they transgressed to his rock-hard thighs. She was astounded at her boldness. Never before—

"Go ahead, Morgan—don't stop—" he grated hoarsely.

Carefully she averted her gaze and sought his deep gray eyes. "Grant, please . . . I—"

He stood and stepped out of the discarded briefs then sat down beside her again, his large, brown hands encircling her ivory shoulders. "I know, Morgan. I can hardly wait for you, too." He lay next to her and fervently pulled her on her side, into his welcoming arms. As the lengths of their bodies molded together, she realized the confirmation of his unyielding desire for her. "I crave you. But this moment is too beautiful to be rushed. I want to enjoy you slowly. And I want you to enjoy me, too." His mouth covered hers hungrily, his tongue teased her lips open until she welcomed him, touching the tip of his tongue with hers. A low moan escaped from his chest as he allowed her to tease, tempt, and plunder his mouth with her reckless, flicking tongue.

His hands caressed her back and stretched over her curved hips to pull her ardently to his own volatile warmth. He molded her silky softness to his firm, lengthy frame, thrusting his hips toward her instinctively.

Morgan buried her face in the curling hairs on his chest and inhaled the close male scent of his skin. It was a sensuous, heady fragrance that increased her already-excited desires beyond believability. She ran her hand possessively down his side, delighting in the feel of the warm slope of his back, claiming every rib, every muscle, as her own. Moving her trembling palm in massaging strokes, she caressed the narrowness of his waist, the flare of his hips, and kneaded the muscled tautness of his thighs before exploring the tensed contours of his buttocks. She was astonished at her own willingness to make him a part of her.

From the depths of her feminine instinct, she was acutely aware that Grant's passion was rising to the summit of his endurance. She could feel his hard-muscled thighs, his firm chest, his masculine physique pressed excitingly against her. His lips found hers, his tongue outlining the softness of her mouth, as she breathlessly parted her lips to receive him. She tasted his sweet warmth and stretched out her arms to pull him even closer to her soft curves, but moaned aloud in pain.

"What is it?" he asked anxiously. "Did I—"

"No," she whispered with a sigh. "It was me. I forgot I have broken ribs. Can you believe I forgot so soon? I just wanted to pull you closer to me." She laughed lightly and rested her forehead against his solid chest, breathing deeply of his fragrance until the sharp pangs of pain subsided.

"Little one . . . little one . . ." He cradled her easily against his chest. "Come, let me make you my wife . . . officially . . . consummate our marriage. Mrs. LeMaster, tonight you are mine. And I am yours. We won't hurt those ribs, I promise." He gently pulled her on top of him, her breasts pressed into his chest. She felt him moving ever so slightly, easing her carefully until their bodies blended together. She smiled faintly, grateful for his gentleness.

He tilted her head up and looked deeply into her eyes, stroking the back of her neck, sending quiet ripples of desire down her spine. "Morgan, should I protect you? We never discussed it, since we hadn't planned on this."

Her voice was subdued. "I'm taking the pill, Grant, for medical reasons, and have been for a long time . . . Grant, could I make a small request? Please . . . turn out the light."

"Why? You have a beautiful body, and I want to see you when I love you, little one."

Morgan's bronze eyes traveled over his face, reaching his eyes in a pleading gaze. "Please, Grant . . . make it dark."

With an exasperated sigh he turned and switched the small lamp. "There! Is that better? Nothing in sight."

Morgan's voice sounded small in the darkness of the room. "Yes, Grant, much better . . ." How could she tell him that her lack of experience precluded any preference?

The bed dipped slightly when Grant shifted beneath her. He lay quietly for a moment, and she could feel the heat radiating from his body. Oh, God, what was she doing? Suddenly old fears welled up inside her to replace the confidence and desires she had felt with Grant only moments ago. His hand stroked her back and she gasped audibly at his touch. *Should she tell him?*

His fingers made sensuous circles on her buttocks. "Easy, little one. Just relax, honey. I told you, I won't hurt your ribs."

"Grant, I . . ." *She had to explain her reluctance.* "Can your wife make a confession?"

"Of course, darling," he murmured, his lips excitingly caressing the curve of her neck, as his tongue drew glistening patterns on her silky skin.

"I'm not very . . . experienced. There's been only one other man in my life." *There. That should be enough.*

His voice was muffled as he nestled his face at the base of her throat. "Only one? In your life . . . or in your bed?"

"Grant, this is serious." She giggled nervously. "In my bed!"

"Honey, I must admit, I didn't think you were entirely innocent. But I'm still jealous! I want you all to myself!"

Morgan twirled her fingers in the hair on his chest, and raised herself slightly, then lowered her head to caress a hardened nipple with her lips. "Don't be jealous. This is where I want to be . . . with you, Grant."

"Where? In Europe? Was it . . . were you in love?" His raspy breathing halted, but she could feel the heated pounding of his heart.

Her hand moved up his strained neck, along the squared jawline to outline his lips with her eager fingers. "Yes, in

Europe," she managed, then paused to take in a tremulous breath. "It was . . . awful."

"Damn!" Grant hissed, his hot breath steaming her cheek. "Damn, I hate him! That's why you've held back from me. Even tonight. You're scared. Morgan honey, I'm sorry . . . I hope I can make you want to love again." There was a gentleness in his tone.

Morgan's fingers silenced his lips. "Grant, I . . . I held back for . . . love. And I'm not scared of you. Please love me tonight. Teach me to be your wife."

"Yes, little one, I'll love you . . . gently and completely." And he nuzzled her earlobe, kissing a fiery path to the throbbing hollow of her throat. His purpose was different now. He wanted to give, not just receive.

Grant carefully eased her onto her back and stretched alongside her, propping himself up on one elbow.

His finger slowly traced the outline of her trembling body, stopping finally at the soft cushion of her breast where it lightly awakened her nipple into prominence. He knelt beside her, bending forward to continue his teasing game with his tongue, going from one satiny slope to the other, lovingly flicking her nipples.

His hands caressed her abdomen, causing a fluttering to begin deep within her. With one hand he gradually provoked the warmth of her femininity, carrying her to a height of passion that threatened to consume her. She strained toward his touch as it liberated her to joys she had never before experienced. Finally she cried out to him . . . softly . . . but it was a plea nevertheless. Grant responded by carefully moving her over him, acclaiming the triumphant glory between a man and his wife. He had long awaited her touch, her response, and now, as she pressed her body into his, he knew the ecstasy was shared by both of them. Oh, how he had longed to take her, to claim her body. She was his wife, and now he would truly know her as he should.

The waiting was over, and as he lifted her to meet his urgent need, he exalted that there was no stopping now. Forgotten were the hateful words, the unfair reasons for their marriage, the unfulfilled past. Nothing mattered in those frenzied, mindless seconds when the lovers reached the once-distant peaks of satisfaction . . . together. *Together, at last!* A sharp cry escaped

Morgan's lips. A cry of love . . . a cry of pain. But there was no stopping, for either of them. Finally Grant, in the moment of complete release, clutched her shuddering body to him and they slumped exhaustedly against each other, riding out their sharing of the exquisite passion that slowly eased out of their bodies.

Morgan sighed, totally at peace, as she sensuously slid down the length of his body and curled on the mattress beside him.

Grant shifted to look at her face. "Are you all right? I didn't mean to hurt you."

She gazed lovingly into his passion-darkened eyes. *Did she see love there?* "I'm fine."

He kissed her nose affectionately, then her lips. "I always knew it would be like that with us, Morgan . . . perfect."

Shyly she answered, "I know I wasn't much of a lover, Grant, between my damned cracked ribs and lack of experience." Suddenly she was filled with a rush of emotion, and unavoidable tears swam in her large, bronze eyes. Was it body-wracking passion or the joy of love . . . fulfilled at last? She squeezed her eyes shut.

"Morgan, look at me." Grant's voice was still thick with emotion. Framing her face with his large hands, his thumbs wiped away the tears. "Was it that bad, little one? I want you to enjoy our love as much as I do."

She pulled his hand to her mouth and kissed the palm. "It was wonderful, Grant. These are tears of joy. It's just that . . . I . . . wanted love . . . not lust. I want your love, Grant."

"You have my love, Morgan," he murmured huskily against her cheek, moving his lips to hers. "You're a wonderful lover, little one. Next time will be better, I promise."

"Next time? Promise?" She smiled through her tears.

"Oh, yes, Morgan. This is just the beginning for us. We have a lifetime of love ahead. You'll enjoy it more . . . I'll see to that."

"I couldn't enjoy you more, Grant." *A lifetime together? Not just one short summer?* Her heart skipped at the thought. She could feel them both relaxing, and it filled her with a deep feeling of contentment.

"The first time is never the best, honey. Each time we love will be better than the last. I promise. But in order to improve we have to practice."

"Practice, huh?" She giggled. "Don't forget you have an injured wife who knows as much about making love as she does about breaking wild horses!"

"Forget the horses. I'll teach you the rest."

And he did. Grant's kiss was as gentle as his love for her, and Morgan eagerly responded to his promises and passions throughout the night.

CHAPTER EIGHT

Grant glanced up from his early-morning coffee. "Well, good morning, little one! What are you doing up so early?" He sat alone at the table while Willa busily prepared her usual breakfast feast in the kitchen.

Morgan smiled happily at her husband, placing one affectionate arm on his shoulder. "I'm missing too much by staying in bed all day. And that's no fun."

He rose and kissed her sweet, smiling lips thoroughly. "I figured after last night you'd need a few more days of recuperation," he murmured just loud enough for her to hear.

Morgan blushed, but responded smartly, "After last night I should be capable of anything, short of horseback riding!"

Grant grinned devilishly at her. "Well said!" Then he glanced at the polite sounds nearby. "Look who's up, Willa!"

The older woman smiled broadly. "Morgan, honey! Good morning! How are you feeling? Don't you think it's too soon for you to be getting up? And so early in the day!" Willa was obviously concerned about the welfare of her self-appointed charge and continued to hover like a clucking hen, even though her charge was determined not to be hovered over any longer. At least not by Willa.

"I'm much better, thank you, Willa, thanks to excellent nursing care from you and Grant. And you're right about it being awfully early. I think a cup of coffee would help to wake me up."

"Oh, sure!" Willa hurried for the coffee while Grant helped Morgan sit comfortably.

"Morgan, I think Willa's right. It's too soon for you to be up and about," Grant commented seriously.

"You didn't think so last night," she countered.

He leaned close and jibed, "I'm for keeping you in bed all the time, myself!"

David's happy voice interrupted the loving look and mutual desires smoldering between them. "Hi, Morgan! Are you going to have breakfast with us? Are you well now?"

She smiled a happy greeting to the youngster. "Hi, David! I'm not completely well, but I'm much better. And I'm tired of lying around in bed all day. I miss all the fun!"

Grant's eyes caught hers with a teasing glimmer as David joined them at the table and continued talking. "Can we go fishing today, Grant? And can we have another picnic? Huh?"

Morgan sipped her steamy coffee. "I doubt it, David. There's too much work to be done. I'm anxious to get back to work."

Grant refilled his own coffee cup and pondered aloud, "As a matter of fact, there isn't much happening today. You'll be happy to know that we've sold Blue Velvet. They're coming after him tomorrow. Next week Boyd and I are picking up several horses from a ranch south of Bayfield. So today will be rather slow."

"Then we can go! Oh, boy!" David's face was exuberant.

"Now hold on, pardner," Grant hedged, trying to calm his son. "I don't think Morgan's up to tromping across the fields and climbing on rocks to fish."

As Willa set heaping plates of eggs and biscuits for everyone, she suggested, "Morgan definitely needs to take it easy, but I'll bet she's up to a ride over to Mesa Verde. I could pack you three a picnic lunch and you could spend the day."

Grant greeted the idea enthusiastically. "Willa, that's a great idea! How does it sound to you, Morgan? Would you like a little ride to the Indian ruins? I think David will find it very interesting."

Morgan nodded in agreement. "I haven't been there in years, and I'd love it. I'm sure David would, too."

"Indian ruins? What's that? Can you fish there?" David asked curiously.

Grant shook his head. "No. No fishing. But there's lots to see."

"No fishing?" David puckered his small face. "Then why would I like it?"

Grant reached over and tousled his son's dark hair. "Just wait and see. Trust me, David. You'll like it."

It was a couple of hours before they were ready to set out for their excursion. Grant and Boyd quickly finished up morning chores, Willa prepared the picnic lunch she promised, and Morgan dressed very slowly, with a little help from her husband. The project was delayed considerably as Grant admired and savored the newly discovered, warm curves of his wife. He spent substantially more time dressing her than he had undressing. And of course, in a conscious effort to avoid hurting her injured ribs, Grant took the time to be abundantly careful. And impassionately romantic.

Finally a small, impatient voice outside the bedroom door rushed their efforts. "Morgan! Aren't you ready *yet*?"

"Almost ready, David!" called Morgan, giggling against her husband's chest. "Come on, Grant. David's waiting."

"Kids!" groaned Grant, good-naturedly. "Oh, all right. This day is for him. But don't forget, the nights are reserved for us, Morgan." He tweaked her nose and began to pull on his jeans.

As the three left the ranch house, Grant pulled Boyd aside. "You and Willa take the day off, Boyd. You both deserve it. Take your wife out to eat and to a movie this evening." He winked and clapped his friend on the back before joining his small family in the car.

The trip to Mesa Verde took about two hours. In that brief time they traveled from the lush woodland of the San Juan Mountain area to the semiarid land of mesas and canyons. Morgan was always amazed at the transformation of the landscape between Durango and the green table, as the Indians called it. Aspens and ponderosa gave way to piñon and scrub oak and juniper and cactus. It was a strange, yet beautiful, transformation.

As the winding road hairpinned to the flat top of the huge

mesa, there was a growing anticipation to witness the centuries-old villages hidden deep in the canyons. There, tucked into widemouthed sandstone arches in the sides of the cliffs, lay proof of the lives of ancient people in this rather hostile land. It was a secret concealed from modern civilization until this century.

Morgan glanced across the front seat at the dark-haired contour of her husband. He seemed lost in thought today as he quietly guided them to the place that time forgot. She wondered what secrets of his past were hidden by time, and if she would ever know all about him. She already knew he was a different man from the one she thought she had married. He was definitely his own man and would not be dominated by her. Mysterious, yet magnetic, tough and obstinate, Grant was also very sensitive and passionate. Who was this man she had married? Morgan would probably ask herself that question a hundred times before she knew the answer.

Actually they had just begun to know each other last night. *Last night!* She tingled inside and felt her cheeks tinge at the remembrance. The passions Grant had awakened in her were beyond her wildest yearning . . . even her most wanton imagination. She had never believed it possible for her to desire a man as she did Grant. And, even as he had predicted, she had brazenly gone to him! She had actually asked him to make love to her! And oh, God—*did he!*

But was it love? Was it really Grant's love that influenced his intense and skillful lovemaking? Or was it his passion gone wild? How could she be sure?

Morgan had always dreamed that the man she loved would elicit her passion and her love, the feelings she now had for Grant . . . had felt last night. And yet she wasn't even sure of her own love. It was all too new. She glanced again at him, remembering his words spoken in the quiet satisfaction of her embrace. *You have my love, Morgan.* Did he really mean it? Or did he intimate that they were lovers driven together by their own desires?

Maybe it was her own desires thrusting her into this man's arms—this man who was her husband. It had happened before. Only . . . with André, there had been no fulfillment. And the intensity of their relationship was nothing like what was happening between her and Grant. It had ended long ago in Greece. . . .

"Would you like to walk down to Long House with us, Morgan? This is the largest of the cliff dwellings here, and it's like taking a walk back in time."

The warm sound of Grant's voice jarred Morgan back to the present, and as she gazed at him with love in her eyes, she knew she didn't want to leave the present time and place. She wanted to be here, in love with Grant, and receiving his love. She smiled and nodded, enticing him with her glow of love. Unable to resist, he kissed her lips instinctively.

His voice was a bare whisper. "Save that look for me tonight. Right now we'd better hurry to catch up with David."

Hand-in-hand, they followed him into the ancient silent city that was nestled in the arched cave of the huge sandstone cliff. After listening to the guide's exposition, the three milled around the ruins on their own. It was easy to imagine ghosts of the past going about their daily lives. Morgan sat on a shaded wall as Grant tried to explain the significance of the Indian ruins to David in terms the boy could understand.

"People lived in these little stone houses seven hundred years ago, David!"

David looked around with renewed interest. "Did kids live here, too? Kids like me?"

Grant nodded. "Sure, David. Entire families lived here with their kids. Doesn't that sound like fun?"

"You mean whole families like us and Morgan? Yeah, that would be fun! Would you like that, Morgan? If our family lived here instead of the ranch?" David's large, dark eyes were positive reminders of his ancestors.

She smiled at his exuberance. "Yes, it would be fun, David. Climbing up the steep rocks using those little footholes might give me some problems, though!"

He looked straight up at the small indentions in the rocky cliffs. "They might be hard for me, too. I think I'd miss the ranch . . . and the ice cream!"

Morgan tousled his straight, raven hair and laughed. "That's right, David! There was no ice cream in those days! We'd both miss that!"

He propped small fists on his hips and assessed the situation in his own, youthful insight. "I think I like our family just the way it is right now. Don't you, Grant?"

The man looked gently at his young son, then seriously at Morgan. "Yes, David. I like things just the way they are right now. Couldn't be better, huh, Morgan?" His hand slipped around her hips affectionately, while the other hand encircled his son's shoulders.

"Yes, the Anasazi missed a lot living here in these rocky cliffs." Grant heaved himself up to sit beside Morgan on the wall, their legs touching intimately.

David climbed up beyond where they sat and curiously peeked into a small, square window. His voice was filled with wonder. "Where did these Anasazi people put the TV?"

Both Grant and Morgan laughed at the child's twentieth-century view of routine life. "They didn't have TV in those days, son. They didn't even have electricity," Grant explained.

"Wasn't it awfully dark up here at night?" David's ebony eyes scanned the ancient block buildings that towered above them.

"I'm sure it was," Grant conceded. "But they had campfires that provided light and heat as well as a place to cook. There are still traces of campfires. Do you see the groove in this big rock? The Anasazi women used another round, smooth rock, like this, to grind their corn by hand. It made a cornmeal for their bread. These rocks are called *mano y metate.*"

Morgan eyed the demonstration skeptically, grateful that she didn't have to hunker over the *mano y metate* to grind their food today. However David was far more interested in what the ancients ate than the process of preparing the food. "What kind of bread? Was that all they ate?"

Grant shrugged. " I suppose it was flat bread, like a tortilla. But they also grew corn and squash along the top of the mesa." He pointed at the brush-covered land above the sandstone arches and cliff dwellings. "They ate corn on the cob."

David nodded, for obviously some of what Grant was explaining was familiar. Most Indian children knew tales of their ancient ancestors, and David was no exception. "My grandmother grew corn and squash, too. We had a campfire sometimes and she let me roast marshmallows." The small, brown boy walked around the peculiar circular wall where Grant and Morgan sat. When he reached them, he hunkered down solemnly. "She also told me stories about the Anasazi. She said that in the round *kiva* strange things happened. Sometimes good, sometimes bad. Do you believe that?"

Grant tried to dispel unfounded fears in the mind of his small son. "No one is really sure, of course, but they think the *kiva* —this area here—was a ceremonial place. And I suppose things that are strange to us happened here. But look, David, we're sitting in a *kiva* right now, and it seems perfectly safe to me."

David picked up a tiny rock and tossed it. His smile reflected the relief he felt. "Me, too! Did my mother have ice cream and TV?"

"I'm sure she did." Grant's large hand rested securely on David's small shoulder.

An eerie silence settled over the abandoned Indian ruins, broken only by the plaintive call of a red-tailed hawk, which circled overhead. All of the visitors had gone, leaving Grant and Morgan and David sitting alone atop the ancient wheel-shaped wall.

"What about my father? Did he ever take her to get ice cream, the way you do Morgan and me?"

Morgan caught the gasp in her throat before it became audible.

"I don't know, David," Grant muttered gruffly, aware of the acute crisis that had suddenly been created.

"Where is he? Could we ask him?" David began to climb down off the wall.

"No, David. I don't think so." The silence around the words was deafening.

There was a shocking honesty in the small, brown face as David declared, almost casually, "Well, I don't care. He didn't love me and my grandmother, so I don't love him. Anyway, you're my new father, and I love you, Grant. And Morgan. I like this family best of all. I hope we're always like this."

He was too young to notice the dark concern in Grant's face, and the stricken astonishment in Morgan's. His statement was made, and, childlike, his attention rambled quickly to other things.

"Can I climb down to that big flat rock over there?" He pointed down the arroyo.

Grant nodded silently, avoiding Morgan's alarmed, questioning eyes until David was out of earshot.

Morgan's voice quivered slightly. "Grant? What was he talking about?"

Grant looked at her and sighed heavily. "Out of the mouths of babes . . . come remarkable truths. I think that was a beautiful compliment from David, Morgan. We've only been a part of his life a short while—"

Morgan's tone was alarm filled, and her statement flat. "He's not your child, is he, Grant?"

Grant pressed his lips together tightly. "Not yet. I'm in the process of adopting him."

Rage shook her being. "Adopting David? Then why didn't you tell me? I'm only your wife!"

"You weren't until last night!" he accused.

"Grant, please. I am your wife! We've shared—" Her voice quivered as she recalled the intimacy they had shared the night before.

But his voice was steel-edged. "Morgan, you've got to admit, until last night we'd shared nothing!"

She shook her head slowly, ignoring his inference. "Why . . . why couldn't you tell me such an important thing as this? Adopting David . . . adopting . . ." She mulled the words aloud as if trying to digest them. And indeed she was. The whole idea created a huge knot in her stomach.

"Morgan, try to understand me. It's because this issue is so important and sensitive that I held back until the timing was right. There are a lot of legal ramifications involved here. I needed certain credentials for this adoption."

Yet Morgan could not hide the hurt and resentment she felt as she snapped, "And now's the right time? It seems to me David picked the time and, in his innocence, revealed more than you wanted me to know!" Her voice echoed against the empty stones around them.

Grant's voice was lower, gentler. "This isn't exactly how I planned to tell you. But I did want you to know—of course I did! And now I'm . . . I'm glad it's out in the open."

"It doesn't matter now, does it? At least, it's after we've been to bed together! After the bonds of our marriage have been sealed! After you've—"

"No!" he interrupted. His large hands reached out to her, trying to grasp her shoulders. "My God, Morgan! Our relationship has nothing to do with David!"

Morgan twisted away from his touch. "The hell it doesn't! All the time I thought . . . I thought we were . . . like a little family. Just as David said—" She choked on the knot that had now settled in her throat, causing tears to fill her sorrel eyes. But she continued. "I thought things were beginning to work out for us. We—you and me—were just starting. And David seems so happy, and it's like we really belong together."

"We do belong together, Morgan. It's all still the same."

"No! It's not the same! You lied to me! You lied by not telling me all about David! How do you expect us to build a relationship without truth?"

Grant's lips stiffened angrily. "I did not lie!"

Defiantly she answered, "It's all the same! You were unfair to let me believe what was wrong!"

"Unfair? You have the nerve to accuse me of being unfair? You—who asked me to alter my life long enough to marry you so you could get your own life straightened out? You have a warped sense of fairness, Morgan!" He moved to his feet like the lithe Indians that stalked this land so many years ago.

"Is that how you think of me, Grant? Of our . . . marriage? That it's unfair—that I've inconvenienced your life?" Hot tears trailed her cheeks as she fought for control of her wildly raging emotions.

Grant's gray eyes narrowed as he commented cruelly, "You'd better think again before you call what we have a marriage!"

Morgan pulled herself to her feet. "Well, I think you just saw the opportunity to grab some quick bucks and a chance to crawl into my bed as well!" With a deep sense of abhorrence she regretted her capitulation last night. Oh, how could she have been so stupid . . . again?

"Frankly, Morgan, you can think what you damn well please because I don't care! And my business with David is none of your concern!" His heartless words ripped through her, leaving Morgan feeling as vacant and empty as the Indian ruins surrounding her.

As she watched Grant's back disappear, she muttered angrily, "Damn you, Grant LeMaster! I hate you!" But her words were snatched up by the wind and flung against the sandstone arches and never reached him.

Strong gusts swept through the deep arroyo and whined around Morgan's lone figure, drying her bitter tears and whipping her long blond hair around her head in an unruly aura. She began to walk, aimlessly following the circle of the *kiva.* Overpowered by the crush of intense silence, the impact of her conversation with Grant left her chilled and bereft. It had all happened so fast . . . one minute they were a happy little family, the next there was an abysmal chasm between them. One moment Grant was declaring that they belonged together, the next he was asserting that this business with David was none of her concern! How could he possibly expect her to simply excise all interest and affection for David? After all, she cared deeply for him—had grown to love him, as she did Grant.

No, what she felt for Grant couldn't be love. He made her feel too awful . . . like now. The things he said and did were too cruel, too harsh for love. What had happened between her and Grant could be summed up in one word—sex. Shamefully Morgan admitted it to herself. They had each responded to the passion of the moment without regard to sensitivity. What they'd shared was an emotionless reaction to physical closeness. *Or was it?* They had exchanged words of love . . . words *about* love. There was a difference.

Suddenly Morgan was overwhelmed with an eerie sensation. The ghosts of the vanquished seemed to hover all around her, crying with the wind, screaming at the fair-haired intruder. She was encroaching on their sacred land just as she was invading the lives of Grant and David. And she didn't belong.

She looked around, half expecting to see a bronze, leather-clad body lurking in the crumbling ruins. But she was alone. Maybe David's Indian grandmother was right, that strange things did happen in the *kiva.* After all, it was here in the ancient ceremonial place that the truth had been revealed. Truth Grant had tried to hide from her. What else was he hiding? Oh, dear God—who was this man she had married? And what other secrets was he hiding?

Impetuously another thought struck her. Maybe Grant was David's real father, after all! Maybe he was the man who had fathered the Indian child, then abandoned him! And now she was caught in the midst of Grant's personal guilt and legal battle to compensate for the sins of his past! Damn him, anyway! No, she couldn't love him. All she wanted to do was to get away from Grant . . . and the exotic, prehistoric, Indian cliff dwellings. Both were formidable.

Slowly Morgan climbed the carved-out stone steps alone, returning with dread to face Grant and David, who waited by the car.

Grant generously handed her the remainder of his Coke and offered, "Here, finish this. I know you're thirsty."

She accepted the drink silently and gulped thirstily. *Do you also know how much I'm hurting inside?*

"Let's have lunch, Morgan. I'm hungry," David suggested.

"Good idea, David!" Grant agreed before Morgan could respond. "Why don't we find a nice place for a picnic. Maybe we can hike down into an arroyo. There are other cliff dwellings around here, you know."

They found a place to park the car and hiked in seclusion to Mug House, another of the cliff dwellings. Their picnic was quiet and tense with David doing most of the talking. Afterward David and Grant explored the rugged, rocky-cliffed terrain while Morgan waited in the shade of a huge boulder. It gave her some much-needed time alone to mull over today's revelations.

Finally they returned, David leading the way. "Morgan! Are you ready to go home?"

"Sure." She smiled lovingly at the weary little boy. No matter whose child he was, he had worked his way to her heart. She began gathering the picnic supplies.

As Grant approached, he added, "David's had it for today. He's exhausted!"

Morgan glanced caustically at the tall, perspiration-drenched man who followed the still-active child. "Looks to me like David's not the only one who's exhausted. I dare say he's done better today than you!"

Grant doffed his straw cowboy hat and wiped his dripping brow. "Undoubtedly!" he admitted with a devilish grin. "Of course, my energy was expended before the day began!"

Morgan's spicy brown eyes condemned him as she asserted, "Well, we'll see that you get plenty of rest from now on!"

David took her hand, pulling her impatiently along the path. "I wish you could have come with us, Morgan. We saw some broken pots that the Anasazi used. And I looked for arrowheads!"

"Sounds like fun, David."

"Uh-huh. But this isn't funner than fishing, is it, Morgan?"

Morgan smiled at the tired but truthful child, then cast a glance at Grant. "Well, David, this has been . . . enlightening, but not as much fun as fishing. I see at least one of us is being completely honest today."

"Can we stop in Durango for ice cream, Grant? Can we, huh?" Anticipation lit David's ebony eyes.

"Sure, David," Grant acquiesced. "Maybe it'll salvage the day."

"Yeah! Ice cream!" David ran ahead up the path.

"Nothing can salvage what's been said today," Morgan claimed icily.

Grant grabbed her arm and made her turn to hear him. "How about the truth?"

"I think I've heard enough confessions for today!"

His hand tightened on her wrist. "You haven't heard nearly enough, Morgan!"

"You're hurting my arm!" Morgan hissed under her breath. "Let go, damn you! I don't intend to listen to any more of your half-truths! Anyway, David's waiting."

The long trip home was silent and strained. Both Morgan and David had reached their maximum endurance and settled comfortably in the roomy Suburban. David curled in the backseat and was asleep in no time. As the sun dropped from view in a glorious, red-orange blaze beyond Mesa Verde Indian Ruins, Morgan dozed. Through the treacherous, hairpin curves, the flat farmland, the rise of mountains around Durango, Morgan slept soundly against the shoulder of the man she wanted to hate.

The journey home was interrupted by the brief, promised

stopover in Durango for ice cream. When the Suburban finally jolted to a stop in front of the Rocking M, Morgan roused and pushed herself away from Grant.

"Are we home yet?" David asked sleepily from the backseat.

"Okay, you two sleepyheads, wake up! We're home!" Grant announced as he turned to help David out and unload the picnic supplies.

Home? Morgan wondered vaguely as she stumbled inside the dark ranch house. *How can Grant call this home? He's here under duress. But then, so am I.* With a wearisome sigh she entered her bedroom alone. She heard the muffled sounds as Grant packed David into bed and pondered sadly how long they would occupy this house and her life. She felt now that it had been a big mistake to involve them. At one time it had seemed so simple. Grant could help her achieve her goal, she would pay him handsomely, and he would leave with no regrets. *No regrets!* She hadn't counted on her own emotional involvement and concern for this man she now called her husband. And his son . . . she shuddered at the thought and the deception.

Morgan stepped into the shower, attempting to wash away the futility of her relationship with Grant and the exhaustion of her body. However she accomplished neither. Her muscles still ached for rest, and her soul longed for reprieve from Grant's possession. Sleep, she reasoned, would satisfy both desires. She pulled her robe over her nakedness and turned down the covers of her bed just as Grant entered the bedroom.

Morgan faced him wearily, exhaustion obvious in her face, but spirit in her voice. "Get out of my bedroom! I've had enough of your lies today!" She wondered where she got her bravado, for inside she trembled. He seemed to tower ominously over her and had proven he could overpower her. Now, with her rib injury, she was completely helpless. *What was she thinking? He was her husband! He wouldn't—*

"Oh, no!" Grant laughed wickedly and leaned arrogantly against the dresser. There was a heartless quality to his voice that was both alarming and infuriating. "I've come to see if I can help *my wife* out of her clothes! Do you need a man tonight? Or maybe you need me to bandage your ribs! I'm good at wrapping ribs!

Or maybe you just need a wrangler who'll bust his ass on your goddamn ranch for room and board!"

Morgan raised her chin defiantly. "You got more than room and board last night! Now what do you want? I told you to get out of here! If you think this night will be as rewarding as last, it'll have to be by force! You'll have to rape your wife, Grant LeMaster!"

His lips curled contemptibly. "Don't flatter yourself, Morgan! I'll never take you by force. I came to talk. Then you can go to bed *alone.*"

Her brown eyes flashed. "We have nothing to say."

He folded his long, powerful arms across his solid chest. "Yes, we do. I have some things to straighten out with my wife . . . David's adoptive mother."

"Don't . . . don't call me . . . that." She nearly choked on the words.

"Why not, Morgan? Does being an instant mother scare you? Well, don't worry. It won't be for long. In fact I came very close to just taking him with me and leaving this place tonight. I feel an urgency to go somewhere that no one can find us . . . so they can't take him away from me." Grant's voice ended with a sober, hard-edged tone. When Morgan didn't answer, he continued. "But I know that won't help David. Most of all, it won't help the adoption. It would only serve to confuse him even more. And, God knows, he's confused enough about his life already."

Angrily Morgan defended the child. "What do you expect? Even I am confused. If you'd start telling the truth—"

"David knows the truth! He knows his father was a white man who left before he was born. He knows his mother was a beautiful Navajo woman who died when he was born. And he knows that I'm trying to adopt him and . . ." Grant's voice became strained and somewhat hoarse. ". . . that I love him."

Morgan folded her arms boldly. "Does he know you're his real father? That you fathered him and left his mother alone when she was pregnant, then became plagued with guilt after all these years?" Morgan knew she was drawing heavily from her own speculation and, by the shadow on Grant's face, treading dangerous ground. But she wanted the truth this time from Grant and was willing to risk his wrath.

Grant's steel-cold eyes hardened at her accusation. He took a step closer and gripped her forearms angrily. Through clenched teeth he muttered, "David's not my child! Damn you, Morgan! Haven't you had enough of unfounded allegations from your family? Now you've done the same to me!"

His stinging reply smacked across her as if he had raised his hand physically against her. Suddenly Morgan felt sick and miserable at the truth of his accusation. She hadn't even given Grant a chance at the truth, just as they had never listened to her.

"Grant . . . I . . . I'm sorry. . . . I just . . ." she stammered, groping for the right words, which never came.

His face came within inches of hers, and once again his musky scent reached her. "I will tell you this, Morgan. David is not of my blood—but that doesn't matter a damn to me! He will be my *real* son very soon. And it will be accomplished with your help, too!" He released her then, and shoved her away as if repulsed by her closeness.

She touched her throbbing arms where he had gripped so tightly. "My help? Hardly!" What did he want from her now?

"Oh, yes! You'll sign the adoption request saying you're my new wife . . . and David's prospective mother. I upheld my end of the bargain. Now it's your turn!"

Bargain? Is that what he thought of their . . . relationship? Had she imagined it was more? Oh, what a fool she had been! "I don't see how you can ask anything of me. Why would I help you, anyway?"

Grant's answer was simple and hard-hitting. "Only for David's sake. I am all he has."

Morgan sighed raggedly. "Grant, why didn't you tell me the truth? All this time I thought he was your child. And now—"

Grant spread his hands with a shrug. "Why should I tell you? And risk that you wouldn't marry me and give me what I needed most for the adoption—a wife? You probably wouldn't have signed that marriage contract. But you were willing to sign anything in exchange for my name on your marriage license."

Morgan shook as she realized what she had done. "You're very devious, Grant LeMaster. You knew that if I didn't sign the contract, I would have as much legal claim to David as you . . . if we ever end this marriage."

"But we don't have to worry about that now, do we? I'll never let you have him. I'm the one who fought for him. I'm the one who'll keep him. Don't you understand? No, I . . . I guess you couldn't." He looked away and ran his hand through his dark hair.

"Try me."

Grant looked at her deeply, trying to analyze her sincerity. Then, he sat on the edge of her bed, heaved a sigh, and began to speak, as if in a daze. "I was in Ignacio at the Ute tribal office working on a story when they brought him in. Someone had found him eating out of . . . the city dump . . . and he looked like a wild boy. You wouldn't have recognized him. His hair was long and matted, and he was just skin and bones. All you could see were those big, brown eyes. The Sheriff's Department determined that David's grandmother had died two weeks earlier in the mountains where they lived. The clincher was that he isn't Ute. He's Navajo. So they had to return him to his tribal government down in Arizona. Since he had no family, and was obviously a half-breed, he would probably end up a ward of the state, white man's problem. I watched them toss around the options for this little kid all afternoon. Well, the chief and I had become friendly, and I managed to convince him that I would take good care of the boy. But one look into those eyes of David's, and I was hooked. Within the week I filed for adoption with the Indian Child Welfare Department of the Navajo Tribe. The hearing is set for next month."

"And I came along just in time to provide the stable family life you needed to prove yourself a fit father for that adoption," Morgan finished bitterly.

He shrugged his admittance. "Something like that."

"Damn you, Grant! Why didn't you just tell me? Why weren't you truthful right up front? We could have worked something out for David. Instead you used me! And managed to get into my bed, too!" Tears filled Morgan's sorrel eyes.

Grant rose and faced her menacingly. "How the hell can you stand there so self-righteously? You used me, too! You wanted a husband for your own personal gain and a strong back to run this damned ranch! Well, you've got both! You're just angry because I turned the tables on you and took advantage of the marriage, too. You selfish bitch! It's all right for you, but not for me!"

Morgan blanched at his accusations. "No! That's not what I meant. I just want us to be truthful—"

"Truthful?" He laughed scornfully. "Okay, Morgan. Let's be truthful. As for last night in your bed—I was there because I wanted to be. And so were you. I didn't have to go through all this hell to get into a woman's bed. I wanted *you.* And don't forget you invited me there! There was no force and you damn well know it."

"Grant, please—"

"Let me finish, Morgan dear, and you can go to bed alone, as I promised. I'll assure you of one thing. I love that kid in there. And you'd better not try to do a thing to interfere with my keeping him or . . . you'll regret it. I'll do anything to keep him, Morgan, and don't you ever forget it!"

"Anything?"

"Anything!" And he stalked out, keeping his promise to stay away from her bed.

However, as tired as she was, Morgan found sleep elusive.

CHAPTER NINE

Despite her sleepless night Morgan stumbled to the breakfast table early. She had no desire to lie in bed for another sleepless hour. "Just coffee, please, Willa." She averted her red-rimmed eyes from Grant's sharp gaze and concentrated on the steam rising from her coffee cup.

He refused to ignore her and reached over to cover her shaky hand with his. "What are you doing up so early?" There was no softness in his voice, and Morgan was aware of the exchange of knowledgeable glances between Willa and Boyd.

Damn! Why did Grant have to be so obvious about their conflicts? There was a world of difference between his sweet, loving greeting of yesterday morning and now. Morgan was determined not to be intimidated by Grant or their personal clashes. She slipped her hand from his warm touch. "I've stayed in bed too long already. This dude ranch needs a lot of work."

"You're in no shape to do any work, Morgan, and you know it."

Her sable eyes flashed at him. "I'm fully aware of what I'm capable of doing . . . and what I'm not able to do." How dare he question her!

He sighed as if dealing with a recalcitrant child. "Well, if you insist on being up and around, why don't you work on the books? Nobody has had time to organize an accounting system for the Rocking M Ranch. There are already several bills that should be paid and a brand-new ledger is on the desk. Do something useful today." With that he walked out, his heavy boot step punctuating his taciturn statements.

Morgan gripped her coffee cup, repressing the primitive urge to hurl it at Grant's receding back. Instead she clutched it tightly, gathering control of her raging emotions. This lack of control seemed rampant whenever she clashed with Grant, which was quite frequent. But then he was so demanding and harsh, living with him was nearly impossible. That almost ended last night, yet Grant went about his work this morning as if nothing had happened between them. Oh, but it had. In the last two days they had drawn together into intimacy, then hurled apart with vicious accusations. She couldn't dissolve the question in her mind of how they would manage through the summer. Then David joined her at the table, and she wondered with inner pain what would happen to them all by the end of the summer.

After forcing some breakfast with David, Morgan ambled into the small room they had turned into the office. She surveyed the disarray of papers scattered about and the neat, never-opened ledger and realized with a jab of anger that Grant was right. Someone needed to work on the books. And it might as well be her.

Morgan spent most of the next two days at the desk, organizing, figuring, writing, filing, working herself into exhaustion so that she could fall asleep nights. It was the only way she could get any rest.

"We'll be working in the red until late July or early August at this rate, Morgan," Grant assessed, pouring over her neatly penciled ledger one evening.

Morgan's solution was her old standby. "I can just borrow—"

"You can't keep dipping into the trust fund, Morgan." His tone was disparaging.

"That's what it's there for." She shrugged.

"But, Morgan, our goal is to function in the black, remember?"

She looked at him sharply. "*Our* goal? Somehow I lost sight of *our* goals. I thought you had yours and I had mine!"

He gazed at her thoughtfully. "Neither of our goals are

fulfilled yet, Morgan. We have until the end of the summer to make them realities. That's what you estimated, remember?"

"But I didn't figure on some of the obstacles we've faced." Her eyes met his steadily. She was determined not to back down in front of him, no matter what her insides were doing. She wouldn't let him know he had bested her in any way, or that she was jelly under all her crusty facade.

"Can't we discuss the business of this ranch without involving our personal lives, Morgan? We have a long time to go yet. And if we can't discuss the ranch, we may as well give up now." His hands shrugged helplessly.

Morgan answered stoutly. "Well, I'm not ready to give up. And I would be delighted to achieve our goals and run this business without getting personal. In fact, I think that was my purpose in the beginning."

Grant's gray eyes darkened, reminding her of clouds over a stormy ocean. "It's too bad you're married to a temporal man instead of a steel robot, Morgan. Then he could easily turn away from you! And there would be nothing emotional . . . nothing personal."

"It's only your heart that's made of steel, Grant! There has been nothing between us but pure, unadulterated lust! Now could we get back to the business at hand?"

He tossed the ledger back on the desk. "Okay. You handle the books and I'll check in with you from time to time. If you have any questions or problems, just ask. I'll do the same. Otherwise I won't bother you. And I expect you to return the favor. I don't want to be stumbling over you every time I turn around. Now, we have six new horses coming in tomorrow and six more next week. They'll keep me busy most of the time. We have to train them and shoe them—"

"Are they broken?" Morgan asked quickly. Even though things were strained between them, she didn't want to face that experience again.

His answer was a curt nod. He turned to leave, then paused and glanced back at her. "Incidentally . . ." He pulled a long envelope from his shirt pocket. "Here's the petition for adoption from the Navajo tribe. It's just basic info about his . . . about you.

Would you mind filling it out and dropping it in the mail?" He flipped it onto the desk and was gone.

She looked at the white envelope and burned inside because Grant was so assured that she would comply. Her conscience wouldn't allow otherwise, for she couldn't let David suffer because of matters between herself and Grant. And he knew it. He had the upper hand, and she hated him for that!

Temporal, indeed! Diablo was more apt!

During the next two weeks Grant was occupied with the new animals, as he had predicted. And Morgan spent her mornings going over the accounting and her afternoons planning the activities for the dude ranchers. She visited several other ranches in the area, meeting the owners, making friends, studying their procedures, and merging their ideas with different ones of her own.

So Morgan and Grant managed to stay busy, their paths never crossing, their personal lives never touching except for a terse word occasionally. Morgan lay awake nights listening to the staccato pecking of Grant's typewriter. Many times it clicked late into the dark, lonely nights. Apparently he had decided that being a writer was superior to being a rancher and was attempting to renew his former career. Or perhaps he was preparing for summer's end. Morgan lay awake long after his typewriter was silent, worrying about what time would bring.

A loud pounding jarred Morgan from her nightmare-filled, restless sleep. Before she was fully awake, she was struggling to rise, for accompanying the thunderous noise was Boyd's alarmed call.

"Grant! Grant! Wake up, man! Hey, Grant!"

Morgan's heart pounded wildly, and her hands shook as she struggled with her robe. She first thought it was fire! *Or vandals! Or Willa's sick!* With her imagination running rampant, Morgan stumbled out into the kitchen where Grant was listening intently to Boyd's breathless explanation for the disturbance.

"... and they busted down the north fence and followed that white devil up into the mountains—" Boyd's words were elaborated by both arms flying excitedly in the air.

Grant's countenance was calm, sleepy. "All of them gone?"

"Yep! Even the mules! They're heading for the San Juans as hard as they can go!" Morgan had never seen Boyd so animated. "And you should see the mess they made of the fence! The *new* fence! We've got to go after them before they get too far ahead!" Eager anticipation of the hunt was written on his wrinkled face.

Grant raised his hands, gesturing for calmness. "Okay, okay, take it easy, Boyd. We'll get them. But, first, let's get organized. Morgan, you make some coffee. Boyd, call the Haroldsons. See if we can borrow a couple of horses. And let's get dressed. It looks like a long day."

Morgan seethed inside as the men left her to prepare the coffee. While they were off taking care of the emergencies, she was obliged to feed them and take care of the kitchen. Well, she wouldn't let them have all the excitement. Quickly she primed the coffeepot, then hurried to dress, colliding with Willa in the process.

"Throw some breakfast together, will you? We're going after the horses!" And she was gone to dress for the excursion. She would show Grant LeMaster!

Morgan stepped out of her bedroom just as Grant opened his door, and they faced each other. She was dressed to the teeth with a shirt, sweater, jacket, jeans, and boots. It was obvious that she didn't intend to hover over the scrambled eggs. For a long moment their eyes met . . . questioned . . . clashed.

"Where are you going?" he growled.

"I'm going after the horses with you," she announced solidly.

"That's ridiculous!" he scoffed. "We've got to go into the mountains on horseback after them. You can't do that!"

"And why not? I'm perfectly well!" Her hands pounced jauntily on her hips. "Boyd certainly can't do that much riding. Don't forget his crippled leg."

Grant's face scowled, and she could see him relenting inside. "Are you sure you're up to it? Are your ribs still bothering you?"

"I'm fine," she half lied.

"It's going to be a hard trip, Morgan."

"You'll need some help. You can't do it by yourself. Anyway, they're my horses, too."

He sighed and, without a word, acquiesced by just leading the way out to the breakfast table. Morgan followed him, satisfied and smug. She had gotten her way . . . and that wasn't easy to do with Grant.

Grant and Boyd discussed the strategy for retrieving the horses around the early-morning breakfast table. The plans, by necessity, included Morgan, as Grant assumed the role of decisionmaker. "Willa, could you pack us some food? Morgan and I will follow their trail into the mountains. Boyd, you take the Suburban and scout the area for any stragglers and the mules. I'm sure they're around here somewhere. They couldn't make it into the mountains at the same speed as the horses."

"You're taking Morgan?" Disappointment was obvious in Boyd's eyes.

Grant nodded, taking full responsibility for the decision. "Yeah, Boyd. I need you to take care of things around here at the Rocking M while I'm gone. You'll have the responsibility of getting those mules as well as repair of the fence."

"Sure, Grant." Boyd nodded, trying to mask his true feelings. He rose and murmured, "I'll drive over to the Haroldsons now and lead the horses back so you can get started. He said he'd have them saddled. Good neighbor. Said he'd come over later and help repair the fence."

"Good. I want it secure by the time we get back. Eat up, Morgan. We'll leave in about ten minutes. And you definitely need nourishment today." As Boyd left the kitchen, Grant cast an accusing look toward Morgan that would cut steel.

Defiantly she responded to his unspoken blame. "Would you rather take Boyd with you? You can always change your mind."

Grant's eyes touched her flaxen hair, the unusual deep chestnut eyes, her pouting, sensuous lips, and knew he desired her more than any woman he'd known. "Now, you know I'd rather be in the mountains with you. Boyd will get over it. I'm not so sure I will, though." His tone was soft and low.

His expression told Morgan more than she wanted to know. "We have a job to do, Grant. Don't forget—"

"I haven't forgotten *anything,* Morgan."

"Then you'll recall that we decided to keep our activities strictly business." She bent her head to eat the breakfast before her. Even after Boyd's temperamental display and Grant's roguish replies, she was determined to make the best of the excursion.

She would make every effort to prove herself helpful to the men, especially after winning—or was it taking—the opportunity. Stubbornly she admitted to herself that she didn't regret taking Boyd's place. After all, she would rather be active in the search than sit at home and wait for someone else to return her own horses. She longed for the adventure . . . the excitement. Even if that meant following Grant into the mountains.

There was noise outside and she knew that Boyd had returned with the horses she and Grant were to ride. Her husband rose with the admonition that they'd be leaving soon. With one last gulp of coffee she followed him out into the frosty, dark morning.

Willa pressed two bulging saddlebags into her hands.

"This ought to take care of you for a while. Are you sure you're up to this, Morgan? It's not too late to back out. Boyd could always go along." She couldn't help hovering just a little.

Morgan shook her head, but before she had a chance to say a thing, Grant moved close. "We'll be just fine, Willa. Thanks for the food. This early-morning breakfast is above and beyond the call of duty, but we really appreciate it. Take good care of David."

Willa's smile of gratitude was grand. "You know I will, Grant. You two be careful and . . . good luck."

"Oh, we'll get them. We can't afford not to," Grant said confidently, swinging his long leg over the horse's back and settling easily in the saddle. Morgan hurried to mount her horse, vaguely noticing the small, tight blanket roll tied securely behind the saddle. It didn't occur to her that they wouldn't be back, with errant horses in tow, before dark.

"See you later." She smiled and waved. Morgan was happily off on the adventure she sought! No more sitting behind the desk all morning!

"Be sure to get that fence fixed, Boyd," Grant called, already fifty feet away.

Morgan kicked her horse and followed Grant's lean, straight back as they made their way into the rugged San Juan Mountains. The Colorado sun sent streaks of light across the trail and reflected a pink glow on a distant peak, but it would be hours before they saw and felt its warm glow on their backs. Up the steep and rugged terrain, down plunging ravines, across natural arroyos, edging narrow trails, farther and farther they traveled, deep into the giant ponderosa pine country. Quietly they shared part of the huge lunch Willa had prepared and placed in Morgan's saddlebags. The sun glowed enthusiastically, lulling them, and Morgan longed for an hour's nap in the quiet, peaceful place.

"Couldn't we stay here for a little rest, Grant? We've been on those damn horses for hours."

He shook his head curtly. "Don't have time. Those beasts haven't stopped, or we'd see signs. They can't just keep going, though. They've got to stop soon."

Morgan sighed with exasperation. "Why are they keeping up such a pace?"

Grant looked at her for a long moment, then a crooked grin broke his straight face. "They are just following their male leader. What's wrong, Morgan? Aren't the mares liberated enough for you?" His wicked laughter echoed off the towering rock cliffs.

Her chestnut eyes narrowed angrily in response to his mocking jabs. "I just thought they'd have more sense than to follow blindly, that's all!" Morgan grabbed the saddle horn and swung herself achingly into the saddle again. She could ride as long as he could, by damn!

Grant moved his mount alongside hers. This time he attempted seriousness. "Are you feeling all right, Morgan? Are your ribs hurting you?"

"Oh, of course not! That's not the part of my anatomy that's hurting!" She bolted out in front of Grant to lead the way. Let him stare at her backside awhile!

Grant's laughter again rocked through the craggy mountains. It was as if they were alone in the entire world . . . nothing or no one to disturb them. . . .

They continued along the treacherous mountain paths for the course of the afternoon, stopping once for drinks and to rest the horses. Grant hiked to a nearby cliff and spent the time looking, never halting his search, even when Morgan slumped wearily against a tree trunk. Then he mounted his horse impatiently, not waiting for her to catch up, but leaving her to struggle alone.

Finally Morgan called to him. "Grant? Don't you think it's about time we started heading home? We have a long distance to cover. It's getting dark and . . . cold. We can get an early start tomorrow morning."

He wheeled around to face her, an amused expression on his square-jawed countenance. "Go back? Do you want to lose them completely? We're not far from them. I just know it."

"But, Grant—" she began.

"We're not going back, Morgan. Pick a campsite."

"Campsite?" she gasped. "Sleep up here?"

He shrugged and again that devilish grin spread across his face. "That's the usual reason for a campsite. 'Course, I'm game for more activity if you are!" He turned his horse and trotted over the next hill and out of her sight, chuckling.

She followed him, still protesting. "But, Grant, we're not equipped . . . and it's going to be cold up here tonight."

Grant had already dismounted in a lovely little glen cushioned by millions of pine needles and canopied by the spreading ponderosa pine branches that stretched upward to the darkening sky. Morgan was taken aback by the gorgeous, quaint place. It was like a dream . . . or a western location from a Louis L'Amour novel. They were all alone and left to the wiles of the mountains. A slight shiver ran through her then, and she could feel Grant's hand on her leg, urging her to dismount.

"Come on, Morgan. We're more equipped for keeping warm than you realize."

She dropped the reins and slid off her horse into Grant's waiting arms.

"Willa packed more food in my saddlebags, and we each have a sleeping bag. As for the cold . . ." His arms tightened around her. "I'll be glad to keep you warm." His head lowered to hers and those lips that had mocked her all day covered hers hungrily.

An inner lament escaped her lips as Morgan responded to his warm kiss, reaching up to clutch his shoulders, involuntarily pulling him closer. Oh, why did she respond so eagerly to him when she hated him so? But she didn't give herself time to figure it out. She was too busy enjoying his touch, his kiss, his warmth.

Grant's lips breathlessly trailed hot kisses down her neck to the pulsating hollow of her throat, and she moaned his name softly. She parted her lips, willingly receiving his gently probing tongue. Voltaic sensations spread through her limbs, exciting

Morgan to meet the depths of his passion. His large hand sought her soft contours, cupping her soft, warm breast under her many layers of clothing, impartially exploring one mound, then the other, until the rosy tips met his palm with relish.

She murmured his name aloud. "Grant, Grant . . . love me . . ." She knew they should stop . . . she should stop this growing surge of electric passion between them. . . .

As if saying his name aloud broke the spell, Grant groaned softly. "Morgan, we've got to . . . make camp before dark. There'll be time for this later." He kissed her lightly on the lips before moving away.

Morgan took a deep breath of the cold, fresh air. As it cleared the sensuous cobwebs that enmeshed her entire being, Morgan wondered what had come over her, responding to this hateful man that way. She certainly hadn't intended to . . . didn't want to . . . Oh, God, what was happening to her? She had to get control of her emotions—and of her actions.

"Gather some firewood, Morgan, while I take care of the horses." Grant called instructions from where he worked to unsaddle the animals.

Orders! Same old Grant, Morgan thought wryly as she bent to retrieve a variety of small kindling twigs and a larger tree limb to keep the fire burning longer. *That's what has happened to me,* she mused. *My love for Grant was ignited long ago . . . even before our marriage. Now, even though I try to turn away from him . . . to hate him . . . one little spark is enough to rekindle my love . . . and desire . . . again. Maybe it's just desire. I know that he has no love for me. He admitted his reasons for marrying me were as far from love as mine were. And he only went to bed for . . . what were his words that night? "Pure unadulterated lust"! And that's what came over me, too. Lust!* Morgan glanced over at the sight of Grant bending to care for their horses. Ah, but he was such a scandalously virile man, it was difficult for her to force her mind from him, especially since she had gone to bed with him. She knew the ecstasy of his warm, hard body on hers, the fire-trails of his kisses, the skill of his lovemaking. Grant had made her think his love was real that night. However because of her lack of experience, Morgan doubted if she could judge his true feelings. He had never admitted any love for her. Not really.

Morgan's breath choked in her throat. *That's because there isn't any love.* Sighing raggedly, she bent wearily to her task, the aches and pains of the entire day on horseback descending on her. How would she fare through the solitary, chilling hours tucked away somewhere in the San Juan Mountains with a man who didn't love her but persisted in stirring her emotions to a boil?

Grant interrupted her meandering thoughts as he gazed in agitation at her small pile of sticks. "Is that all you could get, Morgan? This won't keep the fire going an hour. Come on, honey. Let's get with it! I'll help you."

Honey? Her heart thumped expectantly . . . hopefully . . . sadly.

Together, silently, they worked to build a decent fire with plenty of wood stockpiled to endure throughout the frigid night in the mountains. They ate quietly, yet ravenously, their appetites spurred as much by the cold as by hunger. Near the glowing warmth of the campfire, Morgan huddled on her sleeping bag, its down-filled layers insulating her from the earth's chill. Grant loomed opposite her, perched impatiently on a cold rock, his elbows braced on widespread knees, his eyes dark with desire. He sat hunched like a coiled spring. No words were spoken between them, but the timeless timbre was obvious, the understanding was clear. Evocative tension stretched thin in the mountain air, as tight as a leather strap, wet after a sudden storm. They were alone in the world and needed each other this night . . . for warmth, for protection . . . perhaps even for love.

By the time they finished dry ham sandwiches, water bubbled merrily in the small collapsible pan on the fire. As if that simple chemical reaction were a signal, Grant stood, an impending destiny rising with him. He brought his sleeping bag to Morgan, draping it across her back, letting his hands linger on her shoulders, touching her cheeks lightly.

"Is that better?" His low, sensual voice enhanced the spell that captured them both as silvery, undulating smoke cast about languidly.

Morgan nodded and lifted grateful, mahogany eyes to his, a faint, shy smile on her lips. One look into Grant's taut face, and she knew he was within her power. It was obvious that he desired her tonight. She had only to acquiesce. But did she really want to tease her own emotions again? Did she want to fool herself with acts of love? Somehow as she stared into his smoky-gray eyes, Morgan felt as though she was caught in *his* spell . . . she was instead within *his* bewitching power.

Abruptly Grant turned away from her and stooped near the blaze with a low, aching grunt. After preparing two cups of hot chocolate, he handed one to Morgan, then settled purposefully beside her. He tucked the sleeping bags snuggly around them, cocooning them from the frosty air. Their shoulders and thighs touched, and Morgan could feel Grant's arm move against hers as he brought the drink to his mouth. She smiled to herself when he groaned low and shifted from one aching hip to another. She was experiencing those same pangs throughout her body and appreciated their kindred miseries. It drew them closer.

They drank wordlessly and the tension between them mounted. Why was she being so foolishly mute? She had so much to say to Grant. There were many questions to ask. There should be a lifetime of communication between them. She knew so little about this unusual man she had married. And yet Morgan was captivated by the sweet enchantment of being alone with Grant, deep in the San Juan Mountains. Their hidden little world was lit only by the crackling circle of fire near them. Morgan was lured toward the warm energy radiating from his body, and she longed to feel him against her again.

She attempted to initiate conversation. "Grant . . ."

He turned to her, his gaze lingering on her lips before meeting her eyes with a passion-filled, unasked question.

"Oh, Grant, don't—" Morgan gulped hard, forgetting whatever she had in mind to say to him, knowing what was inevitable.

His lips were close to hers as he murmured hoarsely, "Don't deny this feeling between us, Morgan. Forget our differences tonight."

As his kiss deepened . . . lengthened, Morgan swirled in the lovely magic that ensued. Oh, how she wanted to forget that harsh words had ever passed between them. His lips crushed hers ravenously, blocking out all thought except of the glory of the moment. Responding to her own wild desires, Morgan's arms opened to receive him while her lips parted to ensnare the tongue that sought her sweetness. His hard body stretched out, and he pulled her to match his length.

Once again his hand sought her silky warmth, slipping under her layered clothes and caressing her thrusting breasts and taut nipples. He pressed his palm against her, and she matched his pressure. Uttering a soft moan, she arched toward his compelling touch.

"Come to me, Morgan, my little one . . ." he persuaded, raining her flushed face with kisses. "Take these clothes off. I'll keep you warm . . ."

She struggled, but his leg sprawled over hers, pinning her to immobility. Oh, God, it was hard to think when he touched her like that . . . when he spoke those words. Could she forget—even briefly—that he didn't love her? Could she . . . was it possible to *make* him love her?

Grant's ragged voice whispered in her ear. "Morgan, I want you . . . I need you so badly . . ." His hand slid from her taut-nippled breasts to her waist and unsnapped the jeans. He unzipped her jeans and tried to eliminate their encumbrance.

She tried, futilely, to move away from him. "Grant, we . . . we shouldn't—"

"Shouldn't? My God, Morgan! I'm your husband!" Grant's hand moved roughly inside the jeans he had managed to open, caressing her intimately. Morgan gasped with the unexpectedness of his boldness, giving his other hand opportunity to pull the jeans over her slim hips. "Morgan, don't fight it! I want you . . . and you want me, too, so don't deny it for both of us!"

He was right, and Morgan ruefully admitted it to herself. She allowed him to help her discard the layers of jackets and shirts from her silky bodice. He even strained to remove her boots, then tugged again on her tight-fitting jeans.

"I could stand, you know." She giggled.

"Naw, that would make it too easy," he asserted with a satisfied retort as the cumbersome jeans finally slid free of her legs.

She reached down for his head and ran slender fingers through thick, dark hair, luxuriating in the curls that bent so near to her contours. "Grant, oh, Grant . . . Grant," she whispered, letting his name rustle past her lips.

"My God, Morgan," he rasped with a sharp intake of air as

his steel-sharp eyes discerned the pale, exposed image. "You always tear me up when I see you like that!" He gazed, intrigued, as her creamy curves danced with crimson flickers of light from the campfire. Kneeling beside her, he jealously sought her vibrant softness. His hand comprehensively ranged the length of her naked body, exploring from her knees upward to her hips, the warm, feminine juncture at the tops of her legs, her quivering belly, the tender rib cage, tantalizing her breasts' burgundy peaks to fiery firmness.

Boldly she reached for his warm hands, compressing them unflinchingly atop her heaving bosom. "Now it's your turn to undress. We'll both freeze together."

"I'll make sure you aren't chilled, little one," he replied, squeezing her alert nipples between thumbs and forefingers. Small spasms rippled through his muscles as her inquisitive hands pushed the shirt from his shoulders and lingered delicately on the lean sinews that predominated his upper torso.

"Looks like you need someone to keep you warm, too, Grant," she teased. Her hands encircled his throbbing rib cage, forcing his bare chest against hers. With audacious purpose Morgan writhed until her soft breasts were crushed to his solid chest. Her tongue bedeviled his half-open lips as he reached frantically for his belt and those binding jeans.

"Morgan, you're a witch! Hold on! Just wait until I get— Oh, damn, the boots!"

Instantly Morgan was up on her knees. "Here, let me. I'll help you, darling. It's the least I can do since you so courteously divested me!" She grasped one of his boots with fervor and pulled with all her might, but nothing happened.

Grant laced his hands beneath his head and watched the antics of his ivory-skinned wife. "Morgan, you have to turn around with your back to me and pull on the heel. It's the only way to get those tight boots off."

Obligingly she stood, turned her back to him, and hitched up one heavy, booted foot. Taking the heel firmly in both hands, Morgan hefted her weight futilely to remove the offending item. It didn't budge. Once again she pulled. This time something cold and flat shoved against her bare buttock, forcing Morgan, with boot in hand, to stumble free!

"What in hell—" she gasped as she wheeled around, hobbling over the rocks with bare, tender feet.

Grant shrugged, with the most faultless expression he could muster. "It was the only way, honey. I had to help—"

"Damn you, Grant LeMaster! You put your dirty boot on me!" she exclaimed, horrified.

His laugh was a guttural chuckle. "Let me brush it off . . . there . . . I didn't mar a thing! Smooth as a baby's!" His large hands stroked both rounded buttocks intimately to Morgan's delight, and they both ended up laughing joyously. "Now, the other one, honey. This time, no boot, see?" He wiggled his toes at her, and Morgan knew that unshod foot would be the brace this time.

She bent quickly to grab the other dusty boot, and just as she expected, his bare foot sank into her gently curved bottom. But she was prepared for his thrust this time and shored herself suitably. "Aha!" She held the boot up triumphantly, then tossed it casually with the other. "Now, the only obstacle is this—" Morgan grasped one pant leg, then the other, shifting, scooting, maneuvering, until the jeans slid past his hips and revealed Grant's bulging manhood, still covered with his skintight Jockeys.

Morgan feigned dismay. "Underwear, yet! All right, get rid of those, too! If I have to freeze, bare-butted, so do you!" She made a rapid dive at the sleeping bags and the man she knew would warm her tonight.

Grant shed his underwear and lovingly ran his hands along her shivering body, which was already pressed against his. They came together, breathless and trembling, seeking comfort and intimacy. They were just two people alone in the world, their conflicts laid aside for the night, perhaps forever.

"You're cold," he rasped. "Come on, Morgan. Let's get inside the sleeping bag where you won't get chilled any more."

Suddenly shaking from her exposure, Morgan nodded in agreement. Grant scrambled in first, then slithered Morgan down his length, kissing and teasing her body as she went. With a low, satisfied groan he pulled her onto him, letting the weight of her body excite and arouse them both.

Morgan tormented him with kisses . . . his eyes, his cheeks, his chin, nipping at his lips and neck and chest. Enthusiastically her probing fingers massaged the corded muscles of his neck until he groaned, "My God, Morgan, you're a fast learner. You're driving me crazy!" He rolled them over, cradling her body under his. "This way I can keep you warm all night. I want you so, I could love you all night long."

"You wish!" Morgan laughed as he kissed the wildly throbbing hollow of her throat.

"Oh, God, yes, I wish! Do you want me, too?"

Morgan relished the pulsating desire that rushed through her whenever he touched her, and she arched against his male hardness. "I want your love, Grant. You know I do," she whispered shakily.

"Oh, yes, little one. I can feel it. I want your love, too." His arms molded her to him, guiding her ardently, feverishly, in the ways of love until they both reached passion's pinnacle.

Morgan exalted at Grant's unreserved words of love, as she interpreted them to mean what she wanted to hear. His kisses ignited the dormant flames within her, and she moved seductively against his extravagant blaze of warmth. Willingly, eagerly, Morgan gave in to the age-old glories of loving. Her wild desires matched Grant's that night. They were two lovers lost in their own hidden world.

Later they lay curved together inside Grant's down-filled sleeping bag. "Are you warm enough now, little one?" he murmured against her ear.

"Hmmm . . ." She snuggled even closer, cherishing the way the hair on his chest and belly tickled her back.

His hand feathered her smooth, silken skin. "Ah, Morgan, look at all that we miss by arguing. This feels so good to have you close to me . . . responding to me."

"Um-hmm . . . nice." She cupped his hand over one breast.

"Morgan," he began, his voice suddenly tight. "Something has been bothering me for some time now."

She giggled teasingly. "Why, Grant, that's been settled. That's what tonight was all about."

"No. This hasn't been settled at all."

Morgan turned to lay on her back and gaze up at him. He was serious. "What's wrong, Grant?"

His hand rested on her flat belly. "Who is André?"

With a nervous little laugh she asked, "How did you know about him? He's . . . he's nobody."

"Oh, I think he definitely is someone in your past. How important is he to you? You . . . you called his name when you were sick. I thought he'd been your lover but . . ."

Morgan reached up to trace his lips with her index finger. "Oh, no, Grant. No one was my lover before you." She took a deep breath and his hand rose and fell with her ribs. She supposed she had to tell him about André. Now seemed an appropriate time, when she was nestled in his arms, able to let him know that he meant more to her than anyone. "André was a man I met in Europe. I thought I was in love with him. He was very handsome and . . . and we—"

"Morgan, please—"

"It's okay, Grant. I want you to know," she explained honestly. "André convinced me he cared for me, too, and I agreed to become his lover. But he was selfish and rough—not at all like you, Grant—and he left me crying that first night. Afterward I found that he was married! I was very upset, feeling used and manipulated . . . and stupid. I fled to Amsterdam and was staying with a couple who are old friends of my family when we received word of Daddy's death."

Grant's once-relaxed hand had clinched into a fist on her stomach. "Then you came home to the sadness of losing your father and the unfair will," he encouraged.

"Yes. Actually the will stated that if I wasn't married or the ranch wasn't profitable within a year, I would share its ownership with my brothers. But I was too stubborn and proud for that to happen. This ranch was the only property Daddy left me, and I decided I'd be damned before I'd let my brothers take over it, too. So I made up my mind I'd do it myself. Adam had agreed to help."

"But then Adam broke his leg."

"Yes, and you came into my life." There was a smile in her voice. "I must admit, by that time I was convinced that Daddy hated me, and my feelings ran pretty much the same for the entire male species. You included. But I knew I needed help from a man . . . and, Grant, I'm glad I chose you."

His fingers roamed in teasing circles around her belly and navel, then slowly lower. "So am I, my little one. So am I." He lowered his face to hers, kissing her completely at great length.

"Now it's your turn," she plied. "Where did you grow up? And what were you doing during those years that I was in Europe?"

His hand stroked her smooth, silken skin and the soft triangular mound. "I was gathering creative experiences for my writing," he murmured, nuzzling her ear.

She wriggled, trying unsuccessfully to escape his maddening manipulations. "Come on, now. The truth—"

"I grew up in Boulder with my grandparents. I left home at eighteen and ended up in Nam. By the time I came back, my grandparents had died. I finished college and did some freelancing for a few years. Then my old college buddy called to see if I'd like to go skiing one last time this season. I said, 'Sure!' Then Adam broke his leg and . . . I'll bet you can guess the rest!"

She placed a smiling kiss against his neck. "I know the rest. Some crazy dame asked you to marry her! Now, tell me about your writing. What are you writing about that takes so much of your time? I've . . . I've heard you typing late into the night." Did she dare tell him that she lay there in her lonely bed, longing for him while he paid homage to that damned cold, clanking machine?

"I'm writing the great American novel," he muttered sarcastically. His hand slipped up to cup her splendid breast, teasing the tip slightly.

"Grant!" His name was a sharp gasp. "Grant, I wonder if you're writing about me . . . about us."

"You?" He laughed. "No, little one. You're my private life. You're too special to share. I want to keep you to myself." His feathery kisses fanned the smoldering embers deep inside her, making concentration on anything outside their sleeping bag impossible.

"I don't see how you can write at night . . . so late . . . after a full day of ranching." She found speaking increasingly difficult when he touched her like that.

Grant grasped her hand and pressed it to him intimately. "I don't expect you to understand, Morgan, but sometimes when

I'm writing, I don't know where I am or realize that I'm tired. Writing is my life. I love it and can't seem to stop, even when I've been a wrangler all day."

"Grant—" Morgan's voice wavered as she became acutely aware of where her hand rested and Grant's subsequent masculine response. "Are you . . . are you writing again so you can become independent enough to leave me?"

"What?" He turned to her, his breath quickening. "Whatever gave you such a crazy idea?"

"Don't leave me, Grant," she begged, her hand moving over him of its own accord. "Please don't leave me. . . ."

His arms wrapped tightly around her, pulling her face close to his. "Oh, Morgan, I'm not going to leave you," he rasped hoarsely, desire gripping his body and affecting his irregular breathing. "I want you . . . need you. And I'll be here with you as long as you want me, little one."

He lowered his head and left a fiery trail of kisses from one placid nipple to another until each perked up alertly, meeting his flickering tongue with eager anticipation. His lips adored the entire swell of each breast, over and over, bringing them to firm mounds of burning impatience. Morgan thrust them upward to augment the sensations of his teeth kneading those cherry points ever so gently. Soft sounds escaped her lips when Morgan thought she couldn't bear his finesse any longer.

But endure she must, as Grant carefully brought her to the brink of passion. Again and again he led her to the edge, then allowed her brief relaxation, then seduced her to the razor-sharp edge once more. Each time he lengthened her ascent, heightening her unconstrained longing and enjoying her complete and total capitulation under his tutelage.

Finally, in anguish Morgan cried out, "Grant . . . oh, Grant . . . *now*!" Her legs crossed atop his. With a soft laugh of satisfaction he pulled her over him, filling her with his love and keeping promises made in the heat of passion. Together they ignited flames of passion that warmed them throughout the cold, mountain night.

"Morgan . . . come, little one," Grant urged. He spent the night gratifying, spoiling, teaching his sensitive bride; and she in turn satiated him, convinced of his love for her.

* * *

Dawn came chillingly to the inner mountain ranges and Morgan stirred, seeking the warm length that had curled against her nakedness all night.

"Morgan! Morgan! Wake up!"

"Hmmm." She smiled, snuggling for the warm body of her husband.

"Hey, little one! Wake up! I've found them!" His voice was loud but definitely not beside her in the sleeping bag. Morgan opened her eyes, searching. How dare he leave her so cold? "Grant?"

He answered her from across the glen, where he was saddling the horses. "Come on, Morgan! Get up! They're eating in a small meadow about five miles away!"

"Who?" And then she recalled that the purpose for their trek into the mountains was to find runaway horses. But who cared about them this morning? It was much too early. Morgan couldn't bear the thought of crawling out nude into the chilling morning air. Why, she could see her breath in a stream of misty fog! She lay very still until she heard his footsteps approaching.

"Morgan? Are you awake? Hurry up and get dressed!"

She looked up at him in aggravation. "Don't I even get a cup of coffee before I have to climb on that damn horse again?"

His voice was demanding. "No. We don't have time. We'll lose them if we wait too long."

"Grant!" She gritted her teeth and ventured out of her warm cocoon.

He laughed as she tore into the discarded clothes, her bare, shapely legs and hips glowing in the morning chill.

"Don't laugh at me, you beast!" she shouted.

He grabbed her sleeping bag and began to force it into a tiny roll. "Hey, no one would like to stay here better than me! But I'm going after your horses, my dear!"

"*Our* horses!" she flung after him, scrambling to mount her horse and follow him.

"Okay. Let's get *our* horses and go home!" He flashed a marvelous, sleepy grin at her and led the way.

They found the mares grazing contentedly in a hidden meadow. On a rise, keeping watch, stood the magnificent form of the white stallion that had led them astray. He raised his fine head at the first sight of Morgan and Grant. Their presence spelled danger, and with a flash of his tail, he wheeled and galloped up an opposite slope. Nickering to his new mares, the stallion rose, pawing the air, then galloped over the far hill and out of sight.

Grant quickly roped the lead mare and, with Morgan bringing up the rear of the bunch, kept the group together and headed them out of the meadow and away from the wilderness. The greater part of the day was spent leading the mares back to the ranch. Lunch was a brief exchange of food and water, then on toward home.

It was late afternoon when Morgan and Grant finally reached the ranch. Boyd shouted a typical cowboy salutation and opened the gate to the newly repaired corral. Morgan was numb with hunger and exhaustion and her limbs were weak. Grant reached a supporting arm around her, steering her toward the house.

Willa greeted them on the doorstep, a worried, unusual expression on her face. "Is she all right, Grant?"

He nodded tiredly. "Coffee, Willa. We need coffee, food, and rest."

Morgan smiled faintly at Willa. "I'm okay, just tired. And sore! What I really need is a hot bath!"

Willa smiled grimly and answered, "Sure you do. Supper's warming in the oven. Grant . . ." She placed her wrinkled hand on his arm.

His response was immediate. "What's wrong, Willa? You look —"

The woman's mouth tightened as she nodded to him. "Grant, the caseworker came here to see about David while you were gone."

CHAPTER TEN

Grant's hand knotted into a fist as he involuntarily gripped Morgan's shoulder. An angry shadow darkened his tanned face and a muscle flexed ominously in his squared jaw. But in his eyes there was a tinge of fear as he demanded, "She didn't take him, did she? Where is he? Where the hell *is* he, Willa?" He stormed through the living room like a bull elephant on the rampage, arms gesturing violently, calling, "David! David!"

Willa hurried after him, frightened by his sudden, explosive temper. "Oh, no, Grant! She didn't take him. He's over at the Haroldsons playing with their grandson. He'll be back in a couple of hours. Is that all right to let him go to the neighbors' to play?"

Grant turned and stared at her for a full minute, as if determining whether David would be allowed the freedom of playing.

Placing a comforting hand on Willa's shoulder, Morgan gently took command of the uncomfortable silence. "Of course he can go play with a little friend, Willa. That's fine—"

Grant's fury turned instantly toward Morgan. "Who are you to interfere with my son—"

Morgan's steady, brown-eyed gaze bore into him as she met his anger with her own. "Oh, look at yourself, Grant! You're acting absolutely paranoid! Of course a child can play with a friend without cause for alarm. And David is no exception. Now,

Willa, come sit down and tell us all about this caseworker who came here."

Grant clamped his jaw broodingly and followed the women to the seating area, knowing deep down that Morgan was right. He was being an alarmist. This raging reaction was so unlike him. But the thought of losing David . . . that little rascal had wrapped Grant around his little finger—tightly. "Go ahead, Willa," he muttered, trying to regain his control.

"She came about two yesterday afternoon," Willa began. "At first she thought Boyd and I were the . . . adoptive parents. She just sat at the kitchen table and had a glass of tea with us and . . . talked and asked a few questions. She was a real nice lady."

"What kind of questions?" Grant sat tensely on the edge of his chair and leaned his elbows on his knees. Forgotten was the two-day trip on horseback, the renewal of his relationship with Morgan, even his exhaustion.

Willa continued. "Oh, she wanted to know things like how long David has lived at the ranch. And how long Boyd and I have been here. And what we had observed about your family. I guess she was sent to make sure no one was cruel to David or something."

"Damn!" Grant exploded again. "Who do they think we are?" He was on his feet, pacing the floor like a wild man.

And again Morgan intervened. "Grant, calm down! This is perfectly normal for an adoptive child. They question everyone who knows the families. That's usual procedure. It doesn't mean that they think any particular thing is going on with David. It's common to check on them. They have to be very careful in the placement of these kids. You wouldn't want it any other way. It's just that we weren't here, that's all."

"There's one other thing she did ask about, though," Willa admitted.

"What? Asked about what?" It was Morgan this time who jumped. *Damn!* How she wished they could have been at the ranch yesterday to meet that caseworker.

"She asked if you left David in my care often."

Grant raged again. "Well, what the hell does she mean by that? What in the name of the stars was I supposed to do with him? Drag him into the wilderness, just so I could keep him with me? What the hell does she think we do? Leave him all the time? What did you say, Willa? Did you tell her we take good care of him?"

She nodded obediently, quickly, to appease him. "Of course! I told her you always take David with you. That this was the first time you'd left him overnight as long as I could remember."

"That's right." Morgan nodded in agreement. "Including our . . . wedding." She started to say "honeymoon," but caught herself, remembering there had been no such occurrence for them.

Grant's eyes settled on her for a brief, understanding moment, then he smiled defensively. "You're right, Morgan. We didn't even take a honeymoon and leave that kid. I wonder if that would satisfy the Indian agency!"

Morgan turned to Willa. "Is that all she talked about?"

"Well, that's all she asked us. Then she sat with David and talked to him awhile." Willa spoke hesitantly, knowing Grant would be furious again.

And he didn't disappoint her. "Talked to David? What in hell did she talk to him about?"

Hesitantly Willa admitted, "I don't really know, Grant. They sat on the sofa here, and I was out in the kitchen."

"You left him alone with her? And you couldn't hear what they said?"

She shook her head. "But they only talked about fifteen minutes, and he seemed real happy the whole time. She didn't say anything to upset him."

"And then she left?"

Willa nodded again. "But, Grant, before she left, I told her that you and Morgan . . . love David very much. Of that I'm sure."

A curtain of relief veiled Grant's face, and he took Willa's hand, encouraging her to stand. "Willa . . . thanks." He paused awkwardly before repeating, "Thank you. It's . . . it's true, you know. I . . . we love him more than *anything.* And I'm sorry I've been such a jackass today. I'm just tired and . . . worried." His long arm swept around her, and he hugged her long and hard.

Willa's face was flooded with relief and she smiled. "I understand, Grant. I'm worried, too. I hope I said and did the right things. Now, how about that cup of coffee?"

Morgan watched them walk to the kitchen, Grant's arm draped over Willa's bent shoulder. She had felt those secure arms of his around her in joy and passion. But could it ever be called love? *Ever?* She was haunted by Grant's emotional confession to Willa. It reverberated in her weary mind: "I love him more than anything." *Or anyone?* she wanted to ask, but didn't dare. Morgan feared the answer.

When David arrived home, Grant questioned him extensively until the boy complained that he wanted to have a snack and not talk about "that lady" anymore. Grant relented but spent more time than usual with him during the evening. When he finally tucked David into bed, he closed himself in his old room. Morgan could hear that infuriating *peck-peck* of the hard, cold typewriter. Frustrated because he turned to that inanimate object instead of her, she curled between the sheets alone. She sank wearily onto the pillow and fell asleep listening to the staccato, rhythmic sound she was growing to hate.

Hours later Morgan was awakened by a scuffling in her room, near her bed—and Grant's plaintive, "Morgan, are you awake?"

"Um-hum," she mumbled, trying to rouse herself. Before she could wake fully, Grant's warm, hard body slid into bed beside her, engulfing her immediately in his sweeping arms.

"Hold me, Morgan. Oh, God, love me . . ." he mumbled into her long, tousled hair as he buried his face against her cozy neck.

Still half-asleep, she reached up, opening her arms instinctively to him. Her heart pounded at the abruptness of the interruption of her exhausted sleep and his earnest request—*love me.*

Ardently she responded. "Oh, yes, darling . . ." Morgan placed eager kisses against his ear, then the dark hair that strayed near her mouth.

Grant didn't lift his face to hers, but continued to awaken her with fiery kisses . . . and his bedeviling, blazing tongue. Quick, sure strokes encircled her breasts, spiraling wildly to the lively, flaming peaks. A gentle suckling immediately brought them to tight, uncomfortable knots. He hastened downward, leaving her breasts burning with unrelenting desire, igniting her navel and flat, tense belly.

Yet on he moved, relentless in his tongue's exploration of her sleep-drugged body. Morgan moaned with the unexpected pleasures that suddenly gripped her as his hands grasped her knees, impelling them apart.

Grant was masterful in his ability to agitate her, tormenting in his drive to intensify her desire for him. And Morgan remained passive, willing to submit to this immobilizing ecstasy. She twisted her fingers in his hair. "Oh, Grant . . . don't stop . . . don't—" she gasped, writhing with the unassuaged tightness that clinched her entire body.

Yet stop he did, giving each firm nipple one last gentle tugging before he crushed his muscular chest against them. His hands gripped her fiercely, raking down her back, reaching for her sore hips and kneading them impatiently against him.

His lips had set a hot trail of kisses across her body, waking Morgan to greater pleasures than she had ever believed possible. Roughly Grant's insolent lips accosted her, tempting her senses, arousing her fiercely. She felt his teeth chafe her own soft lips, while his hands grappled her thrusting breasts, teasing them to ripened perfection. When he forced her to a quick submission, a soft whine escaped her lips, but was lost in Grant's overpowering passion and exultant groan. His lovemaking was rough and abrupt, not gentle and skillful as in the past. He seemed to take his anger out on Morgan physically, as he aggressively took her and made her his own.

Afterward, as the tension in Grant's taut body relaxed against her, he slipped to her side, cuddling while he dozed. His raging passion had left Morgan weak and perplexed, and she gazed, now fully awake, at his shadowed form. Impulsively she ran slender, digging fingertips through his dark hair, spreading her fingers over the noble head that slumped against her shoulder.

She relished these quiet, precious moments alone with Grant and her private thoughts. Without the ever-present passion between them she could honestly evaluate her feelings for him. Her index finger traced his eyebrows, the jet-black lashes curved against high cheekbones, his long, straight nose.

Inevitably he had become her haven of strength. She looked

to him for guidance and direction around the ranch. He had, by combination of their marriage and honest, physical labor, unselfishly saved the ranch for her. *For them.* Without him . . . she shuddered at the thought.

And, unexpectantly, he had become her lover. That was the most precious surprise of all. He taught her about loving— physically as well as emotionally. Her finger outlined his well-shaped lips, recalling the ecstasy they had created for her. Just tonight . . . but tonight's lovemaking had been different. Turbulent and stormy . . . almost like their life together. Her hand wrapped around the cords in his neck, easing down to the crisp, curly hair on his chest. She dug her nails into the inky mat, raking lightly with a growing temerity.

Morgan tried to understand Grant's need for punishing . . . for lashing out. She, too, had felt like lashing out when life's circumstances were beyond her control. But she had been rewarded—surprisingly—in one of those instances. Affectionately she ranged the span of muscles that banded his chest, marveling at their masculine shape.

Her reward was her marriage to Grant . . . for this man she had chosen to be her husband had introduced her to loving. Her curious hand followed the ebony, hairy trail that led down the center of his well-formed torso. Morgan was discovering the wonders of Grant's male physique and her own powers to titillate and arouse. It was a wonderful, heady feeling to know that she could manipulate him in such a way. She, too, possessed the skills to captivate him at will, as she had been mesmerized by this virile man in her bed.

In return she loved him—even his savage touch—more than she had ever imagined possible. And she couldn't understand it completely. More times than one she had wondered if his affection for her was merely for someone who filled his needs at the time—whether it was a "wife" in the adoption, or lover in his bed. But no, she had to believe . . . wanted to believe that he loved her.

Shamelessly Morgan stroked Grant, delighting in his response. She needed his love now, not just his angry, raging passion. She wanted his compassionate, abundant love. Swallowing a sob, she turned to him, embracing his sleeping form. He moved instinctively into her open arms, thrilling her with his intimate confirmation of her bold ramblings.

"Ah . . . Morgan . . . you're enough to drive a man crazy—" His voice was a hoarse rasp in her ear.

"I thought you were asleep."

"Nobody with any life in them could sleep through that!"

"Well, how was I?"

"How? Hmmm . . . passable . . ." he growled.

"What?"

"Well, honey, there's always room for improvement—"

"Grant—" Her hand tightened.

His laugh came from deep within his chest. "How about fantastic . . . creative . . . romantic? Come here, I'll show you—"

The assurance of his touch, his need for her this night, his masculine response, gave Morgan peace and a deep happiness that Grant was here in her bed. He was hers . . . even if just for tonight.

The next morning Morgan stirred enough to see Grant dressing in the semidarkness. "Grant?" Her voice was thick with sleep.

He turned to her and gazed solemnly for a moment. "I didn't mean to wake you, Morgan. Go back to sleep."

She smiled serenely at him, remembering their renewed love . . . and the previous night. "Grant, come here . . . please." There was a promise in her tone.

He strode over to her relaxed, inviting form and stood wide-legged, gazing down at her. *God! He was handsome!* "I can't, Morgan. I have too much to do today. I . . . hope I wasn't too . . . rough last night, little one. I don't know what happened to me . . . just lost my control, I guess."

Morgan licked her bruised lips with a frown. Didn't he remember the gentler embrace—the sweet lovemaking? "Grant? Are you all right?"

"Yeah," he muttered, rising. "I have some early chores to do. Later this morning, I'm going in to town to see my lawyer." He walked out of her bedroom quietly, leaving Morgan to wonder and worry in the early-morning darkness.

Why was he going to see his lawyer? Was he trying to arrange to leave after all? He wouldn't leave her now—so close to the opening of the dude ranch! Surely he couldn't just end what they had started of their relationship! Or could he?

By the time Morgan struggled down to breakfast, Grant and Boyd were working in the barn. She tried to catch a few moments alone with him, but he rode to check the far range. There was no time for talking, explaining. Certainly Grant made no moves toward that end. So she watched in dismay and concern as he eventually drove toward town, taking David with him. Apparently he was taking no chances that anyone would check and find that he had left the child again. *Or was he taking David away for good?* Why did that thought always haunt her?

It was with great relief when hours later Morgan spotted the familiar burgundy Suburban drive up and park beside the ranch house. She wanted to rush out and grab them both up in her arms, hugging David's tousled black head close, taking Grant in her arms reassuringly. But she refrained. Instead she watched as they ran chasing each other into the barn, only to emerge minutes later with two horses to saddle. They worked together, then mounted and galloped over the far range, out of sight. They enjoyed each other tremendously and it was plain to see the love from both sides. David idolized his new father. Grant adored his little son. And Morgan was nowhere in the picture.

After dinner Grant followed his usual routine with David. With the playing, the bathing, and the reading behind them, he finally tucked his son in bed and entered Morgan's bedroom. Left on her own, Morgan had showered and was in the process of drying her hair. She was scantily attired in a shortie gown that did nothing to hide her sensuous curves. Her breasts were covered with pale blue net, the nipples hidden by lacy embroidered butterflies. With her arms raised to complete the job of drying her long hair, she made a very alluring picture.

Grant stopped midroom, drinking in the sight of her. He took a deep gulp of air, then turned away from her and sat on the end of the bed. It was as if the sight of her repulsed him, and she was puzzled by his strange actions.

"When you finish that, I'd like to talk to you, Morgan. And put on a robe," Grant ordered.

Morgan halted her task, leaving the hair slightly damp, cascading down her back like a honey waterfall. She walked slowly, deliberately, to stand in front of him. His eyes climbed guiltily as far as those lacy butterflies. Morgan propped her hands on her hips and asked pointedly, "What in hell is wrong with you, Grant? Why are you acting so strange? Coming in here to finally explain what you're up to, telling me to put my clothes on! Usually it's the other way around! You didn't mind taking them off up on that mountain, even at the risk of pneumonia! And last night, in this very room, you were happy to take me au naturel!"

Grant's cloudy gray eyes traveled from her face back down to those butterflies, and involuntarily he reached for her. But he was slow and Morgan easily stepped out of his reach. His eyes sought hers, almost pleadingly. "It's hard for me to talk to you when you're . . . like that, Morgan. My God, woman, I'm only human! And you're . . . very alluring. It's almost a sin for anyone to have such dark brown eyes when everything else is blond."

Morgan wheeled toward the closet. "Sorry, that's just the way I am. You have to accept me like this." She grabbed the satiny robe and wrapped it around her tightly. "Okay, everything's covered. So talk."

Satisfied that she had covered herself sufficiently and he could try to concentrate on what he had to say, he began. "As I told you this morning, I went to talk to my lawyer today. And I'm going to need your help, Morgan."

Morgan's heart beat rapidly, fearing what he would say next. Hadn't she helped him enough? Hadn't she done his bidding as a wife? And more! What if he wanted her to cover for him while he took David far away! *Oh, dear God, No! Don't leave me now!* She tried to keep her voice steady and calm. "What kind of help, Grant?"

"We've got to stop this bickering and present a loving family atmosphere at all times."

"What?" Morgan's head whirled with the incoherence of his words. "You're not leaving?"

He ran his hands through dark, disheveled hair. "Leaving? Why would I do that? I told you I needed to stay. Listen, Morgan, I've got to remain here and see this adoption through. It's the only way I'll get legal custody of David. This place and . . . you . . . are my only chance. And I need your help."

Relief flooded through Morgan at his commitment to staying —and his admission of needing her. All she wanted was to hear him say that he was staying. Now that he had fulfilled her hopes, she wanted to wrap her arms around him and tell him she would do anything to help him—anything at all! Instead she restrained herself with a quiet, "What kind of help do you need, Grant? Money?"

"Money?" he expounded in disgust. "If that's all I needed, there'd be no worry. No, what I must have is a little more complicated than that. According to my lawyer, we have to look like an ordinary, loving, happy little family trying to adopt a kid."

Falteringly she said, "I . . . I thought we were that already."

"Ordinary? Ha! Happy? Hardly!" His words were scornful and cruel. "We're anything but an ordinary family, Morgan! Surely you realize that!"

"But I'd like to think there's love—"

"Love?" he scoffed. "With all the fighting we do?"

"But, Grant, that's over—"

He shook his head. "For now maybe. For tonight. But what about tomorrow . . . or next week? It's on again, off again, and that just won't do. We need a unified front."

"A . . . unified front?" Morgan gulped. It sounded like he was outlining strategy for a war. Maybe he was.

He nodded. "That's exactly it, Morgan. The caseworker will be back, you know. She'll come unexpectedly, unannounced. Just like the last time. We'll never know when she's going to pop in. But next time I want your assurance that you'll be . . . that you'll help me . . ."

Morgan's voice was hollow as she finished his statement. ". . . by being your 'loving wife.' "

"Exactly. If they suspect trouble in this marriage, or—"

Morgan interrupted. "—or an arranged marriage . . ."

Impatiently Grant seethed, "Oh, come on, Morgan. Surely we're beyond that now. I just want to put away our battle gear. After all, we've shared a very intimate relationship. Doesn't that mean anything to you?"

"What does it mean to you?" Morgan's voice was quivering, matching her insides.

"Morgan, we've lived together for months now. We've slept together. You know me."

Morgan's voice was barely above a whisper. "I hardly know you at all, Grant." She didn't like the way this conversation was going.

Grant was on his feet, pacing, expostulating loudly. "You know that I love that boy. You know that I'll never let harm come to him, and I'll be the best parent he could ever have. Do you realize what will happen to him if they take him away from me? From us? He'll become a ward of the state, tossed from one place to another. That is if they can find a foster home who'll take a kid his age. Otherwise he'll remain in an institution. I'll do *anything* to keep that from happening!"

"Anything?"

"Anything!"

Morgan raised her chin defiantly, afraid to ask—knowing the answer. "Would you even go so far as to sleep with me to establish a 'loving relationship'?"

His eyes were steely gray and his lips thin. "If I have to."

"You bastard!" she exploded with deep inner anger and pain. "You slept with me just to gain an intimacy to bind us together purely for your own needs! You tried to make me your 'loving wife' because that's what you needed for David. You never really cared about me."

Painful realization spread across his face. "You're wrong about that, Morgan."

"Wrong about what? That you never loved me? That all you care about is yourself . . . and that kid in there? I think, for the first time ever, I understand you and your motives! I really know you tonight!"

"No, Morgan—"

But she wouldn't be stopped. "You cared nothing about me! Or about my feelings!"

Grant's slate-gray eyes narrowed. "Morgan, I've helped you this entire summer. I've worked my butt off for you and put this ranch in order. You've got to admit, I haven't shirked my end of the bargain. The dude ranch opens next week, and by damn, we're ready. The building, the trail rides, the big barbecue, the singing around the campfire, the horses are broken—everything is ready for guests! The very least you can do—"

Morgan interrupted. "Never mind that I've given you and your son a home and warmed your bed during all this!"

He spread his hands in explanation. "What I need from you now—"

"I know. You need a unified front, a certain loving appearance from me, not a warm bed. Well, let me remind you, Mr. LeMaster, the bargain included fifty thou at the end of the summer, not a 'loving wife'!"

"Morgan—"

"Listen to me for a change, Grant! Just shut up and let me have my say in this!" Morgan folded her arms and paced in front of the contemptible man she called her husband. "I'll agree that you've done a remarkable job on the ranch this summer. Without you I could never have done it. And I appreciate that. But things are different now. Different from what I thought they were between us. Actually I also fear what would happen to David without us because, believe it or not, I care about him. Since I know that you love him, I will be a part of your unified-front idea and play the role of your 'loving wife.' I will do my part to help you become the legal father."

"Oh, Morgan—" His voice was raspy.

Her tone was hard and firm. "I'm not finished, Grant. I'm doing this for David, not you! And you won't have to sleep with me anymore to manage that feat. I will be the epitome of your loving wife, but you will stay away from my bed. That's not necessary anymore. And I won't be used any longer!"

"Morgan, surely—"

"If you come near me again, I'll scream the whole sordid tale to the Social Welfare departments of Arizona and Colorado! And to the Navajo Tribal Council!" Her chestnut eyes narrowed. "You stay out of my bed. Agreed?"

His gray eyes seemed to shoot daggers at her. But Morgan was strong in her conviction. She met Grant's gaze steadily and stood firm before him. She would not back down now. If he wanted something else from her, he had to give up something. And apparently her love was not high on his list of priorities. Therefore she would eliminate it.

"Damn you, Morgan," he muttered gruffly. "Agreed!" Then Grant turned on his bootheel and stalked out of her bedroom for good.

Angrily she tore the loving ring from her hand and flung it tearfully against the door.

CHAPTER ELEVEN

The glorious warm weeks of the Colorado summer passed busily. The opening of the Rocking M Dude Ranch kept everyone hopping, including the four newly hired ranch hands. Weekends were unbelievably busy, with "ranchers" filling the guest bunkhouses and activities filling every waking minute. To the public Grant and Morgan presented a beautiful, loving couple, hard at work and deeply in love. There was laughter, light kisses, frequent touching of arms and shoulders for everyone to see. They were a fun-filled, delightful addition to the dude ranch experience, and most people left with promises to return again next year. Some even made reservations. Morgan's financial statement moved rapidly to the black.

For all the loving facade Grant and Morgan exhibited, there was no affection when no one was looking. Grant disappeared whenever there was a spare moment into his room to type.

Morgan closed her bedroom door and sat alone to brood silently. She ached for a kind word or touch, but received neither from Grant. Many times she wished she had never banned him from her bedroom. She longed for his touch, his warm body next to her, even though he didn't care a damn about her. And yet Morgan was sure she couldn't live like that. She knew she was only torturing herself with those thoughts, but couldn't help it. She loved him deeply, and it was tearing her up inside. She was willing to do almost anything for his love.

How many times had she gone to the bedroom door, hand on the knob, preparing herself to tell him she didn't care what he thought of her if he would just come and hold her through the night? And yet each time she lost the nerve it would take to do it. And she knew it would just destroy her even more to know that he took her to bed and still cared nothing for her. So, morosely, Morgan went to bed alone, listening to that goddamn, clanking typewriter late into the night until she fell asleep to its rhythmic beat.

"Grant, she's here." Willa's quiet voice interrupted his poring over the books in the study.

It was one of the few quiet days they had enjoyed since opening the Rocking M. The time off would be spent, as usual, getting ready for the next "ranchers." Morgan had asked Grant to review her figures before she made a trip to the bank. Grant, lost in the realism of credits and debits, murmured, "Hmmm? Who's here, Willa?"

"That woman who came before. David's caseworker."

Grant's head snapped up and his attention was immediate. The late-night hours he had been keeping were taking their toll on him. His eyes were bleary and his face showed signs of strain. A brief glance out the study window, and he muttered to Willa, "Why isn't she coming to the front door? Where the hell is she going around the side of the house?"

Willa smiled and shrugged. "Maybe she sees David and Morgan. They're in the corral, practicing roping."

"Roping? My God!" Grant rolled his eyes and moved hurriedly through the house.

The woman propped her arms casually on the fence railing, watching Morgan and David's antics. They were unaware of anyone's presence so far and, like two children, were taking turns trying to circle a post end with an unwieldy rope.

The woman turned, smiling, as she heard Grant approach. "I think David's at least as good as she is." She laughed, amusement lighting her dark eyes.

"At least," Grant agreed, chuckling. "Before long he'll be teaching her."

"I wouldn't doubt it at all. David seems capable of doing

anything he sets his mind to. You must be Grant LeMaster. I'm Cora Whitefeather of the Navajo Agency Branch of Welfare. I'll be reporting on David's case to the Tribal Council in Arizona." She extended her hand to him and he shook it, liking her informality instantly, in spite of himself.

He nodded. "I'm Grant LeMaster. Nice to meet you, Ms. Whitefeather."

She smiled graciously. "Please, call me Cora. Is this your wife with David?"

"Yes, that's Morgan with David," Grant said, watching with satisfaction as they laughed and played together. Morgan was certainly keeping her promise about being the loving wife and mother. She actually looked like she was having fun.

It was a few more minutes before Morgan spotted their audience. She waved and Cora returned the gesture.

"Come on over, Morgan!" Grant called, beckoning. "This is Cora Whitefeather, David's *caseworker.*" His emphasis was implicit.

Morgan smiled warmly and extended her hand. "So nice to meet you. And I understand you've met David." Her eyes sought Grant's briefly. Their "unified front" was in force!

Cora smiled and exchanged greetings with Morgan, then turned her attention to the boy. "Hello, David. Do you remember me?" Her raven eyes matched his, and the resemblance of their shared heritage was obvious.

David grinned confidently at her and nodded. "You're the lady who was going to bring me a white feather, just like your name. Did you bring it?"

"David . . ." Grant looked uncomfortable.

However Cora Whitefeather adeptly ignored Grant's discomfiture and acknowledged the child's request seriously. "I wondered if you would remember it, David. I brought you a beautiful eagle feather today. It's in the car. Come with me, and we'll get it." David accompanied her eagerly, leaving Grant and Morgan to gape nervously at the two bronze-skinned figures.

"Grant, I like her. She seems very nice. And she obviously cares for David," Morgan said when they were out of earshot.

"Obviously. But don't forget why she's here, Morgan. Her job is to find out whatever she can about us!"

Morgan's reply was acute. "She's here to make sure this is the best home for David. She is not our enemy. Give her a chance, Grant."

His face was taut as he murmured through clenched teeth, "*You* give her a chance, Morgan. I'm prepared to be more realistic!"

"There you go being paranoid again. Take it easy, Grant. We're working on this thing together, remember?"

He nodded tersely as Cora and David approached, chattering happily. "David and I will show Cora the stables and horses. Why don't you make some coffee for us, Morgan? And maybe a little lunch." His affable smile flashed white teeth her way.

Morgan returned his smile with a warm expression of her own and acquiesced agreeably to her husband's suggestion. But she burned with frustration down to her toes as she watched Grant lead Cora to the activity centers of the dude ranch while she was again relegated to the kitchen. She slammed the kitchen door and jerked the parts of the coffeepot into action. Trying to speak calmly, her voice squeaked and she stopped to clear her throat before starting again. "We'd like some lunch, Willa. And do we have any of that coffee cake left?"

"I've already made sandwiches. But the cake is frozen. I'll stick it in the oven right away. It'll be warm enough by the time they've toured the ranch." Willa eyed her young boss skeptically, fully aware of the strain this visit was creating in both Morgan and Grant. Things were not exactly right between them, but she just couldn't figure out what it was. Maybe it was just all this adoption business.

Morgan answered tensely, "Yeah, and I'll bet Grant will be as nervous as a caged tiger by the time he's toured the ranch with that woman. He's already so irritable no one can stand him."

"He is a little tense, isn't he?" Willa agreed.

Morgan sighed. "He's a regular coiled spring, Willa. I just hope he doesn't say the wrong thing and offend Cora today with some offhand remark."

"Oh, he won't do that, Morgan. He knows this visit is too important." Willa confidently patted Morgan's arm.

"Too important . . ." echoed Morgan as she turned to slice fresh celery.

Without further comment they prepared the simple lunch. Each was lost in her own thoughts as to the consequences of the caseworker's visit and the adoption hearing. Of course Morgan knew that even if they were awarded custody of David, that would not end the turmoil between her and Grant. With a heavy sigh she tried to force her thoughts back to the present.

Lunch was kept lively solely by David's enthusiastic participation with their guest. Cora had proven her caliber by remembering to bring him the feather. She was obviously interested in him and, typically, he eagerly took advantage of her attention.

Morgan and Grant were gracious, smiling—and tense. They tried to pretend to be completely at ease, but neither was a very good actor. Cora Whitefeather's alert eyes assessed the couple. *She knew.* She had seen those same taut faces before, as prospective adoptive parents tried to be calm in her presence. And she smiled inside. It was a good sign.

As they finished the meal, Cora took the initiative. "David, why don't you run along and play while we grown-ups have another cup of coffee?"

Run along and play? No one ever told him that! David looked up at her, clear disappointment in his dark eyes. He glanced quickly at Grant, who nodded affirmatively.

"You could practice the roping and get a jump on Morgan," he suggested.

"Yeah!" Renewed interest lit his small face.

"And we'll check to see how good you are before I leave," chimed in Cora with a smile.

"Okay!" With a scuffling of chair and feet David left the room.

There was an uncomfortable silence broken only by the tinkling of someone's spoon stirring coffee.

Grant finally spoke, his voice low and strained. "You wanted to talk?"

Cora sipped her coffee, then, "Yes. I want to assure you of a couple of things. One is that even though I'm definitely looking out for David's welfare, that doesn't mean I'm against you two as the parents at all."

Morgan squirmed, but dared not look at Grant as Cora reiterated Morgan's earlier statement.

Cora continued in a serious voice. "I'll admit I am very concerned about this child who so far has been deprived of a normal childhood. That doesn't mean he was without love, but we know he was quite isolated living with his grandmother. Now special care and education will be needed to acquaint David with the real world. Then there is the fact of David's heritage. That must not be ignored. It's quite a challenge."

Grant rushed to the defense of the child he loved. "Cora, let me assure you I'm willing to accept any challenge where David's concerned. I know he has some problems. And I'm willing to give him whatever he needs—and more! And that includes all the love he can handle!"

Cora smiled tolerantly at his outburst. "I believe you, Grant. And I can see the loving relationship he has already developed with you and Morgan. And I like what I see."

"You do?" Morgan asked eagerly, almost childishly. She was so anxious that she could hardly think straight.

"I do. And that's what I'm going to report to the Navajo Tribal Council." Cora paused, waiting for the effect of her words to sink in.

Morgan found her voice first. "You are?"

"Yes. And I don't see any problems delaying this adoption. Now let's say good-bye to David. I have a long trip ahead of me."

Bubbles of giddy joy and laughter filled Morgan with effervescence and she was vaguely aware of her own impulsive giggles. Grant was pumping Cora's hand, mumbling hoarse words of thanks, and Willa was clapping her hands in the kitchen, where obviously she had overheard every word.

Wisely Cora moved ahead, leaving Grant and Morgan alone for a brief, exuberant moment. Their eyes met, hers brimming with tears of joy. His arm encompassed her shoulders, squeezing her to his warm chest. His voice was husky. "Did you hear that, Morgan? We've done it! It's almost over! Thanks, honey! I'll never forget it. You gave it your best shot—and it worked!" He removed his arm as swiftly as he had engulfed her and was gone.

Morgan stared silently after him, the tears spilling over and rolling down her cheeks. A huge knot formed in her throat, choking normal breathing. *Damn you, Grant LeMaster,* she thought morosely, *I gave it my only shot! I love him, too! Don't you know that by now?* She breathed deeply several times, openmouthed, trying to move that choking knot.

"Are you all right, Morgan?" It was Willa.

Morgan turned away and wiped the tears away quickly. "Yes, I'm fine," she managed, and headed out the door. With a sinking heart she knew the answer to her own question.

Within a month David's adoption hearing was held in Durango's old courthouse, via transfer of jurisdiction. It was almost anticlimactic. Of course it was more official than the verbal promises of Cora Whitefeather and her follow-up letter, but they had known. Willa and Boyd accompanied Grant and Morgan, sitting grim-mouthed while David squirmed on the hard bench between them. In accordance with the laws governing the Navajo tribe, Grant and Morgan LeMaster were awarded custody of David. The joyous occasion was celebrated at Swenson's with four ecstatic adults and one raven-haired, brown-skinned little boy toasting spoonfuls of Hot Fudge to Raisin Rum, Bubble Gum to Pistachio.

Yet the jubilance that Morgan felt was clouded by inner turmoil as she wondered what would happen to them now. She just couldn't escape the claws of apprehension that tore at her insides. After all, summer was almost over, and their agreement had been fulfilled. What she hadn't bargained on was falling in love with Grant and his little son as well.

Another week passed before the roof caved in on their uneasy, contractual marriage. Willa and Boyd had taken the day off, their first in many weeks. Morgan was poring over the books, as was her usual morning habit. She reached absently for the ringing phone.

The voice was obviously long distance. "Hello, there! Grant LeMaster, please. This is Jack in L.A."

Morgan wrinkled her brow . . . *Jack?* "I'm sorry, but Grant is out somewhere on the ranch right now. Can I take a message?"

"You must be his new bride I've been hearing about! Tell him I called and he'll be glad to know the deal is set. He'll need to be here in L.A. by Friday to sign. Have him return my call and we'll work out the details." The voice was exuberant.

"Uh, Jack . . . who?" Morgan's mind puzzled over his voice and name. Neither sounded at all familiar.

There was a slight pause. "Just tell him Jack Myer called, sweetie. He'll know."

"Jack? What deal?"

"Didn't he tell you? That sly devil! He must have wanted to surprise you."

"Yes, that sounds like him. Are you going to tell me what deal?" Morgan snapped, perturbed by the glib tongue of the caller.

Another slight pause. "Uh, I think I'd rather not, my dear. I'll let your hubby disclose the little surprise. But don't worry. It involves a great deal of money. I think he'll be happy with the deal we've set. And you will be, too."

"Money?" Morgan's mind whirled. *Gambling?* What the hell was he talking about?

"Just have him call me."

"Yes. I will." Morgan dropped the phone into its cradle, an ominous chill of dread spreading from her scalp downward over her body. Hugging her arms closely, she rocked back and forth slightly and watched the first yellowed aspen leaves of autumn float languidly to the ground.

After lunch Morgan waited until David had eaten and dashed off to play before approaching Grant. "Who is Jack Myer?" she asked bluntly.

Grant was caught off guard and raised his eyebrows curiously. "Jack?"

"Jack Myer called from L.A. Now, who is he?"

He shrugged and spread his hands innocently. "He's my agent."

"Agent? I didn't even know you had an agent."

"Well, Morgan, I didn't think it necessary to explain all of my business to you. So far it hasn't mattered."

"Now, obviously, it does. Jack says the deal is set, and you are to fly out to L.A. by Friday to sign. You are to call him for details. Does that make sense to you?" Morgan's voice was tinged with anger, for none of it made any sense to her.

Grant smiled eagerly at her words. "It certainly does. He's been trying to sell my screenplay for a movie. Sounds like he did it! This is great news, Morgan. Looks like things are working out!"

Icily she asserted, "Things are certainly changing. What else have you lied about in your life? Maybe there's a wife and kids somewhere I don't know about, and you didn't bother to tell me because it didn't matter until someone found out."

"That's a hell of an accusation, Morgan. What's gotten into you?"

"I . . . I feel as though you've led a double life. One that we see . . . and one that creeps out by bits and pieces."

"Don't be ridiculous, Morgan. I don't have any more secrets. No other wife! No other kids! I'm just a screenwriter who happened to get mixed up in a crazy marriage scheme, the likes of which I could never have created in my wildest imagination!" His words were stinging.

"You're not at all who I thought you were—"

"What's wrong with you, Morgan? Afraid you'll be left out of a chance to travel? Miss some excitement? Well, don't worry. I'll take you and David to L.A. with me."

Numbly she answered, "My business is here. I have 'ranchers' coming through September."

He shrugged angular shoulders in a noncaring attitude. "We can make some kind of arrangements. Cancel the weekend or something."

"Cancel? You know I won't do that!"

His slate-gray eyes cut into her. "Look, Morgan, David and I are going to L.A. by Friday. I have business there and I'm going to take care of it. You can tag along if you want to, Morgan. I don't give a damn what you do."

Morgan felt as though her feet had been knocked out from under her. Grant was missing her entire point. He was raving about some damn trip, while she was upset over the continued revelations. *What next?* "Grant, I really don't know you. I've lived with you, been the loving wife you needed for David, even slept with you—and I don't know you at all. At each turn it seems I'm finding out new and different things about you that I never realized. Now with this . . . screenplay thing—"

He interrupted cruelly. "What difference does it make, Morgan? I did your bidding! Even in bed!"

She ignored his reference to the bed. "What difference? I thought you were a free-lance writer. I thought you did travel articles and human-interest stories about the Indians. You . . . you deceived me."

"Look, Morgan, I'll admit I led you to believe I was a freelancer, but—"

"That's exactly what you told me when we first met! A freelancer! You lied to me then. And you haven't stopped lying yet!"

He tried to explain, but it was too late for justification. "Morgan, I don't go around blaring to the world that I write screenplays. In fact I was a free-lancer for many years. At the time it was an easy answer."

"An easy answer!" she mocked. "To find out you've been writing plays and negotiating movies while all the time I thought I was doing you a favor by hiring you and providing a home for David . . . It's just too much." She shook her head as much to clear it as to get things straightened out in her mind.

"Morgan." His voice was gentle. "You have done us the greatest favor you could ever do! You played the best acting role I've ever seen as loving wife and mother to David. Without you it would have been hell for me to get custody of David as quickly as I did. It probably would have taken me years. I will never forget it, Morgan. I can't tell you how much I appreciate it. We both do—"

"Acting!" Morgan's voice was shrill. "Don't you know—yet —that I wasn't acting? Don't you understand that I love him, too?"

"Morgan, you're getting hysterical."

But he couldn't hush her. "Why—why couldn't you tell me about *anything*? Your writing . . . your life? After all, I am your wife!"

"Wife?" he jeered. "Hell, we haven't lived together as husband and wife for weeks! You can't claim intimacy. You knew I was working on a project. Surely you could hear me typing. But you never cared enough to ask me once about it."

She nodded and murmured in a toneless voice, "I heard you typing every night . . . every night . . ."

Grant moved to the telephone. "I'm tired of this lashing out at each other, Morgan. If you'll excuse me, I have some calls to make. Should I include you in the reservations?"

She turned her back to him. "No. I belong here, not in L.A."

His words were emphatic. "David and I are going to L.A. with you or without you!"

Her tone was dull, lifeless. "Then go ahead. You never really cared for this ranch . . . or me. You have a different kind of life to lead."

She could hear him step closer to her, but she kept her back to him. "Does that mean what I think it does, Morgan? Without you? Is this it?" His voice was flat with the realization.

She shrugged, her shoulders looking small and burdened. "You certainly don't need me to run your life. You have all you need from me."

"Looks to me like it's mutual, Morgan." Grant grasped her elbow tightly and turned her around to face him. "You don't need me, either! And summer's over."

Her bronze eyes narrowed, carrying all the spite she could muster. "Oh, how I hate you, Grant LeMaster! You'll do anything to get what you want! You are undoubtedly the most ruthless man I've ever known! Why, you even surpass my own father! You both used love to get your way!"

"Don't try to lay that guilt trip on me, Morgan. You used me too, don't forget. You got what you wanted. So did I. Now I have everything I want. So David and I will get out of your life. No more demands, no more deals. Incidentally, about the money . . . just keep it. Maybe you can buy a few more unbroken horses and find some fool to risk his neck to break them for you!"

Morgan's face stung with the hot lash of his words. "Grant, surely—"

His squared jawline was etched menacingly in her view. "While we're gone, go ahead and file for the divorce, Morgan. I'll do nothing to stop you—or interfere with your life again. Just don't interfere with mine." He released her elbow and shoved her away roughly. Reaching for the phone, Grant began to dial.

But Morgan didn't stay long enough to hear him reach his destination. She ran blindly outside, ending up at the barn. Impulsively she threw herself astride a mare, bareback. She rode hard, the wind stinging her tear-streaked face and whipping her long tresses out in a golden stream behind her. Finally, breathlessly, they approached a stream and she allowed the animal to slow naturally. They followed the stream at a walk, both heaving for breath. This was the same mountain stream where she and David and Grant had fished . . . and laughed . . . and loved. And she despised Grant for all that he had done to her life. At one time she had thought he could simply solve her problems. But, oh, how he had complicated things. Now she knew what the end of the summer held for them all. They would part. They would be a little family no more. And David . . . David . . . oh, God, what would happen to him? Whatever did, she wouldn't be a part of it. Oh, how could Grant do this to her? Didn't he know it would tear her apart? But what did she expect? She had known—*felt*—all along that the man she had chosen for her husband wouldn't stay forever. Why should he? There was nothing more for him. And he was right. They both had what they wanted . . . what they had bargained for. And now what? Grant had said it. *Divorce!*

Morgan glanced down at her hands and the green and silver Thunder Mountain turquoise sparkled—the ring with the legacy of love. What had Grant said that day so long ago when he placed it on her hand? *The one who wears this ring will be forever loved.* Tears filled her eyes, and she knew the legend was false. "We could make it happen," he had said.

Wrong again, she thought.

CHAPTER TWELVE

The evening sun was dipping low and an autumn chill was in the air when Morgan arrived back at the ranch. The first thing she saw was the open-doored burgundy Suburban, ready for loading. A large brown box was already tucked in the back. *The toys!* So soon? They were leaving so soon? Morgan walked slowly, wretchedly, toward the ranch house.

Inside the kitchen things were in a general uproar. Willa and Boyd had returned and both were questioning Grant at the same time. David was hopping around the kitchen like a little brown frog. *What a circus!* she thought dizzily.

Morgan touched Boyd's sleeve. "I left Lady in her stall, but she needs to be rubbed down. I rode her pretty hard. Would you take care of her for me, Boyd?"

When David caught sight of her, he flung himself against her, hugging her legs and exclaiming, "Oh, Morgan, please come with us to California! Why don't you want to come? We're going to have so much fun!"

Morgan's hands caressed David's raven hair, and she wanted to cry . . . to wail. Never did she think she would ever be so attached to a child . . . but this one was different. He was special . . . like Grant. And she had helped Grant fight for him. "I . . . I just can't go with you David," she mumbled, glancing at the boy's father. But Grant kept his head turned, eyes averted from hers.

"I'll go take care of Lady," grumbled Boyd. "Would you like to go with me, David?"

"Yeah! I've got to tell my friends where I'm going! Do you think they'll miss me?" He hopped beside Boyd, taking his gnarled hand.

"Sure they will." Boyd attempted a smile.

"Don't forget, I've got your favorite chicken-noodle soup for supper, David." Willa was wringing a dish towel nervously.

"And the cookies! You promised chocolate chip cookies!" David reminded her with a huge smile.

"Oh, yes, the cookies," Willa muttered weakly as they trotted out the door.

"Well, I've got some more packing to do," Grant announced gruffly and strode away quickly.

Willa's sorrowful eyes met Morgan's.

Morgan blinked and propped her fists on her slim hips. "And I've got some talking to do. Take your time with those cookies, Willa." She took a deep breath and stalked off, following Grant.

His bedroom door was open and Morgan glanced furtively inside, gathering her strength for what she had to say. Grant was flinging clothes haphazardly into the open suitcase on the bed. His face was taut, his angular jaw set squarely. He moved with jerky, angry motions.

Morgan took a deep, sobbing breath. "Grant, don't do this. Don't . . . take David away from us . . . from the ranch. I love . . . him."

He didn't even pause in what he was doing. "Morgan, you knew this would end."

"I didn't know anything of the sort! At least I hoped not," she declared. Suddenly her tone was hard, tinged with viciousness. "Have you forgotten that I was also awarded custody of David? If you take him away from me, I'll sue you!"

Grant's tone was low and cruel. "It'll be a vicious court battle, Morgan, because I'll fight you. Don't—don't drag David through that. Not after all he's been through already."

Morgan blinked angrily, knowing deep down that she could never make David suffer through a lawsuit, as much as she wanted to cling to him. She was bluffing, and Grant knew it. She turned away from his steel-edged glare. "You're right, Grant. I could never take him away from . . . his father."

She kneaded her sweaty hands together nervously and felt the ring. *The loving ring!* She jerked it off her third finger and whirled around to face him. With hand outheld she charged sorrowfully, "Here's your ring, Grant. Maybe you can get your money back. The legend lies. There's no love connected with it."

Grant stared at her, obviously shaken, for long moments. It was unutterably quiet. There were no words, only eyes meeting in sad expressions of lost joy. Then he looked down at her outstretched fist holding the ring. His large tanned hands, both of them, enclosed her small fist, keeping it knotted tightly around the legend ring. "Yes, there is, Morgan. The legend doesn't lie." His voice strained to speak normally. "The ring was given to my wife. Keep it as a reminder of my love, little one."

Morgan's heart pounded wildly and her head reeled dizzily for a moment. "What are you trying to say?" she rasped.

He cleared his throat and his voice sounded more reasonable and strong. "I'm saying I love you, Morgan LeMaster. I'll admit, I hadn't planned on falling in love with my wife, but it happened. The ring is a symbol of my love. You can do with it what you will."

His hands still held hers securely, warmly. "Why didn't you ever tell me you loved me?"

He sighed. "You didn't give me a chance."

"I . . . I begged for your love." *Oh, Grant, did I ever tell you that I loved you . . . ever?*

"You had my love, but you twisted it, then rejected it. These separate bedrooms were your idea, you know."

Morgan smiled weakly, agreeing. "I thought . . . I thought you didn't love me. I didn't want to force you into sleeping with me anymore."

"Forced to sleep with you? My God, Morgan! It was all I could do at times to keep from breaking the wall down to get to you! To touch you! These last few weeks have been hell!"

She smiled broadly at the mental image he created. "I . . . I wish you had. I . . . wanted you so much. I hated the sounds of that damned typewriter so late at night. I'm afraid I fell in love with my husband, too."

He placed her hands on either side of his neck and pulled her close. "What fools we've been, Morgan. Look at all the loving time we've lost arguing and . . . sleeping apart. Oh, God, Morgan, I love you so much!"

She hugged him closely, joyously inhaling his musky masculine aroma. "I've missed you," she whispered.

"I've missed you, too. And this . . . and this . . ." He kissed and touched her intimately. "And this . . ."

Morgan arched against him and stood on tiptoe, tilting her head back to greet his longed-for kiss eagerly. His lips crushed hers breathlessly in a sweet, delicious, probing kiss. When he finally lifted his lips to kiss her cheeks and nose and eyelids, she murmured, "Oh, Grant, I do love you. *I love you!* Don't ever . . . ever leave me!"

"Oh, no, Morgan. Never. You and David are going to L.A. with me . . . but we'll postpone that trip at least another night. We have some catching up to do!"

"If we all leave, what will we do about the dude ranch? We're expecting guests."

He nuzzled her ear. "To hell with the guests. We'll arrange something for them. I want you with me. And when we get back, we deserve a honeymoon. How does Cancún sound?"

"Sounds wonderful!" She pulled her hands between them and slipped the loving ring back on her third finger.

Grant held her fingers admiringly, then kissed the beautiful ring and her fingers lovingly. "You will be forever loved, little one. I promise. We can make it happen."

Morgan kissed him boldly. "Now! Let's start making it happen now, Grant. You said yourself that we have a lot of catching up to do!"

"But what about David? And Willa?"

Morgan kicked the door shut. "Don't worry about them. Willa's letting David help her make cookies. If we're not back soon, she'll know what to do." Morgan smiled confidently.

"Well, if that's the case." Grant swung Morgan up triumphantly in his arms. "Let's catch up! What a sweet, sensuous, little wife you are, Morgan! Someone must have taught you well!"

She laughed and kissed his neck. "The best!"

He carried her over to the small bed, and with one nudge of his boot the suitcase slipped to the floor, scattering Jockey shorts and T-shirts over the floor. But the mess was ignored. There was a lifetime ahead for cleaning up the messes. Right now it was time to catch up on love!

CAPTIVE DESIRE

To Roger, who never doubted me; and Mary Lynn, who was midwife to this birth.

CHAPTER ONE

The car lunged backwards, tilting to the back right corner. Charly pressed the accelerator, but the vehicle refused to move, and she heard a dragging sound. She hopped out quickly, fearing the car had sunk into one of those ruts. Charly stared long seconds at the limp tire, then kicked it angrily.

"A flat! Out here in the middle of nowhere!" she wailed aloud. Her irritated voice echoed from the towering pines and thick oaks and through the Tennessee mountain air. Then there was a quiet stillness, and all she could hear was water rushing in the stream that ran parallel to the rutted road. "Damn!" she muttered, stalking back to the open car door to turn off the ignition.

The discreet rustling of dry leaves attracted her attention and Charly looked up apprehensively. Seeing nothing, she whirled around, brown eyes searching frantically through the thick summer-green foliage. A clatter from above caused her to crane her neck. There, sitting arrogantly on a tree limb, was a bushy squirrel, his furry tail curled behind his back. He fussed at her in rapid-fire chatter, then scampered away.

"Whew!" breathed Charly, relief flooding over her. Haunting visions of the movie *Deliverance* sent a chilling shiver through her slim frame. For a moment she imagined someone hiding in the leaves, watching her. She managed a little laugh at her apprehension. Still, it was awfully quiet.

At least I can change a tire, she thought bitterly. So I may as well get to it. There is no one out here to help me . . . except that stupid squirrel.

Charly secured the emergency brake, then opened up the trunk. Pulling with all her might on the spare tire, she dragged it out of the car, letting it bounce and flop on the ground. She fumbled with the jack, fitting it together and pushing it under the sunken fender. A furious pumping motion impelled the jack to work and it began to raise the rear of the small compact car. Then, moving around to the deflated tire, she pried around the hub cap. It popped off and clattered across the rocks.

"Damn! A fingernail!" Charly muttered, grabbing her stricken finger. The nail had been ripped off, tearing into the tender skin beneath. It began to throb, and blood oozed slowly around the painful nail.

Abruptly, distant dead leaves rustled again, this time accompanied by the distinct crack of a dry stick. Fearfully, Charly froze in a half-bending position, holding her injured finger. The noise was approaching, getting louder. Someone—or something—was definitely coming toward Charly!

The ponderous silence was rent by the resonant sound of a male voice. "Are you all right?"

Charly whirled around to face him, brown eyes wide with fright, heart pounding loudly in her ears.

"Well, are you? Do you need help?" He motioned toward the car.

Charly could only stare, speechless, at the rugged man who had emerged from the woods. She took a step backwards, preparing to run. Possibly she could lock herself in her car until help came. But *what* help? Panicky fear gripped her, and she completely forgot about the injured finger, which by now dripped small spots of blood to the rocks beside her feet.

"What happened?" He motioned to the bleeding finger and started toward her.

"N-nothing. It's—it's just a broken fingernail. It's all r-right," Charly stammered hoarsely, taking another step backwards.

The man stood over six feet tall and was dressed in faded jeans, a well-worn tan sport shirt, and scuffy shoes. He seemed overpowering, for his dark hair dominated his appearance. Only intense blue eyes were visible beneath the shaggy, black hair that hung over his forehead and framed his entire jawline. The rich sable beard and thick hair framed his craggy features and accented his lean, muscular body. There was a light scattering of dark hair on both corded forearms, ending with small inky patches on each long finger. Charly shuddered involuntarily, fearing that her worst nightmares had suddenly appeared before her in an almost macabre reality. Tales of mountain men flashed through her wildly racing mind, and she wondered recklessly if she could possibly outrun him. Charly couldn't shake the terror that gripped her as the man's all-encompassing gaze flowed from her to the car and back again.

"Do you want me to change your tire?" His voice was a low rumble.

Charly froze, not knowing whether to accept his help or run for her life.

He spread his hands toward her and claimed, "I won't hurt you, lady. I'll just help you with this tire so you can be on your way."

As he spoke, Charly's confidence grew slightly. He was obviously educated and somewhat refined in his manner and . . . there was something in those daring blue eyes that reflected a spark of credibility. Actually, if he was willing to change the tire, perhaps she should accept his aid. He seemed sincere.

"Okay," she said haltingly. Honestly, she didn't have much choice.

Charly stayed near the car door apprehensively as he bent to the job. The man reached for the discarded tool and finished loosening the bolts that attached the tire to the car, working rapidly with skillful, precise hands. He grunted softly as he lifted the heavy tire from the hub, then looked inquisitively at Charly. "What are you doing up here by yourself?" he asked.

"I'm . . . I'm here on business," Charly admitted.

He furrowed ebony eyebrows as he continued working, never looking up at her. "Business? What business could you possibly have way up here?"

Charly pursed her lips thoughtfully. Just how much should she tell this stranger? "I'm here to meet someone. What are you doing up here in this wilderness?" She could play the question game, too.

He lifted the spare tire and slid it onto the axle, his muscular arms bulging with the strain. "Hand me that tire tool, will you?" he directed Charly.

Reluctantly, she handed it to him. As her hesitant brown eyes met his sharp blue ones, he answered, "I was fishing when I heard your noise." His rough hand graced hers as he took the cold metal tool.

Charly watched silently as he tightened the nuts that secured the tire until they squeaked. She pondered the credibility of his explanation. Fishing? Yet she knew that there were trout streams nearby and many people came into the national park to fish. It sounded reasonable. Still, the stranger had appeared mysteriously. Could she trust anyone who looked as rugged as he did? Undeniably, she was a little awed by him. He had been nice enough to fix her tire. And underneath that shaggy appearance, she suspected, was a reasonably handsome man. His eyes certainly held an arresting appeal.

With a heaving grunt, he lifted the flat tire into the trunk along with the tools. Then, turning to face her, he directed assertively, "There is a widening of the road up ahead by that curve. You can use it to turn around." He slammed the trunk, punctuating his decisive remark.

Charly eyed him defiantly. "Oh, I'm not turning around. I am going on to the end of this road. But, thanks for changing my tire, Mr. . . . uh . . . what is your name?"

The man's dark brows came together in a frown. He looked at her for long moments, carefully assessing the chestnut hair piled on her uplifted head, the slim neck, the high breasts hidden behind a white cotton blouse. His arrogant eyes continued down her frame, taking in her slender hips, long straight legs, and ending with the smart, wedge-heeled shoes that revealed neat pink-nailed toes. His lips thinned with contempt and his voice was unrelentingly hard. "The person you are meeting couldn't possibly be up here. This road isn't open to the public. It doesn't go anywhere of interest."

"Oh, yes it does," Charly disputed stoutly. "It leads to Walter Simms's house. And if you're through stripping me, I'll be on my way." Her brown eyes flashed and she flung open her car door. She crawled into the small car and grabbed a tissue, wrapping it around her injured finger.

Although the bleeding had stopped, it throbbed uncomfortably. By the time she looked back up, the bearded stranger was gone. He had vanished completely. Charly looked around, overcome with an eerie feeling. Where had he gone? And why had he disappeared so quickly? How strange . . .

She shrugged and started the car, proceeding on her journey up the rugged mountain road. She glanced at her gold watch. Had it only been two hours since her small compact car had rolled to a stop at the forest ranger's house? Somehow it seemed much longer as she reflected on her meeting with the ranger, who had directed her to this remote area. He had issued warnings and offered to accompany her. Now why had she refused?

The screen door had creaked as a tall uniformed man emerged from the house and stood in greeting on the roofed porch. "Howdy." He waved one hand, then rested it on a nearby post while Charly made her way to the ranger's house.

"Hello," she answered with a friendly smile. "I'm Charly Ryan, from the Bureau of Land Management's regional office. Did you get my letter?" She squinted in the bright Tennessee sunlight, shading her brown eyes.

The man's crinkled smile faded to a solemn acknowledgment. "Yes, ma'am. I got your letter last week. But from the name I expected . . . well, I didn't expect a girl."

Charly smiled good-naturedly. "I always get some reaction to my name. Actually, it's short for Charlene, compliments of my younger brother."

"I see," he responded, scrutinizing her trim form. "Did you drive all the way from Atlanta?"

She shook her head. "I flew to Knoxville, then drove over here yesterday. I'm staying at The Azalea Inn until my business here is finished." Charly's voice couldn't hide her annoyance at having to rent a car and drive the hundred miles from Knoxville. The small town she sought was nestled in the mountains on the border of North Carolina and Tennessee, far from airports and, in Charly's opinion, conveniences. But she was determined to make the best of it. After all, sometimes inconveniences came with the job in order to prove flexibility in any situation. And it was Charly's intent to prove her flexibility, as well as her ability, with no complaints.

The man raised his graying eyebrows at her words, as

if he read more into them. "Would you like to come in for a glass of tea?" he asked kindly.

"No, thank you." Charly declined, tucking a loose strand of chestnut hair back into the neat twist where she had piled her thick curls in an effort to get some relief from the humid late-August heat. "I just stopped by to report in and find out how to reach Walter Simms. I tried to find his number in the phone book, but he isn't listed."

The ranger ran his hand over his face, briefly smoothing out the wrinkled cheeks. "Well, now, the only way you're going to see Walter Simms is to go after him. He lives up on the mountain. And there's no phone." He waved his thick-veined hand toward the green and yellow mound rising high behind them.

"That's fine. Just tell me how to get there, Mr. . . . uh . . ." Her eyes traveled down to the metal nametag attached to his uniform pocket. " . . . Crockett."

"Are you sure you want to go all the way up there? It won't do you any good, I can tell you right now."

Charly drew herself up, trying to elevate to his tall frame. But there was no way to stretch her five-feet, four-inch length to match his six-feet, two or three. Arrogantly, she looked up at him and said, "Let me worry about that. All I need is directions to his house."

Crockett's eyebrows furrowed, and his eyes took on a friendly glow as he drawled, "I'm not very busy today. Would you like for me to take you up there? It's a long distance."

Confidently, she declined his offer. "No, thank you. Just give me directions and I'll be on my way." It was obvious that the ranger didn't think she could manage this trip alone. However, she had dealt with his typical male attitude before and just humored him patiently.

"Well, I guess that's how a girl like you got such an important big-city job. You're spunky, aren't you?" His gray eyes twinkled as his face softened slightly.

Charly couldn't help smiling at his old-fashioned adjective describing her. Actually, his assessment seemed fairly accurate. She had to be *spunky* to make it in the man's world in which she worked. She considered herself equal to any of her co-workers—even her boss, Lewis Daniel. Maybe her attitude was "spunky" after all. *Tough* was the word Lewis had used.

"I'm just doing my job, Mr. Crockett. Which way to Mr. Simms's?"

The tall ranger motioned toward the road and, unavoidably, the mountain. "Well, now, you just follow this road all the way to the top. It's about thirty miles. When the blacktop road ends, you'll cross a bridge, then go on another half-mile on the graveled part. You'll see the dirt road that takes you to the left, up Simms Hollow. It follows Little Creek all the way up to ol' Walt's cabin, about five miles. By then you'll cross the state line and be in North Carolina."

Charly nodded briskly at his directions, given in his slow Southern drawl. "Thirty-five miles. That's not so bad, especially after the trip I just made from Knoxville." She felt reassured that the man she sought was so close.

"It's a slow-paced drive. And the last five will be the longest. That road's pretty rough."

"Thanks for the directions, Mr. Crockett." Charly turned to go, then looked back with a smile. She was in the Smoky Mountains, and it was just too much of a coincidence to pass. "You aren't related to *Davy* Crockett, are you?"

He grinned, revealing furrowed crow's-feet around his gray eyes. "I always get comments about my name, too," he quipped. "Ol' Davy was from Cumberland way, not the Smokies. But you never know—maybe one of his sons roamed over this way, leaving his kin in these mountains."

Charly's eyes twinkled at the ranger's suggestive comment. "It might be interesting to research your roots, Mr. Crockett. Thanks for the directions."

"Sure thing. Drive carefully and . . . oh, Miss Ryan . . ."

Charly glanced up from the car door.

"Watch out for the weather. Don't get stuck up in Simms Hollow if it rains." He pointed toward the sky, where faintly gray-edged clouds dotted the blue expanse. "Looks like we could get rain before the day's over."

"Okay." Charly nodded, immediately forgetting his warning. She backed out of the driveway and headed for the curvy mountain road that led to her destination. The sky was mostly blue, and the sun beat down unmercifully as she drove away from the sleepy little Tennessee town.

She left the farms and stretches of fields that nestled at the foot of the mountains and immediately started winding her way upward into the elevated forests. A brown wooden sign announced her entrance into the Great Smoky Mountains National Forest and she sped onward. Humid air from the open windows swirled around her, loosening short hair around her neckline. It was a good feeling and the beauty of the scenery raised her spirits.

She flipped on her car radio, and the only station that penetrated the deep recesses of her remote location was a country music station. With singular guitar accompaniment, a man sang in sad tones about Smoky Mountain rain and his lost love. However, the woeful notes contrasted with Charly's buoyant mood, and she switched it off again, humming her own happy tune.

She mused over her conversation with Mr. Crockett, possible distant relative of the eminent Davy. He had called her "spunky." In such a remote region as this, he probably hadn't seen many women who held positions of influence, especially in government. Charly prided herself on her job and her ability to carry out proposals and make decisions. She would show Lewis Daniel that she could complete this assignment, however unpleasant. He had expressed some doubts about her ability to do it. As her boss, he had even suggested that she take the assistant regional manager with her. But she would show him! She could handle these backwoods people and accomplish her goal—with their endorsement. He'd see.

The trip turned out to be slower than she had anticipated. The further she went, the more narrow and winding the road became. Charly found that she couldn't speed around the mountainous curves and was forced to take them slowly. Eventually she decided to make it a relaxing trip and enjoy her surroundings. She even stopped several times to view the spectacular mountain scenery.

Charly watched in awe as white frothy water cascaded over Bald River Falls, emitting a fine mist spray that glittered in the morning sunlight. The water pelted downward, finally rushing loudly beneath the bridge where Charly stood. From there it slowed its pace and washed over rust and gray rocks, lingering in the deeper pools.

She had studied maps of the area and knew that this large river was fed by numerous smaller tributaries that ran down from the mountaintops. Little Creek, where Walter Simms lived, was one of those tributaries. Breathing in the cool, moist air, Charly felt very close to nature as she continued her trek into the interior of the southern Appalachian range.

Her quest for the home of Walter Simms had led to this secluded road and, ultimately, the flat tire and the mysterious mountaineer. When would she reach the end of her journey? The rutted road jolted her to the present.

Finally, Charly could see a clearing ahead. Thank goodness she had reached the end of the road. What a nerve-wracking trip it had been. She tried to dismiss the strange, bearded mountain man who had helped her, then disappeared so suddenly. But his relentless blue eyes and rough appearance remained with her, even though she had not learned his name.

Charly emerged from the dark tree-shaded road into a bath of sunshine and spotted a weathered cabin nestled against the side of the mountain almost hidden by the trees. She parked near an old yellow truck of 1950 vintage and walked around to the steps that led to the high porch, where a man stood. He watched her every move. She noted that he must be the sought-after Walter Simms.

She took a deep, confidence-building breath and smiled. "Hello. I'm Charly Ryan. Are you Walter Simms?" She gazed at the stoop-shouldered man and marveled at the eighty-nine-year-old countenance before her.

"Howdy," he answered in a creaky voice. "Yep, I'm Walter Simms. Y'say your name's 'Charly'? Funny name for a girl." He shuffled over to a wood-slat rocker and gestured for her to sit down. "Come on and join me. I was just about to have some lunch. Would you like some, and a glass of tea?"

Charly smiled in acceptance. "Tea sounds great, Mr. Simms. Let me help you."

"No, you have a seat. I can do it." He stepped into the house, leaving Charly alone on the porch.

She could see a small barn, the nearest wall of which was lined with stretched-out raccoon skins. She shuddered at the thought of the little masked animals. Slumping into the wooden rocker, Charly was surprised at how comfortable it was—or maybe she was just tired from the oppressive humidity and her long hours in the car during the last two days. There was a peaceful yawn in the air, punctuated only by the buzz of flies gathering in the heat of the day. The sound of the screen door shooed them away and alerted Charly that Mr. Simms was returning.

He set a platter piled with tomato wedges, cheese slices, and crackers on a table between them and handed her a tall glass of tea that was graced with a green mint leaf.

Gratefully, Charly gulped the cool liquid, then set the glass on the table, watching the pungent mint leaf float languidly to the bottom of the glass. They ate the simple food quietly for a few minutes before Charly broke the silence.

"Mr. Simms, I'm from the Bureau of Land Management in Atlanta. That's the organization that oversees the use of this government land." She motioned toward the surrounding hills.

He nodded and reached for a wedge of tomato. "The government?"

She watched him manage the juicy tomato without so much as a dribble. "Yes, sir. The government."

His lively blue eyes caught hers. "What do you want with me?"

"I . . . I came to see . . . to check on the proper use of this land." She would not be intimidated by this man. She came up here for a reason and she would not back down. Reaching for a piece of pale yellow cheese, she bit into it.

"Is that all? Well, I can show you that right quick. Come on," he said enthusiastically. He reached for a cheese wedge and placed it on a cracker before leading the way down the steps to the yard.

She followed the spry old man, hurrying to keep up with him.

"Here's my garden. I have to work all the time to keep the deer and rabbits from eating the whole thing." He pointed to the ample plot of ground, tilled and completely fenced in. There wasn't a weed around any of the plants and Charly was amazed that, at his age, Walter Simms could prepare such a beautiful garden and coax so many vegetables to grow. The garden would go into her official report.

They walked past the barn with its covering of raccoon skins. Irritated at the gruesome sight, Charly remarked, "Mr. Simms, don't you know that killing animals in a national forest is against federal regulations?" Raccoon skins would certainly be included in the report.

He stopped and flashed his blue eyes at her. "I've been huntin' 'coons all my life, lady, and I'm not gonna quit now." After a pause, he added quickly, "Besides, I killed them on my own property."

"Still, Mr. Simms, these animals belong to the forest. How could you possibly kill them?"

"Survival. It's all survival. I only take what I can use. And I'm surviving in the forest, too." He turned and led her to a row of perfectly square white boxes.

As they approached, she could hear the buzzing and knew their purpose. "Bee hives!" she exclaimed in recognition.

"Yep," he nodded proudly. "They keep me in honey all year and I still have some to sell and trade. There's basswood, poplar, and sourwood trees all around here and my bees produce the best honey you'll find anywhere."

Charly watched in awe as he opened one of the drawers and casually brushed aside a small group of bees with his bare hands.

"Here, taste this." He pinched off a small portion of the honeycomb with its sweet filling. "Put the whole thing in your mouth. That 'comb' won't hurt you. It's just wax . . . beeswax . . . hee-hee." His laughter was high and slightly squeaky.

Charly obeyed and popped the entire thing in her mouth, chewing on the wax while the marvelous sweet honey oozed onto her tongue. She continued to chew on the wax until it was a small, tough ball. The bees, too, would be a part of the report. Following Walter Simms back to the house, she tried to prepare him for what she had to say.

"Mr. Simms, don't you miss civilization way up here all by yourself?"

"Nope. People just get in my way."

"But you must get lonesome sometimes."

"I'm too busy to get lonesome. I'm getting ready for winter right now."

"Winter?" Charly made a mental note, for here was another tactic she could use in the report. "The winters up here must be awful. How do you get to town for supplies?"

"I don't." He climbed the steps, holding on to the gray weathered railing with a gnarled hand.

"You can't get down for supplies?" she asked incredulously. Another item for the report.

"Nope. Snow's too deep." He paused at the top step to catch his breath.

"Then what do you do? It's dangerous for you to be up here like that."

"That's why I get ready for winter. I store up firewood, supplies, food—everything I'll need for the winter months. Then I don't worry about it." He sat in his straight-backed rocker and looked peacefully over the land.

"Mr. Simms, as a representative of the government, I have made an assessment of this land and the best use of it. I am also concerned about your welfare. Therefore, I would like to make a proposal. We will pay you for your land, your house—everything here. We will help you to relocate down in town where you'll be closer to friends, supplies, and medical facilities. It'll be for your own good."

"Hold on, young lady!" Alarm filled Simms's cracked voice. "I have a lifetime lease—from the government—that says I can stay here until I die. Then"—and he shook a crooked finger at Charly—"and, *only then* can the government come in here and take over my land."

Charly nodded. "Yes, I know about your lifetime lease. And we will uphold it. But you are abusing the land. You are killing raccoons, plowing up the land, depleting this area of its wildlife."

He hit the flat of his thick sturdy hand on the chair arm, making a loud *spat.* "I'm *not* depleting this land! I'm just living here! It's survival of the fittest! Haven't you ever heard of that?"

"Yes, but this is now protected public domain. Federal laws protect the land and animals, trying to save them for the next generations." Charly knew her explanations sounded feeble to this stubborn old man.

"This is *my* land! What about *me?* What about this generation . . . *this* old man?" He poked himself on the chest for emphasis.

"Believe me, we are concerned about you, Mr. Simms. That's why we want you to move to town. Then you can be closer to people who can care for you—your family, friends, doctors."

"I don't need anybody to take care of me. And I don't have much use for doctors. I've got my own remedies from the mountain. I'm staying right here. I won't let anybody drive me off my land."

Charly smiled. "I'm not trying to drive you off your land. I'm only trying to help you."

"Help me? The government? Huh!" He looked away disgustedly. Abruptly he stood up, gesturing in the air as he spoke. "I've lived on this mountain for over sixty years and never asked for help from the government or anybody! And I don't intend to start now. I won't let you drive me from my land!" With that, he stomped angrily inside the house, letting the screen door bang loudly.

Charly blinked, feeling a little sorry for the old man, who embodied such bitterness. Although his words to her were harsh, she understood his deep feelings about the land. It didn't make her job any easier. She knew what her boss, Lewis, wanted—had demanded. Sighing, she rose. She knew it was futile to continue today, for her visit with Walter Simms had come to an end. She would return to town and give him some time to cool off, but she wouldn't admit defeat yet. The initial report could be filed while she regathered her forces. She might have to consult with Lewis after all.

As Charly reached her car, the oppressive humidity closed in on her. Flies buzzed near her head and she swung her hand to shoo them away just as the first large raindrops started to fall. She hadn't noticed that the dark-edged clouds had covered the blue sky and cast a gray shadow over the afternoon. Now huge wet drops bounced on the dusty car, plopped on the dry earth, and ran over her arms before Charly could jump into the dry shelter of the car. She sat for a moment in silence, listening to the rain as it pelted the car, recalling the ranger's warning not to get caught in the rain in Simms Hollow. Well, thank goodness she was leaving just in time. She started the motor, drowning out the soft patter of a million raindrops hitting the roof and windows.

When she reached the dirt road, she plunged swiftly ahead, dodging ruts and large rocks. The rain had turned the road into a soggy path where her car slid and skidded its way along the muddy rivulets. Charly leaned forward, straining to see through the gray haze caused by the severity of the sudden downpour.

Charly had traveled about a mile down the slippery road when she felt the car swerve. She struggled with the steering wheel, wrestling impotently to control her vehicle until, at last, she felt the helpless swing of the car out of control as it slid first one way, then the other. Finally, after what seemed like a slow-motion eternity, the car slumped securely to a dead halt. Fear knotted in the pit of her stomach as the little car tilted threateningly on one side, sinking even further into the mud. She worked feverishly to open the door, but it was wedged shut against grass and mud, which were closely visible outside her window. She struggled over to the passenger side of the car and opened that door, climbing out into the driving rain. She assessed the extent of the damage, eyeing the little car, which leaned precariously on its side in a water-filled ditch next to the mud-slick road. As the wind blew swirls of wet leaves against her and cold rain sent chilly streams of water down her back, Charly knew that it would be risky to crawl back into the small compact car with it so dangerously tilted.

Consequently, she reached inside and grabbed her purse and locked the door securely, leaving her scattered portfolio in the back seat.

The wind was cold and Charly was immediately drenched from head to toe as she stood stewing over her predicament. There was only one thing to do. She would have to go back to Walter Simms's cabin and wait out the storm. She dreaded the thought of facing him again, but there was no alternative. The car was stuck—and so was she.

Charly started hiking through the mud, her stylish, wedge-heeled shoes proving to be impossible for clomping through the mud. The only reason she left them on was to protect herself from the rocks, for she had to stop periodically to scrape thick mud from the sides and bottoms. As she trudged through the cold rain, darkness closed in. The rain was steady and hard, and occasionally the gray-black forest blazed with the flash of lightning or echoed with the rumble of distant thunder.

Charly was chilled thoroughly, teeth chattering, hands and arms shaking, and legs almost rubber from fear and cold. How could it be so cold when only a few hours ago the heat had been oppressive? The ranger, Crockett, had been right when he predicted rain. And she should never have come up the mountain alone. Suddenly, an additional fear gripped Charly. She remembered the bearded man who had appeared and disappeared so suddenly in the forest! What if . . . ? But she refused to think of it. Frantically, for more than an hour, Charly struggled on up the road to the security of the old man's cabin. She tried not to imagine what might be behind every tree and bush.

She moved faster, almost running up the road, fearfully looking over her shoulder every few minutes. What if he was watching her, stalking her? Every time the lightning flashed she took advantage of the light by searching through her pitch-black surroundings. The storm, the cold rain, the random lightning were no longer her enemies. *He* was—whoever was out there!

Whatever had convinced her to come to this remote, uncivilized place by herself anyway? She should never have let Lewis . . . but he tried to tell her. Damn him! He should have insisted. But would she have listened? Probably not. Next time . . . if there *was* a next time! Oh—what a terrible thought.

It seemed forever before she spotted a weak light shining from the distant cabin, beaming warmth and comfort out into the cold, miserably wet night. Breathlessly, she ran to the house, slipping out of her ruined shoes, leaving them on the bottom step in the rain. She stumbled clumsily onto the porch and knocked loudly at the door. Her voice rose to a wailful, rather frantic, "Mr. Simms, Mr. Simms! It's me, Charly Ryan!"

Walter Simms opened the door slowly and stared at Charly. What a mess she was. What a dripping, shivering, muddy mess! But, thank goodness, she was safe!

Her chestnut hair was torn from its chic twist and hung drooping over her shoulders. Her face was streaked and mascara smudged into two inky blotches beneath her eyes. Her white blouse clung wetly to her body, outlining her breasts and heaving ribs. The once-clean gray slacks were mud-speckled and wrapped tightly around her thighs. And her bare feet were covered with brown oozing mud.

"M-Mr. Simms, I had car trouble," she muttered through chattering teeth. "C-Can I . . . come in?"

He looked at her for a long minute, assessing the young

girl in his old, slow way. He rubbed a gnarled hand over his rough chin stubble. Finally, when she thought he would never answer, he said, "Guess I don't have a choice. You don't have any other place to go." He stepped aside. "Come on in."

Charly stepped gratefully into the warm room, which glowed with the flames from a huge fireplace. The welcoming blaze enticed Charly and she was drawn involuntarily toward it.

Abruptly, she stopped short, a muffled cry in her throat. There, kneeling before the fire and placing logs in a certain neat order, was the dark, foreboding form of a large man. He swung his head around to look at her and the fire's glow lit his shadowed face, revealing the same bearded fisherman who had changed her tire earlier that day! Charly gasped, fear rising within her once again. Just when she thought she had reached safe harbor, her sanctuary in the mountains was invaded by the menacing figure before her. She sought refuge in the cabin with the very man from whom she was trying to escape! And she was trapped miles from civilization and no chance of help from anyone except old Walter Simms!

CHAPTER TWO

"What are you doing here?" Charly questioned disdainfully.

The dark man's steely eyes raked over her drenched, accentuated curves as he answered, "It happens to be where I live. What are *you* doing here?"

Charly was all too aware of her wet, suggestive appearance. She crossed her arms to hide her breasts from this stranger, whose eyes chilled her. She clutched both forearms. It made her realize just how cold she really was. "You live here? This is Walter Simms's house. I thought he lived alone. Who are you?"

The man turned away from her indifferently and continued to complete his task with the fire. Ignoring her question, he asked his own. "Who are you, and what in the hell are you doing here at this time of night?"

"I'm . . . I'm Charly Ryan. My car is stuck in the mud about two miles down the road. I had to leave it there and walk back here through the rain. Do you think you could help me get it out?"

"Tonight? No way! Looks like you're stranded. What is your business up here?"

Charly wasn't sure why she felt compelled to tell this stranger about herself, but she did. Maybe it was his overpoweringly dominant attitude or his gruff appearance. Maybe it was just his indifference as he turned his broad back to her.

"I'm from the B.L.M.—the Bureau of Land Management—and I'm here on assignment. When I came up here earlier today, I didn't notice the impending storm. Now that road is just awful. Once my car started sliding, I couldn't control it."

"So you want to spend the night," he finished, as a statement of fact.

"No, I don't *want* to, but I guess I have no choice," Charly snipped, hugging her arms around her, trying to warm her chilled body. She shivered visibly just as he looked back at her and she cringed under his all-consuming gaze. "Unless, of course, there is a motel nearby!"

Once again, his eyes traveled down her, ending with her muddy feet and the growing pool of water gathering on the floor around her. He stood up and his dark presence significantly dominated the room.

"Come over here closer to the fire and I'll get you a towel." His voice was a sharp command, which she unwittingly obeyed. "There isn't a motel within a hundred miles of this place."

He left the room and Charly turned around to warm her backside. She noticed that the old man was nowhere to be seen in the spacious room that served both as living room and kitchen. She looked down with dismay at the muddy puddle she had made on the floor. Suddenly she was shivering uncontrollably and felt very close to tears. What in the world was she doing, getting herself into a predicament like this?

In a moment the grizzly-looking man reappeared with several items draped over his arm. He was speaking to her as he walked closer. His words were rebuffing, denouncing, but the tone was somehow soothing, gentle. "This was really stupid, you know—coming up here by yourself. A woman like you has no business in these mountains alone and whoever sent you is a fool."

Charly smiled secretly to herself as she imagined Lewis's face if he could hear this stranger's assessment of his judgment. And he would be appalled if he could see her right now, in a cabin alone with this ruffian and an old man. She could hear him now. "What a damn-fool thing for me to do . . . let you go off alone to that mountain!"

"Here is a towel and a change of clothes." The stranger held the towel for her and she moved closer to the warmth of the fire and the burly man.

"I . . . I couldn't help sliding in the mud," Charly answered defensively. This man certainly had a way of intimidating her and she wasn't easily bullied. Maybe it was because she was so cold and miserable.

He draped the large dry towel around her shoulders. "You've had trouble with that car all day. Does that tell you anything? Maybe you don't belong on this mountain. I don't want you interfering."

She again felt his rebuff of unfriendliness. How could he be so unpleasant when he didn't even know her . . . and she was so cold . . .

Shivering visibly, she muttered, "I'm not here by my own design, I can assure you. But I can't see that *you* belong here either." That was a matter she intended to take up at a later date. "Mr. Simms is supposed to live alone."

"Well, as you can see, he doesn't." He pulled her closer to the fire.

Charly hovered near the fire, muttering through chattering teeth, "Thanks for changing my tire today. You left too soon for me to tell you how much I appreciated it. Only now the car's mired in mud that covers the tires. Oh, what a mess." She watched the reddish licking flames and tried to absorb their warmth. But her body was too wet, too chilled. All she could do was shake.

His voice was almost consoling. "We'll check out the car tomorrow. But right now you must get these wet clothes off or you'll never get warm." As he spoke, he began unbuttoning her blouse.

Mentally Charly agreed with what the man was saying, although she didn't answer. She could only nod, for she was too chilled to respond to anything but physical warmth. His voice soothed her and she stood still until his hands brushed her cleavage.

Shrinking away from his touch, she tried to cover herself, but the buttons were already undone, and the blouse was hanging loosely open down her front. Before she could grasp the moment, his rough, responsive hands were on her shoulders, pushing on the blouse.

"W-What are you doing?" Charly gasped, knowing full well what he was doing. "Get your hands off me!"

His voice was low and calm. "I'm *only* taking these wet clothes off. You can't keep them on. You're chilled. Come on, now."

"I can take my own clothes off, thank you!" she shrilled, oblivious to the humor in her words.

But the mountain man was fully alert to her words . . . and her body. He stared at her with a bemused expression, his blue eyes penetrating her . . . undressing her further.

Abruptly, the expression changed and a dark, foreboding veil covered his face. Roughly, he draped the large towel around her shoulders again. "Do it, then," he rasped. "Get all of your wet clothes off and—for God's sake—cover up those damned nipples!"

Charly looked down at her disheveled appearance. Her thin, wet blouse and lacy bra clung to her shape, outlining her breasts and pointing out the prominent nipples. Under cover of the towel, she quickly shed her blouse, letting it drop to a soggy heap by her feet. Her wet bra was next, and she huddled into the thick towel, trying to wring some warmth from the thing. It had a fresh, clean fragrance, reminding her of fields of flowers.

"Here are some dry clothes," the man commanded, shoving them into her arms. "Put them on."

He walked away from her and into the kitchen, which was just an open area in the far corner of the big room.

Charly turned her back on him and, with shaky hands, donned the shirt he gave her. It was a soft blue chambray, obviously well worn. It felt deliciously warm and soothing to her cold back and arms and it, too, had the marvelous fragrance of fields and flowers. In a moment her once-gray front-pleated slacks joined the wet pile of clothes and she pulled on jeans that hugged her hips but gaped widely at her slim waist.

Once again the bearded man was by her side. She hadn't even heard him approach.

"Here, drink this," he ordered, handing her a small glass.

"What is it?" She sniffed at it curiously.

"Wine," he answered shortly. Stooping down, he began to roll a cuff on each of her pant legs. "How do these fit? They're a little long, but this will help." By the time he'd finished talking, he was standing again. "Do you need a pin for the waist or will they stay up without it?"

"They're fine, thank you," Charly murmured. She didn't want to inconvenience him any more than she had already.

"Go ahead. Drink your wine. It'll be good for you." He scooped up her wet clothes and made another trip to the kitchen. Soon he returned with a small pan. Setting it down beside her, he again issued an order. "Wash your feet here. I'll get you some warm socks."

Charly sipped the pungent wine and did as she was told. By the time he had returned with the socks, her feet were washed and snuggled into the towel. She was just realizing how icy cold they were. She finished off the wine, then stuffed her feet into the large woolly socks he offered.

She smiled with pleasure. "Oooo, those feel good. Thanks. And what kind of wine was that? It's very good."

"Blackberry."

"Blackberry? I always thought blackberry wine was very sweet."

"Not the way we make it up here."

"You made it?" she asked incredulously.

"Sure. Drink it all. It'll help warm you up. There's plenty more. Whenever you're ready to eat, supper's on. Just help yourself." He refilled the wineglass, then walked away, leaving her to sip the wine and stare into the fire, pondering her situation.

Vaguely, Charly could hear sounds of the two men eating in the small kitchen area, and wondered where Simms had disappeared to. Finally the savory aroma of whatever they were eating reached her and she realized that she was starved. If she was waiting for another invitation to eat from the men, she soon realized that she wouldn't get it. So she rose and walked meekly across the room to them.

"Do you mind if I eat, too?"

Walter Simms didn't say a word to her. He didn't even look up at her. His attitude clearly told her that she was basically unwelcome here.

Well, she thought remorsefully, I certainly don't relish the idea of being here either, so we're even!

The bearded man motioned toward the stove. "I told you to help yourself."

"So you did. Your politeness overwhelms me. Please, don't get up. I can help myself." Charly stalked angrily over to the simmering pot and dipped some of the savory stew into her waiting bowl. No one spoke, so she sat at the huge round table with the two men and ate quietly. No one said a word for long, merciless minutes of agonizing silence. Finally, in an effort to redeem the situation, if not the evening, Charly attempted conversation.

"You know, I've met Mr. Simms, here. But, although you've changed my tire and I'm now wearing your clothes, I still don't know your name."

The man gazed at her for a moment, a devilish gleam barely detectable in his intense blue eyes. "I'm Noah Van Horn. And this . . ." He paused, giving dramatic emphasis to the sounds of rain still pelting the tin roof of the cabin. "This is Noah's ark." He laughed heartily and poured another round of blackberry wine. "How do you like it?" He motioned to the wine container.

Charly's brown eyes caught his. "Which?" she asked smartly. "The ark or the wine?"

He leaned forward, his elbows resting on the table as he grinned. "Both!"

She shrugged indifferently. "The wine's fine."

He raised his dark eyebrows. "And the ark?"

Charly was not amused by his line of dialogue. "I'm not here by choice, remember."

He leaned back in his chair and motioned dramatically with his hand. "Well, city lady. You may as well get comfortable and enjoy it, because it looks like we're here for the duration. All of us together! Forty days and forty nights it rained! And they came into the ark, two by two. We haven't figured out just where you fit into the scheme of pairs, Miss Ryan. But we'll work something out, I'm sure."

Charly cringed at his wicked grin, which was barely visible under the mass of his beard and mustache. She could feel her cheeks tingle with anger as she retorted, "You don't have to worry about me, Mr. Van Horn, because I'm leaving this barbaric place tomorrow. And you can be assured that the reports I file will not be favorable toward Mr. Simms and whatever is going on up here in the mountains!" She shoved her bowl away.

"Oh, come now, Miss Ryan. Let's not get snippy!

Would you like more squirrel stew?" Noah offered politely.

"Squirrel stew?" Charly choked out the words. "*Squirrel?* No!"

"Yes. It's the house specialty," he admitted with a proud smile.

He lifted the wine decanter again and Charly eagerly held her glass out to be refilled. Something had to take away the funny taste in her mouth and help soothe the sudden flip-flopping of her stomach at the thought of having eaten squirrel stew. She gulped at the wine, losing count of the number of times her glass had been refilled. But right now she really didn't care. Just the thought of what she had eaten sent chills down her spine, and she wanted to drown out the sensations.

Charly sputtered angrily, "This . . . this meal will be included in my report that goes to the Bureau of Land Management in Atlanta tomorrow." She couldn't bring herself to say what it contained, but it would certainly be written in the report.

Noah folded his arms across his chest. "I'm just curious to know how your report is going to make it to Atlanta tomorrow, when you won't even be able to plow out of here for days." His mouth curled into a mocking grin.

Charly's eyes rounded in alarm as she snapped, "I am leaving this place tomorrow! With my reports! Squirrel indeed!" She shoved her chair back with a clatter and, taking her wine, stomped over to the fire, where she plopped into a stuffed chair with her back to the men.

She burned with indignation as she could hear them laughing at her outburst. But she didn't lower her dignity to give them a glance. Charly curled her feet under her in the big chair and was surprised at its comfort. Maybe she was just so tired and frustrated from the events of the day that the cozy chair provided just the security she needed. In the background she heard faint sounds of the men moving around the kitchen. As she slowly sipped her wine, Charly actually began to relax. The fire crackled busily, and soon the sight of the licking flames and the snapping noises they made consumed all of her attention.

She thought of Lewis and what he would say when he found out about her predicament. She cringed inside as she thought about facing him again and what he would say after "I told you so!"

Why had she fought his opinions? Why did she really feel so strongly that she had to prove her superiority to him? Now she would have to admit defeat, which was worse than accepting help at the outset. Damn! What it would mean was that he was right. His judgment, at least in this particular situation, was farsighted and correct. Everyone in the department would know it. And Lewis wouldn't soon let her forget this mountain situation.

Stubbornly, she didn't care. She would handle the job—and Lewis—when the time came. Right now, she'd give anything to see his handsome face and feel the security of his arms. Do I really mean that? she thought. After the way I fought his dominance, his advances? At least he would rescue me from this mountain prison, and that's what I want right now.

Charly knew that she had wanted to prove herself to Lewis. He had been relentless in his efforts to seduce her. Maybe if she had agreed to his wishes long ago she wouldn't be in this predicament. She had always been strictly business whenever she was with him. Now, in a moment of weakness, she wondered why she had refused him. Perhaps it had to do with love, or lack of it. He had promised that he would take care of her.

Still, she had resisted his every advance, and it had put her in a very difficult position with her boss. She wanted him to guide her in her career, to be her leader, her boss, not her lover. But he had other ideas for the attractive lady who was the new deputy assistant. Tonight, however, she would welcome him with open arms, just to get away from here. Oh, Lewis . . . Lewis . . . where are you when I need you?

Charly heard music floating faintly through the darkness. A radio . . . no, was it a harmonica? Anyway, it was nice and peaceful. She sipped the last of the blackberry wine and settled back in the comforting arms of the old chair. Eventually the wine and the flames worked their magic, mesmerizing her, and Charly drifted to sleep.

Vaguely, she felt herself floating, or was she being lifted? She grasped hard shoulders and snuggled against the warmth of a broad chest. A faint whiff of the smoky, masculine scent reminded her of the fire and the lovely flames that enticed her, captivated her.

Then she was being carried away from the flames, the heat, and tucked into a cool place. Frantically, she clutched at the warmth, embracing it, pulling it to her. She had been so cold, so wet, and she didn't want to lose that delicious warmth again.

Fervent hands pushed her legs straight into the cold bed, trailing, caressing the length of her limbs, lingering on her thighs, hips, waist. Subconsciously Charly clung to his warmth. Immediately, his responsive length stretched beside hers, wrapping long arms and legs around her, warming her with his passionate body. As his lips met hers, soft hair tickled her face and she accepted his hearty affection. The sensation was so lovely, so pleasing . . .

Then, with a sharp cry, she was awake, pushing against his firm chest, trying to break the steel-hard arms locked around her. She struggled—fought—against him for a moment. Abruptly, he grabbed her shoulders with a fierce jerk.

"Calm down, you wildcat! I'm here tonight by invitation!" His voice was thick and his breath fell in raspy spurts on her face.

"You . . . you are not! Get out of my bed! Why . . . you . . . you barbarian!" Charly sputtered.

He loomed over her menacingly, his entire body leaning prominently against her. "This is *my* bed, and I'm here at your insistence."

"No you're not! I didn't—"

He was so close that she could feel his hot breath on her face. "Oh, yes you did. I have the claw marks to prove it! Don't tempt me like this again or there will be *no* stopping!"

Angrily, he abandoned the bed, leaving a cool draft where his warmth had been. And Charly was fearfully alone in the dark.

CHAPTER THREE

Muted light filtered through the tiny square window, spreading a small ray of grayish luminosity over the bed where Charly lay. She blinked, focusing on the unfamiliar room, the strange sounds around her, her preposterous situation. As she tried to pull it all together in her mind, she looked around the room at the crudely built bookshelves along one wall, full of thick, hardbound books. Somehow they seemed incongruously out of place in this backwoods cabin. Perhaps it was the strings of dried onions, peppers, and some kind of—was that *meat?*—hanging at intervals along the bookcase that created the absurd kaleidoscope. There was very little else in the room except for one small desk littered with papers, pencils, and a few more books along with the bed where Charly curled, warm and dry.

She listened intently for a moment and was startled wide awake at the steady plunking, almost rhythmic beat of rain on the roof. It was quite distinct when she concentrated on the sound. Rain! *Still* raining? It just couldn't be! Charly had to get out of this place today! And how could she if it was *still* raining? Instantly, she sat up, her mind racing. She just *had* to get down off this mountain today! She threw back the covers and glanced carelessly at the bed, which, until now, she had taken for granted. It was comfortable, dry, and warm, and—had she really crawled into this bed with *that man* last night? She shuddered visibly at the thought. Yet she remembered clinging to his warmth, her actions inviting him to join her. And he had! But then he had left her alone. Hadn't he? She checked her clothes and, with some relief, found them intact. With great determination she climbed out of the big bed. She had a lot to do today, the first of which was to get her car unstuck so she could leave this loathsome place.

There were other sounds that struck her as she reached for the door. A cheery, crackling sound obliterated the rain noises and Charly curiously peered into the big room. A rich aroma reached her nostrils and she was aware of the marvelous morning smells of fresh-brewed coffee and fried ham.

"Mornin'," came the almost cheerful greeting from the kitchen, where old Walter Simms was clattering around, obviously cooking breakfast.

Apparently he had decided to speak to her today, and Charly answered agreeably, "Good morning. Is it *still* raining, Mr. Simms?"

He nodded. "Yep. We've got us a real toad strangler out there. Looks like we'll be here for a while, so why don't you just call me Walt? Noah does."

Charly looked curiously at him. His figure of speech amused her, but she disliked the thought of being stuck there long enough to understand the old man and know him on a first-name basis. She just *had* to get out of here today—and she would, too. Mention of Noah's name reminded her, with chagrin, of her encounter with him last night and their eventual seductive involvement. Yes, she *had* to get away from here. If she landed in bed with that man on her first night, what would happen if she stayed longer? Well, she certainly wouldn't hang around to find out, Charly told herself. She was determined to leave today.

"Have some coffee," Walt offered, handing her a cup of the hot black liquid.

"Thank you, Walt." She ambled over to the window and gazed outside, where everything was lost in a misty gray background. "Speaking of . . . Noah, where is he this morning?" She tried to sound casual instead of curious.

"Oh, he's out huntin'," Walt answered.

"Hunting? In the rain?" Charly wrinkled up her forehead. She couldn't imagine going out in that miserable weather.

"Sure. Best time for huntin' squirrels," Walt answered easily.

Suddenly Charly was jolted back to the awful reality of her location and her reason for being there. *Squirrels?* And he was *hunting!* That was part of the problem with this particular lifetime-lease situation and now she was thrown right into the heart of it. Lewis would be interested to learn all she had to say about this place.

"Oh, Mr. Simms . . . where is your . . ."

Walt looked up curiously at her for a moment. Then he nodded knowingly. Motioning toward the back door, he said, "Out there."

"What?"

"Out there. You can go out there. Wear my old coat and boots. They're just outside the door on the porch. Go ahead."

Charly stood dumbfounded for a long moment, her eyes traveling from Walt's face to the back porch, past the neat garden, to the little outhouse, which she could barely see through the fog and rain.

"Go on before the rain gets harder. And call me Walt."

Charly was appalled at the thought of having to use outdoor facilities! It was uncivilized—crude. This was modern times and people didn't live like this anymore! As she stood there, staring outside and stewing inwardly, Charly realized that if she was to get any relief she would have to go down that path! Furiously she jerked the door open, and with angry, shaking hands she pulled on Walt's stiff coat and boots and proceeded to slosh through the mud down the path. How in the hell could she have let herself get into a predicament like this?

Later, as Charly stood by the fire warming her chilled body, frustration mounted within her and tears threatened. She pursed her lips, trying desperately to keep from crying when the unwelcomed tears burned her large, brown eyes. Walt had refilled her coffee mug and, as she sipped it, she couldn't help thinking of it as somewhat of a peace offering. His old gray eyes seemed to know of her dismay. What a way to start the day! It just made Charly more determined to leave as soon as . . . But it was *still* raining outside.

She looked up bleakly and Walt stood before her again, handing her another offering—a plate of food.

"Here, have some breakfast."

"Thank you," she mumbled weakly.

Without hesitation, Charly took the dish and sat on the edge of the hearth, remaining close to the warmth of the fire. For some reason she was starved and the ham, biscuits, and honey smelled delicious. Walt sat quietly nearby and drank his coffee. He offered no apologies, no opinions, no suggestions for her deliverance from the mountain prison. Apparently it didn't occur to him that anyone would want to escape his abode. Between bites Charly questioned him.

"Who is that man living here with you, Mr. . . . uh, Walt?"

"Name's Noah Van Horn," he answered simply.

"I know that. I mean, who is he to you? A relative?" she probed.

"Nope. A friend."

"How long has he been here?"

"About two years, off and on."

Charly squinted at his expression. "Off and on?"

Walt was not prone to long, involved communications

and tended to converse in short, terse statements. "Yep. He comes and goes."

"Then he doesn't live here all the time? He uses this place as a—a lodge?" Charly figured aloud.

Walt stirred, irritated with her persistence. "Look, Noah comes here and I don't question him. He leaves, and I don't question him. He is my friend and can come to my home anytime he wants to and stay as long as he wants. And I don't ask half the questions you do!"

Charly answered him firmly. "Walt, you must know this changes the account I'll have to make. You were reported to have no one else living here, but the presence of Noah changes all that. It appears that he is using this place as a recreation domicile from which he can pillage the land. It makes the chances of your staying here in jeopardy. There isn't supposed to be anyone else living off this land and it certainly isn't to be used as a . . . hunting lodge."

Walter Simms leaned back and squinted his gray eyes angrily at her. "That so? Well, let me tell you something. I won't let any city gal with a bunch of big words come up here and tell me what to do with my land or my house!"

Charly blinked, knowing that she had struck a brick wall in trying to convince this old man that her words carried a great deal of authority. So she decided on another tactic. "Where did Noah come from? Why is he here?"

Walt studied her for a long moment, anger still visible in his eyes. Then he answered tersely, "Mournin'."

"Morning?" Once again Charly couldn't understand the old man's meaning.

"Yes. He's mournin' his wife and child."

The words hit Charly like a thunderbolt and she muttered weakly, "Oh." It didn't change the facts, her goal, her predicament. But it did change her point of view—for a moment, at least—as she imagined anew the presence of the dark-haired man who had eagerly taken her to bed.

Sounds of thunder interrupted her harried thoughts and she glanced toward the door, which Walt was in the process of opening. She could see Noah stamping his wet boots on the porch and realized that the ponderous noise came from him. He grinned through his beard and held up three dead squirrels by the tails for her to see.

"Ooooh," Charly gasped, and quickly turned her head away to block out the grisly sight. Then she hopped up and dashed to the door, angry words lashing out at the rough woodsman. "You . . . you jackass! How could you do such a thing as . . . as this? And don't hold them up for all to see! I'm not impressed with your cruel and savage activities! What kind of man are you, anyway?"

He looked at her for a moment, his blue eyes moving wickedly over her slight frame, which was still attired in his clothes. "I am a normal man, make no mistake about it. But don't be offended by these." He gestured toward the animals. "I'll fix them in a dish tonight that you'll love."

Charly could feel her hair rise, prickling the back of her neck. "Don't bother! I'll be gone by then! It'll be a cold day in hell before I eat . . . that!" She motioned, still unable to say the words that offended her so. "Anyway, I'm leaving today."

The man laid the offending animals aside. "Oh, really? And how do you propose to do that? It's still raining, or haven't you noticed?"

"I've noticed. But at least it's daylight and I can see to get the car free. If not, you can just take me in that truck. Or I'll walk if I have to, but I'm leaving this damned mountain today!" Charly's cheeks glowed pink in her angry tirade toward the man who viewed her with mirth in his half-hidden face.

"We'll see, Wildcat. We'll see. Now, do you want to help me clean these?"

"No!" Charly fairly screamed at him and wheeled back into the house.

She retreated furiously into the little room in which she had spent the night and slammed the door so she could pace the floor alone. Back and forth she walked, from the door to the desk, the desk to the door. She looked up at the small window, where occasional gusts of rain blew against the panes, reminding her that the water continued to fall and she continued to be a prisoner. Well, she wouldn't be for long. She would force that barbaric man to drive her back down the mountain. Force him? She rearranged her thinking slightly and acknowledged that she would ask him—kindly. But she was sure he would do it. After all, he probably wanted to be rid of her almost as much as she wanted to get away. Could she trust him to drive her? But she quickly put that thought away. Of course she could. He hadn't bothered her when she had told him to leave her bed. She shuddered to think of what might happen if he wanted to take full advantage of her. It was up to him, for she would be practically helpless to defend herself. She should be grateful . . . *No!* She would only be grateful if he helped her get out of this godforsaken place.

Charly could hear noises on the back porch and her imagination went wild. She had to get away from the sounds—all the sounds. So she opened the door to the room and dashed out onto the front porch. Now! All she could see—and hear—was the rain plunking on the tin roof, pelting the foggy clearing and whispering on the misty forest. She settled into an old rocking chair at the far end of the porch and rocked furiously while she stewed over her helpless predicament.

Eventually a noise at the front door gave notice that she would have company. She refused to look in the direction, but could feel the dominant presence of Noah as he took a chair near her. He offered no conversation at first, but soft sounds told her that he was eating.

Finally Charly broke the strained silence. "Will you help me get my car unstuck today—please?" Her voice quivered slightly with emotion.

Noah didn't answer at first, and she glanced his way to see if he heard her. When he had her attention, he said in a low, serious voice, "I'll try to help you out. But with no letup in this rain, the chances of doing that right now aren't very good."

"Oh, I can wait. When the rain stops, can we go down and see about the car?" Charly felt almost like a child, asking for an ice cream cone.

He paused before answering. "Sure, when the rain stops we'll see about it. Meantime, why don't we try to be civilized toward one another?"

Charly looked at him sharply. "Somehow I feel like I'm the only civilized one around here! What are you suggesting, now that the squirrels are skinned?"

He ignored her stabbing remark and leaned toward her. "We can start with your telling me exactly what you're doing up here alone. What is your business?"

Charly took a breath, determined to be convincing in her explanation of the importance of her job. Although she hadn't been successful in convincing Walter, Noah was younger and probably more reasonable and aware of the power of her influential position. "I'm from the Bureau of Land Management's regional office in Atlanta. I've been sent up here to evaluate the proper usage of this land and recommend viable alternatives." There! she thought with satisfaction. That sounds official enough.

But Noah was unimpressed. He was concerned with other aspects of the job rather than its importance. "Alone? They sent a woman—like you—alone to do a job like that?"

"What do you mean, 'like me'? Of course. This is just

a routine job, Noah." Charly pulled herself up indignantly.

Amusement played at Noah's lips as he countered. "Is it routine for you to spend the night in your client's bed and wear his clothes?"

"No. You know this has turned into a very nonroutine experience!" Charly stormed at Noah's arrogant, laughing face. "But usually my 'clients,' as you call them, are more accommodating than you!"

His eyes penetrated her harshly as his words mocked her. "Why, I don't know how anyone could be more accommodating than Walt and I. We have fed you, and I have given you my clothes and my bed. What more do you want from us? The very land we live on?"

Charly stood up, shaking with fury at the impudence of the man. "For starters, I'd like to leave this damned place!"

"Believe me, Wildcat, I'll do everything in my power to accomplish that!" He stood, towering over her, and stalked into the house, followed by a discontented Charly.

"That reminds me," she blazed at his back, ignoring his mocking name for her. "Where are my clothes?"

Noah left the plate he had been using in the kitchen. "Out there." He nodded toward the back porch.

Charly peered in the direction of his nod and then gaped in horror. There, stretched from a short, makeshift clothesline on the back porch, were her blouse, slacks, panties, and bra!

His voice pulled her horrified eyes back to his amused face. "I washed them out for you last night, but, with all the dampness in the air, they just haven't had a chance to dry. We can hang them in front of the fireplace if you want."

Oh! She had completely forgotten about her wet, muddy clothes! And he had taken care of them himself—had washed them! How could she have been so careless? And now they dangled seductively, dancing in the wind—the thin blouse, the long legs of the slacks, that lacy bra—why did she ever choose such a frilly thing?—and her bikini panties. "I'll take them!" she gasped, lunging for the door. She couldn't imagine which was worse: to have them suspended across the windows, swinging merrily, or draped in front of the fireplace for close inspection. Of course, Noah had already done that! Damn him!

She grabbed the offending garments and hustled inside with them. She would put them in her room—well, *his* room—oh, hell—the room she was using for now. She tried to find a suitable place in the small room for the wet clothes, but finally settled on a couple of hooks from which the dried vegetables hung. As she once again paced the floor, the sight of her lacy bra draped intimately with a string of dried peppers was almost funny. Almost.

Suddenly she knew what she had to do. She yanked the damp clothes off their inappropriate driers and folded them altogether into a small, compact package and stuffed them into her purse. Emerging into the big room, she confronted Noah. "I'd like to go now. Will you take me to my car so that I can leave?" Her pink lips thinned into a determined line and her bronze eyes seemed darker than before.

Noah looked up with a surprised expression. "But it hasn't stopped raining. I told you . . ."

"I don't care what you told me," she interrupted. "I want to go now. If I have to wait for the rain to stop, I may never get away from here. At least it's daylight and I can see where I'm going."

He shook his dark head. "I don't think it's wise. That road is in poor condition and hasn't improved during the night. In fact, with all the rain it's much worse. You see, the roadbed isn't packed enough. There's no base of rocks underneath. It's just a graded path through the trees. I doubt if we can get your car out." He sat back leisurely on his haunches and Charly could see that he'd been sharpening a huge hunting knife. He made no effort to move.

There was something about his arrogant, leisurely, know-it-all attitude that infuriated Charly and she found herself raging at him. "Get up! You can take me down there in your truck! And if we can't get the car out, then you can just take me all the way back to town! After all, I'm . . ." Her voice was shrill and almost out of control.

Immediately he was beside her, grabbing her forearms with his powerful hands, shaking her slightly. He pulled her close to him and Charly found herself looking directly into his forceful mouth; past the black beard, which appeared wiry, but she knew it felt like velvet; past the white, white teeth, the occasional flip of his pink tongue as he at once assailed her and calmed her with words that tumbled in short breaths on her face.

"Hey, Wildcat, get ahold of yourself. You're not going anywhere in this rain. Didn't I tell you last night we're in for *days* of rain? Now, just calm down. You'll leave here when I *say* you can and not until."

Momentarily Charly was mesmerized by his power and the absolute authority of his words. Involuntarily she swayed toward him, seeking his strength. Then, abruptly, she was shoved away from him. She stood before him, drawn magnetically toward him, although they weren't touching. Finally she found her voice. "I . . . I want to leave. Will . . . will you take me?" She felt weak, drained, like a child again, this time not asking but begging for a treat. She hated that feeling, and at that instant she hated this ruffian called Noah.

He looked at her steadily. "No. I will not take the truck out onto this mountain road and risk getting it stuck, too. That's insane." He turned away from her and stooped to continue the job he had started.

Charly spoke above the nerve-wracking grinding of

steel on steel. "Well, I'm . . . I'm going. I'll just go by myself." She paused, waiting for his response.

There was none. He didn't even look up at her.

"Thank you for everything—the food, the clothes . . . Oh, I'll see that you get your clothes back." She looked down at her attire—the blue worn shirt, the baggy jeans, her bare feet. "I'm going now."

He still didn't give her any recognition, continuing his hateful chore.

She walked to the door alone and onto the front porch, where occasional gusts of wind blew wet spray into her face. She looked at the steps and there, on the bottom step, were her smart wedge-heeled shoes, pelted into an unhappy heap where she had left them last night in the rain. She skipped over them as she scampered purposely out into the rain. Before she had gone any further than the clearing, while the house was still in sight, Charly heard a shout. Turning, she saw Noah striding toward her through the rain. He held a coat in one hand and a shovel in the other. As he reached her, she could see he was angry—extremely angry. Charly turned away from him and felt something slap her on the back, and she was roughly pushed into the heavy, stiff raincoat that belonged to Walt. She had worn it earlier in the day for her trip down the outhouse path. She allowed herself to be dressed in the coat, but refused to look again into Noah's face until he turned her himself, buttoning the front.

Forced to look into his rain-streaked face, Charly noted with distraction the drops of water that glistened and clung to his curly beard. She had a brief, wild desire to lick those silvery drops away and bury her face in his dark beard.

But he broke the spell, railing angrily at her, flashing those white teeth. "You are the damnedest, stubbornest, most hardheaded female I've ever seen! Don't you have any sense in that thick head of yours? I told you what it was like out here! Don't you believe me? I guess you don't, or you wouldn't be out here. Well, let's go and I'll show you that this is absolutely impossible, futile, and a useless waste of time." He pushed her along with him as he strode across the mud and rocks. "This is crazy and one of the most damn-fool things I've done in a long, long time. I've never met such an obstinate female!" He continued his tirade as they sloshed along. She guessed it made him feel better to justify why he was following her. So Charly was quiet. She made no comment and allowed him to vent his anger and frustration on her while they made the arduous slow trek through the mud. At least he had come along with her, and he had brought a shovel, so he intended to try to help her. And that's all she wanted. For she knew that with a little help she could dislodge the car and leave this damnable mountain. And she wanted that fervently.

At last the white compact car was in sight—barely. It was tilted sharply to one side and appeared to be buried up to the fenders in mud and tall grass. The futile, sad sight of the vehicle made Charly want to cry. She knew—at that moment—it was absolutely, totally useless for them to try to release the car from its muddy grave. Noah was right.

She stood immobile, gaping forlornly at the sight as Noah made some attempts to free it. With the shovel, he dug around each sunken fender. Then he walked around the car, assessing the extent of the problem.

Finally he straightened and returned to her, his boots and pants legs covered with mud. "It's impossible for us to get it out alone. Even if I could dig down to the tires, we would need another vehicle to help pull it out of the hole it's in. The car slid into the drainage ditch to the side of the road and . . ."

His words spelled the dismal future to Charly and she hated to face the inevitable. With tears in her brown eyes, she said stubbornly, "Then I'll just walk out of here." Her words were punctuated by a loud crack as lightning flashed somewhere near them, followed by a ponderous thunderclap.

His voice was thunderous above the sounds of the gathering storm. "Another electrical storm is brewing. You can't walk out of here. It's too far and too dangerous."

"I'll show you! I'll go where I want to go!" Charly answered fervently and brushed past him.

She had barely taken two steps when she felt a strong force on her arms, wheeling her around.

"You are not walking out of here. I'll see that you get out safely, but not now. Not today. You'll just have to wait." His voice was a threatening rumble.

Charly jerked free of his grasp. "I won't wait! You won't tell me what to do!"

"I just did!" His arm shot out to impede her passage.

Suddenly, before she knew what she was doing, Charly was screaming at him, flailing at him, kicking his legs. The more viciously she fought him, the tighter, closer he held her. She twisted, slapped, kicked, tried every trick she ever knew from fighting with her brothers as a child. But he just held on to her, not letting go, holding her close. His restraint checked the force and damage of her lashings, but that didn't deter the vigorousness of her assault. She vented every frustration of the last twenty-four hours on the man who held her, preventing her from leaving.

Eventually the force of her energetic flinging plummeted them to the ground and they rolled together, fighting, sliding, oozing through the slimy mud. Heaving with exhaustion, Charly finally stopped fighting. She was defeated. She felt the mire under her neck and hands and in her hair as Noah sat lightly astradle her, pinning her arms above her head.

"Okay, Wildcat, are you ready to go back home?" he hissed.

"Home? It's not my home—nor yours either!" Charly

spat through gritty teeth. "I hate you, Noah Van Horn. I will never forget this . . . this atrocity. You'll be sorry you ever stopped me! I'm a government employee, remember, and I'll report every bit of this . . . assault. People will be looking for me."

"Oh, shut up. I'm already sorry! I'm sorry you ever set foot on this mountain with your big brown eyes and skinny hips and big breasts! Now get up and come on. You're a miserable sight now." He pulled Charly to her feet and held tightly to her wrist as they made their way, stumbling back up the mountain through the storm, back to the cabin prison.

CHAPTER FOUR

By the time they had worked their way back to the cabin in the storm, Charly was thoroughly wet, even though she wore the old man's coat. She could feel her hair matted with the spiteful mud and she resented the fact that, in her mind, Noah had caused the mess she was in now. The storm bristled around them and Charly cringed as a streak of lightning flashed in the clearing. It hadn't occurred to her that if she continued down the mountain road she would be in the midst of this same storm—by herself.

Once again she was wet and cold and tired, and once again she was seeking shelter in the remote cabin. As they ran around to the back of the house, Charly wondered briefly if Lewis had tried to reach her, if there was a faint chance of her being rescued tonight. No, he probably wouldn't even miss her yet. She'd only been out of touch with the world for twenty-four hours, and yet she felt that she'd stepped back in time and had been away for days.

"Just leave the coat here and I'll get a pan of water for your hair. We have to wash that mud out of it. Then I'll show you the shower." Noah's tight, commanding voice interrupted her rambling thoughts and she looked up to him. But he was too busy to give her any more attention, removing his muddy boots and entering the house to emerge moments later with a small pan of water.

This time he looked at her, his blue eyes sharply cutting into her as he snapped, "Well, come on, Wildcat. Get with it. We have a job ahead getting that pile of hair clean. Drop the coat, sit down here, and lean your head back. I'll get most of the heavy mud out now, and you can shower it cleaner in a few minutes."

Charly did as she was told. The fighting spirit was gone out of her now. She had been defeated and knew she would be spending another night in the loathsome cabin. She wasn't sure when—or if—she'd be leaving her unusual prison. Oh, God—what if—but *no,* Lewis would find her . . . eventually. He would surely alert the authorities. She wouldn't have to remain here forever.

Charly felt the gentle tugging on her hair as Noah worked to clean it. She gasped as its icy chill touched her scalp. He hadn't even bothered to warm it up.

"Sorry the water's so cold. One of our inconveniences up here is lack of hot water. And I didn't take the time to warm it." Noah apologized and continued his task of washing her hair.

"*One* of the inconveniences?" Charly snapped harshly. "The biggest inconvenience is *being* here!"

"Oh, come on, Wildcat. When you get used to it, it's not so bad up here. Why don't you try to enjoy the simple pleasures? Haven't you ever had to make the best of a situation?" His voice had mellowed as the anger faded.

Apparently he had decided to make the best of it—or, Charly feared, take advantage of it. The first pan of water was tossed out and another quickly replaced it. This one was warm. Charly was lost in the pleasurable sensations of Noah's hands working with her hair, massaging her scalp, tugging, stroking the length of it. She closed her eyes briefly, daring to enjoy the hypnotic motions of his long fingers. She signed, relaxing in spite of her anger, her tenseness. Perhaps she should just make the best of it and resign herself to another night here.

"There!" His rumbling voice interrupted Charly's trance. "That's as good as I can do. You'll have to clean the rest off in the shower. Come on, and I'll show you where it is."

She rose and followed him down the steps and under the eaves of the house to a small square platform of bricks. Charly looked up and saw with alarm the bare shower head.

"Not very fancy, but this is it," Noah admitted.

"This . . . this open-air contraption is the shower you expect me to use?" Charly sputtered.

"Sure. Why not? You turn it on here and soap and shampoo are here . . ." He proceeded to show her what she needed. "The one drawback is that we don't have hot water, so you'll have to make it quick."

"*No* hot water?" Charly gasped.

He shrugged. "Sorry. I'm not very much of a plumber. I did well to rig this shower with piped water. You see, it hooks in with the piped water to the kitchen directly above. Actually, a cold shower is good for you. It gets your blood flowing and is invigorating." He grinned at her while she gaped from Noah's taunting face to the shower head to the pipes above them and back to Noah's face.

"You're crazy if you think I'm going to shower here," she concluded.

"Where do you propose to do it?" he challenged, folding his arms and eyeing her with one raised eyebrow.

"I'll . . . I don't know. But I won't shower here, with no hot water and . . . no curtains!"

"Don't worry, Wildcat. I won't look. I'll get you a towel and a change of clothes." He was gone before Charly had a chance to protest.

She again examined the open-to-the-woods shower and decided that she would not strip down and expose herself to the world—whatever "world" was out there in the forest. She met Noah on the porch as he returned with the promised items. "Don't bother," she informed him. "I'm not using that thing."

He examined her skeptically for a moment, then nodded. "Suit yourself. But you really need to get your hair clean. And it wouldn't hurt the rest of you, either."

Charly's bronze eyes snapped as she propped her fists on her hips. "I suppose so! And if it weren't for you rolling me in the mud, damn you, I wouldn't look like this! You aren't Mr. Clean, you know!"

He grinned agreeably. "You're right, Wildcat. We both need a shower. Let's take one together. I'll help you get your hair clean and you can scrub my back!" His long arm draped around her shoulders and he attempted to turn her around.

But she stood firmly. "I'm not amused. I told you, I'm not showering there. And certainly not with you!"

"Well, if you're going to be so stubborn about it, I think I'll go ahead. Why don't you come down and hold my towel for me? If you promise you won't look." His rumbling laughter followed him down the steps while Charly looked away angrily. He was getting his laughs at her expense, and she was furious—furious at him for making her return to the cabin and furious with herself for getting into this predicament in the first place.

Charly folded her arms and sat stubbornly on a nearby stool on the porch. She knew she was too muddy to go into the house and wasn't sure what her next move would be. She could hear the splash of the shower beneath the back porch as it mingled with the continued, steady rainfall. It was accompaniment for faint sounds of a male voice singing about Smoky Mountain rain. It reminded her of the country tune she had heard on the radio as she headed up the mountain the first day. Was that only yesterday? She tried not to pay attention to the low masculine singing and concentrated on what to do next. Somewhere in the back of her mind she knew that she would eventually have to give in and bathe in that infuriating shower. And, of course, Noah knew she would, too, which made her even more resentful toward him. He was an arrogant, despicable, always-right ruffian who happened to be one of the most virile, sensuous males she had ever known. And she hated him for being that way.

Soon the sounds of water and singing ceased and Noah emerged fresh, clean, and—nude. Charly gawked at his bare body coming up the stairs toward her and only realized when he reached the top of the steps that he had a beige towel tucked low around his waist. Her eyes followed the dark trail of hair upward from the towel, the length of his flat belly, to the hairy patch that spread across his chest. His penetrating blue eyes stood out sharply in the mass of dark hair that surrounded his body and seemed to be fully aware of Charly's provocative thoughts. She felt her face blush pink and tingly as he stopped close beside her.

His hand reached out and cupped her chin, ever so gently, tilting it upward as he murmured, "You promised you wouldn't look. Go ahead and take your shower while I dress. I left your towel and clean clothes down there on a stool, so you won't have to come up like this. But you'd better hurry before I take back my promise not to look, *too.*"

He left her dazed and embarrassed until she realized that he probably meant what he said, and, if she was going to take a shower—without him—she'd better hurry.

The first blast of icy cold water took her breath and a loud shriek involuntarily escaped her lips. She was tempted to stop the shower immediately to get away from that bitter blast, but she had already soaped her hair. She rinsed it quickly, letting the water trail from her scalp, down her back, like a thousand icy needles nipping at her. She tried to discover the invigorating pleasure Noah referred to, but the chilly tingling was almost painful to her sensitive skin. "Invigorating" indeed! She was thoroughly chilled. It was such sweet relief to cut the water off.

Forcefully, she scrubbed her body with the towel, trying desperately to rub some vitality back into her cold limbs. She grabbed the clothes Noah left for her and hugged them to her. The jeans were soft and faded, and a red plaid flannel shirt had never looked so welcome and warm. Once again she gratefully donned his clothing, basking in their comfort. Wrapping the towel around her thick, dripping hair, she trooped upstairs to seek out the warmth of the fireplace.

"Have a seat by the fire and get warmed up while I fry these squirrels for supper," Noah remarked easily from the kitchen.

Charly looked at him sharply and tried to ignore the fact that he stood barechested, and that she was alone with him. It seemed that since her arrival, Simms was spending more and more of his time in his bedroom. "Don't bother frying any of . . . that for me, because I won't eat any of it. I won't." She tried to emphasize her pronouncement. He would not persuade her to change her mind about this. Taking a cold shower when you are covered with mud is one thing, but eating . . . She shuddered involuntarily as she thought about it.

He walked toward her with two small glasses of wine, amusement playing at his lips as he pressed the glass into her hand. "Well, then, how about some wine? Or is it too domestic for you?"

Charly took the glass without letting her eyes leave his. "Thanks," she murmured, raising the glass to him. "This seems to be the only pleasant thing up here."

"Oh, it's too bad you feel that way. I'd like to change your mind. You aren't offended by my being shirtless, are you? It's not exactly cocktail attire, but then we're hardly at the Ritz." A devilish grin spread across his face, lighting those flashing blue eyes.

Charly snapped him a disgusted look. "Hardly. But I'm

getting accustomed to the hairy bears in these mountains."

He sat on the hearth, propping his elbows on his knees, and motioned her toward the comfortable stuffed chair. His matter-of-fact answer to her caustic remark caught her by surprise. "Well, we'll have to do something about that. You can cut my hair tomorrow. I've needed a trim for a while anyway, but just haven't had a chance to get to town for one."

Charly sat in the soft chair and curled her legs under her. She answered slowly and distinctly. "When you take me to town tomorrow, you can just get your hair cut. I'm certainly not doing it."

"Don't make idle threats, Wildcat. You seem to make it a habit of eating your words! I'll show you how it's done."

She lifted her head defiantly. "Oh, I know how it's done. I could do it, if I wanted to. I just don't choose to. I have a younger brother and trimmed his hair for years until he got to be a teenager and wouldn't let me touch it anymore."

"A younger brother, huh? Is he the one who gave you the name? Short for Charlotte?"

Charly nodded with a soft smile. "Yes. Stevie couldn't say my name—it's Charlene. Sounded like 'Charly' to him and it seemed to fit, so everyone picked it up."

"Where is Stevie now? Atlanta?"

"Steve," Charly corrected. "He's trying to make me realize that 'Stevie' doesn't fit a six-foot-three twenty-two-year-old. I'm finding my old habit hard to break. He's at home in Pennsylvania. Actually, he's at Penn State."

"You're from Pennsylvania? How long have you been in Atlanta?"

Charly nodded. "I'm from Philly, and I've been in Atlanta four months now. Before that I worked out of D.C., so I've been away from home over ten years. It's funny.

Both of my brothers still live within shouting distance of our home, while I've been away and on my own since I was eighteen. I guess I'm too independent to stay."

"So you're the kid in the middle, huh? That makes you independent, you know. Makes you want to prove that you can do what anyone else does."

"I thought that was the oldest child who developed the strongest traits—leadership qualities and all of that." Charly smiled and sipped her blackberry wine.

Noah shrugged and walked over to get the wine carafe to refill their dwindling glasses. "Naw. Maybe leadership. But who wants to lead? Middle kids grow up proving themselves, and when they're adults they know they can do it and spin their wheels proving it to the world."

"That's a lot of psychological introspection for a backwoodsman who spins his wheels hunting squirrels."

"Hunting gives me a lot of time for thinking. Maybe that explains why you were willing to tackle this mountain as a routine assignment. Who are you trying to impress this time? Not your parents." He halted, giving Charly an opportunity to answer.

Charly replied eagerly, not realizing that she was relaxing for the first time with Noah and enjoying a conversation with him. "No. I'm beyond that. I guess I'm trying to prove myself to Lewis—my boss. He—" Charly stopped abruptly and reversed her line of conversation. "I want to show him that I can handle anything that comes into the office—that field work is something I can do, too—not just paperwork."

Perceptively, Noah asked, "Is that all you want to prove to him?"

Charly's brown eyes met his. "Yes. That's all," she answered shortly, denying with her eyes what he seemed to know. But it was left unsaid. Charly looked away, feeling that those blue eyes of Noah stripped her to her soul and knew what was going on inside her—maybe even better than she did. Yet she had only known him less than twenty-four hours. How could he be so all-knowing? It was those eyes—those devil-blue eyes that had stripped her clothes the first time she met him. Now they delved even deeper.

"Well, I'd better get busy if we're to have supper tonight." Noah rose and pulled a T-shirt over his head before going into the kitchen.

"Don't bother with me. I won't eat what you're preparing."

"Oh, come on, Wildcat. You'll like it if you give it a chance." He persuaded with humor in his voice.

"No. I won't." Charly was adamant about that. Suddenly she remembered her still-wet clothes packaged-up in her purse. She went out onto the porch to retrieve the muddy purse and the items within. Thank goodness, at least her clothes were still relatively clean. Wrinkled, but clean. She busied herself with their care, turning her back on the darkness outside, where rain continued to pelt the wet forest. When would it ever stop?

On returning, she questioned Noah. "Do you mind if I use this . . . your room again tonight?"

He smiled rakishly at her. "Of course you may use it. We backwoods people want you to know how accommodating we are! I'll even warm the bed for you . . ."

Charly turned away from his mocking face and stalked into the little room, trying fervently to escape the sounds of his laughter. She didn't think the joke very funny at all. In fact, part of her feared that he would do just that—warm her bed and her along with it sometime during the night. Another part of her desired it. After all, he was aggravatingly appealing. And both of those reasons were why she absolutely had to leave the mountain tomorrow, she resolved as she again hung her lacy bra on the hook alongside the dried peppers. She looked at the sight and laughed. Lewis wouldn't believe all this. And there were times when Charly could hardly believe it, either.

Lewis will probably be horrified when he learns everything about this miserable little excursion of mine, she thought. He is so . . . refined and smooth, damn him. In fact, in his own slick, superior way, he had been trying to get into her bed for the four months she had been in his department. And this backwoods ruffian had managed it in one night. Of cou.se, nothing had happened—what was she thinking? It was almost as if— *Oh, no!* She just had to get away—soon! And where? Back to Lewis? Now, after this assignment failure, she might not be able to resist his advances any more. And she felt sure it would cost Charly her job if she continued to refuse him. But she was determined not to fall into that trap of his. She knew that one of the office girls spent an occasional weekend with him. The girl had not been able to keep her mouth shut, for going to bed with the boss was enough to brag about. Charly refused to join that little group. She'd request a transfer first.

Charly took the towel off her wet hair and bent over at the waist, drying it vigorously with the towel. From that position she noticed some of the books lining the wall. There was an odd assortment of everything from architecture and art to law, as well as several books on the preparation and preservation of natural foods. She supposed they all belonged to Noah and gave a general perspective of the man and his interests. But why would he need *Black's Law Dictionary* alongside *Preparing Wild Game? Foxfire* and *The Architectural Sourcebook? Drawing in Perspective* and *You and the Law?* The collection was a strange one.

Curious, she straightened and walked over to the cluttered desk. She riffled through some of the papers, with pencil sketches of everything from a simple flower to a large woolly bear rearing on two legs. Some of them were very good; some were mediocre. She assumed that they, too, were the product of Noah. This was a strange and complicated man she had encountered. Actually, he wasn't a backwoodsman at all. Then who was he? And what was he doing in a place like this? He puzzled her, yet attracted her . . .

A knock at her door startled Charly, and she jerked her hand guiltily away from the desk. She moved away from it, feeling for all the world like a guilty child with her hand in the cookie jar. Purposefully, she began rubbing her wet hair with the towel. "Yes?"

Noah opened the door slightly, giving her an outline of his towering form. "Supper's ready. Walt's not feeling well and has gone to bed. I'm all alone. Come on and eat with me."

She glared at him, trying to discern just where those deep blue eyes were in the darkness that surrounded him. "You can go to hell alone, for all I care! I told you I'm not eating any damned squirrel, and I mean it!"

"How about a little more wine?" He raised the hidden carafe.

Charly eyed the wine for a moment, then nodded, agreeing silently and trying to ignore the marvelous aroma that entered the room when he opened the door. But no! She would never admit it was a marvelous aroma! Never! And certainly not to this ruffian who poured her wine so steadily, then turned away from her without another word.

Noah ate in silence without her. Charly combed the tangles out of her hair and stood in front of the fireplace to dry it. She wondered what it would look like without the benefits of blow dryer and electric curlers. Well, she couldn't worry about that. Who cared if she looked like a witch anyway? She certainly wasn't trying to be pretty for anyone up in these mountains. She wondered briefly about Walt's illness, but Noah didn't seem concerned about him, so she dismissed her own concern. After all, he was a very old man and was entitled to feel bad occasionally.

Charly busied herself during the evening, drying her thick hair, checking on her clothes, pacing the floor. She spent a lot of time at the latter. She was extremely hungry, but wouldn't admit it and ignored the loud grumbling in her empty stomach. She hadn't eaten since the late breakfast of ham and biscuits, but that was long since gone. She had hiked—and fought—and expended a lot of energy arguing with Noah since her last meal. But she would never admit that she was hungry, especially to that arrogant man, who persisted in crossing her. And most of the time he had gotten his way. She was still here, which is what he had predicted. Damn him! He knew it all. He knew she wouldn't be leaving anytime soon. What if she were stuck here in this remote cabin all week? What if she couldn't get away from Noah? What if . . .

Suddenly Charly resorted to her remaining emotional response—tears. She had fluctuated from anger to determination to frustration during the course of the day and the only thing left to vent her feelings was to cry. It was a sudden, unavoidable, uncontrollable sobbing that racked her body and reduced her to a huddled heap on the bed. She was grateful for the darkness that enveloped her and the lonely bed where she could be alone in her misery. Her weeping continued into the night. Charly lost track of time and wasn't sure if it had been an hour or less. She just knew that she was terribly unhappy over the turn of events and wanted to obliterate it all by washing it away—with tears and the miserable, hateful rain, which still pelted the tin roof.

Charly didn't hear the door open quietly, nor did she see the large figure that gathered her in his arms. She only knew that someone was holding her close, comforting, warming her. She sought the offered solace, clung to it, cloaked herself in his protecting, secure arms.

"There, there, Charly," he murmured softly.

It was the first time he had ever called her anything but "wildcat" or "city lady." And it was nice—so nice. Her name rumbled from his low voice and vibrated from his body directly into hers. "Charly . . . Charly . . ."

She buried her face against his hard chest with its cushion of soft hair and inhaled his clean, slightly smoky, masculine scent. He held her securely, without moving, until her sobbing ceased, and she continued to cling to his security.

No words passed between them. It wasn't necessary. Shared feelings were all that mattered. They lay together for a long time, enjoying, drawing from each other.

Finally, she moved, raising her tousled head from the muscular chest that pillowed her. The crying had left her voice hoarse and she felt abashed by her stereotypical feminine actions. "Noah, I'm sorry. I didn't mean to . . ."

Noah's hand caressed her hair, pushing back a part of it that fell across her face. "You don't have to explain, Charly. I understand. I do understand."

She smiled wanly, saying, "I don't see how you possibly could. You hardly know me . . ."

He sighed, trailing his finger along her cheek. "I know you're soft, and feminine, and resent the fact that you're stuck with the inconveniences of this place. You're just too refined to find anything redeemable in a place like this—or someone like me."

She sat up and smiled. "Now, I'm not that 'refined.' You forgot what a wildcat I am."

He laughed a low rumble. "Oh, no. I haven't forgotten that. You've spiced up my dull life remarkably since you arrived, Charly."

"I know I've caused you some trouble, but . . ."

He sat up. "You've opposed me more in the last twenty-four hours than anyone has in the last two years. Everyone has been sickeningly nice to me, agreeing with me, catering to me. It's true! I know you won't believe me, Charly, but I've enjoyed your challenges. I lead a simple life now. No one here challenges me. Sometimes I miss that."

"Well, if a challenge is all I've given you in exchange for safe harbor, clothes, food, and a dry bed, you're hardly being repaid," Charly said, laughing softly.

"Oh, Charly, you've given me much more than a challenge. You've inspired me."

"Inspired you? To what? How about being inspired to fix me a little something to eat?"

He smiled and winked. "I'd love it. Come with me."

Dutifully, Charly followed him into the big room.

CHAPTER FIVE

Charly awakened to a quiet morning, with daylight filtering softly through the small window. She lay there for a moment, wondering what seemed so unusual, so stark about the place. Obviously, she was still in the mountain cabin where Noah had held her again last night, had comforted her when she cried.

She closed her eyes and smiled to herself, recalling her warm feelings of pleasure when he embraced her and held her close. Sometimes just holding, just being close to someone could be comforting. He seemed to know that, for holding her was all he had done. He made no other advances, although she knew he wanted her. She had felt his desire, known of his wishes while they were close. And yet he hadn't used his strength to overpower her. Strange man, this Noah. Strange and . . . sensual. Oh, yes, very sensual. Oh, my God! What am I thinking? I've got to get out of here—soon! Her eyes popped open and she listened.

What was so different from the other mountain morning? What—then she knew! *No sounds of rain!* There was no water hitting the roof after more than forty-eight hours! Was it possible that the rain had stopped and—

Charly bounded excitedly out of bed and ran to the window. She searched the gray sky where, for the moment, no rain was falling. She was ecstatic and quickly dressed, then opened the door into the big room, which was empty. All was quiet—not even a fire in the blackened fireplace. The back door was open and she glanced outside.

Noah stood on the back porch with his back to her. He was shirtless and faced a mirror that he had hung on the support post. Charly moved closer, watching him with interest for a few moments. She couldn't help but admire him. Noah was a very virile, handsome man. His straight back was muscular and hips slim as he stood with long legs apart, concentrating on his task. The muscles flexed with his movements, and Charly realized—with inner alarm—that he must be shaving! That marvelous beard!

Charly gasped audibly and caught those intense, blue eyes of his smiling at her from the mirror's reflection. She wondered if he knew how long she had stood there, gawking at his body.

"Morning," he greeted her.

"Good morning." Charly joined him on the porch. "You're not shaving your beard, are you?" She tried to sound casual, but the question itself was defensive.

He turned around to face her, small silvery scissors in his hand. "No, just trimming it. Don't you think it's about time? Or do you think I should shave it off completely?"

Charly shook her head and answered a little too quickly to be casual. "Oh, no! I like it. It looks nice . . . on you, especially now that you've trimmed it. It adds some interest and a little mystery to your image."

He turned back to his project in the mirror. "Mystery, hmmm? I thought I let it get too shaggy. Guess I didn't realize it—or care—until you showed up."

"And now you care? Since when did you start caring about my opinion?" Charly folded her arms and leaned against the house, eyeing him boldly.

His response was slow and deliberate. "I care how you feel about the beard because I don't want you to be offended by it . . . when I kiss you. Women have certain feelings about these things and I'm interested in yours."

Charly answered him with a sassy grin. "I told you, it looks nice. But it doesn't really matter what I think about the way it feels . . . because I'm not interested in touching it. And you can just forget about the kissing . . ."

Noah turned around to face her again, a slight smile pulling his lips, which were more visible after the trimming. "Oh, I find it hard to forget about the kissing. You're a very attractive—and kissable—woman, Charly, and I don't want to repel you with something as controversial as a beard. Come on. Surely you want to touch it." He moved forward and, taking her hand, placed the palm against the black velvet of his beard.

His quick movement and electric touch sent jolts of fire through her, and Charly tried to respond to his taunt calmly. Her fingers caressed, then dug into the soft, dark matt. "Now. My natural curiosity has been relieved. Are you satisfied?" Her voice was tight, and she pulled her hand away quickly.

But Noah stepped closer to her. "How about satisfying *my* natural curiosity," he answered quietly, pinning her against the wall.

Charly put both hands on his bare chest as he closed in on her. Although she pushed on him, she only had time for a quick, protesting "No—" before his lips met hers in a soft, wonderfully tender morning kiss.

When he finally spoke, his voice was low. "I'm not satisfied with that, Charly. It doesn't relieve my natural desires at all. It only whets my appetite for more."

"Noah, please . . ." she begged. She couldn't believe that here he was, kissing her, at this hour of the morning—and aspiring for more. And here she was, enjoying it.

"That's my line. Charly . . . please . . . don't stop me . . ." He moved his head toward her again and she knew it would mean another kiss.

Charly pushed again, this time aware of the soft hair on his chest between her fingers. "Noah . . . Noah, stop it.

Please, don't. I . . . did . . . did you notice that it stopped raining?" She sputtered inanely, trying to change the subject.

"Who wants to talk about the weather at a time like this?" His voice was husky.

"I do. I have to talk to you about . . . please, move. Move back a little, Noah. Move back so I can talk to you. It may mean I can go home." Charly couldn't even think straight with the man so close that she could feel his breath on her face. She actually wanted to bury her face in that dark beard and feel those strong arms around her again. She had never before been aroused to such free abandon by anyone, and it scared her. What this man did to her actually frightened her.

Noah sighed heavily and took two steps back from her.

"Much better." Charly smiled, trying to appear calm and collected, when underneath it all she was a wreck. "I . . . I think I'd better take a walk. Then we can discuss my leaving."

"Take a walk?" he puzzled.

She nodded quickly and headed down the steps. "Take a walk down your damned little path to your damned little out-house. Oh—I hate this place!"

His rumbling, low laughter followed her and he promised, "I'll get us some coffee and maybe we can continue this *stimulating* conversation!"

There was something in his manner, his infuriatingly arrogant words that filled her with fury as she stomped down the path. He aroused such passions within her—rage, fear, desire—oh, God! the desire—that she felt almost out of control whenever they were together. Actually, she was out of control of her feelings, as well as her crazy situation. Usually she remained cool and in command of her emotions—even her desires. Never had she wanted a man like she wanted this one. Oh, yes, she was certainly glad to be leaving this bewitching place today.

"Here, have some coffee. Do you take it black?" He met her at the back steps, handed her the cup of steaming liquid, then sat on one of the lower steps, sipping his coffee. He had donned a shirt—blue to match his eyes.

"Yes. Thank you." And she joined him, gazing morosely out at the misty forest, where it had started to rain again. "I should have known it was short-lived. The break in the rain. How long does it rain in this damn place?"

"Hell, I'm no weatherman! I told you forty days and forty nights. After that, we'll see!"

"Oh, God! Spare me forty days in this cabin!" she exclaimed, horrified.

His voice was tinged with humor, but he didn't look around at her. "How about forty nights? They could be pleasant—exciting if you'd allow them to be." He drank deeply of the dark brew.

Charly raised her eyebrows. "If I'd allow *what?* This place isn't pleasant, it's boring."

"I'm offering to make things more exciting than last night—and much more satisfying. It wouldn't be boring, I promise." His voice was low and matter-of-fact.

"Guaranteed?" she laughed. "Actually, Noah, all I want to do is to leave here." It was a lie. She wondered if he knew it, too.

He emptied his cup. "You may as well resign yourself. You're here for a while. The rain doesn't show any signs of stopping—at least any time soon."

She gazed futilely out at the forest, knowing he was right. "I'm just so . . . frustrated at being here. Don't you find this boring?"

"I'm here by choice, and I don't find it boring. I'm not here to be entertained."

"Then what are you doing here?"

"Let's take a walk, Charly." He stood and turned to her.

"In the rain?"

"You didn't mind it yesterday. Anyway, it's not raining very hard. Just a light drizzle. It's a nice time to walk in the forest."

Gamely, she followed him away from the cabin, and they entered the quiet green tunnels provided by the thick growth of oaks and red maples and black gums. Charly hurried to catch up with Noah's long strides. "You didn't answer my question, Noah. Why are you here?"

"I lost my wife and child in an accident two years ago. I tried to escape from my grief and ended up here."

"Noah—" Charly halted and reached out for his arm.

He stopped and looked at her, his eyes deep and dark.

"Noah, I'm sorry. I didn't mean to . . ." Charly was at a loss for words, but her expression told Noah her feelings of sympathy.

His voice was gentle, almost consoling her. "It's all right, Charly. Really, it is. My wife and two-year-old son were killed in a car wreck. I couldn't handle my grief very well."

"If it's too painful to talk about it, please don't."

Noah took her hand and helped her up a sharp ravine before answering. "Not unless it's too painful for you. It's been two years since the accident. I can handle it now."

"This is none of my business, Noah . . ." Charly felt uncomfortable, but Noah obviously had settled it all in his mind.

He continued to hold tight, leading her along rapidly. Then, as if something pulled him back toward her, he slowed and looked at her. "Listen—stop walking and listen to the wind and rain, Charly."

She obeyed and stood with him, both of them tuning in to the almost imperceptible sounds of the wind whispering through the trees somewhere above them and the rain faintly falling on the leaves. It was extremely quiet.

"I . . . I don't hear very much, Noah," Charly finally admitted.

"I guess that's what I was looking for when I first came up here. Quiet, and not much of anything. About a week after my family was killed, I left my business and came here. It was the only place I could escape to where nobody could find me."

Charly knew she was treading on highly emotional ground with Noah, and she was reluctant to question him further. She was just quiet and let him talk whenever he felt like it.

"I will admit I was escaping—trying to. There's really no escaping, though. And I felt guilty."

"Guilty?"

He nodded. "Guilty because it was them instead of me. You know—the typical 'why am I still alive?' syndrome everyone goes through when they lose someone they love. Well, I wallowed in it, and it took me a long time to realize that I wouldn't die, too, just because I wanted to. Oh, God, I wanted to!"

"Why did you come here to the mountains?"

"Oh, I guess I wanted to punish myself, as well as escape from civilization. This seemed to be a good place for that. No civilization, or signs of it. No electricity, hard to live, no hot water—all of that."

"How did you meet Walt? Did you know him?"

"No. He ran across me. I had been sleeping out for about a week. I was sick and a sorry sight. He nursed me with some god-awful herbal tea—I still don't know what it was—and, in spite of myself, I lived."

"And you've been here ever since?"

"Not exactly. After about a year, I pulled myself together enough to go back and settle things with my business partner. Needless to say, he was surprised to see me. But I wasn't ready to enter the world again—not permanently —so I just appear occasionally, to straighten my business out and get supplies for Walt. He doesn't know it, but I've been looking out for him for the last year. He would hate to hear me say that, so don't let it slip. He thinks he's still responsible for me. And I like it that way."

"And you're telling me you're not bored up here?" Charly countered.

"Hummm, maybe. But I'm too concerned about Walt to leave him indefinitely now."

Charly stopped dead still, pulling her hand from his grasp as she motioned excitedly. "Noah, the solution is simple. Just help me move him off this mountain. He would be paid a fair market value for his home, giving him a nice nest egg, and we would see that he is placed in a good nursing home or something. Then, with him taken care of, you'd be free, and my job here would be finished. I could go back to Atlanta."

Noah's stone-blue eyes cast viciously at her. "No!" he boomed. "Walt belongs here on this mountain! It would kill him to make him leave! Can't you see that?"

"But, Noah, he'll be closer to medical facilities and . . . people. It'll be for his own good!" Charly couldn't imagine anyone, of his own free will, choosing to live so far from civilization—except Noah, of course. That she understood completely—and was sympathetic toward his reasons. But Walt—

Noah loomed menacing near her, his lips spitefully thin. "I won't be a part of his leaving this mountain. And I'll do everything in my power to keep you from changing his home. He has lived here most of his life and—by God—he'll die here!"

"Well, he just might, we're so far from medical care," Charly flared.

"So be it! It's his own choosing! And no high-assed government official—and a woman at that—is going to come in here and tell him what to do! The man is old. He doesn't have too much longer to live. Can't you leave him in peace?"

"Is that what you think of me?" Charly spewed indignantly. "Well, let me tell you, you backwoods ruffian . . ."

As Charly began to verbally bombard him, Noah turned his back on her and strode away. He didn't even turn when she called him an arrogant bastard and a goddamn fool. He just kept going, out of sight.

It then occurred to Charly that she'd better follow him if she wanted to find her way back to the cabin. So she hurried after him, rounding a large poplar tree to see Noah's receding figure with its blue shirt and shock of dark hair. "Noah—Noah, wait!"

Miserably, angrily, she trailed him back to the cabin. Finally, she reached the porch, pausing to catch her breath. She could hear Noah inside, clanking pans in the kitchen, then a muffled exchange as he talked with Walt. He was probably telling the old man about their latest encounter and her proposal. Damn him, anyway! If Noah wasn't here, she probably would have persuaded Walt to her way of thinking by now. She was still stewing over the situation when Noah appeared on the porch.

He began peeling off his shirt. "Get those scissors over there and trim my hair," he instructed, without a glance her way.

"Just who do you think you are? You don't order me around. Are you crazy?" Charly was still furious and this last insult was all she needed to set her off again.

He glanced at her, his eyes cutting into her. Then he pulled the stool close and straddled it. "Nope. Are you through calling me names?"

Charly's brown eyes narrowed and she propped her fists on her slim hips. "Are *you?*"

He sighed patiently. "Yes, Wild . . . er, Charly. And now I'm ready to get my hair trimmed. The scissors are over there. By the way, I enjoyed the walk. You make such stimulating company."

"Well, you don't! You are rude. You've been away from civilization so long, you've forgotten how to act reasonably."

"Maybe. But there are some things I haven't forgotten."

"I'm sure there are! But what can one expect from a ruffian like you?"

"I don't know. What does one expect?"

Oh, he was maddening! Arrogantly, infuriatingly irritating! Charly seethed at him. "I expect to be treated with respect."

His reply was very blasé. "So do I. Now would you please get the scissors? Trim just a little here, not too much around the ears, and even it out in the back."

Through clenched teeth she muttered, "Now why should I cut your damn hair?"

"Because I asked you to. Come on, Charly. I have a day's work ahead of me. I'll fix your breakfast when we're through—unless, of course, you can cook on a wood stove."

Charly grabbed the scissors with an angry jerk. "No, I haven't had much experience with wood stoves lately. That was more my great-great-grandmother's job!"

Charly was so angry that she fairly shook as she ran her slender fingers through his thick, black hair for the first snip of steel. With measured purpose, Noah grasped her hand with his viselike grip. He pulled her around to face him. "Charly. Calm yourself. I don't have any desire for clipped ears or a Mohawk haircut. So just cool it."

"How do you think I'm going to react when you treat me like a—a child!" She recalled all the times this infuriating man had intimidated her, including now.

He spoke precisely, dragging out the words. "Ah, so that's my mistake? Do you want me to treat you like a woman?"

Charly's undoing was her next challenge, and she knew it the minute she uttered the words. "I don't think you know how. You've been away from a woman for a long time!"

"Not as long as you think. I haven't claimed celibacy yet." In one swift movement he stood, his arms encircling her, his lips kissing hers with such skillful fervor that Charly clung weakly to his back. Her heart beat rapidly against his own powerful pounding and she responded to his demanding lips in spite of herself. His tongue demanded entry, which she readily admitted, unable to resist, unwilling to stop him. His tongue separated her lips and probed her willing mouth, setting up an undeniable motion. She felt his teeth painfully hard against her sensitive lips, and a soft moan escaped her. In another breathless moment it was over, and Noah's fierce, demanding mouth moved above hers.

"Now, let's get on with the business of the day—unless you want to finish this now."

"Noah—" His kiss had left Charly weak-kneed. And she had never—*never*—had such sensual feelings pulsing through her.

"Come on, Charly." Noah sat back heavily on the stool. He had proved a point, and she dare not press him further.

Charly rested her nervous hands for a moment on his bare shoulder. Then, slowly, carefully, she proceeded to clip his hair. As she moved around his seated frame, she began to concentrate on her job, making sure it was straight and not too short, that both sides matched. Charly wasn't even aware of her thigh brushing Noah's leg or her soft breast caressing his shoulder.

But Noah was. He had shut his eyes in a pained expression and there was no conversation between them.

That didn't bother Charly. After all, what would they discuss? That indeed, yes, he knew how to treat a woman like a woman. Or should she admit her inability to respond to anyone like she had to this ruffian? No, these things were better left unsaid. Charly diligently concentrated on the raven hair she ran her fingers through, forcing herself not to look into the sensuous face a few inches below her working hands.

Finally, in a loud rasp, Noah said, "For God's sake, Charly—*hurry!* What do you think I am, a robot? My neck's getting stiff."

She stood back and admired his hair, evaluating her job. "There . . ."

Immediately he was on his feet groping for the broom. "Thanks, Charly. Here, sweep it up while I get breakfast." He reached for the door.

"Aren't you even going to look at it?" she asked, disappointed at his abruptness.

"Ah, yes." He acquiesced and glanced in the little mirror. "Yes, Charly. Nice job. Not too short. It's good. I'll get breakfast." And he was gone.

As Charly swept, she wondered if she was going crazy. Maybe being away from the city—the challenges of her job, the various people she constantly encountered—truly had had its effects on her. First, in a walk in the rain, this stranger had revealed his sensitivity to her. He probably had not discussed his family's tragedy with many people. But he had to her. Then he ordered her to cut his hair, kissed her into submission, and left her to clean up the mess. And yet her anger had diminished and she didn't really object to the sweeping. It was just something that had to be done. Maybe it was Noah's kiss that melted her defenses. God—he aroused her senses! If she didn't leave this place soon—

"Ready to eat?"

"Uh, yes. Just a minute." Charly snapped back to the reality of her imprisonment as the rain started up again in earnest.

As the two of them ate the hearty meal alone, Charly asked about Walter Simms.

"He's still not feeling well. I took his breakfast in to his bed."

"It's not just because I'm here, is it? I hope my presence hasn't been upsetting to him. It seems he's spent a lot of time in his bedroom since I've been here."

Noah shook his head. "He has a bad heart. This happens occasionally. He just feels weak, with no energy. Anyway, I assured him that I'll handle you, and that no government agency will run him off."

The assurance of his voice jolted Charly. He seemed so positive of his ability to prevent her from accomplishing her job. They finished the meal in silence with Charly pondering his statement about "handling" her. Was that his goal? To "handle" her? Or just to protect his friend Walt? She suspected the two meshed into one effort.

They spent the day at various physical labors around the cabin. In spite of the rain, Noah chopped wood. Out of sheer boredom, Charly helped him stack it, donning the funny old straw hat Noah handed her. She even hauled in a load of wood for the fireplace, while he carried some to the kitchen's wood stove.

Noah led her to the cellar, a dank, earthen storage area dug into the side of the mountain. They chose some smoked meat for the night meal, which Noah called "supper," and Charly teasingly corrected him with "dinner."

The garden required some weeding, and Charly bent in the misty rain to help Noah. They loaded themselves with red-ripe tomatoes, fresh, leafy lettuce, and long, green cucumbers for a marvelously fresh salad for "supper."

By evening, Charly slumped into a stuffed chair, her aching body bordering on exhaustion. It had been one of those days where the physical activity had kept her busy, and that in itself kept her happy. There was something gratifying about the hard work done with her hands, and it hadn't given her time to worry about getting off the mountain. She stared into the fireplace where Noah worked patiently to kindle a flame. Soon his efforts paid off and yellowish flames commenced to flicker, growing in size and intensity as they engulfed the carefully stacked logs. It was a peaceful sight, and Charly stared magnetically at the flames and the man who coaxed them.

Noah turned around and casually placed his hand on her knee. "I'm going to take a shower before dark. How about you?" It was a casual 'will you have a cup of coffee, too?' kind of question.

Charly hesitated. She knew that after the hard working day she'd put in she certainly needed a bath. But she couldn't avert the natural protest. "Oh, Noah, that water's so cold . . ."

He smiled at her and she felt the flame's glow spread over her. "Tell you what. I'll give you a pan of warm water from the kettle that's been heating on the stove. You can take a 'bird bath' in your room. How's that sound? Warm enough for you?"

"*Bird* bath?" Charly laughed.

"That's another one of Walt's expressions. Frankly, none of it sounds nearly as much fun as 'skinny dipping'!"

She smiled at him, her bronze eyes dancing with yellow highlights in the firelight. "The 'bird bath' sounds just fine."

"We'll delay the 'skinny dipping' to another day," he warned as he braced himself on her knee and climbed slowly to his feet. "Ahhh, I'm not getting any younger after a day like this."

Charly was delighted that he evidenced the same exhaustion that she felt. It made her feel better to know that she could compete with this mountain man in his everyday life and feel no worse than he. She wondered briefly if he could compete in hers. But it really didn't matter.

By the time Charly emerged clean, if not entirely refreshed, from her little bath, Noah was returning from his shower. His hair was wet and he dripped steadily across the room. His attire consisted, once again, of a small towel strategically wrapped below his waist.

"Noah—" Charly gasped at the sight of his bare body.

"I know—I'm dripping water everywhere. Grab that towel over there and dry my back, will you?" He turned around and presented his wet, brawny back to her, the corded muscles prominent and glistening with moisture.

Charly fumbled with the towel, trying to be casual about her task. She dropped the towel, grabbed it up quickly, rubbed his back, trying to be only concerned with the water that dripped to the floor.

Finally, he turned around to face her, a devilish glow in his blue eyes. "That's fine. Thanks. Now, if you'll let go of the towel, I'll use it to dry my hair."

Charly smiled sheepishly. "Oh. Oh, yes. Sure." She released her firm grip on the towel and watched him disappear into the room she used.

"You don't mind if I use my room to change, do you?" he called.

"No, not at all," Charly hastily affirmed.

Dinner was quiet. Noah prepared a dish for Walt in his room, leaving Charly and him to eat alone again. They cleaned up the dishes together, and as they finished Noah offered, "How about after-dinner wine on the patio?"

"The patio?" laughed Charly. "Sounds magnificent!"

"Of course, in simple mountain terms that's the back porch." He chuckled.

Charly went ahead, inhaling the cool, clean mountain air. She could hear the rain falling lightly on the already-saturated earth, but the blackness made it impossible to see the forest that surrounded them. She felt lost—lost in a hideaway filled with soft, pattering sounds and slow calmness that allowed her mind to roam with no interruptions. Maybe this was just what she needed. A break, a total escape from her hectic life was rejuvenating. Noah joined her with the wine, and his very presence reminded her that she was not alone in her hideaway—nor did she want to be.

Charly took the offered glass, touching his fingers casually in the exchange. "Thank you. As much as I hate to admit it, Noah, it's very pleasant here. Even the sound of the rain is relaxing. Two days ago I hated it." She laughed and sipped from her glass. "I could become addicted to your blackberry wine, you know. This is getting to be an every night's occurrence."

"It's not Chablis Premier Cru, but it'll do, I suppose. I could easily get accustomed to a habit like this, Charly." He stood close to her, their sides touching. "You're right, you know. I have been here a long time. I have almost forgotten how nice it is to have a woman around all the time. I've enjoyed having you here, Charly."

She turned slightly, not quite able to make out his features in the dark. "Noah, you know I've been an aggravation from the beginning." She laughed nervously, trying to lighten the conversation, for she could feel the sexual tension between them.

"But I've enjoyed this . . ." His voice trailed away as he cupped her chin with one hand and kissed her lips. Charly stood motionless as his beard brushed her face and his lips caressed hers gently. It was not the fervent, intense kiss of the morning, but a languid, tender touch that kept her desire smoldering while her senses begged for more. His hand trailed her neck, leaving a hot stream of fiery passion, stroking the cleavage between her full breasts until a small gasp of pleasure escaped her lips. The kiss intensified as his hand encircled one breast, his thumb massaging the tip to ripened perfection.

Charly strained against his hand, wanting him to stop,

yet desiring him to continue. She moaned softly and tried to move away, but a gentle tugging on her nipple forced her to stay. "Oh . . . oh, Noah . . . please . . ." she murmured, trying to talk under the force of his lips.

He moved to kiss her cheeks, her eyelids, her forehead. His hand slid from her breast to around her waist, pulling her closer to his full length, so that she could feel his rising passion. It gave her a chance to speak, but her words came out in a hoarse whisper. "Noah, please—don't. I—we—we mustn't. This is too soon."

He held her close, his lips resting against her temple. "Charly . . . Charly, don't deny what's happened between us. It's too good, and it's not too soon. It's been too long in coming for me. I want you . . . I need you . . ."

"No! Please. You'll spill my wine. Let's go inside." The earnestness of his voice scared her and she knew that if she stayed much longer, if he touched her again, she would give in to his desire—and her own burning passion. She started to move toward the door, but Noah stopped her and pulled her into his arms. This time the power, the appeal, the desirability of the man overpowered Charly's rational protests and she clung to him, returning his ardent kiss.

In a flash, she was swept up in his arms and, as he groped for the door, he murmured, "Don't spill the wine, Charly."

Instinctively, she held the glass upright behind his back, where her hands clung for support. As he lay her on the bed, she gasped, "Oh, Noah, the wine—the wine!"

He halted and moved his lips away from hers, half-expecting to feel the cool liquid splashing down his back. But she brought the glass around him with a satisfactory smile. "And not a drop spilled." She laughed triumphantly, sitting up to drink the remaining drops.

"My, my, what a marvelous sense of balance you have,

Little Wildcat," he teased, nuzzling her earlobe.

"Just natural reflexes to save good wine, Mr. Van Horn." She smiled.

"Speaking of natural reflexes . . ." His lips claimed hers, drinking hungrily of her sweetness, and the empty glass fell abandoned on the bed.

As his lips moved against hers, she allowed them to part for his tongue's penetration and exploration of her mouth. Charly became enraptured, caught up in her own longing for this man whose beard tickled her face and whose obvious desire responded to her own. She wasn't aware that his hand easily manipulated the buttons of her shirt—*his* shirt—until she felt the gentle tugging on her taut nipples as his fingers sought first one, then the other rosy tip.

Gasping with pleasure, Charly allowed his kisses to deepen, gave more room for his hand to roam, responded like she never had to any man's touch. She closed her eyes and reveled in the splendid pleasures Noah created as he brushed her eyelids with his lips, her cheeks, her earlobes, her neck—her breasts and their hard, rosy tips. She lay back flat against the bed, giving him the invitation she knew he wanted as his hand trailed lightly over her body, pausing only a moment to unzip her jeans—*his* jeans.

As his hand probed even further, he shifted to stretch to her length, one leg draped over hers. His exploring fingers discovered the extent of Charly's responses, introduced her to even greater heights of ecstacy.

"Noah . . . oh, Noah . . ." she murmured as his lips set her on fire. She arched her back to increase her pleasure but realized that his hands had stopped probing, strategically eliciting her sensuous desires to the peak he sought. Then she knew why. He lay over her, prying at her legs with his knee, and she felt him against her stomach. She knew—too late—what she had done, what she had led him to. He had warned her that there would be no stopping.

"I want you, Charly—need you . . ." he rasped, close to her face.

"Yes . . . oh, yes, Noah." And she knew that she didn't want him to stop.

CHAPTER SIX

Charly's peaceful sleep was invaded by the feathery-soft caress of a butterfly on her eyelids, inviting her to awaken to greater pleasures. The butterfly refused to go away. It continued to provoke and tickle her until her brown eyes popped open to see that the annoyance wasn't from an insect, but the light touch of a man's lips. The sleepy-eyed face of Noah was only inches from hers, and he kissed her nose and murmured, "Good morning, Wildcat. Have some coffee?"

He moved back, and Charly blinked and smiled at him. "Morning. Do you always wake your houseguests this way?"

He grinned slightly, and she could see a faint glimpse of white teeth beneath the beard. "Sorry. I lost control. Your eyelids looked so alluring, just laying there, tempting me. Anyway, I figured I shouldn't have to face the morning alone while you sleep peacefully through it all."

She paused and narrowed her eyes. "Do I hear rain—still?"

"Yep. Beautiful morning. At least, in here it's nice."

"Is that my coffee you're holding?" Charly shifted up on the pillows and reached for the steamy cup. Modestly, she tucked the sheet under her arms, hiding what he had already seen—touched. She lowered her eyes and sipped, murmuring, "Thank you. It's very good."

Noah's hand caressed her cheek, and she looked up into

his intense blue eyes. Suddenly she was filled with embarrassed constraint with this man she barely knew. She remembered the intensity of their lovemaking the previous night and knew she certainly hadn't shown any constraint then. She could see that he was fully dressed, and she wondered when he had left the bed. Last night or not until this morning? She really didn't know.

Her eyes must have told him what she was thinking, for his voice was low and gentle. "Don't be ashamed of what happened last night, Charly. It was a very honest and natural consequence. After all, I'm just a man. . . . It was very beautiful. *You* are very beautiful, Charly."

She bit her lip and looked away, catching sight of the incongruity of the books and dried peppers. *Just* a man? *Hardly!* "But I don't know you. I . . . I can't believe I let myself . . ."

His hand stretched around her jawline and turned her face back to him. His thumb gently followed the shape of her lips. "But that doesn't matter, Charly. The important things are the feelings between us right now. And those are good, aren't they?"

She looked at him quietly for a moment. Unmistakable magnetism definitely attracted her to him. She smiled broadly. "The best, Noah. The best!"

Immediately, his lips met hers in a fierce encounter that left her gasping for breath. "Oh, God, it was good. You are the best, little Wildcat!" he murmured against her face.

"Noah, the coffee! I . . . we're going to spill the coffee!"

He kissed her nose and eyelids again. "Why, you managed to handle the wine last night and didn't spill a drop! You should be able to juggle a simple mug of coffee!"

One hand weakly pushed against his chest, slipping between the shirt buttons to the dark mat of hair that cushioned it. "I don't think I have the same sense of balance this early in the morning," she said, laughing.

He sat up and clasped his hand over hers, guiding it

further inside his shirt and holding it firmly against the hardness of his chest. She felt the taut muscles and the hard nipple surrounded by velvety hairs and enjoyed the magnetic warmth of his body. She ran her hand down his rib cage to the unnatural barrier of his belt, then back up again where the steady pounding of his heart filled her palm. It was a nice feeling to caress him freely, to know he enjoyed her touch as much as she did.

"You'd better finish that coffee quickly or we'll be making love with coffee dripping from our bodies," he warned hoarsely as he set his cup on the floor.

Charly giggled. "Sounds like fun," she managed, and took one big gulp before he relieved her of the responsibility of the thing and lowered his body to hers. "Noah . . . it's . . . it's too early . . ." She squeezed the words between his kisses, and then he left her lips to make a hot trail to each uncovered breast, then returned to her protesting lips again.

"Never—never too early. It's still raining, and there's nothing else to do." His raspy voice was teasing, as was his tongue.

"Oh—oh, Noah. . . . What do you mean, 'nothing else to do'?" She tried to be insulted, but his never-ceasing kisses left her weak and willing to please and be pleased.

He undressed and came to her quickly, urgently. This time there was no hesitancy or reserve as Charly opened her arms to him. The rain beat steadily on the tin roof of the little cabin, obliterating the world from the lovers, who escaped to their hideaway only to discover everything important in each other. Their passion ascended to the zenith of their emotions, leaving them clinging to each other for the affection and acceptance they shared. It was what they both wanted—needed—and they drew from each other. Somehow it seemed exactly right, too.

Afterward, Charly dozed in his arms, her head pillowed on his chest. When she awakened, she could still hear the soft sounds of rain on the roof. It was almost like a sweet song now, serenading their lovemaking. Only a few days ago she had hated that sound. But now it was pleasant and romantic. Many changes had taken place in the last few days.

Charly looked up at Noah's still-sleeping face. He encompassed the biggest change that had come over her. Someone who had frightened, angered, and fought with her had turned out to be appealing and engaging and—sensual. Unable to resist the touch, she traced the straight line of his nose and down to where his lips parted slightly as he slept. What an interesting man you are, Noah Van Horn, she thought. And what a crazy thing I've done! I must be losing my mind—but I love it!

Unexpectedly, his mouth opened further, and his teeth nipped her finger lightly.

"Ouch!" Charly jerked back in surprise. "I thought you were still asleep. Hey! You tried to bite my finger!" She grabbed a handful of his velvety, curly beard.

He smiled, his eyes still closed as he nuzzled her earlobe. "I don't bite—just nibble around a little."

"Speaking of nibbling, I'm hungry. What does a girl have to do to get breakfast around here?"

"Oh, I guess you qualify by just doing . . . this. I think I'll finish what I started earlier this morning . . ." He started to move.

Quickly, Charly sat up in bed. "Now just a minute!"

He laughed, a deep, rumbling laugh. "Calm down, Wildcat. When I brought you coffee, I intended to prepare your breakfast and bring it to your bedroom suite. But I got sidetracked by a bewitching beauty with thick chestnut hair and big brown eyes. She's a real wildcat, too, with claws and sharp teeth!"

"Oh, yeah? Then keep her out of this bedroom! This is my domain! Where's my breakfast?" she demanded, laughing delightedly.

He bent to pick up his jeans. "At your service, ma'am. How about another cup of coffee while you wait?"

"Sounds fine," Charly agreed, and leaned back leisurely on the pile of pillows, pulling up the sheet to cover her breasts. "Just bring it into my luxurious bedroom suite, sir!" She laughed at the thought of calling the humble little room a "suite."

She looked very happy and alluring against the white sheets with her dark hair spread over the pillow. Noah gave her one last longing look, then disappeared to do her bidding.

They spent the morning leisurely, eating, laughing, talking. Charly helped Noah clean the antiquated kitchen. Looking in dismay at the old wood stove, Charly said, "I don't know how in the world you cook a thing on this. It looks like something that belongs in a museum."

"It probably does. I had to learn how to fire it up and gauge cooking times differently—slower."

"Well, if you'll fire it up, I'll start some vegetable soup. This seems like a good day for soup—and I don't have a taste for squirrel! Of course, I'll need some vegetables from the garden, Noah." Charly felt very domestic today for some reason and began to busily prepare the soup. "Anyway, it'll be good for Walt," she deducted, thinking of the old man, who still refused to get up. She wondered how much was actual illness and how much was stubborn insolence. Humming merrily, she covered the huge pot and left it simmering, while she and Noah sat on the back steps, watching the silvery rain. It was a pleasant, comfortable day. And Charly didn't mind the rain at all.

Finally, Noah offered, "I'll take Walt his lunch. Looks like he isn't going to make an appearance again today."

Charly laid her hand on his sinewy arm. "Let me, Noah. I made the soup for him, so I'd rather take it in to him. I have a feeling that part of his ailment is my being here. This will give me a chance to talk to him."

Noah looked at her honestly. "I know he's not too happy with your being here. And, frankly, he probably doesn't want to talk to you, Charly, so don't be offended if he's short. You don't exactly represent his ally, you know."

"But I'm not his enemy!" Charly protested.

Noah shrugged and let the matter drop. "Walt really does have a heart problem and is sometimes in bed for days at a time. When he says he doesn't feel well, I respect that. The doctor says there isn't much he can do for it except rest and take his medicine. And I've seen to that. He's just a stubborn old man."

"I don't care. I want to see him. Please." Her voice was tender, yet serious. "After all, Noah, I am using his home."

Noah hooted tauntingly. "I can't believe you, of all people, said that! Ms. government official, friend of the mountaineer, prepares vegetable soup for last supper! Sure, Charly, go ahead! Walt will never suspect a thing!"

"Damn you!" she shrieked, lashing out at the large man, who easily pinned her arms to her sides and kissed her lips.

"Can't you take a little teasing?" he rumbled close to her.

"Not . . . not about this . . . about my job and . . ." she sputtered.

"To hell with your job!"

"Too bad I can't say that! My job happens to be the way I live!" She jerked free and gave him a nasty look before going inside. She could hear his low-rolling laughter as she prepared a tray for Walt. Damn his insolence anyway!

Charly concentrated on making the lunch offering for Walt attractive and appetizing. She even added a small wild violet and smiled approvingly at the feminine touch. Apprehensively, Charly walked into the semidark space that Walter Simms occupied. The room was larger than the one she and Noah had shared, but not as interesting. It included a very old dresser and chest of drawers, a wooden rocker, and a lamp with an old yellowed shade. One time, many years ago, the furniture and lamp must have been new, but now they, like Walter, were withered with age.

"Mr. Simms—er, Walt, are you hungry? I've made some great vegetable soup. Everything in it came from your garden." Charly's voice cheerfully punctuated the heavy silence in the room.

Walt made no move to take the tray, so she set it on the table beside the bed. His sharp blue eyes followed her and she felt their gaze raking her back. Turning to him, she said agreeably, "Can I prop your pillows up for you? You'll need to sit up if you're going to eat."

"I can sit up by myself," he answered shortly, and began to peel back the covers. Charly was amused to notice that the old man was fully dressed. She didn't comment, but took his elbow and assisted him to the chair, where he plopped, obviously ready to receive the tray.

He eyed the soup and asked, in his short, terse way, "Say this is vegetable soup?"

"Yes." Charly nodded.

"Hmmm, haven't had vegetable soup in a long time. Bessie used to make it once a week—straight from the garden in the summer, like you did."

"Bessie?" Charly sat on the edge of the bed, relieved that she had penetrated the wall between them, even if only a crack.

"My wife," he answered between bites, as if she should recall his wife, deceased for over ten years now.

Charly vaguely remembered reading in a report somewhere that at one time Walt had had a wife. She listened as he told about Bessie and their simple, gentle mountain life. She could tell how important the life was to him—even the remembering. He talked throughout the meal.

And Charly communicated, but not too much, and asked the right questions at the pauses. It was the most Walt had conversed in days—even with Noah.

As she took the empty tray from him, he gazed at her for a long moment. Then, tersely, he said, "Thanks. That was pretty good . . . for a city girl." He turned and hobbled toward the bed and Charly left, not knowing if she had succeeded or not.

She set the tray in the sink and sought Noah, who was still on the back porch. She needed some kind of reassurance, but it was doubtful she would get it from him.

He looked up and grinned devilishly at her. "Undoubtedly, Walt decided to talk. For a while I was worried about you. Thought he had you cornered! You never know about these mountain men!"

"Oh, you!" She tried to tweak his ear, then slipped her arm through his as she sat near him. She snuggled against his shoulder, enjoying the fresh, woodsy fragrance of him. He made her feel good even when he teased.

"Actually, he had a lot to say—mostly about Bessie and their life together."

"Well, you must have said just the right things to bring him out like that, Charly. He can be an ornery old cuss sometimes, and nothing—or no one—can open him up."

Charly shook her head and part of her hair fell on Noah's shoulder. "I don't think it was anything I said. It was something I did. The vegetable soup reminded him of the kind Bessie prepared for him frequently. I think that brought him around. He seemed surprised that a 'city girl,' to use his phrase, could do such a thing as cook."

"So am I. Let's go in and try it. I want to see what kind of potential you have. I know what a great lover you are—but a cook, too? I may just kidnap you forever!" They rose and he swatted her playfully on the rear.

Charly smiled, but ducked her head in embarrassment at his compliments about her loving. It was too soon, and

Charly was still trying to adjust to this new relationship with Noah. Actually, her own behavior amazed her. She had never let her emotions run rampant like this. But then she had never felt like this before either.

Soberly, she admitted, "I'll bet my office in Atlanta thinks I've been kidnapped. They haven't heard from me in days. But then . . ." She paused, thinking. "Lewis has been out of town, too, so maybe no one else will worry about me."

"Who is Lewis?"

"My boss."

"And he's the only one who would worry about you?" There was an edge of concern in his voice and another question in his words.

"Well, I usually keep in touch with Lewis. So, for a few days, he's the only one who would realize that I haven't reported in or that I'm unreachable."

He pressed. "Is your boss the only one who would care?"

Charly took a deep breath and nodded slowly. "Lewis is the only one who will care. However, he will care very much that I'm staying in a cabin with two men!" She laughed lightly, but both of them realized that there were others who would one day invade their lovely hideaway world.

"Does that bother you?"

She reached up and caressed his cheek and the dark beard. "Not any more. I could stay here forever! I don't care if it never stops raining!"

His hand covered hers possessively and he moved it to his lips, kissing her palm fervently. In a moment they were in each other's arms, kissing, caressing, clinging. Forgotten were Walter Simms, their waiting lunch, the world outside. They were aware solely of each other and the passion of fire ignited by only a touch.

The days lengthened and Charly wasn't aware, nor did

she care, if the rain still fell. She was happy and busy and had found a kind of freedom that she had never known in a strange and different mountain world. And she had discovered an unmatched relationship with a man she loved. Or did she? Was it possible to love someone this soon? This intensely? Was it love—or lust? Oh—she didn't want to think about that. All Charly knew was that she was gloriously happy with Noah.

They were free and open and loving, and there was no interference from the outside world. There were no time schedules, no meetings or parties, no people except Walt.

The old man kept very much to himself. It was as if he knew intuitively, through his vast years of life experiences, that the two were in love. Sometimes he prepared dinner, then left them alone while he took a walk. Other times he serenaded them at night with the plaintive sounds of his harmonica. Who would say it was romantic? And yet to Charly the music, mingled with the quiet sounds of the mountain nights, was as romantic as Nancy Wilson's "Midnight Sun." And now she knew the meaning of the lyrics that spoke of a brilliant flash of the midnight sun as her love for Noah reached new heights every day . . . and night.

"You've been here for a week, Charly. I can't believe so much has happened in so short a time." There was wonder in his voice as they walked through the quiet woods. The constant rush of water from the mountain stream they followed was the only sound for a few minutes.

"It has been busy, hasn't it?" Charly agreed. Busy falling in love, she thought.

"Now that the rain has stopped, we should check on your car."

"Tomorrow." She answered firmly, taking his hand as they walked along.

"That's what you said yesterday. Charly, you've got to—"

"No, I don't!" she interrupted, putting her fingers on his lips. "Not today! Tomorrow, or in a few days, I'll worry about the car and . . . everything. But not now. I just don't want to! Now, are you going to show me how to catch rainbow trout or not?"

"Well, I don't know. After that loud outburst, they probably have hidden in the deepest, darkest hole they can find," he admonished her.

Charly's hand flew to her mouth apologetically. "Oops, sorry. Do you think I scared them all away? Darn! There goes our fun!"

"There goes our supper!" Noah pointed with the long fishing rod in his hand. "We'll go on upstream a bit. Maybe they couldn't hear you this far away. But remember—quiet. They can hear you."

Charly nodded, trying to be serious, but a devilish gleam lit her brown eyes. "Okay. Those little fish are clever fellows, aren't they? Just don't mention . . ."

"Leaving," Noah finished, catching her eyes knowingly.

She looked deep into those blue eyes she rapidly had grown to love and nodded. "Yes, leaving."

The conversation failed to put a serious damper on their usually jolly mood. It just pointed up—briefly—Charly's aversion to leaving or even talking of it. They climbed through thick green underbrush and over huge gray rocks to reach the small river's bank, where Charly watched solemnly as Noah cast his lure skillfully across the dark rushing waters. He pointed to a specific spot where the water ran deep and murmured in hushed tones that it was a "good hole" and likely spot for a trout. She watched spellbound as he patiently and expertly flicked the silvery lure to the exact spot time after time, reeling it slowly to skim the water's surface, then casting again to repeat the action.

Abruptly, the repetitious, monotonous action of casting

and reeling was broken as a splash shattered the water's surface and the rod bent with the weight of an obvious catch! Slowly, patiently, Noah reeled and worked with the fighting fish. Charly wanted him to raise it high out of the water so they could view it triumphantly, but he humored it, finally wading out into the icy stream to meet it halfway and dip it quickly into the net. Only then was there a triumphant smile on Noah's face as he showed her the fish with its beautiful rainbow-colored stripes that glistened in the afternoon sun.

Charly gazed wide-eyed into the net. She was like a child and everything in Noah's mountain world was a wonder. "Oooh, Noah, it's beautiful! I . . . I don't think I can eat it!"

Noah rolled his eyes. "Oh, no! Don't tell me that— Charly, that's ridiculous! This is the sweetest, best-tasting fish you've ever had—especially these mountain trout. They're delicious! Surely you've eaten fish before!"

"Yes," she countered. "But not the ones I've looked in the eye!"

"Oh, my God, Charly! What a sentimental fool!"

She folded her arms defensively. "I can't help it. I just . . ."

"I suppose if you spent much time up here you'd turn into a complete vegetarian! And then, if the carrots waved at you in the breeze, you wouldn't eat them either!"

She narrowed her eyes at him. "I suppose so!"

He shook his head and proceeded to unhook the fish and drop it into a bed of damp leaves in the creel that hung from his shoulder.

She watched him silently, then decided she would be a good sport about it and prove her willingness to adapt to his life-style. "Let me try to catch one. Teach me to fish, Noah."

He raised his eyebrows and gazed at her for a minute,

then nodded. "If you catch one, you have to eat it. Rules of the game."

She eyed him skeptically for a moment, then determinedly agreed. "Sure." Her facade was much more assured than she felt inside.

Fortunately, with the first cast of the rod, Charly was saved from her promise to the "rules of the game." The lure, hook, and thirty feet of line were hopelessly tangled into the branches of the oak tree, which spread its limbs majestically over Charly's head and half the small river. Noah spent forty impatient minutes trying to untangle it. Finally, he cut the line, leaving a portion of the mess in the tree for posterity.

"Noah, I'm sorry. I don't know how that happened! It just looked so easy to see you flip that little thing over your shoulder right to the exact spot where you were aiming." Her brown eyes were innocently rounded.

"It takes years of practice to cast the way I do, Charly. I tried to tell you—"

"You aren't mad at me, are you?"

He looked disgustedly at her for a moment, then his face broke into a smile. "No, Charly. I'm not mad at you." What could he say when she looked at him that way? Those eyes . . .

She kissed him quickly. "Good! I think I'll watch you awhile longer. I'll learn to cast another time."

"Good idea," Noah agreed tersely as he tied on a new float, weight, and lure.

Charly lounged comfortably on a huge gray rock, observing quietly as Noah repeated the casting procedure until he had netted three more large trout in the next hour and a half. It was a slow process, requiring considerable patience. Perhaps it wasn't the thing for Charly after all.

Finally, Noah turned to her, where she dozed on the sun-warmed rock. "Come on. Let's go home, Wildcat."

There was something exciting and secure and loving about his statement, and indeed, Charly felt as though being with Noah—even on this alien mountain—was "home." Immediately, she curled an arm around his waist, and arm in arm they walked through the woods toward home.

CHAPTER SEVEN

The days melded into one glorious, loving experience for Charly. Some of her time was spent in quiet reflection, alone. And Charly enjoyed that. It was like an unexpected vacation for her and a welcome respite from the dailiness of her job.

She also spent many hours with Noah, and that time was almost like a honeymoon for Charly. She grew to know him and love him, as they shared their lives with one another. He had eased his way into her heart.

During one of their pastoral walks through the forest, Noah opened a small crevice of his past. It was just enough for Charly to realize that the way to Noah's heart would not be easy. She had to climb a mountain first.

Charly's laughter echoed against the trees. "I guess I was a tomboy. With two brothers, what else could you expect? They even let me play sandlot baseball with them, but insisted that I play right field. One time, there weren't enough players for all the fielding positions to be filled. I begged for them to let me play first base. They finally agreed, and I made four outs in the game! After that I played first base every time!"

"Were you Phillies fans?"

"Oh, my God, yes! Our big—and only—family event was to go to a Phillies game. It wasn't often, but as we kids got older we worked odd jobs to pay our own way. I think it bothered our dad, but we were such a gregarious bunch, he couldn't help but go along with us. We'd pitch in and buy him a hot dog and couple of beers, and he'd be in heaven!" Charly smiled as she recalled the fun they had had together.

"What about your mother? Did she go along?" Something in his voice said he couldn't imagine such a thing.

"Oh, sure! She loved it, too. Or maybe she just went along to be with us. I'll have to ask her about that someday. Anyway, she seemed to have fun. She worked, too. She was a teacher, so she didn't make much. But it helped keep us in jeans and tennis shoes. I dressed like my brothers. Thought everybody did until I reached junior high."

"Are you still close to your family?"

Charly nodded. "As close as I can be when they're in Philly and I'm in Atlanta. My older brother Jack is a lawyer in Philly. He watches after Mom since Dad died a few years ago. Steve, the youngest, is in college this year. We keep in touch. Actually, I've been gone from home since I was eighteen."

"Why? It sounds as though you had a marvelously happy family life."

"Oh, yes," Charly said enthusiastically. "Happy but poor. By then my folks were struggling to put Jack through law school. So, I went to work and college at the same time. After graduation, I was lucky enough to get a job with the government in D.C. I worked there for six years until I was transferred to the Bureau of Land Management office in Atlanta four months ago. End, story of my life."

"Aw, and it was so intriguing, too. You were just getting to the part I liked best."

Charly raised her eyebrows. "The part where you come into the story?"

"Naw, the part about your job in Atlanta. Do you like it?" It was a loaded question.

She narrowed her eyes and stopped, arms akimbo. "If

you're expecting a confession about how I hate my job, sorry to disappoint you. It's a good position, and I like it." Her emphatic tone hid her disillusionment with the job and disagreements with her boss, Lewis. Nor did she mention that Lewis wanted to be her lover. That complication was far away as she stood next to Noah, hidden deep in the Smoky Mountains.

He draped his arm around her shoulder affectionately. "Oh, no, Charly. I wasn't looking for a confession. I just wondered if you would quit the rat race and move to the mountains with me."

"Sounds like heaven," she murmured, knowing that deep inside she meant it. "But how would we live? On love?"

He reached around her neck and drew her face close to his. "Hmmm, I'm for that." His kiss was sweet and tender, then he turned and led her on through the woods.

"Enough of my fascinating life. It's time for your exposé," she encouraged.

They walked awhile before Noah spoke, surprising her with stories of his aristocratic Southern family.

"My sister, Missy, and I went to the best prep schools in North Carolina. Fine education, but dull."

"A preppy? You?" Charly hooted with delight. She grabbed his arms and examined him thoroughly, her eyes lingering on the dark beard. "Somehow I never imagined you, of all people, a preppy! A hillbilly, maybe. But not a—"

"Southern is not 'preppy.' Eastern is 'preppy.'" He glared at her.

"Yes, Noah. Anything you say." She acquiesed, grinning delightedly at him. Here was more teasing material—later.

"Do you want to hear this or not?"

"Of course I do. You were just getting to the interesting part." She turned and continued walking.

"If you think that's interesting, wait till you hear this. I even went to The Citadel, military college! While the rest of the world was breaking away, I was marching. God—I hated it! And my dad for sending me."

Charly was appalled at the thought of one's life being so planned. "Did you have to go?"

He shook his head. "There were no alternatives. Missy and I had certain family traditions to uphold. We were groomed to carry on the family name. We spent summers at the Outer Banks' seashore and Sapphire Valley."

"Sapphire Valley?"

"It's a beautiful old resort hotel. There were supervised children's activities to keep us occupied. We were instructed in tennis, golf, horseback riding, and gold mining."

"Gold mining? You're putting me on!"

"Gold mining, yes! Didn't you know that the first gold in the U.S. was discovered in North Carolina? Where have you been all your life, city girl!"

"Well, not looking for gold in North Carolina, that's for sure!" Charly laughed.

"You missed a lot. As a kid, I used to think I'd discover gold in some obscure creek and be rich. Panning for gold was my favorite pastime."

Charly sniffed indignantly. "Sounds to me like you were rich enough."

Noah shrugged and stuffed his hands in his pockets. "Probably. Although I didn't know it. All of my friends lived as I did. I didn't have much personal money. We were just quite busy all the time. I thought everyone spent winter vacations in Ashville or Gatlinburg."

Charly sighed. "What a glorious life you had."

Noah ambled off the path, stepping over tree stumps and roots until he found just the right grassy spot to sit. Charly joined him.

"Not really. My mother drank a lot. Unhappy, I suppose. My sister and I stuck together during that period."

Charly shook her thick hair and let it flow down her back. "Are you and Missy still close?"

He shook his head. "Just friends. When I graduated from The Citadel, I had some hell raising to do. So I spent a few years traveling and getting the hell knocked out of me—one way or another. I rode a rodeo circuit for a while through the West and Canada. That was some experience." He chuckled at some private remembrance. "I was in Alberta, Canada, when they finally reached me that my parents had been killed in a plane crash in the Bahamas."

Charly looked up sharply. What a jolt in the glorious life. Noah was staring through the trees as he talked. She decided not to interrupt with sympathetic comments. Not now.

"So at twenty-five I took the reins of the second largest furniture manufacturing plant in the South. For the first time in my life I worked. And did I ever work! I knew nothing about the business and had to start from scratch."

"Why did you leave it?" Charly asked with trepidation.

"Actually, that's when my glorious life began. I managed to get the business under control, made Missy's husband a partner, and married my high-school sweetheart. By then both Vera and I were around thirty and wanted to start our family as soon as possible. So we had Noah Wade Van Horn the Fourth. Within two years they were both dead. So was the meaning of my life."

"Noah . . ." Charly's voice was gentle as she scooted closer to him and slipped her hand in his.

"So I escaped to the only refuge I knew—these mountains. Here I've found a renewal for my life and strength to continue."

Charly moved to her knees and wrapped her arms around him, cradling his head gently against her breast. "Oh, Noah," she murmured. "I'm sorry about your family—your child . . ." Tears filled her eyes as she empathized with the pain he must have experienced.

But he pushed her away, his blue eyes as intense and fierce as his voice. "Don't sympathize or mourn for me, Charly. I've done enough of that already. I've wallowed long enough in my own sorrow and depression. I'm beyond that now. It's a part of my past and I won't go back. I have found new meaning in life—and you have given me new joy. From the moment I saw you with your damn car trouble and when you trooped in covered with mud, I knew that my life had been invaded. No more escaping." He pulled her down to his level and kissed her nose. "But it's been a nice invasion."

Charly smiled through her tears. "What else can you say to me? I'm still here—invading your privacy. But what about when I leave?" She moved away and leaned against the trunk of a giant oak tree that spread its arms over their moss-covered glen.

"What about it?"

"I guess the proof of our . . . relationship . . . will be then." She was scared of the thought, afraid to say it aloud. Her constant fear was that when she left the mountain, she would never see Noah Van Horn III again.

"I guess." Noah lay back on the green mossy bed, using her lap for a pillow. His discerning blue eyes searched for answers in the multitude of tree branches above them and beyond.

Charly ran her fingers through his raven-black hair, relishing the touch. Her other hand lay casually on his muscular chest, tracing small shapes in the hairs.

He shuddered and turned to her, reaching up to cup her breast. "Come here, Charly. I need you . . . want you close. I need you now . . ."

Eagerly, she came to him, burying her face against his chest, clinging tightly to his warmth. The musty smell of the moss-covered earth beneath her mingled with the fresh pine's fragrance, and Charly thought the forest floor was a lovely, natural place to make love. Her passion soared to the heights of the trees above her as Noah caressed her, matching her fervor with his own. Their lovemaking was intense and extravagant, an almost desperate attempt to perpetuate what they feared they would lose. It was as if they sensed this was the last time they would make love— and they lay gratefully, fearfully in each other's arms, trembling at the thought of parting.

Their love was now visible to the world—the trees, the animals, the aged mountains. It was hidden no more. And Charly wanted to shout it to the universe—*I love you, Noah.* But she didn't. She just held him, hiding her tears of joy and passion, hoping she would never, never lose him.

It wasn't the last time Charly and Noah made love. There were other days—and nights. But Charly was staying on borrowed time, and they both knew it. There were no solutions, no offers of relinquishment, no declarations. They just enjoyed the time they had with each other and didn't talk of her leaving.

There were times when Noah or Charly felt entirely content being alone. It was a comfortable feeling, for there was a sense of security between them. Noah had gone off by himself earlier one day and Charly made her way around the clearing, searching purposefully for him. The early morning sun revealed where Noah had secluded himself, and Charly made her way toward him.

"A-ha! Thought you could hide from me, eh? What are you doing up at this hour?"

"Shhh . . ." He held his hand up to stop her, and Charly hushed and eased slowly to the grassy knoll where Noah sat. There, not ten feet away, was a wild, brown rabbit with big ears and a twitching nose. Noah sketched him with quick, sweeping strokes. The light swishing scrawl of the pencil moving across the paper was the only sound they heard, as the forest dominated their presence. Suddenly something spooked the little animal, and he was gone.

Noah and Charly looked at each other, disappointed at his brief debut. Then Noah laughed. "Damn crazy rabbit. Doesn't know when he's in good company!"

"Let me see your drawing," Charly commented, examining the sketches. "Hmmm—not bad, Noah."

He cocked his head, assessing his work. "No. And not good, either. Except for the ears that are too long, the back that's too humped, and the legs that are out of proportion —oh, and the crooked nose—he's perfect!"

"Hey! He's kind of like you, Noah!" Charly teased, and pinched his nose.

Instantly, they were rolling together in the grass, shrieking, wrestling, laughing, kissing . . .

"I meant the 'perfect' part—honestly, Noah! Perfect!" Charly giggled as Noah pinned her arms above her head and kissed her soundly.

"Hmmm—that *was* perfect." He smiled when he finally moved from her willing lips. "Perfect, but not complete. Let's make it complete."

But Charly struggled to be free. "Let me go, Noah. We have to do something for Walt."

"What?"

"Let me up, and I'll tell you," she sputtered, straightening her white blouse and brushing debris from her shoulders. "This is the first time I've dressed in decent clothes in days."

"Are you saying you don't like my clothes?"

"No—yes!" More giggles. "But mine do fit me better. I'm trying to look nice, and you roll me on the ground!"

He grinned at her slyly. "You should be used to it by now. That's the way with us mountain men. Actually, you didn't have to go to all the trouble of putting on decent clothes for me, Charly. I like you in nothing!"

She ignored his teasing remarks and continued to fuss. "I hope I didn't get grass stains on this blouse!"

He inspected her flagrantly, his hand roving over her, lingering on her shoulder. "This does fit you better. I like it!"

"Do you want to hear what Walt wants?"

"No—yes, go ahead." It was hard for him to be serious. Obviously this would be another laugh-filled episode in Charly's mountain fantasy.

"He wants us to go over to the Crismans', wherever they live. Something about trading."

"Sure," Noah agreed, and he began to gather the scattered sketch papers. "We exchange honey and vegetables for eggs and meat and . . . wine."

"Bartering?"

"Yep. It's always been a part of the mountain way. You'll enjoy meeting our neighbors, Ralph and Helga Crisman. And they're just a healthy six-mile hike away." They started for the cabin.

Charly stared incredulously. "*Six* miles?"

"Um-hum. One way."

"Twelve miles in one day? You've got to be kidding me, Noah!"

"Nope. We can't take the truck because there aren't any roads. But you'll love it. It's a nice trip—what a beautiful view from the top! Come on!"

"*Mountain* top? Do you mean we're not on top now?"

Noah turned to her and there was a special glow of appreciation in his deep-blue eyes. "Oh, no, Charly! We're all surrounded here with thick woodlands. You have to climb into the open—on top—before you can see the real beauty."

So both Noah and Charly loaded backpacks full of "barter" and set off on the six-mile hike to Walt's neighbors. Noah was in high spirits, even breaking into song at one point, as the morning sun rose high to humor them and warm their backs.

Charly felt as though she were removed from herself, watching her image go through the paces of being back in time at least a hundred years. In the modern days of jets and space flights and computers, she and Noah were hiking six miles over rugged terrain to the nearest humans. And no one knew where she was. She felt far removed from civilization. It was almost—*almost*—unbelievable.

By the time they arrived at the Crismans' mountain home, Charly was well aware that she had hiked six miles through the rugged Smokies. She slumped exhaustedly on the old porch and gulped the marvelously wet iced tea that Helga offered. She and Noah listened respectfully as first Helga, then Ralph talked nonstop to their first visitors in days.

The old couple insisted that their guests stay and eat. Charly admitted to being starved and offered to help Helga prepare a lunch. The meal they set on the table would have fed six field hands! Charly sat amazed as they all dug in, as if they hadn't eaten in days. There were two kinds of meat, four vegetables, two huge pans of corn bread, and chocolate pie with a beautiful five-inch meringue!

As Helga started to clean the table, Charly murmured to Noah, "Many more lunches like this and you can just roll me off the mountain."

He smiled appreciatively toward Helga. "It was delicious, wasn't it?" Then, to Charly: "I didn't see you holding back! I believe you tried everything!"

Charly smiled sweetly and muttered through her teeth, "I didn't want to hurt her feelings."

They helped clean the kitchen, took a quick tour of the small farm, completed the bartering, and bid the Crismans *adieu.* After all, they had another six-mile trip ahead of them.

"Let's go back a different way. There's a beautiful waterfall I want you to see," Noah said, leading the way.

Charly shook her head wearily, thinking of the miles she had yet to cover. "Y'know, a helicopter could take us home in ten minutes." She dreaded the long hike back, and it was obvious in her lack of enthusiasm.

Noah turned and looked curiously at her for a moment. "A helicopter could take you out of these mountains in ten minutes," he commented tersely.

She caught his sharp eyes for a moment, then looked away. "But, then we'd miss the beautiful waterfall, wouldn't we?" she asked weakly.

His hand gently turned her face toward him again. "It won't be long, Charly. You know that. It's been nine days. The rain has stopped . . ."

"Noah, please! I don't want to think about it. Not yet. I'm not ready to . . ."

"Yes, you are, Charly. I think you are." Abruptly, Noah turned his back and continued along the tree-lined path.

Charly followed, brooding and silent. She knew—fearfully—that he was right. That one day—soon—their odyssey would come to an end. *Then* what?

"Look, Charly," Noah whispered, and pointed toward a small group of deer who looked at them solemnly with large round eyes, then bounded away.

Charly stared, amazed. But it wasn't the deer that drew her curiosity.

"Noah—"

He gazed in the direction where she pointed, but didn't answer her.

"What's that?" She gaped at the huge contraption nestled among the trees beyond where the deer had stood.

"It's what you think," he confirmed, shrugging unconcernedly.

"A . . . a whiskey still?" Charly whispered, suddenly apprehensive of their proximity.

He nodded, then turned to continue the trek. "Moonshine. Come on, Charly. It wouldn't be wise for a government official such as you to be caught here."

"My God! Noah! Do you realize—"

"I do! Come on, Charly. I hope you'll forget about this." His tone was terse.

Charly followed, knowing that she wouldn't forget about it, but not quite sure what, if anything, she would do about it. Once again she felt distinctly as though she had been plummeted back in time to another world. Noah's world.

Charly's mind whirled wildly. How long would she stay—should she stay—in the cabin? How in hell would she explain it? Did Noah—or Walt—have anything to do with the illegal whiskey still? After his comments today, was Noah ready for her to leave? Did he dread it as she did? Would he beg her to stay? Would he—oh, God—go with her? Did Noah love her? Or was the love one-sided? *I love you, Noah! Can't you see that?*

"There!" Noah's voice interrupted her confusion. It rose above the loud rush of water as he pointed out the lovely waterfall. "It falls in three levels. Come on. Let's hike down to the final pool." He began the descent through the thick underbrush.

With considerable assistance and effort, Charly finally emerged onto the floor of the narrow, hidden ravine, where the final plunge of the waterfall formed a deep, circular pool. The main rush of the water crashed above them, scattering fine, misty spray everywhere. It was a lovely, enchanted place. Another fantasy in her odyssey.

Charly couldn't resist. The boots she had borrowed from Walt were off in a flash, as well as her backpack. She took one look at the emerald pool framed with gray boulders, sprinkled with silvery mist, hidden from the world, and knew she had to be a part of it.

"Ohhh, it's beautiful, Noah! The water is so inviting—I want to go in!"

Noah shrugged. "Go ahead and wade."

"No . . . I mean I want to swim in it!" Charly was excited at the thought.

He smiled knowingly. "Charly, it's very cold . . ."

"Hell, I'm used to cold water after all those awful showers at the cabin! Come on, Noah! Come in with me!"

Slowly, he smiled. "There's only one way to go, Charly. In the buff!"

She looked at him for a moment, then met his challenge with a devilish grin. "I'll beat you in!"

Impatiently, feverishly, they stripped. Charly was determined to be the first one into the beautiful water.

Noah's low tone was intended for another warning, but it only served to spur her faster. "Charly, this water is *ice* cold. Are you sure . . ."

"Yes, I'm sure! It's beautiful, and I'm hot from all this damn hiking! It's just too tempting to pass up!" She laid her clothes carefully on the pack and hesitated only a moment before plunging, nude, into the misty, sunlit pool.

Noah laughed as Charly shrieked and howled when the icy water immediately chilled her hot body and practically took her breath away in the process.

"Oh—oh, my God! This is freezing! Damn—it's cold!" she gasped at him from where she treaded water in the deep center of the pool. Then she smiled and teased him sweetly, "Come on in, Noah, the water's fine! Once you get used to it—" Her words were cut short by her chattering teeth, but she managed a smile.

Noah looked at her skeptically, for he knew the truth. He hesitated on the bank, for he knew the full impact of the icy water and tried to delay it as long as possible.

He climbed onto a boulder and Charly admired his

muscular, masculine form as he stood poised. But she wasn't about to risk that he wouldn't join her. "You'd better get in here—or I'm coming after you!" she yelled, wondering how she would ever force him to do anything.

With a shout that echoed off the rocks above them, Noah dove in and swam swiftly through the water. He stroked evenly across the pool, then back to where Charly huddled on an underwater rock.

"You have to move around, Charly. Get the circulation going or icicles will form . . ." He grinned and clasped both of her breasts teasingly.

Together they swam a few laps, touching, teasing, chasing each other in the breathtakingly cold water.

"I . . . I think I've had enough, Noah," Charly finally admitted through chattering teeth.

"Thank God—I thought you'd never want to get out! I'm afraid my masculinity is ruined for life!" He pushed her through the water toward the bank.

They sat in the evening sun, drying each other with Noah's shirt, rubbing vigorously to revive their chilled senses. Soon their efforts gave way to soothing caresses and gentle touches that aroused passions. Noah couldn't resist kissing Charly until her lips parted with willing desire and her chilled skin tingled with warm passion. Charly wrapped her arms around his neck and clung to him, molding her lithe figure to his muscular frame. She enjoyed the warmth that radiated from him and wriggled with pleasure.

"It's so warm here with you. Feels so good," she murmured against his cheek as he lifted her off the ground and carried her to a soft, grassy spot. Her feet touched the cushioned earth and he reached to loosen her grip on him.

"Let go, Charly. I'll spread my shirt." Clumsily he made a crude bed for them. Then he turned to her, his passion strong and virile. "Come here, little Wildcat."

Eagerly she knelt on the shirt beside Noah. He ran his

hand along her thigh and pulled her to him, igniting the flame that burned in her.

"I'm yours, Noah. Just yours—for always," she murmured in his ear.

He answered in a hoarse whisper. "Don't say 'always.' Right now. Be mine *now.*"

She shuddered and surrendered her love to this man who wanted her now, but not forever. Or so he said.

But Charly wasn't like that. The man who elicited such wonderful heights of emotion—delight, excitement, passion—would always have her love. She was convinced of this and gave to him freely.

Later, as they lay in each other's arms, she stroked his chest and murmured, "I can assure you of one thing, Noah."

"What's that?" His voice was still low and dreamy.

"You weren't ruined for life by that ice water! Maybe stimulated!" They chuckled and snuggled together, gathering warmth from each other.

"We'd better start back soon, Charly. It's getting late."

"I know. But I hate to leave this spot—and you. I may just stay here forever and never go back to civilization!" Her voice was full of love.

His hand titillated her creamy breasts as he talked. "Oh? You love those cold showers, eh?"

"Hardly! Maybe I do miss civilization and my nice, warm scented bath."

His hand trailed to her face, around her lips, tracing their shape. "Do you remember when you fought me to let you go? Wasn't too many days ago."

She smiled sheepishly. "I know—but that was before . . ."

"Don't make any commitments now, Charly. Just enjoy the present." His fingers stroked her flat stomach.

"Is that what you're doing, Noah? Just enjoying the present?"

He smiled and nuzzled her ear. "You bet I am. Let's get dressed, Charly. We need to start back before dark."

They dressed quietly, regretfully. Noah tied the wet shirt around his waist and led the way over the remaining mile to the cabin. It had been one of those exhaustingly perfect days. Charly felt so at ease, so totally wonderful with Noah, she couldn't imagine leaving him. Oh, how she wished they could be together forever. Did he really mean it the time he had said, "Quit the rat race and move to the mountains with me?" Could she really do that? Would she?

As they approached the clearing where the old cabin stood, the soft silence of their forest world was interrupted by the unmistakable drone of a vehicle's motor.

CHAPTER EIGHT

Charly stood numbly as Lewis Daniel embraced her fervently, backpack and all. He held her at arm's length and examined her, his eyes traveling over her five-foot, four-inch frame. He ogled at her braless mien, where her firm-shaped nipples were outlined naturally, tantalizing him.

Charly's cheeks were pink, her face slightly flushed. She was hot and grimy, her clothes less than tidy after the twelve-mile hike. Her chestnut hair hung loosely curled around her shoulders, the way it had dried after her dip in the mountain stream. Was that a leaf entangled in a tousled wave? She presented an unsophisticated, vulnerable appearance, as opposed to her usual polish and grace. Yet Charly's natural beauty was never more obvious.

A band of tiny beads of sweat was barely visible across Lewis's forehead as he exclaimed, "Charly, have you been here all this time? I've been worried sick about you! I can't believe this has happened to you! Are you all right?" There was emphasis on the "all right" and Charly knew that Lewis meant more than the words implied. He hadn't changed.

There seemed to be a crowd of men, all talking and exchanging greetings. Walt and Noah shook hands with Lewis, then someone else. Charly turned her attention from Lewis and recognized the forest ranger, Crockett. He had been kind enough to drive Lewis up that "dangerous" road to rescue her. *Rescue?* Crockett said something of assurance to Lewis about being confident all along that Charly would be all right. He had known Walter Simms a long time and . . .

Lewis wrapped his arms around her again, and she was engulfed with the fragrance of his expensive cologne. Suddenly it was overpoweringly unpleasant, and she pushed him away from her. Charly was accustomed to Noah's fresh, natural smell, and any other was now repulsive.

Lewis was still the same intense, powerful person. In a low voice he asked urgently, "Charly, are you really *all right?* I mean . . . have you been held here against your will . . . or has anything *else* happened to you that I should know? Have you been here, in this hovel, the entire two weeks?" He couldn't hide the exasperation in his voice.

"It's only been nine days, Lewis." Somehow, it sounded so short to her now.

His voice was urgent as he rushed to explain. "I would have been here sooner, Charly—you know that—but I was in D.C. all last week. Hell, I didn't even know you hadn't reported in until Monday. We wasted two days trying to reach you at the Azalea Inn. Lovely place. They didn't know anything about you. Same with the dumb bastards in the office. Finally, I knew I had to come find you myself. Damn! I'm glad to see you!"

There was a definite message in his story of "how and why" and Charly detected it immediately. She was to thank him for "rescuing" her, but she just couldn't bring herself to do it.

Instead she smiled reassuringly at him. "I'm fine, Lewis. I've just been stranded up here because of the rain. Didn't you pass my car on the way? It's been mired in the mud since the first day. Walter Simms and . . . Noah . . . have been very nice. They've taken good care of me." She felt good that she hadn't let Lewis intimidate her. But why didn't Noah speak up? Where was he, anyway?

Lewis still talked the same, but he looked haggard. His

dark hair, tinged with gray at the temples, was slightly awry from the rough trip up the mountain, but he was impeccably dressed in brown slacks and expensive beige sport shirt. His face, tanned from every-Friday-afternoon golf matches, was clean-shaven and lean, edged with worry lines. He ran the office operations with an iron hand, and Charly had caused ripples since her arrival. He was dedicated to another tactic for ruling her. She shuddered at the thought.

She stood, as if in a daze, while the men talked. She was vaguely aware that her backpack had been removed and Noah wasn't beside her anymore. She looked around for him, but he wasn't to be seen.

The arm around her shoulder squeezed tightly to get her attention, and Lewis's commanding voice directed her, "Get your things, honey, and let's go. Mr. Crockett wants to get off this mountain before dark. And I *know* you don't want to spend another night in this place."

Another night? Just one more night . . .

Charly nodded and a strange, faraway voice said, "Let me get my purse."

In the big room Noah stood wide-legged with his back to her, looking intently out the back door. What is he thinking? she wondered. Why doesn't he let me know? Why doesn't he stop me? He would, if only . . . if only . . . A small sob welled up within her.

Charly allowed her gaze to leave Noah's broad back and drift about the room, conjuring memories of nights curled by the fireplace, cutting Noah's hair, drying his back, cooking together, making love in the small book-filled bedroom. Her eyes returned to Noah and the muscular back she had rubbed and caressed. It angered her that he wouldn't look at her, talk to her.

"Noah, it's time to go. I . . . I have to leave now." Her voice was slightly shaky and she moved across the dark room to stand close to him.

He turned to her then, arms folded across his chest, dark blue eyes interposing and nonemotional. It was as if he dared her to love him.

He said nothing, so she stammered, "I . . . I don't want to . . . to leave you."

He shrugged. His voice was low, but steady. "But you must go, Charly. You know that. And I understand."

Charly was beside herself! "You sound as though you don't even care!" Damn him! His laissez-faire attitude was infuriating!

His eyes met hers steadily. "Oh, I care. You have renewed the joy in my life, Charly. I wish our little odyssey could last forever. But we both know that's impossible. Oh, yes, I do care. But it's no use. There is nothing I—or you—can do about it."

Was there a touch of emotion, concern . . . oh, God, *love* . . . in his tone? Charly's hopes rose. "Then will you come back with me, Noah? Will you leave this place? We can make it together. I know we can."

He hesitated and took a deep breath. A low, mocking chuckle escaped with his first words. "Back to 'civilization'? No, Charly. I won't leave Walt now. At least, not for long. My responsibilities are here. You know that."

In that second her hopes were dashed. All her dreaming, hoping, loving were for naught. "Nothing we can do about it"! The words would haunt her. Nothing! It's all for nothing! A sob caught inside Charly's throat, almost choking her, for she now realized that, indeed, they were parting. Her old fear of never seeing him again—never loving him—returned to smother her. Defensively, she explained, "I have responsibilities, too. My job . . ."

"I know, Charly. I knew all along that you would leave. You have to go, and I understand that. I have to stay. I hope *you* understand." His voice was gentle.

Understand? To hell with understanding! Charly didn't want understanding and lashed at him bitterly. "So, you have enjoyed our little fling while it lasted. Just like you said earlier in the week. And now it's 'Good-bye and good luck.' Just like that!"

Noah looked at her for a long moment, assessing her anger, deciding to allow it. It made the parting so much easier for both of them. "You have a job to do, Charly. So do I," he answered quietly.

She grabbed her purse, her only personal possession in the cabin for nearly two weeks. "Well, you don't have to worry about my job, Noah. I'll ask to be removed from this case. I'm not a disinterested party anymore. I'm trying to be, but I'm not."

The jeep horn blasted loudly and impatiently, reminding them that Lewis and the "civilized" world awaited her. Charly slipped her feet out of Walt's clumsy boots and walked purposely over to Noah. She touched his hard chest and stood on tiptoe to kiss him one last time. It was a dry, unresponsive kiss—just lips touching, brushed by a velvet beard, then gone.

"Good-bye, Noah," she whispered.

She padded barefooted out the door and hugged Walt quickly on the porch. "Thanks for everything, Walt. I'll . . . I'll try to help you." Her voice was husky and strained.

The old man stared at her intently, his blue eyes shining defiantly. "For a city gal, you did pretty good up here. And you fix good vegetable soup—for a city gal."

It was the closest he would come to a compliment. Charly smiled her appreciation and left the cabin, not knowing what, if anything, she could do to help this old man—not knowing if she would ever see Noah again.

She crawled into the jeep, barefooted and bedraggled, and slumped unhappily into the seat beside Mr. Crockett. He shifted gears and the vehicle jostled roughly away. Charly purposely didn't meet Lewis's eyes, fearing her expression would show her true feelings. She was very close to tears and didn't want these men to see her crying. They might misunderstand.

Noah watched darkly from the window as Charly climbed into the vehicle and it started to roll away. He stood unblinking as Lewis draped his arms securely around Charly and kissed her. She didn't resist the affection Lewis lavished on her and remained in his encircling arms until the jeep rolled out of sight down the mountain road. Noah stalked outside then, letting the door slam behind him, jerking off the binding shirt as he moved. His muscles flourished as he raised the ax high overhead and brought it crashing down with all his might, again and again, until it was so dark that he couldn't see the pile of wood he had chopped. Then he lit a kerosene lantern and chopped until exhaustion overtook him and he dragged his spent body to the ice-cold shower.

Charly reclined against the back of her large old tub, relishing the luxuriant feeling of the warm water lapping over her sensitive skin. The millions of bubbles caught the various colors from the small candle that glowed on her vanity and clustered in pinks and violets and yellows around her legs, breasts, and shoulders. How much of this self-indulgence would it take to obliterate those nine days she spent without what she considered the necessities of life. She was exhausted after the long trip back to Atlanta. She and Lewis had driven relentlessly through the night, finally catching a midnight flight from Knoxville to Atlanta. Lewis had hovered, and Charly had let him. She functioned in a shocked state. But he understood. He had assured her of that. But he didn't—not really. Oh, God—did *she*? Was it a dream?

Returning to Atlanta and seeing her familiar belongings had jolted Charly back to the realities of her life. After living in the simple cabin, the modest apartment Charly called her own was such a welcome sight. The long east window, with its glass étagère full of plants, was the city version of her two-week odyssey close to nature. Thank goodness Mrs. Kline, her landlady, had kept them watered and alive. And her cat, Mitts. He sat behind the elephant ears and occasionally swatted a leaf, refusing to come to her right away.

"Dumb cat." She fussed. She unloaded the small suitcase and cosmetic case—neither of which had been touched during her entire trip—that she had taken from the trunk of her abandoned car.

Charly looked in the mirror at her miserable appearance. The natural face, free of makeup, the windblown hair, a slight tan on her nose, and an unmistakably healthy glow to her cheeks contrasted sharply with her eyes. Oh, God, those eyes! They were red-rimmed, dark-hollowed reminders of the pain she felt inside.

She pinched her pink cheeks. "Maybe there was something good for me in all that—maybe," she mumbled, as she began to run warm water into the marvelous old tub. It was an ancient one with legs and deep enough to cover her body with water—almost.

Without delay, Charly had stripped off her bedraggled clothes and stepped into the shallow water. She settled in the near-empty tub and closed her eyes, letting the warm water creep slowly around her aching body. All she wanted to do was to wash away the entire mountain experience —as if that were possible.

Oddly, she now lived in the lap of luxury just because she had hot running water, a flushable commode, electricity, and a stove that heated immediately without hauling wood to it. Thank God, she was home!

And no more cold showers! Actually, Charly thought she would never get enough of her warm, fragrant, relaxing baths. Oh, she had really missed this. She opened her eyes and the candle's glow flickered light shadows on the wall. The lemony scent permeated the room. Suddenly, she shut her eyes tightly, pinching the vision of Noah by the fireplace, making love to her with his eyes. She heaved a sigh. Oh, when would he go away?

Charly's favorite Nancy Wilson records filled the background with soft, romantic sounds. It was definitely more pleasant than a harmonica! Enormously so! Charly swayed slightly to the hypnotic beat, trying not to slosh her bath water on the carpeted floor. *Oh, yes . . . this is the life . . . so nice . . .*

But there was one memory that her easy, comfortable life-style couldn't obliterate. Noah. Noah Van Horn. Were those two weeks in the rugged mountain cabin a dream? But life there was harsh. It wasn't the sort of place one dreamed of. Was Noah her fantasy? He had never declared his love. Never.

Charly ran her hand over her body, slick from the bubbles and oil. Shuddering, she recalled his caress and knew he was real. Brief, but real. She had never responded to anyone like she had to Noah. His touch warmed her, thrilled her, tore at her reason, intensified her passion. Suddenly, she missed him terribly, longed for his gentle hands on her, craved his lean, dark body next to hers.

Tormented in her longed-for tub, with scented candles and ever-relaxing music, there was nothing strong enough to make her forget her love. There was no escaping! Great tears welled up in her eyes as she fought the image of his face in her mind. She saw him teasing her, loving her, standing immobile for the last passionless kiss, telling her to go with his eyes. And she cried—great, heaving sobs for the first time since she left the humble little cabin and Noah.

Only now did she realize the full impact of her experience. She had fallen ridiculously, hopelessly in love with a stranger who didn't return her love. And she would never see—or touch—Noah Van Horn again.

* * *

Charly put her hands on the mahogany desk before her and leaned on them. Her brown eyes snapped furiously at Lewis. "I told you before. I want to be taken off this case! In fact, I insist on it!"

Lewis leaned back in his swivel chair and kept his voice calm. "And I told you, Charly, I don't think that's necessary. I'll assign it to Ben if you want. But I want you to work with him on it."

"But why? I've told you everything I know about it. And, after a trip up there, I failed to come back with enough evidence . . ."

Lewis's steady, calm voice instructed her. "Please sit down, Charly. Now, I know that entire episode has left you depressed and uptight. That's to be expected, honey. You've been through a bad experience and I won't send you back. You don't have to worry about that. But I'm not giving up on the case just because you're ready to drop it. We'll work with you to help you finish it."

Charly sat on the edge of the chair opposite Lewis. She gazed out the window of his spacious office, which afforded a lovely view of Atlanta from the tenth floor. The city sparkled with fall sunshine and bustled with the noisy business of the day. She used to enjoy it—thrive on the activity of the city, thrill to be a part of it. But now it annoyed her. It was too loud, and fast—maybe she just needed to get away for a while. But she'd been away . . .

". . . Charly, you're not listening. I think you know a lot more about this case than you're telling. For instance, what is Van Horn doing up there? You haven't explained his presence to my satisfaction at all . . ."

Charly twisted her hands nervously. "I told you, Lewis, I don't know! I just don't . . ."

"You were with him the day we arrived. What were you two doing together? Where had you been? What did you see deep in those mountains?" His voice was sinister and driving.

"Don't grill me as if I were a criminal, Lewis. I don't have to answer that!"

Damn! She'd been impossible lately! "I'm just trying to ascertain some facts, Charly. I think you're holding back info that's pertinent to the case. This lifetime-lease case is important. And, Charly, I intend to find out about that situation if I have to send someone else back up there. I think even more is going on than we suspected—and you may know about it! My God! You spent almost two weeks up there! You *have* to know more about the old man's life-style than you're telling!" Lewis's voice was vicious.

Charly spread her hands. "I only know that an old man lives up there and he deserves to continue to live on his property until he dies, according to his lease."

Lewis's wicked golden eyes narrowed. "You sound like you've switched allegiances, Charly. Two weeks with the enemy and the prisoner becomes sympathetic to his cause."

Charly's voice rose shrilly. "I was not there two weeks! I was only there nine days! And they—he—is *not* an enemy! Walter Simms is a nice, trusting old man who is just trying to live and let live. And what is this enemy bit? You're not still in the army, y'know! I wasn't a prisoner!"

"Then why didn't you leave?"

"I . . . I couldn't! You saw my car! It was a total loss. Mr. Crockett had to hire someone to tow it away! You know I couldn't leave! My papers and everything were stuck in the car." She didn't tell him that she and Noah had hiked twelve miles the day Lewis arrived. In actuality, she could have hiked off the mountain and halfway to town. But then, she didn't want to leave. She only wanted to be with Noah. She even threatened never to go back to civilization. So why *had* she? She had asked herself that a million times already. Her head reeled with the thought, but Lewis's staccato-paced words snapped her back.

"What do you know about Van Horn?"

"Nothing!" Her answer was too quick, too severe.

"Nothing? You were with him . . . hiking, did you say? Bartering with neighbors? Come on, Charly. What *is* Van Horn doing there?"

She looked Lewis in the eye and shrugged. "He's a friend of Walt's. He stopped by to help Walt." She couldn't believe she was being so calm while talking about Noah.

"And you just went along for the walk."

Charly glared at him. He was setting her up, and she knew it. Slowly, she answered. "Something like that. I can tell you one thing for sure, Lewis. I will report on the simple mountain life of Walter Simms of Simms Hollow, North Carolina. But I won't sign a derogatory report on him, because now, after being there, I feel that he is not harming anything or anybody by living there."

"Simple life?" Lewis's laugh was wicked. "I thought we determined there were factors warranting his expulsion before you even made the trip up there. Now, after spending two weeks—excuse me, nine days—up there, you can't tell me one harmful thing the old man's doing. Not shooting animals, not running moonshine . . ."

"Moonshine?" Her eyes widened and she feared betrayal.

"Aw, come on, Charly. Surely you know about that! All of those mountain people brew a little 'shine' and run it occasionally—or regularly! How do you think they make a living?"

"They do not!" Charly was on her feet again. "That's not true! Walt doesn't . . . do that! I swear it!" She tried not to be too emphatic. In her mind, there were already doubts that she could keep up this pressure and not reveal a piece of knowledge that would be used against Simms.

Whether the illegal whiskey still she had seen belonged to him or not, if she let it slip that she had even seen one, Lewis would twist the information the way he wanted it.

Lewis walked around the desk and placed his arm around her shoulders. He could feel her quivering inside and knew he was pushing her too far. But maybe now was the time to find out about Charly's relationship with Van Horn. It gnawed at his gut to think what might have taken place between them. Damn! He had to know! Charly denied cognizance of anything about him, but there was tension in the air whenever Van Horn's name was mentioned. Lewis could feel it.

"Calm down, Charly. Come, sit over here." He tried to lead her to the two-seater sofa.

Charly jerked from his grasp. "Get your hands off me," she said, seething. She was different since her trip, all right. He hadn't been able to take her to lunch, much less touch her. He had tried to be patient, but that was wearing thin. He was sure something had occurred between them in the mountains.

Lewis leaned against the heavy desk, looming near her, yet not touching her. The gold flecks in his eyes gleamed menacingly. "All right, Charly. Tell me about Van Horn. What was he doing at the cabin? What do you know about him?"

"Nothing! I told you, I don't know anything about him!"

"Did you know he comes from a very wealthy family in Charlotte? *The* Van Horns, furniture magnates in the South for over a hundred years? Now what would a man like that be doing in the mountains? Living there? He has enough money to buy the whole damn place!"

Charly folded her arms defensively. It helped steady them and hide her shaking hands. Her voice was derisive as she hid her own shock upon learning how much Lewis knew about Noah. "It is public domain, you know. National Forest means anyone can enter, Lewis!"

"I want to know what he was doing with *you!* Is he living in that cabin? Did you live with him for two weeks, Charly?"

Her eyes narrowed and she worked to keep her voice steady. "I think our conversation is finished, Lewis! I won't answer any more of your stupid questions! And I won't file or sign a derogatory report on this case. The only way you'll get any help from me is to take me off the case!" She wheeled toward the door, but before she reached the handle, Lewis grabbed her arm, his fingers digging through her blazer and into her skin.

"I am not relieving you from this case, Charly. The inquisition will continue. Right now Mr. Van Horn is being investigated. Soon we'll know all about him, and you won't be able to hide what you know any longer. I'm trusting that you will still come around."

"Don't hold your venomous breath, Lewis." Charly snapped her aching arm away from Lewis's grasp and left the office. She was so angry, her entire body shook. And she knew it would be impossible to hold up with much more of this kind of pressure from Lewis. She wasn't sure what she could do about it—would do—but there had to be something.

She flew into her office and slammed the door. Damn him, anyway! He suspected something between her and Noah. If he hadn't cared about her, tried to seduce her, the matter wouldn't bother him at all. He probably wouldn't pursue it. But there was a jealousy apparent—and God knows, there was nothing to be jealous about. Not anymore. What happened between her and Noah had been a fling—she had heard nothing from Noah in the weeks since she had left. It was as if it had never happened. One long, miserable month had passed, and Charly had heard nothing. But what did she expect? Love letters?

Hardly! She knew better! She knew she would never see him again. And it was just as well. But the least she could do was protect Walt. And she would try to do that with all her ability—what wasn't eroded by Lewis.

She was furious that he wouldn't relieve her of the responsibility of the case. There was a purpose in that, and she knew it. He hadn't pressed her on it until now. But she sensed there would be increased pressure as time progressed. Lewis was relentless in getting what he wanted, whether it was a resolved case or personal satisfaction. She knew she was a part of that personal satisfaction he desired. It was still obvious to her, even though she had held him off so far. Lately, she had been downright rude to the man, and still he persisted. She shivered at the thought of Lewis's hands on her. She couldn't even stand his arm lightly around her shoulders. She was haunted by the bearded mountain man's touch—more now than when she had first returned. Memory must do something to enhance the imagination. No one could have been that enticing to her. Surely . . .

Charly fumbled in her desk, drawing out a thick folder full of papers. She had these reports to complete, then there was nothing pressing until next Monday. She could work late and finish them, then call in sick tomorrow. She needed the time off, needed to get her head together. It was getting to be a habit taking Fridays off—three of the last four Fridays had been to "get her head together." It hadn't worked yet. What made her think it would now?

Time. That's what they all said—time will heal the hurt. But so far time had enhanced her hurt. It just meant more time that she hadn't seen him. Oh, damn! What could she do to obliterate Noah from her mind?

CHAPTER NINE

Lewis glanced at the office clock. It read 8:10. He knew it had been dark for several hours, but they had been so busy, they had lost track of the time. He looked across the small conference desk, laden with scattered papers, and smiled. Charly's tousled brown head was bent in intense concentration as she poured over the papers before her. She made notes here and there, checked a long accompanying list, and continued reading, oblivious to Lewis's admiring gaze.

His voice was gentle. "Charly, let's call it quits. I'm beat and I know you are. It's after eight. We can finish this tomorrow."

She looked up and automatically checked the clock, then glanced outside, where the city lights glittered in a sea of darkness. Sighing, she nodded in agreement. Her head felt like a heavy weight. "Let me finish this page. It'll only take a few minutes." She continued her task, not realizing that Lewis still hadn't taken his eyes off her and that they held a special glow.

Lewis smiled with inner satisfaction, his eyes settling on her full breasts, wishing he could get his hands on them. Even with no lipstick and her hair disarrayed, she was attractive . . . alluring . . . sexy. He was taken with her appeal—had been from the time she first came to work for him. Maybe tonight . . .

"It's been a long week, honey. I want you to know how

much I appreciate your working late every night to help me finish this damned project," he complimented her earnestly.

She glanced up and shrugged. "Everyone has put in long hours on it, Lewis. It goes with the job. I just seem to get stuck with the night duty. I'll remember this when I ask for my next raise." Was there a touch of the old Charly—joking, teasing, carefree?

He reached across the table and patted her hand, covering hers while he talked. "Don't worry, Charly. I won't forget. I'm well aware that your efforts have been over and above the call of duty. And now the project is practically finished, thanks to your work tonight. In fact, this calls for a celebration. How about grabbing a bite to eat with me? I'm starved!"

Charly tried not to jerk away from his hand, but his touch jolted through her. She knew she was being overly sensitive. Casually, she started to organize the papers into orderly stacks. What harm would there be in a meal together? She hadn't been out in so long—and Lewis had been nice to her at work. There had been no more confrontations. None. And she, too, was starved . . .

"Sure, Lewis. Sounds great. Give me a few minutes to repair my makeup." She hastened to the ladies' room, then accompanied him eagerly to his car.

The "bite to eat" turned out to be a sumptuous four-course meal at one of Atlanta's finest, taking two hours to eat and accompanied by two kinds of wine. Lewis certainly outdid himself, lavishing Charly with attention and wine. The heavy meal—or was it the wine?—left Charly somewhat lethargic, and she smiled solicitously as Lewis entertained her. He was charming, witty, the proper gentleman. Charly knew she was being pursued, but it was a nice feeling. It had been so long since she had been out with a man, catered to, sought after. She hadn't dated anyone and had remained holed up in her lonely apartment for the past two months, nursing her broken heart. And it had been much too long.

Lewis had let up on his relentless pursuit of her knowledge of the lifetime-lease case. It hadn't been discussed in weeks. She had submitted reports to close the case, but she hadn't heard anything on that. Charly was sure Lewis had received information on the pending investigation of Noah, but it hadn't been mentioned. Charly certainly wasn't going to broach the subject. She was trying her best to forget Noah Van Horn, just as he had forgotten her. And she was sure now that Noah didn't give a damn about their relationship, those lustful days they'd spent together. Nor did he care about her feelings.

She hadn't heard a word from him since the day he'd encouraged her to leave the mountain, saying he understood. Oh, how she hated him for understanding! Oh, God, here she was thinking about him again. Her mind rambled sometimes—beyond her control.

"Charly—hey, Charly! Are you ready to go?" Lewis was leaning anxiously toward her, trying to get her attention. His hand warmly covered hers.

She jerked back to the reality of her location, across from Lewis. "Yes? Oh, yes, Lewis." She smiled wanly and stood so he could drape her tweed blazer around her shoulders.

Lewis kept one arm possessively around her shoulders as they left the restaurant. It was as if he didn't want to let her out of reach. He drove rapidly through the city and halted beside an unfamiliar building. Charly looked at him questioningly.

Calmly, he answered her unasked question by suggesting, "Let's go in to my place and have a drink together, Charly. Maybe some coffee. Or, I have some nice brandy." His expression and tone were casually encouraging, but he didn't rush her. He waited patiently for her answer. He had been so patient for many months now.

She smiled her assent. "Well, maybe just a little brandy. Can you believe that I've never had brandy? But remember, we have to work tomorrow, boss." After she agreed to accompany him, she began to have small doubts. Actually, it was a little risky. She really didn't care if she was with Lewis or not. It could be anyone. Indifference was the way she went through her life these days. But that had to end—someday . . . some night . . .

"Permit me, madam." Lewis was already opening the car door, offering his hand to help her exit the vehicle. Before she knew it, she was inside his apartment, taking the round goblet he handed her. She sniffed the pungent brandy and decided this was going a bit far for someone who happened to like homemade blackberry wine. She smiled to herself and walked around the nice but not entirely elegant room. The decor was distinctly masculine in browns and rusts and dark blues. There was a mixture of old and new furniture, indicating a collection through the years. She wondered briefly if he had ever been married. Funny, she had never asked—never cared. The sofa was old and worn, a nearby brass and glass table shiny and new. Sliding glass doors opened onto a small patio that overlooked the city. The lights formed patterns in the backdrop of blackness and glistened like diamonds on display as cars moved along ribbon streets. Charly turned back to Lewis. She had stalled long enough, gathering her courage.

Lewis stood waiting patiently—oh, so patiently—for her attention. Yes, tonight was the night. He sensed it—felt it . . . He licked his lips in anticipation.

Appropriately, he crossed the space between them. Slowly, his arms went around her and Charly raised her head so that he could kiss her. When his lips touched hers, she involuntarily sucked in her startled breath and tried to step back—away from his lips, his advances. Is this really what she wanted? Not really—not yet! She struggled again, but Lewis seemed prepared for her reaction. He kept his arms securely around her, preventing her escape from his clutches. Wisely, he held himself in check and didn't try to force his kisses on her, for he wanted Charly to come to him willingly. And she was so close. Patience . . .

His voice was thick with passion, and his breath fell in raspy spurts on her face. "Charly . . . Charly. Don't fight me. I won't force you. But I can make it good. I can help you forget him if you'll give me a chance. Let me make you forget him."

Charly gasped audibly and looked at Lewis with wild eyes. He knew! Damn him! He knew about Noah! "I . . . I don't know what you're talking about, Lewis," she managed. She pushed gently on his chest.

"Yes you do, Charly," he cajoled softly. "Your beautiful eyes are those of a woman in love—a woman scorned." He said the word with contempt. "Face it, Charly. The only way you'll forget him is to replace him with someone else—someone better."

Replace Noah? She felt slightly dizzy and rubbed her forehead, pushing again on him. "Oh, Lewis . . . don't—don't rush me. I don't know . . ." She shook her head, puzzled over the turn of events and her own torrid emotions.

Reluctantly, he released her, and Charly stepped back reflexively. She gulped the drink, staring into the glass as if the answers she sought danced inside. The brandy seared her insides, but within moments created a small, growing glow. Help me?

Lewis's voice was low and gentle. "I won't rush you, Charly. I'm here when you need me. Don't forget—when you needed me on the mountain, when you were stranded,

I came for you. I won't leave you, Charly. I'll always be here . . . for you."

His voice was soothing. She liked the things he said. He had rescued her from the mountain and . . . Noah. But he sounded too good. Could she really believe him? Charly drank again, emptying the glass this time, for she wanted to obliterate Noah's memory and . . . what was now happening to her and . . . what she was about to do. *Yes! Help me! Make me forget!* She took a deep breath and a step toward him.

"Make me forget, Lewis. Make me forget tonight. I . . . I don't know why it took so long . . ." She opened her arms to him.

Instantly, Lewis's lean arms were around her, his lips savagely abusing hers, his hands raking over her body. Charly tried to submit completely to the pleasures Lewis had promised. The one thing she wanted in the world was Noah's love. But since she couldn't have it, she would forget him—block out his memory altogether. And Lewis had assured her he would help her do that. He would make her forget. She stifled a sob as he lifted her to the broad sofa, his hands roughly seeking her breasts, fumbling at her blouse buttons. Wildly, she wondered how many others had forgotten their sorrows on Lewis's tattered sofa. His hot groping hands touched the sensitive areas of her breasts, seeking to ignite in Charly the desires that matched his.

Spontaneously, unavoidably, Charly's latent emotions emerged in a single frantic cry. "Noah!"

Immediately, Lewis's ardent motions halted. Damn! Patience, be damned! He wanted her . . . *now!*

In the brief moment of indecision, Charly managed to scramble frantically from the sofa, away from Lewis's grasp. Her brown mane tumbled over part of her frightened face and her blouse hung open, revealing heaving breasts. "No, Lewis! I'm . . . I'm sorry, Lewis. Honest I am! I . . . I just can't! Not now. Not yet. I . . . I hope you understand!" She didn't understand, so why should he? She only knew she couldn't bear his touch. She grasped at her gaping blouse, buttoning it blindly.

Lewis stared at her, anger and frustration written on his tortured face. And she couldn't blame him. She had led him on, then done the unforgivable. But right now all she wanted to do was get away from him. Before he could stop her, she had grabbed her purse and jacket and bolted from the apartment. She emerged almost wildly onto the street, amazed at the amount of traffic at this late hour. The gusty autumn wind chilled her blazing body and she quickly donned her jacket, shivering with emotion as much as coldness. Confused, she started to run along the street, needing only to get home. A car stopped near the curb where she moved and honked at her. Frantically, fearfully, she looked around.

"Taxi, ma'am?"

Gratefully, she nodded and lunged into the cab, spouting off her address without a thought to her safety. All she wanted to do was to get home where she could be alone— alone again!

Charly fumbled for her apartment key, finally managing to unlock the door and breathlessly slip inside. She was shaking like a leaf in a storm. Her ragged emotions were tearing her apart, ravaging her reason. And *he* was the cause! Oh, how she hated him! A sob rose like a suffocating mound in her chest and she wanted to scream. *No! I love you, Noah!* She couldn't even deny it to herself, couldn't escape its binding snare. She was caught in Noah's trap, as helpless as the animals who had made the mistake of getting too close. That's what she had done. She had gotten too close. She had cared too much.

Charly turned toward the welcoming darkness of her small home and gasped, a fearful cry of alarm rising aloud from her open mouth. There, outlined in the dark, loomed the broad-shouldered figure of a man!

The low voice that followed her gasp settled her fears, for she recognized it immediately. "Hey, Wildcat, don't you ever stay at home?"

"Noah? Is it you? Noah!"

Instantly, she flung herself into his arms, clinging to him for dear life, crying tears of disbelief and joy onto his beard and neck. He held her like that until her sobbing hushed, caressing her hair, murmuring soft words. She didn't even wonder where he came from, or why he was there, or how he'd gotten into her apartment. That would come later. Right now she only knew that he was here, holding her. It was like a dream. Yet another dream. But Noah wasn't a dream—she touched him, smelled him, felt his warmth against her. And that's all that mattered.

It was a long time before Charly raised her head from his broad chest. She probably should be mad at him. But she was so glad to see him, she just wanted to cling to him. She felt like the mother who couldn't decide whether to hug or spank her runaway son. Love won out and she hugged the errant boy to her breast. Finally, she broke the silence of the night. "Noah? Why . . . why are you here?" Did she dare ask? Would he tell her what she wanted to hear?

He nibbled softly on her earlobe. "I thought you'd never ask. I came to make mad, passionate love to you, Wildcat. God! I've missed you! Do you know how lonely that damn cabin is without you?"

Charly giggled, feeling almost giddy and light-headed with the excitement of having Noah with her, so close. "I know how lonely the big city is without you! I thought you'd never come here—that I'd never see you again! I thought we'd never make mad, passionate love again! What are we waiting for?"

He nuzzled her ear and neck, his marvelous, velvety

beard tickling her, delighting her. "I'm waiting for you to stop crying. Either you're happy or you're sad. Make up your mind. If you're going to cry, I'll hold you. But if you're happy, we'll make love and make us both happy."

"No more crying, I promise. Couldn't you tell they were tears of happiness? I'm very happy to see you, Noah. I've missed you like you could never in a million years know! And I'm eager!" She kissed him fiercely on the lips, surprising him with her darting, teasing tongue.

Noah returned her passionate embrace, pulling her tightly against his unyielding, muscular body. She was soft, pliable, willing. He was hard, insatiable, demanding. They had been so long without each other, it was as if they were starved. And they indulged ravenously in the gratifying delicacy each offered. Their ecstasy was mutually shared as unspoken consent was agreed upon, and Noah swung her up in his powerful arms. At last! They were together at long last! Gently, he placed her on the bed.

Charly started to unbutton her wrinkled blouse, but his hands stopped her.

"Let me. It's been so long, Charly. I want to enjoy every part of you." His hands moved deliberately down the buttons, gloriously opening her blouse. Briefly, Charly was glad the room was so dark that he couldn't see the wrinkled condition of her blouse. Oh—what she had almost done tonight! Almost.

He deftly unsnapped the front opening of her bra and pushed it back so that her creamy white breasts fell naturally into his hands. Noah caressed them both, admiringly, lovingly. His tongue darted and teased the tips to firm hardness. Charly caught her breath as the sensuous feelings radiated throughout her entire body, reaching an ecstatic peak as she arched against the pressure of his hand.

"Oh, Charly, I want you . . ." His voice was husky and he struggled feverishly with his own clothes.

This time Charly grabbed his large warm hands. "No, you'll have to wait. Let me . . ." And she proceeded to unbutton his shirt. She ran her hands slowly down his chest, her fingernails digging through the soft mat of dark hair, tickling, scraping, loving, sharing the excitement of his masculine body.

With a shudder, he stood and began to loosen his belt and zipper. "Get them off, woman—I can't wait for you another minute!"

Obligingly, hurriedly, Charly scooted out of her remaining clothes, as anxious for Noah as he was for her. Suddenly, after weeks of wondering, of being apart, the longed-for time was nigh, and they welcomed the event joyously and with exuberance. The feverish pitch of their passion reached a rapid and glorious zenith, as they clung breathlessly to each other. Afterward they lay quietly together, their bodies saying what no words could.

Noah stroked her hair, urging an unruly lock away from her temple, where damp tendrils curled. His hand was cool and soothing now, as was his voice.

"I've missed you, little Wildcat. I didn't realize just how much until tonight, when I saw you, touched you. I thought it was my imagination. And I had forgotten what a real wildcat you are!"

"Noah." Her voice sounded very small in the quiet darkness.

"Hmmm?" His was a rumble that vibrated through her.

"Noah . . . I love you. I have been so miserable without you." Would she regret confessing her deepest feelings to him? No. It was obvious she loved him. She hoped, waited expectantly for his avowal of love for her. He kissed her, touched her as though he was filled with love—or was it just his strong passion?

"Well, I'm here now. So let's enjoy the next few days, Wildcat."

"Few days?" A feeling of dread began eroding the joy she felt at having him with her.

"Um-hum. I'm here for the weekend. I have business tomorrow, but after that I'm free."

"Every minute? Just for me?" She ran her finger around his lips.

"If you have time for me!"

"If—of course I do! I want you with me every minute!"

He didn't hide the exasperation in his voice. "Hell, you'll have to cancel your social calendar then. I waited five hours for you tonight! Dozed on your sofa . . . made friends with your cat . . . fixed myself a sandwich."

Charly moaned to herself, remembering how she had spent her evening—and how it had almost ended up. "I'm glad you met Mitts and made yourself at home. If I had only known you were coming—"

"It was a spur-of-the-moment deal. Business in Atlanta. I knew I had to see you."

"See me? And that's not all!" She giggled, running her hand over his chest.

His delighted laughter was a low rumble. "I can't look at you without touching, Wildcat. You do marvelous, uncontrollable things to me!"

She smiled against his neck while her fingers traced imaginary lines through the feathery-soft hair on his chest. "Ummm, I'm glad. It would be embarrassing for me to carry you to bed!"

He pinched her nipple. "And you probably could do it, too!"

She trailed a fingernail down the dark hairline of his belly and further. "You bet I could—if I made up my mind to it."

He grabbed the teasing, tantalizing finger. "Careful, Charly. You'll create a recurrence . . ." He pressed her hand to his mouth, kissing her fingertips.

"Promise?" she teased, caressing the lips and beard she loved to touch.

"Charly . . . it's late. Very late. I have a meeting tomorrow and you have to go to work. We'll have all weekend to talk and catch up." His voice was muffled, low and relaxed.

"Catch up? Let's catch up now, Noah!" she challenged with a laugh. She leaned over him and kissed him long and hard, relishing the delicious taste of his lips.

The temptation was too much for Noah, and his hands claimed her again. They felt hot on her cool body as he artfully compelled her to new pleasures of ecstasy. With a low groan, he pulled her over him. Charly's delightful laughter filled the night as she experienced ultimate pleasures with the man she loved.

Finally, they slumped together exhausted, their craving satiated. But Charly was still unable to relinquish to sleep.

"Noah, did you say you've been waiting here, in my apartment, for five hours?"

"Um-hum."

"How did you get in?" It occurred to her that he didn't have a key.

"I convinced your landlady I was your brother. You're going to have to do something about the trusting souls around here. It's dangerous."

"Mrs. Kline?" Charly giggled. "She would die if she realized her mistake! And probably boot me out! Now I have to go around acting like you're my brother! I can't hang on you or kiss you or . . ."

His voice was relaxed and sleepy. "It's late, Charly . . ."

"Noah, how do you expect me to sleep when you're here with me at last? And I haven't seen you in two months . . ."

"Seven weeks and four days, to be exact. And agonizing

ones at that. But now I'm here and I don't intend to leave until you throw me out!"

"Promise you'll stay? You know I'll *never* throw you out, Noah! I want you here forever!"

"Until Monday—go to sleep."

"Noah—"

"Like this." He turned on his side and curved around her warm body. And Charly slept deeply for the first time in weeks, enfolded in the security and love of Noah's chest and arms and legs.

CHAPTER TEN

"Where's Charly?" boomed Lewis, red-faced and irritated as he banged the phone down again.

His secretary looked up knowingly. She was well accustomed to his temperamental moods and went bustling in to soothe him. She wasn't as concerned about him as about those around him. He had been in the office exactly forty-five minutes and had managed to yell at four of the pool secretaries, bringing one of them to tears and alienating Ben Morrison, his deputy assistant, who told him to "go to hell" before stalking out. Now he was screaming about Charly, for Pete's sake. Maybe Charly had something to do with bringing about all this uproar.

"T.G.I.F." she whispered to the records girl as she slipped into Lewis's office. "Mr. Daniel, Charly hasn't reported in today." She smiled a wide fake smile and set another cup of hot coffee on his desk. "Do you want me to get her on the phone at home? Is it urgent?" This off-on-Friday business had gotten to be a habit for Charly and everyone at the office was aware of it. And resentment ran high that she could continue to do it and keep her job.

"No. Ah, no, thank you, Ann. Sick again, eh?" He nodded and muttered again, "Thank you," his first and only kind words of the day. The secretary quietly left Lewis gazing out at the morning's sun reflecting on the glass of the tall Coastal States Building. He chuckled under his breath. He understood why Charly wasn't at work this particular Friday. Or so he thought.

The late-morning sun finally reached Charly's second-floor window and slipped between the thick poplar branches that shaded it. A shaft of light boldly crossed Charly's peacefully sleeping countenance. She stirred, turned over, and snuggled into the empty space beside her. She reached over to touch him, to make sure he was really there and not just a dream. But the bed was empty.

Her eyes flew open immediately and she sat up quickly, the covers falling from her bare breasts. What if—

"Have some coffee, Charly?" His voice made her smile even before she saw him puttering in the small kitchen.

He walked toward her, shirtless, handsome—real—and smiled as he handed her the blue coffee mug. "Good morning, beautiful," he murmured before kissing her. His gaze dropped to her exposed breasts and she reached for the blue-flowered sheet.

"Aw, don't be modest, Wildcat. I like the view," he laughed. "After last night . . ."

Her brown eyes glowed, and she sputtered arrogantly, "After last night, what?"

Noah sat on the edge of the bed and leaned over her, placing a hand on either side of her, kissing her again, this time long and sensual. "After last night, I never want to leave you, Charly. I don't know how I stayed away so long."

"Then don't. Don't leave me—ever," she answered simply, her eyes very sincere, but her heart knowing the truth. She touched his face, caressed his cheek and velvety beard. Oh, how she wished he would always be within her reach, her kiss. But she was afraid he would not. "Kiss me," she begged, longing for his reassuring touch.

The feathery-light kiss intensified to a flood tide of love's passion. Noah's lips crushed hers fiercely, his teeth threatened to damage her tender skin. His hands savagely roamed her body, then pulled her to him. His dark beard covered her face, smothering her, and she gasped painfully as he pressed her tender breasts tightly against his bare chest. At her low cry, he immediately released his grasp. He lightly showered her face with kisses and his hands gently slid over her.

"Oh, God, Charly, I'm sorry. The last thing in the world I want to do is to hurt you. I just lost . . ." He kissed her eyelids and trailed to her mouth, where his lips lovingly caressed her.

Her hand curved around his neck and she dug into the hair curled there. "It's just been so long, Noah. I want you, too. I wish—"

"Don't—" He silenced her with another kiss. "Don't wish—just enjoy."

One hand removed the coffee mug Charly still clutched and unzipped his jeans while the other threw the blue-flowered sheet back, exposing her luscious curves to the angular morning sun.

"What a way to start the day," he teased as he slid onto the bed beside her.

"Hmmm." She nuzzled his neck. "Beats coffee every time . . ."

Their easy-laughing conversation ceased as lips opened for each other and hands sought to please. Soon their bodies melded together in an ecstatic crescendo of love and passion while the sun rose higher to bathe them in warmth. Leisurely, they descended to a lingering, glistening embrace, not wanting to let go, but knowing they must.

"Please, don't leave me, Noah," Charly whispered.

His voice was still hoarse with passion. "You know I can't make any promises—not yet, Charly. But we will have a good time together. That I can promise."

"I know," she admitted, feeling the immediate gulf between them, although they still lay entwined.

Finally, he shifted away from her simmering ardor and pulled his jeans over his slim hips. "How about that coffee now, Wildcat?"

"Want to try it again, huh?" She smiled, gratified knowing he found her magnetic. It gave her a feeling of a little power over him—at least, as long as she was with him.

"I'll stay an arm's length away this time," he laughed as he moved easily to the kitchen. His lithe motions reminded Charly of the stealthy pacing of a caged tiger.

She chuckled. "I think the wrong person has the name 'Wildcat.' It seems to me that it fits you much better."

He smiled as he approached her again, a steamy mug in each hand. "Maybe you're right, Charly. But those first two days I knew you, you were like a wildcat—rebelling, scratching, fighting everything I said or did. After that, however, you tamed down to a cuddly kitten."

She took the mug and grinned good-naturedly with his teasing. "I just needed someone to cuddle with me!"

"So did I." His eyes still twinkled, but there was a seriousness to his tone. Then, adroitly, he changed the subject. "Don't you have to go to work sometime today? It's after ten."

Charly sipped leisurely from her mug and smiled smugly at him. "I'll call in sick in a few minutes. I don't want to miss a second with you." She didn't tell him that this off-on-miserable-Friday business was common for her. Only this time it was a marvelous Friday to be spent with Noah.

As if he read her mind, he answered, "I have a meeting today, Charly. I can't spend the entire day with you. I have some business to attend to, you know. Business lunch at noon."

She shrugged. "That's okay. As long as you spend the night." She grinned.

"Oh, yes! I wouldn't miss the night for anything!" He winked and Charly thrilled to his delightful teasing. He snapped his fingers as his memory was jogged. "That reminds me, Charly. I have reservations to stay tonight at the Peachtree Plaza Hotel. Would you like to spend the night there? It's very beautiful."

Charly raised her eyebrows. "Is that the one with the half-acre lake in the lobby? Wonder if they'd let me wade?"

"Not if I tell them your wading sometimes leads to skinny-dipping! Well, how about it? They have a pool and, of course, the lake. It's one of the most beautiful hotels you'll find anywhere."

She shook her thick mane. "I'm not hunting hotels." *I'm trying to hang on to my man.* "Would you mind terribly if we don't go public, Noah? I think I want you right here with me." There was something possessive about having him in her own bed, and she didn't want to let go.

He shrugged. "It's fine with me. But I insist on taking you out tonight. I already have reservations at Nikolai's Roof for nine. It's a marvelous restaurant and I want you to enjoy it. Also, I want to show you off a little. That is, if I'm not interrupting any of your weekend plans by arriving so unexpectedly."

"I have no plans this weekend except to be with you, Noah." Should she tell him about last night with Lewis? Her desperation? Her agony over the last two months? No—didn't he say to enjoy the present? "Nikolai's Roof? I've heard of it, but—how did you get reservations? They're booked weeks in advance for the weekends."

"Connections, my dear Charly. Connections!" He reached for something on her coffee table. "Here, I brought you a little something from the mountain country. Thought it might remind you of the halcyon days spent at Noah's ark!" He laughed as he casually tossed a small box in her lap.

Charly sat up delightedly, trying to cover herself with the sheet. "A gift? Great! And it's not even my birthday!" She set aside her coffee mug and tore at the calico ribbon that adorned the simple box. Inside, nestled in blue tissue paper, was an exquisite wood carving of a small wild rabbit. As she lifted it carefully out of the box, she could see the precise detail of the carving, right down to the tiny whiskers. It was quite unique.

"Ooooh, Noah," she breathed. "It's just gorgeous . . ." For a moment she was speechless and gazed at the miniature rabbit through misty eyes. "It's so . . . fine. Thank you, Noah. It does remind me of our days in the mountains together. Remember the little rabbit you tried to sketch on that last morning—" Her voice caught and there was a moment of strained silence between them. They both recalled—all too well.

Noah boldly launched through the heavy reticence. "I'm glad you like him, Charly. He was made by an old man who has carved miniatures for fun and relaxation all his life. Now he's making a good living by selling them. And he's preserving his craft by teaching at the local college. I was very impressed by his work and thought you would be, too."

"Oh, I am! And I'm so glad you brought it to me in person." Her voice dwindled as Noah kissed her lips and nose, then offered to make breakfast.

" 'Never disturb a man who likes to cook' is my motto," Charly laughed, ecstatic to have him near. She wanted to savor every moment with him. She enjoyed just watching him prowl around her small studio apartment as if he belonged there.

"I'm going to find a special place of honor for this little fellow," she pledged determinedly, throwing back the sheet and slipping across the room.

Mitts, the cat, jumped to the back of the sofa, alarmed at the sudden activity of his mistress.

"There. How's that?" She stepped back to assess the little rabbit's position on the glass étagère.

"Perfect! Just terrific!" agreed Noah, openly admiring the spectacle of Charly fluttering around the room nude.

"He does look perfect right there between the violets." She smiled with satisfaction.

"I think he'd be happier between the roses!"

"There aren't any roses—" The amused look on his face told her he was teasing her again. She threw a sofa pillow at him. "Back to your pans, chef!"

He dodged the pillow easily and laughed aloud as he went about his task. "How does a mushroom omelet and biscuits sound?"

"Biscuits?"

"Sure." He padded barefooted and bare-chested around the kitchen, reminding Charly again of the casual, carefree days in the cabin. "Biscuits are my specialty."

"No they aren't! Your talents aren't confined to the kitchen!" She grinned devilishly, knowing she had gotten him back.

"Huh?" He was hunting for pans, making a loud rattling noise as he rustled through her collection.

She gave him a disgusted look, then shrugged. The timing for the joke had passed. Oh, well, there would be other times. "Biscuits sound great, Noah. Fattening, but great. I don't think I've had a biscuit since I left the mountain cabin."

He gazed at her slim, bare body. "Looks as though you haven't had enough of anything to eat, Charly. Have you lost weight?"

How could he be that observant? She swung her long hair defensively and it fell loosely over her shoulders. "I've been busy." She disappeared into the bathroom. How could she tell him of the miserable days—and nights—she sat waiting to hear from him, hoping, crying alone in the night?

By the time she emerged from her shower, Noah was setting the table. She wore a short satiny robe that scarcely hid her bare curves. He had donned a light blue shirt, leaving the shirttail casually hanging loose. Oh, she had forgotten how good he looked in blue, his dark hair dominant and those blue eyes outstanding. This was the man she had tried to forget? Thank God, it was impossible. He filled her mind as well as her imagination.

Slowly, she walked to him and wrapped her arms around his waist, lightly scratching his back with her fingernails, then pressing him tightly to her. Oh, he felt good against her!

Noah's arms enfolded her, and he kissed the top of her head. She leaned against his chest, listening to the heavy beat of his heart as it pulsed regularly through her.

He held her that way for a long time, and Charly felt marvelous in his arms. She wanted it to last forever.

"God, I've missed you, Charly." His voice rumbled in her ear.

"I've missed you, too, Noah." She turned her face to him, seeking the sweet assurance of his lips. His kiss told her what he refused to say, and she clung to that feeling—that hope.

They parted at last and Noah reached for a plain brown sack on the counter. "I brought some gifts from Walt. I think he likes you, Charly. When I told him I'd be seeing you, he insisted that I take these to you."

Noah lifted a quart jar filled with golden honey surrounding a long section of the honeycomb.

"Great! Look! It's beautiful!" She smiled her pleasure and noted that it would take her forever to eat a quart of honey.

"And . . ." He raised another jar—a gallon at least. "Blackberry wine!"

Charly clapped her hands with delight. "Marvelous! Oh, I've missed it. What a lovely color!" She admired the clear burgundy hue of the wine. "You'll have to help me drink this, Noah. I'll never be able to finish it. Nor the honey. It's just too much."

"My pleasure," he said, smiling.

"How generous of Walt to send them."

"Yes, considering . . ." His digging comment was left unsaid as he buttered a delectable biscuit.

They ate finally, exchanging small talk about what they had been doing in the past weeks.

"How's the job?" Nothing was mentioned about the lifetime-lease project that had propelled Charly into his mountain life.

"Oh, fine." She didn't say that she hated it more every day—her precious, valuable job and the continued problems of working with Lewis Daniel. Now, after the episode last night, it would be even worse. "How's Walt?" She smiled at the thought of the gentle old man.

"He's fine. Ornery as ever."

"How did you pry yourself away from the mountain?" Was there a sarcastic edge to her question?

But he smiled good-naturedly. "I gravitate to the civilized world every few weeks to check on the business. This opportunity came up, and it was advisable that I take advantage of it. I don't usually travel, but the fact that you are in Atlanta made the decision to come here much easier."

"But if it weren't for business, you wouldn't have come." Charly couldn't help her acid tone.

"If it weren't for you being here, I would have sent someone else to take care of this," he snapped. "Look, Charly, I don't want to argue with you. I'll be here such a short time, let's not spend our time snipping at each other."

Charly bit her lip, already regretting her sharp tongue,

but unable to control her bitterness that it had taken him so long to come to her. Maybe she was the wildcat after all. "You're right, Noah. I don't want to argue either. I guess I've still got some of the wildcat in me."

"Oh, but I like you that way, Wildcat." He rose to take his dishes to the sink and kissed the tip of her nose on the way.

Like? *Like?* Charly almost broke into tears at his choice of words. But she managed to say casually, "Just leave the dishes, Noah. I'll have time to clean up while you're away."

He readily agreed. "Sounds like a good idea, especially since I cooked the breakfast. Taking turns with this kitchen stuff is only fair, you know. Anyway, I need to shower and change. I have a meeting in an hour."

She motioned toward the small bathroom. "Please feel free to use my *indoor* facilities. The toilet flushes and we even have *hot* and cold running water!"

"My, my! Such modern conveniences here in the big city!"

Charly curled contentedly on the bed. She was totally in heaven with a mug of coffee to sip, watching the man she loved. In less than an hour Noah transformed from the casual, rugged, mountain man Charly knew so well to a distinguished, well-dressed businessman in a three-piece suit who was a stranger to her. She couldn't believe how incredibly handsome he looked as he shrugged into the gray pinstripe suit coat that completed his attire. Yet, with his dark beard, he retained a look apart, a rather mysterious appearance.

It occurred to Charly that Noah was an enigma to her, too. She knew him as one man—rough, natural, sensitive. And yet he stood before her as someone totally different—tough, capable, all business. Which was he—really? She accepted his perfunctory kiss, knowing he was already preoccupied with his upcoming meeting. She stood at the window and watched wistfully as Noah climbed into the rented Caprice. He had the look of a wealthy man who ran his ages-old family business with an iron hand. Was this the man with whom she had fallen in love?

By four he was back, twirling her around the apartment, teasing her, making love to her with such rich abandon that she wondered if she had really seen him as the staid businessman she had earlier imagined. Oh, God! How she loved him!

Later they showered together and Noah helped her wash her hair.

"Ummm, that feels wonderful," she said, purring, as they stood glistening wet and Noah towel-dried her thick mane vigorously. "You're spoiling me, y'know."

"And don't you forget it," he answered, and wrapped the towel around her head before grabbing a large bath towel for himself. He left her in the bathroom and she could hear him rummaging through his luggage.

"How are you wearing your hair tonight, Wildcat?"

She struggled with the brush and blow drier, trying to twist the ends in just the right casual curl. "I thought I'd wear it down. Why? Does it matter to you?"

"Oh, no." His answer was casual enough. "Just wondering."

Finally, Charly achieved the look she wanted and applied just enough makeup to enhance her large brown eyes and rosy lips. She opened the closet door and studied her limited wardrobe.

Noah's voice had a tinge of humor as he advised her. "Wear something feminine tonight, Wildcat. I want to see what you look like in something besides jeans—and *my* jeans, at that!"

Charly sighed dubiously. There wasn't much choice. "Now, where did you say we were going?"

"I'm taking you to the zenith, the top of the town

tonight, Wildcat. First, drinks at the Hyatt's Polaris. Then at Nikolai's Roof, atop the Hilton."

"Sounds terrific, Noah. They say the view's beautiful up there." She selected an off-white, creamy satin gown, long, with a dramatic slit on one side, tied on one shoulder. As she adjusted it, she glanced into the full-length mirror. The dress hung loosely over her curves and clung seductively around her breasts.

"Well, the view's certainly going to be gorgeous tonight," Noah acknowledged, admiring the lovely woman before him.

"How do you like it?" She twirled, the side slit showing one long, alluring leg.

"Yes, I'd say you've made the full transition from mountain girl to lovely lady! You look gorgeous, Wildcat." His eyes traveled over her enticing figure and bare shoulder.

"Speaking of changes, you don't look like the same mountaineer I met in Simm's Hollow."

Charly let her eyes roam his masculine frame from his gray coat and vest to his gray lightweight wool slacks that stretched over his sinewy hips and legs. "You don't look like you came from a mountain, sir." She pulled teasingly on his beard until he lowered his face to kiss her.

"Same man, Charly," he murmured as he ran one hand luxuriously under her mass of hair and pulled her close. He kissed her hard and she melted against him. But before she could gather into his arms, he pushed her away and turned her sideways.

His hand was still around her neck and he instructed, "Hold your hair up, Charly."

She obeyed him and lifted her hair before she realized what he was doing.

"There . . ." he said with satisfaction. He turned her around to face him, a powerful hand on each shoulder. His eyes registered a special glow as he assessed her from head to foot. "Ah, perfect—you're beautiful, Charly."

Anxiously, she sought the mirror. When her reflection focused clearly, she gasped at her own image. The necklace that Noah had attached to her slender neck held a magnificent cluster of diamonds that nestled in the hollow of her throat—three circular-cut diamonds arched above a pear-shaped stone. The splendid display was elegantly suspended and presented a glittering emphasis to the swell of her breasts. The diamonds shimmered with an inner glow of blue-white, giving a complete, harmonious splendor to her dazzling appearance. Charly could only stare, her round eyes traveling from the diamonds to her own shocked countenance and back to the glimmering stones. She touched them gingerly to make sure it wasn't her imagination.

"Oooh, Noah . . ."

"How do you like it, Charly?" he prompted.

"I . . . I love it . . ." But it occurred to her that she couldn't possibly accept such an expensive gift from Noah. Her brown eyes sought his. "Noah, I . . . I can't accept this—it's just too . . . too much." She couldn't imagine the monetary value of such a gorgeous display of diamonds. Several thousand, at least. And Noah gave them to her as a gift? She shook her head in dazed amazement and looked back to her image.

Noah stood behind her, his hands resting on her shoulders near the diamonds. Two fingers caressed her slightly and his eyes were serious and somewhat smoky. "Yes you can, Charly. I want you to have them. And they look gorgeous on you—better than my wildest dream." His voice was low and quieting—persuasive. She'd heard that tone before.

Charly shook her head again. "Noah, I can't—I just—"

He interrupted her. "Charly, listen to me." He turned her around to face him, his hands lightly on her neck, tormenting her with his touch. "We are no longer children. We are adults, with adult desires. One of my desires is to give you this small gift. Please accept it." His voice was barely above a whisper. "Charly, I have never given you anything. And you have given me so much happiness. Diamonds are forever—and that's how I want it to be with us."

His mouth claimed hers then, and Charly knew that she would accept Noah's gift—and whatever he wanted for their life together.

CHAPTER ELEVEN

Their first stop was atop the Hyatt Regency for drinks. They glided through the atrium lobby, two people in love with only eyes for each other. Charly was a vision with her chestnut hair framing her beaming face, the diamond necklace flashing prominently above the swell of her breasts, her satin gown flowing seductively, while every step revealed the length of one shapely leg. She had never been so happy and it was obvious in her face.

Noah was tall, handsome, and enigmatic with his ebony beard and shock of collar-length hair. He seemed to hover protectively around his lady, clearly proud to be her escort. Yet the way his eyes caressed her revealed he was more than her escort. Much more.

Charly hid her face against Noah's sheltering shoulder as they zoomed twenty-two stories in the glass-bubble elevator high above the electric city of Atlanta to the revolving restaurant. The view was magnificent and Charly excitedly pointed out the Omni International complex, the Coastal States Building, Underground Atlanta made up of shops and nightclubs, the Peachtree Center Plaza Hotel, her own office . . . But the view was secondary. They savored every moment together, their eyes revealing the love they shared. People viewed them discreetly, thinking they were a honeymoon couple, breaking away from their privacy for such basic necessities as food and drink. And they were—almost.

They briefly toured the Omni, watching ice skaters swirl on the glassy surface, and ended up at Nikolai's Roof for dinner. They sipped a light French Chablis and tasted delectable mushrooms stuffed with crab, spinach, and cheese. The pheasant was rich and savory and included a pungent hunter's sauce thick with mushrooms and wine. They lingered over coffee and cheesecake, each trying to prolong the enjoyment of the evening to the fullest.

Noah toyed with his coffee cup, running his finger along the edge impatiently. "I have to work again tomorrow, Charly." He could see the disappointment in her eyes even in the dim candlelight.

"On Saturday?"

He nodded. "Something came up and we have to continue tomorrow."

She tried to be gracious. "Aw, shucks. I was planning to take you shopping, tour the Underground, and wear you out climbing Stone Mountain." She smiled, but the disappointment was there.

"Sorry. My day starts early. I have to pick my lawyer up at the airport, then we have a meeting until . . ." He shrugged.

"How long?" Suddenly it was important to know how much time she would have with him.

"It depends. There are some details to be worked out, but a merger is in the works. I'm buying out a company here in Atlanta. They will serve as the Georgia distributor for our plant. Eventually I'd like to see them become the Southern distributor. Location is good, plant facilities—management needs beefing up, but we can handle that."

"Noah, does that mean you will be coming to Atlanta more often?" Her voice rose with expectancy.

He smiled tightly. "It might. There'll be work to do here."

Her smile improved and the disappointment in her eyes dissolved. "Great! I like the idea more every minute. I guess I can spare you a few hours tomorrow. So long as you promise to come back."

His dark hand covered hers. "Of course I will."

Why did she doubt it, even when he looked her in the eyes and said it? She hated herself for doubting him. His blue eyes were sincere tonight. They told her he cared for her—loved her. She could believe his eyes, couldn't she? He had given her the diamonds as symbols of everlasting love. His love. She touched them tenderly—tangible proof of his love even if he refused to say it.

"Let's go home, Charly." His voice was low and urgent. "I've had enough of being public tonight." There was a special glow in his passionate blue eyes that urged her, tantalized her, assured her.

Charly rose and nodded in agreement. Her brown eyes smiled their consent, knowing his desires even before he whispered in her ear as he assisted her with the chair, "I want to rush you home and strip that beautiful gown off your luscious body and take you right there on the floor."

Charly's bronze eyes widened with amazed delight as Noah's provocative language sent goose bumps down her legs. She looked around quickly to see if they had eavesdroppers, then to her handsome escort for the evening. He smiled at her pleasantly, serenely, and murmured quietly, "Just walk out normally and pretend you don't notice the bulge in my pants."

Charly's mouth opened into a small O, as if she couldn't believe Noah was tantalizing her with his words. She didn't *dare* look down at him! She obeyed the pressure of his hand on her back and cut her eyes around to steal a glance at him. The devil! Noah's countenance remained placid as he nodded graciously to the waiter and escorted her from Nikolai's Roof, his arm politely around her waist. The handsome young couple, obviously honeymooners, glided from the public's view, two people in love with eyes only for each other.

* * *

The instant that her apartment door locked them from the intrusion of the outside world, his hands were claiming his treasure, seeking to fulfill his publicly whispered promise.

"Oh, God, Charly. This evening has been pure torture!" One hand cupped her satin-covered breast, while the other slipped under her dark halo of hair and gently pulled her to him.

"Noah, it's been a beautiful evening! I've loved it. Eating high above Atlanta was a special pleasure for me. And everything was marvelous! Your gift—the diamonds—and being with you made me feel like a queen tonight, Noah." Her eyes were dark and provocative, her voice almost a whisper, as Noah's hand continued to hold his prize and his thumb pressed sensitive, soft places. A sharp intake of her breath let him know she was feeling the same sensuous pleasures he felt.

"You were a queen tonight. Didn't you see the heads turn when you walked by? I was jealous as hell." His thumb circled the rosy tip, bringing it to a quick, sharp focus. "You were the most beautiful part of the evening, Wildcat. And that made it torture for me. I couldn't touch you . . ." His entire hand mastered her smooth, silken breast, enjoying the slick feel of the material over her bare flesh. "And I couldn't kiss you . . ." He kissed her lips softly, quickly, tantalizing her lips as his hand continued its pleasurable roaming over her silk-covered body.

"Oooh." A small moan escaped Charly's burning lips.

Her arms climbed the wall of his chest, then slowly her fingers trailed around his neck until they buried themselves in his thick hair. His mouth sought hers again, this time in a fierce encounter that opened her lips to his forceful, probing tongue. She felt powerless against him and met his advances tentatively, cautiously offering her tongue as well as her body. He responded with a shudder to the touch of her tongue against his and slid his hands around to her back, pressing ever stronger.

His power intensified as his arms molded her firmly to his steel-hard frame, crushing her rising breasts to his muscular chest. His hands reached behind her buttocks, lifting until her pelvis fit solidly against his and she could feel his maleness against her.

"Noah . . . oh, Noah," she muttered, leaning weakly against him.

Just when she thought he would engulf her completely, somehow pressing her into him, he abruptly released the painful pressure of her flesh into his. He allowed her tongue to trail the shape of his mouth, tantalizing him, plundering his mouth the way he had hers. She enjoyed being the aggressor.

He lowered her feet to the floor and, with his hands on her rib cage, pushed her from him. His eyes raked over her savagely, and his hands rose to grasp both breasts, almost roughly, then traveled on to her slender neck. She shuddered weakly with the passion his touch aroused in her and swayed slightly, since he no longer supported her.

"Lean back. The wall will brace you, Charly." His voice was thick with passion as his hands roamed under her hair and around her shoulders.

Charly lifted her face to his for another kiss—wet, probing, fierce. She found that she had to obey and lean against the wall for support from his piercing kiss. As her passion heightened, she felt his leg separate hers, his knee applying pressure against her. A low guttural sound escaped her throat, and she knew she couldn't stand much longer, even with a wall behind her for support.

Although his knee remained firmly in its wedge against her, Noah moved back to admire her. His fingers quickly released the shoulder clasp and the dress slowly slid down her body, revealing her full, creamy breasts with their taut nipples, her flat belly. It gathered in a rumpled heap around her hips where his knee stopped the continued descent of the material. When he finally moved, the dress slid rapidly to the floor, a creamy-white circle around Charly's feet.

"Get those hose off." The raspy command was actually Noah's voice.

By the time Charly fumbled to remove the offending panty hose, Noah had shucked his jacket and shirt. He stood bare-chested before her, glistening muscles emphasized by a balanced scattering of dark masculine hair.

Charly looked up into his eyes—dark, passion-filled, showing no reflection of her own bare body trembling before him. She stood motionless, boldly enduring his all-encompassing gaze. She was proud of her body and the assurance that she could please him. This was a brief halt in their lovemaking, a moment when she could revel in the knowledge that ecstasy would soon come for both of them. She said it with her eyes. *I love you, Noah.*

"My God, Charly, what a vision—you're beautiful," he murmured, his hands no longer able to refrain from touching her fiery skin. One hand rested possessively on one of her hips, while the other stimulated her senses to wild intoxication. A single finger trailed leisurely from her parted lips to the hollow of her throat, where the diamonds still nestled as a single adornment of his love. His finger burned the roundness of first one breast, then the other, stopping long enough to punctuate the hard buttons at the tips. The tantalizing finger continued its flaming trail over her feminine hip, then around to the tender, sensitive inner thigh, where an excruciating passion blazed her limbs. She shuddered against him as he continued his trail of sublime arousal.

Her fingers fumbled clumsily with his trousers, the stiff belt, the stubborn zipper. "Hurry, Noah!"

Finally, with one hand, he helped her strip off his clothes, never halting his gentle probing of her willing body. He lifted her buttocks again, fitting her pelvis perfectly against his. This time there were no clothes to prevent their ultimate pleasure. Their bodies locked together in love, and Charly clung to Noah's shoulders as he gently lowered her to the floor.

He kept his word, given so brazenly in the restaurant, and took her before they crossed the small room to the bed. But Charly was glad. She didn't think she would have made it to the bed. Finally, Noah carried her to the comfort of her bed, but it wasn't necessary. They only wanted to be together and slept peacefully in each other's arms. Charly was in paradise, encircled in Noah's arms, graced with the diamonds of their forever love.

The next morning, by the time Charly was awake, Noah was already gone to take care of his infernal business. He left the coffee on WARM and a brief note on the table: GET BACK IN BED, WILDCAT! I WANT YOU THERE WHEN I RETURN! N.

She smiled at his lusty, witty note and looked around the quiet, empty apartment. Her eyes fell on the white dress she had worn the night before. It lay in the same circle where it had dropped from her body. She shuddered with delight just remembering the events that had led up to and followed the discarding of the dress. She rubbed her arms vigorously as chill bumps ran their length. She remembered his electric touch, his slow appreciation of her, his power. Why did he have to leave so soon? She wasn't prepared to awake alone. She didn't want to give him up yet. But would she ever—*ever*—be ready for him to leave? Probably not. No, definitely not!

She felt something tug at her neck and automatically reached to caress the elegant diamond necklace that still encircled her. The stones were cold and hard to her touch, a reminder that they would always be there—forever. But would Noah's love? She walked to the mirror and gazed at the image she saw there: a simple, tousle-haired brunette with a slim, high-breasted body adorned like a queen with diamonds. She fingered them again. If he doesn't love me, why did he give me these? she wondered. Why does he look at me that special way? Why . . . last night? Yes, oh yes! That was an act of love! For me it was! She turned away, afraid to think any further.

When he returned, Charly wasn't in bed as he had instructed. She had been busy cleaning the apartment, picking up discarded clothes, making the bed. Everything appeared neat once again, the way she liked it. She was dressed in casual slacks and a sweater, appeared happily in his arms, ready to take him out and show him Atlanta.

He wrapped his arm around her, leading her across the room. "But, Charly, I thought I left the message clear. I want you there!" With a fast motion, he reached under her legs and lifted her high before swinging her onto the bed in an ungracious heap.

"Damn you!" she squealed. "I can read! But I want to take you to Stone Mountain today. You should be homesick for mountains by now, so I thought I'd let you see our nearest competition to the Smokies!"

He shook his head and kissed her soundly. "I'm only homesick for you, Wildcat. I never get enough!" He began working on her sweater, his hands under it, fingers pressing her soft, braless breasts.

"Noah! No-ah!" she giggled. His hands never stopped.

"Yes—come on, Wildcat! I'll beat you getting undressed!" He bounded off the bed and began stripping.

Charly sat up and folded her arms. "Noah—are you serious? You're crazy, you know! Aren't you going to tell me about your meeting? How did it go? You know, all the important stuff like did you buy that company?"

Noah stood before her, completely nude and waiting. "I'm serious. Come here, Wildcat . . ."

Charly squealed and tried to get away from his grasping

hands. Of course, she couldn't. As he pinned her to the bed and covered her face with kisses, she gasped, "Aren't you going to tell . . . me . . . about your . . . meeting?"

"Not now, woman. I'm busy concentrating on important things. Small talk will come later . . . "

Charly was adamant about taking Noah outdoors in the Atlanta countryside. And Noah obviously wanted to shower Charly with his complete attention. So they compromised. Noah got his way. And afterward he helped her remake the bed. They managed to spend part of the afternoon at Stone Mountain. So Charly was the winner after all! How could she lose when Noah was with her! Delighted, ecstatic, content—her emotional level was at its peak.

They hiked the trails and rode the cablecar and sipped Cokes while admiring the immense Civil War sculptures carved in the huge wall of stone.

"Imagine doing that for a living! How long did it take? What a fantastic job!" Noah was obviously impressed. "So precise, so detailed!"

But Charly had seen the carvings before. She giggled. "What if you were the world's greatest stone sculptor and afraid of heights!"

He narrowed his eyes and viewed it prospectively. "Hmmm, you could always do it blindfolded! Of course, someone like you, who can't even travel in the glass elevator at the Hyatt without hiding your eyes, would be in big trouble! The world's greatest stone sculptor would have to find another occupation."

"Any suggestions?" She tucked her arm into his and snuggled against his firm, warm shoulder.

"Sure." He bent his head close to hers. "You could be the world's greatest lover—and I'd hire you. Now I expect my employees to be loyal—no others could seek your services, of course!"

"Agreed! I think I'm hired!" She smiled happily, tugging on his marvelous beard. "I like your mountain better anyway, Noah. It's more . . . private."

"*My* mountain? My God, Charly! That mountain belongs to the whole country! That's what you were fighting for, remember?"

The tone between them changed immediately.

She looked away, remembering. "Yeah, I know. Well, the battle plan's changed."

"But not the ultimate goal." His voice was hard, knowing, prophetic.

"Maybe. Lewis hasn't mentioned it lately. I hope it's been put to rest." A dread pervaded her being, for she knew the case hadn't been entirely closed.

"So do I." But he, too, knew they hadn't heard the last of the lifetime-lease affair.

After spending yet another amorous night with Noah, Charly was so totally immersed in her love of the elusive man that she became depressed at the mere thought that he would be leaving soon. She was living with him—again —and loving it. Again. They spent Sunday morning just being together. Later she couldn't even remember what they had done. She figured they ate, but didn't know what. She recalled walking among some trees with him, arm in arm. She assumed it was in the nearby park, but she wasn't sure.

What she remembered, all too well, was their final conversation. Later she regretted her words. She hated what she had said, but knew her reasoning was right. It had to be. It had cost her a tremendous personal loss. Perhaps if she hadn't pressed . . .

"Where are you going when you leave here, Noah?" Her voice was tight, for saying it finally made it real.

He walked to the window. "Back to the cabin. I need to check on Walt."

"When will I see you again?" She hated talking to his

back and wished he would turn around so she could see his eyes.

"I don't know. I'll try to get back to Atlanta . . . soon. Since we've purchased the other company, someone will need to make the transition smooth."

"Will that be you?" Her voice was expectant.

His broad shoulders shrugged. "Don't know, Charly. I don't usually do that sort of thing . . ."

"Why not? It would give you reason to be here." Her voice betrayed her anxiety.

But his was low and steady. "I . . . don't need a business reason, Charly. You're enough. I'll come back . . . to you."

"Noah, let me go back with you. I . . . I can't stand the thought of being without you again . . . for God knows how long. Take me with you." She couldn't believe her own pleading voice.

He turned around then, and she could see the pained, almost panicked expression in his azure eyes. "No! You know you can't do that, Charly! I can't . . ."

"Why not? I just want to be with you."

He spread his hands. "It's impossible. Now is not the time."

"Noah, I . . . I love you. Will there ever be a 'time'?"

He ran his hand through his hair abstractly. "I . . . I don't know, Charly. Things are too complicated now—too confused."

"Maybe you're confused, but I'm not! What are you talking about anyway? Love?" She was on her feet now, facing him adamantly. Damn him! What did he think he was doing to her?

"No. I . . . I don't think I'm ready—" He placed his hands on her arms. "Just don't press me, Charly. I'm not ready for the emotional obligation of you . . . or anyone else. I may never be. I don't want it, don't you understand?"

Charly's voice was shrill as she reached near hysteria.

"Oh, yes, I'm beginning to understand, all right! You just want to have a bed to come to occasionally! And the expensive gift was to make sure I'd keep it warm for you!"

He shook her slightly, tightening his grip. "No, Charly, that's not true! I . . . meant what I said about . . . everything . . ."

"Then why did you come here?"

He searched her angry face with obscure, confused eyes, then turned away from her. "I don't know. I just had to see you."

"*See* me?" she railed. "Then why didn't you just rent a car and sit on the street until I came down. Then you could have seen me! Why bother to come in? Why did you have to . . . touch me?" She was near tears.

"I don't know . . ." His voice was low and empty.

"What did you think this weekend would do for *me?* Or did you think of that? Did you want to build me up again, so I could fall flat on my face when you walk out the door? Then I could sit over here waiting and hoping and wishing you would have another business crisis so you would have to fly back over here to Atlanta to 'see' me? Well, I can't stand the uncertainty! I don't want to be built up only to be dropped at the end of the weekend! I can't live like this! I won't be your mistress. I must know—"

"Charly . . . Charly, please—" Hesitantly, he took a step toward her.

But she backed away, her voice harsh. "Don't touch me! If you don't love me, just get the hell out of my apartment —and my *life!"* She trembled with the emotion and shock of what she had just said to Noah. Her love . . .

His face contorted with inner pain. It was as if she had just slapped him and he didn't protest what she said. He looked hurt and knew he was defeated—they were defeated. Yet he did not seek a reprieve.

"I'm sorry, Charly. The last thing in the world I want to do is to hurt you. But it looks like that's just what I've done." And with those words he walked out of her apartment—and out of her life.

Well—it's what she wanted, wasn't it? She told him to make the choice! Demanded that he tell her now! "Oh, how I hate you, Noah Van Horn!" she shouted at the closed door, and in an angry rage she jerked the gold and diamond necklace from her neck and flung it against the wall. "And take your expensive diamonds, too! I don't want them!"

But he did not take them. He left the diamonds with Charly—the solid symbol of their forever love. And the necklace lay on the floor of her apartment, near where her satiny dress had been dropped in a circle at Charly's feet—near where Noah had made love to her. The golden latch was pulled out of shape so that it didn't clasp properly anymore, but the arch of diamonds over the beautiful pear-shaped stone were still intact. *Diamonds are forever.*

CHAPTER TWELVE

"Come on in, Charly. So glad you could make it today." Lewis's voice was edged with sarcasm.

He had been malicious since the night Charly had refused his physical advances. He had never forgiven her that injustice and wouldn't discuss it with her. Charly had even tried to patch it up and offered weak apologies, but working conditions had deteriorated badly. They clashed often and over everything. They just couldn't agree on simple goals, much less on complicated strategy, so she tried to avoid confrontations with him. But this time was different. The lifetime lease in the Smokies had been revived and Charly was requested, in Lewis's domineering way, to sit in on the strategy session. Actually, she wanted to be a part of it. She wanted to know what he was planning. So she struggled to make it to work on her "miserable Friday" in spite of her own strong desire to call in sick.

There were other things to do on Fridays to help her forget—but none of them ever worked. Noah was still on her mind—especially this morning as she slid into a chair opposite Ben Morrison. Lewis paced the floor near the small conference table, his mannerisms asserting his dominant position with those in the room.

"It seems that this Van Horn fellow has been living, full time, at Simms's cabin for two and a half years!" Lewis's mention of Noah's name snapped Charly immediately to the events of the meeting. What was he saying about Noah?

Ben was reading a dossier and making notes on the side. "What is he doing up there?"

"Good question. He runs a furniture manufacturing plant out of Charlotte—" Lewis was interrupted.

"Now?" Ben was trying to be thorough.

"Let me finish, Ben. Now he owns a family business, this furniture company, and uses the mountain cabin as his refuge. About two—"

This time it was Charly who interrupted. "That's not true! He doesn't use the cabin as his 'refuge.' He takes care of Walt—"

"Is that so? Well, Charly, maybe you'd like to tell us more. If you'd been willing to do your job months ago, you could have informed us all about this Noah Van Horn and saved time and the money expended to have this damn investigation!" Lewis's eyes gleamed viciously at her.

"You're so tactful, Lewis. I can tell this is going to be a pleasure."

"Goddamn, Charly! I sent you up there six months ago to do a simple job. You ended up staying two weeks and came back unwilling to complete the case! Not only that—you refuse to give up information you have about the subjects. Now what the hell am I supposed to do—pat you on the back?"

"The 'subjects'?" Charly flamed at his terminology.

"Come on, Charly. What's Van Horn doing up there? Running booze?"

"No! Of course not!"

"Is there any being run? Maybe Walt—" Lewis was persistent.

"No!"

"What, then? Is he using the place as a hunting lodge?"

Charly could feel the anger rising in her and she knew

she had to keep cool. "No! He's just . . . just staying with his friend, I guess."

Lewis dismissed her comment with a shrug of his hand. "Well, Van Horn doesn't bother me that much. He appeared about two years ago after the death of his wife and kid in a car wreck. But he's violating the law just by being there. So he'll be easy enough to dispose of. A court order will take care of him. It's the old man we have to contend with."

Charly lifted her head defiantly. What was Lewis leading up to?

After a pause, he continued, slowly setting up his plan. "Now, Charly, I wanted you to sit in on this session to see if you could shed any light on the situation. Or if you would help somehow. You lived with Simms for nearly two weeks. What is he like? Pretty senile, huh?"

"Senile? Of course not! He's perfectly normal—alert, active . . . witty . . ." A smile spread across her face as she remembered the old man. "And he plays a harmonica—"

"My God, Charly! The old guy's eighty-nine! He can't be alert as all that! You said that Van Horn took care of him. He must need supervision."

"No, he doesn't need supervision. Lewis, what are you getting at?"

He sighed heavily and cast a disgusted look at Ben that clearly said, "This is not going to be as easy as we thought." He cleared his throat. "Charly, you won't have to do another thing with this case. Ben, here, is taking it over for you. You won't have to go back there and face those people. We are going to proceed with the strategy already discussed, months ago, before your . . . uh, excursion. You remember that plan, don't you?" He paused dramatically and looked at her. When she didn't answer, he continued, undaunted. He was in control here and she had better know it. "Well, we are still going to get the land. The methods are going to be different, that's all."

"You are *not* going to get that land! Walt has refused, and by law he can live there as long as he wants to!" Charly was adamant.

Lewis eyed her narrowly for a few moments before saying, "Not if we have him declared mentally incompetent, he can't stay."

Charly's mouth flew open. "Mentally incompetent? But he's *not!*"

"He could be! It wouldn't take much to convince a judge that an eighty-nine-year-old man living far from civilization on government land needs to be in a nursing home. He needs to be watched and cared for! It stands to reason!" He seemed so satisfied with himself.

Charly was furious. "A nursing home? Lewis, you're crazy! I'll never go along with a ridiculous, inhuman plan such as this! Not when Walter Simms doesn't need to be there! I'll fight you all the way!"

"Don't waste your breath, Charly. It won't do any good. If you won't assist, I'll just take you off the project, and you won't have a thing to say about it." Lewis glared at her, his vicious eyes sparking golden daggers in the morning sunlight.

As she looked at him, she realized the extent of his vindictive nature. He was doing this to get back at her! Well, she would fight him!

"Lewis, you can't do this! Walt is . . . is just a nice old man trying to live out his life the way he wants to. He's been there on that mountain for most of his life, and now . . ."

His voice was almost mocking. "Come on, Charly. You're getting soft. What I'm proposing won't hurt him. It'll be better for him in the long haul." Lewis actually believed it. Or did he?

Charly stood and faced Lewis. Her voice was tight as she disclosed painfully, "It'll kill Walt. He'll die if we have him removed from that mountain." She shivered involuntarily, recalling Noah's exact words to her months ago, when they had discussed removing Walt from the mountain.

It sounded innocent enough. Have him taken care of. It even sounded reasonable and nurturing. Lewis had convinced himself of that. Charly's trouble was that she knew Walt too well. She knew him as a gentle old man who wanted to live out his life on that mountain. Was that too much to ask? *No!*

Lewis jeered laughingly, "He will *not* die, Charly. That's a ridiculous assumption. He will be fine. And he'll be cared for."

Charly flared at him, her face glowing hotly, her voice almost a scream. "Damnit, Lewis, he's 'cared for' now! He's fine—and won't live there forever, you know. Can't you leave him in peace?" Charly was amazed at the sound of her own shrill voice, her staunch defense of the old man on the mountain. What had come over her? She was now opposing the very goal she had once sought! And confronting her boss! She was treading on very thin ice!

Lewis's voice was steely. "I want him off that mountain, now. *Now!*"

Charly spread her hands. "But why? What's the big damn rush?" Should she back off a little?

Instead of answering, Lewis affirmed assertively, "I want him gone, and you're going to sign these papers as the assigned agent. Ben will take care of the project, so you won't have to bother with it anymore."

Charly's head spun with contradictions. Lewis was maneuvering her, forcing her to the culmination—now! His mandate was clearly before her. Still, she urged for reprieve, justice. "Lewis, this is preposterous! The government doesn't do such things!"

His countenance was icy. "I do. And since I'm in charge here, you'll do as I say!" He flung the papers to the table in front of her and flipped a ball-point pen on top.

His words chilled her and she folded her arms to ward off the cold that engulfed her. "I'm not signing anything, Lewis. Certainly not something incriminating toward Walter Simms."

"Sign it, Charly." He muttered through clenched teeth.

She looked down at the papers scattered on the table, then back to Lewis's stone-cold eyes. Suddenly it occurred to Charly that she hated Lewis and everything he was doing. Most particularly, she hated his methods. She decided she would not be commanded by him anymore. Nor would she allow him to intimidate her.

Her brown eyes narrowed coldly at him. "Go to hell, Lewis. You can take your papers and serve them on yourself!" With a surprising amount of calm, she walked to the door.

Just as her hand reached the knob, Lewis barked, "Charly! Get over here. We're not through!"

She held her head high and looked him squarely in the eye. "I am through, Lewis. You won't order me around any longer. I won't be a part of this travesty. I just quit."

Oblivious to the shocked exclamations of both men in the room, Charly closed the door and glided on light feet down the hall to her office. Immediately, she began the mechanics of unloading her desk. It was only a matter of moments before there was a short knock on her door. She glanced up to see Ben—not Lewis, the coward—ease inside.

His voice was gentle, concerned. She was sure he felt somewhat embarrassed to have just witnessed this final confrontation between her and Lewis. "Charly, please, cool down and think about what you just did. You quit a government job, honey. This will ruin your career. Lewis will see to it."

She shook her head. "I don't care. Lewis has lost all of his sense of balance, and I won't be a part of his organization anymore. This whole idea is crazy, you know. What is his reasoning? Or should I say, why has he lost his sense of reason?"

Ben shrugged. "Last year, at one of the national meetings, someone made a comment about the government land being better managed when all the lifetime leases are cleared out. After that, Lewis seemed to take it on himself to eliminate any and all lifetime leases in his district. There was no official proposal, methods were not discussed. Actually, no big deal was made of it. Lewis just decided it would look good on his record. It's an ambitious project."

"Record . . ." Charly seethed. "And Lewis is willing to wreck the remaining few years of a man's life for his own selfish 'record'!"

"Charly, that's not so unusual."

She cocked her head at Ben. "Are you sure it's not personal—because of me? We've never gotten . . . along, and—"

Ben interrupted swiftly. "Naw, Charly. He wouldn't let personal things get in the way of his career."

She nodded sarcastically. "You're probably right. He'd step over any of us . . ."

"Come on, Charly. Talk to Lewis again. Tell him you were upset. Your signature isn't required on this project anyway. He just got carried away. Tell him you—"

Charly's voice rose. "I'm not telling him anything of the sort! You sound as if he's properly brainwashed you, too! I don't care what he does to my career! Nothing is so important as a person's life, and when you lose sight of that, as he has done, you've gone too far!"

"You have lost your perspective, Charly. Save me from your 'hearts and flowers' routine. I've got business to think about! But if what you really wanted to do was to help this old guy, you've blown it. Now you won't have anything to say about the lifetime lease project. You're completely removed from it. You'll regret this move. Mark my words." Shaking his head, he huffed out.

Charly organized her work on the desk and left a few notes here and there. She found some boxes and piled her personal items into them. Within two hours, she was walking into her empty apartment, alone and jobless.

Charly paced the floor and worried—not about her job, but about Walter Simms. All she could think about was Walter and the plan Lewis had for his remaining life. Oddly, Charly was unconcerned about quitting her job and ruining her career. She would worry about that later. She was determined not to regret her actions. Of course, it was too soon to actually be affected by joblessness. However, that was a minor inconvenience compared to the deeper issues.

Charly stopped long enough to fix herself a cheese on rye. She continued her pacing, alternating sips of Coke and bites of sandwich. The fact that plagued her most was what Ben had said before he left her office. If she'd wanted to help Walt, she'd certainly ruined her chances. Now she was in no position . . . or was she?

Walter Simms would be defenseless against Lewis's fiendish strategy. But Noah wasn't. He wasn't defenseless at all. Actually, that's what Noah has been there for all along—to help his friend. Perhaps he could hire a lawyer or . . . something. If he knew about Lewis's plans beforehand, he could block the action . . . somehow. But in order to help Noah had to know about it. And she was the only one who could inform him about Walt's predicament. She would have to be the one.

She sighed heavily and stared out the window. But . . . talk to Noah? Oh, God—how could she? She hadn't seen him, hadn't even heard from him, since that fateful Sunday when she had ordered him out of her life. He had complied with her wishes. Yet they weren't really, *really* her wishes. But what she wanted could never happen. Yes, it was best this way. At least she could handle it.

Oh, she had immediately regretted what she had said to him. She had wanted to call him and apologize. But his disclosure that he didn't love her stopped her from making a fool of herself with him again.

He knew that she loved him. She had admitted it. And he had let her know that the feeling wasn't mutual. So she had decided to forget—to make herself forget—about Noah Van Horn. And she couldn't do that by calling him, apologizing, seeing him occasionally. That would surely break down all her defenses. She had been doing so well these last few lonely months. And now, because of Walter Simms, she would have to risk her emotions by calling him. She bit her lip pensively. But she owed Walter that much. After all, she had given up her job for these principles. She had to do all she possibly could.

So, what's the big deal? Just pick up the phone and call him. Tell him what you know. That's it. He can take it from there.

Boldly, she picked up the phone and dialed the information operator. "North Carolina, please . . . Charlotte . . . Van Horn Furniture Company. . . . Thank you." By the time she had dialed the number, her palms were sweaty and the sandwich she had eaten was in an uncomfortable knot in her stomach. Just the thought of speaking to him was unnerving.

"Hello, Mr. Van Horn, please." Her voice was raspy and she cleared her throat while waiting to be transferred to his office.

She repeated her request to the pleasant-sounding Southern voice who answered. ". . . He's not in? Well, when do you expect him . . . ?" A little disappointment, a little reprieve. ". . . Oh . . . No, I'll get in touch with him later. Thank you."

Damn! He wasn't in and the secretary didn't know when to expect him! And she had worked herself up to talking with him. Her mind reeled. *Oh, why did you have to go back up there now? Why can't you stay in your office, like normal people do?—normal people!*

She paced again. A phone call would have been so easy! Now what? Charly knew he was on the mountain. She just felt it. And, she knew there was no way of guessing when he'd be back to civilization.

Charly busied herself during the afternoon. She cleaned the kitchen, then straightened the small apartment, threw a load of clothes in to wash, and went through the boxes she had brought from her office. She even tossed away some of the junk that had been there for years and propped up the inspiring HANG IN THERE plaque someone had given her. Her eye caught another gift: the rabbit wood carving *he* had given her. Immediately her mind raced back to Noah . . . and the mountain . . . and Walter Simms. She knew what she must do—had known all along. She had just tried to avoid the inevitable. But she had to go. With a sigh, she picked up the phone and called the Atlanta Airport.

The little cabin looked exactly the same as the very first time she had approached the clearing. She had played it smart this time and rented a small pickup—a red Datsun with four-wheel drive. She wouldn't be stranded up here again! She laughed nervously to herself. Who cared—now?

She pulled to a stop, got out, and mounted the front steps, remembering the first time she had arrived at the old house and how Walt had stood on the porch, watching her warily. Then he had politely served her lunch.

A chilling wind whistled around the corner of the old house as she knocked on the door. There was an uneasy, eerie feeling in the air, and Charly shivered involuntarily. Receiving no answer, she knocked again, then peered in through the window. The big room looked the same—quiet and empty. Then she saw *him*. She caught a glimpse of his dark hair as he sat on the back porch, looking out over the mountains. He didn't respond to her knock, probably couldn't hear her. So she decided to walk around the house.

He slowly turned to face her, when he heard her footsteps on the porch.

"Noah?" Her mouth felt like cotton and she couldn't believe that here she was facing him again. Now what? Hi-how-are-you-and-what-have-you-been-doing-lately? Her dry mouth made further speech impossible for now.

They stared at each other for a moment, Noah obviously shocked to see her, Charly trying to calm her wild heart.

A faint smile crossed his lips as he recognized her. "Charly—what are you doing here?"

After not seeing him for months, she thought he seemed almost bigger than life. He wore jeans and an old blue shirt—the same shirt she had worn in the mountains! His raven-black hair was a little shaggier than when he had been in Atlanta; the dark beard still framed his face boldly. But there was something about his eyes—still beautifully blue, but now red-rimmed and . . . somehow different.

Charly found her voice and tried to sound normal. "I . . . I tried to call you . . . in Charlotte . . . but couldn't get you . . . and I have to talk to you because Lewis is crazy and I have to tell you about what he . . ." She stopped and wondered if she was making any sense at all. Probably not, from the blank expression on his face. But he was nice about it.

"Sit down, Charly." He motioned to the chair next to him, and she sank weakly into it. His hands clenched uneasily, and she remembered those hands on her, around her, caressing her, and she ached to feel them again.

Charly laced her own fingers nervously and tried again. "I told you that I would do what I could to help Walt in this government lease situation. Well, I tried, but it didn't do much good. My boss revived the lifetime-lease project and is determined to get this land. He's going to try to have Walt declared . . . mentally incompetent . . . and I thought you should know." God! It sounded so brutal! She dropped her eyes and tried not to look at his hands. How could she sit so close to him and not touch him—his shoulders . . . his arms . . . his hands.

Noah's expression didn't change as he looked intently at her. She had assumed that he would be as horrified and angry as she was about Lewis's intentions. But he just sat there, as if he were trying to get it all straight in his head. Hadn't she made any sense at all? Finally, after long moments of pressing silence, she rallied. "Noah? Did you hear me? Lewis—"

Noah's upraised hand halted her midsentence. "I heard you." His voice was strangely dull. "But it's too late. Walt's dead."

The words slapped her coldly across the face. "Oh . . . no! Noah—"

Quietly, he answered her unasked questions. "He died two days ago. Heart attack. I rushed him to town, but . . . too late." He spread his strong hands helplessly, looking out into the forest.

Oh, how she wanted to take his hands—to hold him to her breast . . .

Sudden, hot tears burned Charly's eyes. She hardly knew Walter Simms, yet he was responsible for her being sent to the mountain cabin in the first place, for her knowing and subsequently falling in love with Noah, for her quitting her fine, spurious job. And now he was gone.

An empty quiet filled the wintry air, and Charly finally rasped in a hoarse whisper, "I'm sorry, Noah. I . . . I can't believe he's gone. I know he was your friend."

Noah appeared not to notice the two tears that trailed her cheeks. His tone was flat. "He meant a lot to both of us, Charly. At least, what he represented . . ."

"Yes." She smiled in spite of her tears, recalling how

her life, her attitude, even her job had altered since that day when she first drove up the mountain and met the fiesty old man. And Noah. Abruptly, she turned to him, flooded with an empty, sad feeling. "Noah, was all this for nothing? The purpose of everything is changed now that he's gone. The land will automatically revert to the government . . ."

Noah turned to face her, the pain clearly visible in his intense blue eyes. "No, Charly. Everything has a meaning. Especially what has happened between us. I . . . have done a lot of thinking since I left Atlanta. I . . . now realize that I . . . love you. I know this is not the time or the place, but I need to say it. Without you I have been miserable, and I just hope you can forgive me for leaving you."

"Noah—" Charly couldn't believe her ears and slumped against the back of the crude wooden chair.

His hands rubbed his blue-jeaned thighs nervously. "Charly, listen to me. I want you to understand why. You know I've loved you from the start. You must know that. But I just . . . denied it to myself. I . . . I wasn't ready to fall in love—didn't want to—after the death of my wife. I was hurt too much by losing her—them—and my only defense against getting hurt was not to love again. But it happened in spite of me and my denial. With Walt. And with you." Still he didn't look at her, and Charly was going crazy.

She stood and put her hands in his, tugging pleadingly at them. "Noah, I love you, too," she whispered through her tears.

He looked up at her, painfully, questioningly. "Can you forgive me, Charly?" Immediately, he was on his feet, cupping her face with his sensitive hands. His kiss was gentle, loving, longed for . . . "I love you, Charly. I love you . . ." His words were lost against her tear-stained face. He wrapped his long arms around her, enfolding her with his love and warmth. She buried her face against his chest, savoring the closeness, his fragrance, his caress. Somehow she knew they would never part again.

They stood together for a long time, holding each other, drawing strength and love. They reveled in the admissions of love that were finally out in the open—revealed to each other and the world.

Finally, reluctantly, Noah sighed and pushed away from their embrace. "Charly, I have some unfinished business. Will you help me?"

"What?" Charly noticed the strained expression on his face.

"I promised Walt not to leave any traces of his habitation here on this mountain." He motioned toward two large gasoline cans near the door.

"Burn it?" Charly asked, alarmed.

He nodded silently and bent to lift one of the full cans.

"Noah! You can't!" She grabbed his arm.

He looked at her fiercely and she knew immediately that he would. "I've packed my books and things. What's left was Walt's and he wanted it all destroyed. I promised him." He went inside and she could hear him splashing the flammable liquid against the walls.

Without thinking, she grabbed the other can and helped Noah douse the place with the smelly stuff. Somehow it struck her as humorous. "You know, if I hadn't already quit my job, this would certainly do it up for me. My career ruined. Arson of government property isn't exactly smiled upon by authorities!" She smiled at the thought of Lewis's face if he knew.

Noah emptied his can and tossed it into the kitchen. "Quit your job? When? Why?"

They left the house together, and Charly shrugged. "Lewis and I had one final confrontation—over this lifetime-lease project. I just couldn't go along with him anymore. His latest strategy was the last straw, as Walt would say. I couldn't let him do that to Walt."

"Charly, I can't believe you gave up your job over this . . . this situation."

"Why?"

"Well, it meant so much to you, for one thing." He fished in his pocket for matches.

"I have discovered that people are more important than jobs." She smiled. Reaching up, she pulled his face toward her, kissing him, loving the feeling of his lips and beard.

He smiled devilishly at her. "So the world's greatest sculptress has quit her job? Afraid of the heights, huh? Well, you're in luck, because I'm hiring for the world's greatest lover position."

"You are?" She giggled, remembering their jokes in happier times. "Can I apply? I do need a job."

"Sure. But I require strict loyalty. A lifetime of it. Accompanied by a marriage certificate. Those not qualified need not apply."

"Marriage?"

He kissed her ear and said softly, "You're highly qualified, Wildcat."

"Noah—" She drew back. "Did you mean . . . married . . . us?"

"Of course. How else will I test your loyalty? Are you interested in the position?"

"Yes—oh, yes! I'm definitely interested!" She grabbed him fiercely around the neck and hugged with all her might. He was hers to love forever!

Patiently, he removed her arms from their clutch around him. "Charly, I have a job to finish. Move your car back to safety and I'll light this." His voice was grim. "We'll have to make sure it doesn't spread, so we can't leave until it's gone."

Charly nodded solemnly, containing her happiness until the unpleasant business before them was completed. She moved the rented truck to the far edge of the clearing, away from the house, and was soon joined by Noah. Within minutes the small wooden cabin seemed to explode into flames. It crackled loudly as the huge tower of reddish-yellow flames rose high in the sky, engulfing the walls and roof. Suddenly a wall of choking grief rose in Charly and flowed from her in deep, racking sobs. She turned to Noah, who embraced her, comforting, murmuring softly. She cried until there were no more tears, and when she lifted her head from his chest the little cabin was nearly gone.

"It's all right, Charly. It's what he wanted." Noah's voice was firm now.

"I . . . I know," she agreed. "It's just that . . ." She halted and smiled sheepishly through her tears. "This is where we first made love and . . . I know I'm a sentimental fool." She sniffed and tried to laugh.

"Maybe. But I love you that way, Charly." His hand traveled gently from her shoulder to caress her neck. "The cabin can be destroyed, but, like the diamonds, our love will last forever."

She smiled happily and saw her reflection in his blue eyes.

"Let's go home, Charly." He kissed her again, a tender reminder of their forever love.

LEISURE ROMANCE!

FIND ALL THE GLAMOUR AND INTRIGUE OF THE WORLD'S CAPITALS IN THESE SENSUOUS, PASSIONATE NOVELS.

DIAMONDS by Elizabeth Anderson. Raised in poverty, a young woman fled her backwater roots seeking glamour and wealth. Calling herself Diamond, she entered the world of her fantasies. But in the rhinestone world of Las Vegas, she discovered that although diamonds are forever, love is a fleeting dream.

_3060-8 $4.50 US/$5.50 CAN

MORNING STAR by Sandra Bregman. A stunning blonde model and a wealthy Italian count, Lorna and Tony should have had the perfect marriage. But Tony's love for Lorna soon cooled, and their marriage became a travesty. For Lorna and Tony, the game was over, but for their daughter it was just the beginning, and the secrets and scandals of the past would color all her future.

_3044-6 $4.95 US/$5.50 CAN

LEISURE BOOKS
ATTN: Order Department
276 5th Avenue, New York, NY 10001

Please add $1.50 for shipping and handling for the first book and $.35 for each book thereafter. N.Y.S. and N.Y.C. residents, please add appropriate sales tax. No cash, stamps, or C.O.D.s. All orders shipped within 6 weeks via postal service book rate. Canadian orders require $2.00 extra postage. It must also be paid in U.S. dollars through a U.S. banking facility.

Name _____
Address _____
City _____ State _____ Zip _____
I have enclosed $_____in payment for the checked book(s).
Payment must accompany all orders.☐ Please send a free catalog.

SPEND YOUR LEISURE MOMENTS WITH US.

Hundreds of exciting titles to choose from—something for everyone's taste in fine books: breathtaking historical romance, chilling horror, spine-tingling suspense, taut medical thrillers, involving mysteries, action-packed men's adventure and wild Westerns.

SEND FOR A FREE CATALOGUE TODAY!

Leisure Books
Attn: Customer Service Department
276 5th Avenue, New York, NY 10001